Praise for the novels of

JOSEPH TELLER

"Teller's richly suspenseful story
will leave the reader eagerly anticipating the denouement
and Jaywalker's next adventure."
—*Publishers Weekly* starred review of *The Tenth Case*

"Joseph Teller's stellar *The Tenth Case* sets the standard
for defense attorney procedurals."
—*Mysterious Reviews*

"A glimpse into a different era and a peek into the psyche
of the already intriguing Jaywalker, Teller's novel draws
readers in at the very beginning and doesn't let up."
—*RT Book Reviews* on *Bronx Justice*

"Jaywalker's second legal thriller
is once again an insightful look at the dysfunctional
American jurisprudence system from the perspective of an
attorney whose outlook on defending his clients
is much different than the typical lawyer."
—*The Merry Genre Go Round Reviews* on *Bronx Justice*

"*Depraved Indifference* is an excellent legal drama whose
strength lies in the meticulous plotting."
—*The Mystery Reader*

JOSEPH TELLER

OVERKILL

MIRA®

MIRA®

Recycling programs
for this product may
not exist in your area.

ISBN-13: 978-0-7783-2776-9

OVERKILL

Copyright © 2010 by Joseph Teller.

For questions and comments about the quality of this book please contact us at
Customer_eCare@Harlequin.ca.

www.MIRABooks.com

Printed in U.S.A.

To Jason

1

GUILTY WITH AN EXPLANATION

Jaywalker's sitting in Part 30 when it happens. Part 30 is one of the Supreme Court arraignment courtrooms they have down at 100 Centre Street. It's where you go before a judge for the first time after you've been formally charged with a felony. A felony being anything they can give you more than a year for. Like murder, say.

Jaywalker's there for a sentencing. A client of his, a wiseguy-wannabe named Johnny Cantalupo, pleaded guilty to possession six weeks ago, in order to avoid going to prison for sale. It was cocaine, and not that awfully much of it, and Johnny's white and had no record to speak of, so the assistant D.A. and the judge had agreed to probation and time served, specifically the two days Johnny had spent while he was in the system.

In the system.

Whenever he hears the expression, Jaywalker can't help picturing a huge beast, gobbling up the newly arrested, digesting them for a day or two, and then, well, the rest is a bit vague. Spitting them out? *Undigesting* them into a courtroom? Or even worse, perhaps.

Although he was the first lawyer to show up this morning, and Johnny (under penalty of death by Jaywalker) the first defendant, they have to wait to get their case called. A written probation report first has to complete an arduous journey spanning three entire floors of the building, a feat that can take hours, sometimes days or even weeks. Never mind that the report will have no impact whatsoever on the sentence; its presence is mandated by law. In fact, the appearance before the judge this day promises to be a perfunctory one, the precise details of the sentence having been long ago worked out, recited on the record, and promised to the defendant on the sole condition that he show up today, which Johnny dutifully has. Consequently, Jaywalker will barely speak, having no need to convince the judge to do anything or refrain from doing anything. He's therefore allowed his attention to wander from the half-finished crossword puzzle in his lap to the defendants who one by one are brought out to face the judge, stand beside their lawyers and hear the charges they've been indicted on by a grand jury.

The first thing that strikes Jaywalker as out of the ordinary is when the clerk calls a particular case and a lawyer, instead of simply rising from his seat in the audience and quietly making his way up to the defense table, shouts out, "Defendant!" This immediately brands him as a civil lawyer, unfamiliar with how they do things over here on the criminal side.

The guy even *looks* like a civil lawyer, Jaywalker decides. Not just that he's short and bald; those descriptors apply to plenty of criminal lawyers. No, it's more than that. There's something decidedly shifty about him, something just a touch too practiced. Something that suggests ambulance chaser, or fixer. The old term *shyster* even comes to mind, but Jaywalker immediately banishes it, half forgiving himself only because he himself is half Jewish. Sort of like how African Americans are free to call each other *nigger,* but others need not apply.

They bring the guy's client out from the door to the pen, and Jaywalker's attention shifts to him. He's a kid, a kid who looks no more than sixteen or seventeen. Tall, though, with good posture for a teen, pale skin and closely cropped blond hair. A couple of years older and he could be a marine recruit, thinks Jaywalker, or in his first year at West Point. But the thing that really stands out is how good-looking the kid is. Beautiful, almost. Though having grown up in the homophobic '70s, Jaywalker still has a bit of trouble applying the term to a young man. Handsome, yes. Striking-looking, sure. But beautiful? No need to get carried away. But that's how good-looking the kid is, even after a day or two in the system.

He misses the kid's name, but leans forward and is able to catch the word *murder* as the clerk reads off the charges and asks the young man how he pleads, guilty or not guilty.

Now the thing is, the answer to that question is "Not guilty." Always. Even if immediately after the phrase is spoken, the lawyers were to approach the bench, huddle with the judge, work out a plea, and sixty seconds later the not guilty plea were to be withdrawn and replaced by a guilty plea to some lesser charge with a reduced sentence. Precisely as had been the case with Johnny Cantalupo, six weeks ago.

Only that's not what happens now.

Instead, as soon as the clerk asks the question, the civil lawyer answers for the kid. "Guilty with an explanation," he says.

Now that may work in traffic court, or in the summons part. But here, what happens is the entire courtroom—and it's a big courtroom, pretty much filled to capacity—goes stone-cold quiet.

"Excuse me?" says the judge, a white-haired old-timer named McGillicuddy.

"Guilty," the lawyer repeats, "but with an explanation. It's my feeling that probation would be an adequate sen—"

He gets no further than that before McGillicuddy waves him and the assistant district attorney to come up. Which, to Jaywalker's way of thinking, is a pretty decent thing on the judge's part, deciding not to show the guy up in front of a roomful of onlookers.

Because the thing is, you can't *get* probation on a murder charge, not even if you have the best explanation in the history of the universe. The *ten* best explanations. The range of sentencing on a murder count *begins* with fifteen-to-life, and goes up from there.

Jaywalker can't hear what's being said up at the bench, but he can see that whatever the words are, the judge is saying most of them and is being considerably less charitable than he'd been a moment ago. The civil lawyer has been pretty much reduced to gesturing, mostly with upturned palms and shrugging shoulders. "Who knew?" he seems to be saying.

As for the A.D.A., a prettyish woman with dark hair, dark-rimmed glasses and a thick file under one arm, she's shown the good sense to back away from the two of them as far as she can get, evidently wanting no part of an irate judge chewing out an incompetent defense lawyer. Meanwhile, back at the defense table, the defendant has been given a seat by a thoughtful court officer who must have decided that this sideshow is going to take a while.

Actually, it doesn't.

It ends abruptly, with the judge suddenly standing up and ordering the lawyers back to their places. "Mr. Fudderman is relieved," he announces. Then, scanning the front row of the audience, he looks for a replacement.

Jaywalker's instinctive reaction is to break off eye

contact. He's been in the military, been in law enforcement, and learned long ago that you never, ever volunteer for anything. Nothing good can come from it, whereas the potential for disaster is virtually unlimited. So even as he senses colleagues to his left and right straightening up in their seats and subliminally begging the judge to choose them, Jaywalker locks onto his crossword puzzle, focusing all his energy on coming up with a six-letter word for *annoy*.

"Mr. Jaywalker?" he hears.

H-A-R-A-S-S, he pencils in, never quite sure how to spell it. It could be two *r*'s or two *s*'s, or even two of both. But if it's two of both, it won't—

"Mr. Jaywalker?" Louder, this time.

He looks up, feigning bewilderment.

"Come up, please."

He glances to either side and over both shoulders before looking back at the judge.

"Yes, *you*."

2

WHAT WE HAVE HERE IS AN EXECUTION

It turned out his name was Estrada, Jeremy Estrada. Jaywalker found this out in the pen, sitting across from the kid and conducting what might charitably be called a short-form interview. Judge McGillicuddy hadn't actually *ordered* him to do it, but up at the bench he'd made it pretty clear that in his book Jaywalker owed him as much and more, without spelling it out. As soon as Jaywalker had begun protesting (immediately) that he was much too busy (he wasn't), McGillicuddy had silently mouthed the word "Bullshit." The A.D.A. had smiled just the tiniest bit at that but had quickly recovered by adjusting her glasses. No doubt she chalked up the incident as a pair of alpha males squaring off. But the judge's drift hadn't been lost on Jaywalker. About six months ago, in the midst of a run-of-the-mill larceny case, McGillicuddy had made a questionable ruling on a piece of evidence, and Jaywalker had muttered "Bullshit" loudly enough for the jury to hear. The judge had ignored it, even pretended he hadn't heard it, though surely he had. Instead of clearing the courtroom, holding Jaywalker in contempt and maybe even giving him an overnight to reflect upon his outburst, he'd simply filed the incident away, evidently determined to save it for a rainy day. And though it was clear and dry this particular May morning, it might as well have been pouring. The debt had been called.

That the kid turned out to have a Latino last name came as something of a surprise to Jaywalker; he'd figured from the fair complexion, blond hair and blue-gray eyes that he was dealing with a runaway from Iowa or Minnesota, or someplace like that. But when asked if he spoke English, Jeremy answered softly, "Yes, I was born here," without any trace of an accent.

"Do you understand what just happened out there in the courtroom?" Jaywalker asked him.

"No, not really." In a voice so soft that the words were barely audible.

"Well, for starters, your lawyer tried to plead you guilty to a life sentence. Where'd you manage to dig him up from?"

"My mother found him. She said he helped her after they shut off the electric in the apartment. And I guess there wasn't a lot of time, you know."

Jaywalker didn't know, and was almost afraid to ask. He'd agreed to spend ten minutes talking with the kid before letting McGillicuddy know if he was willing to represent him at assigned-counsel rates. Jaywalker had tried to explain that he was no longer on the panel of lawyers who took assignments, having been kicked off some time ago for turning in his payment vouchers months after they were due, sometimes years. But the judge had brushed him off. "Maybe the family has some money," he'd said. "Or you could always do it pro bono. It certainly sounds like a manslaughter plea, from what that other clown was saying. In other words, an appearance or two."

That other clown, by which he had to be referring to the

civil lawyer, seemed like something of a backhanded slap, but Jaywalker had held his tongue. More to the point, the shutting off of the electricity pretty much answered the question of whether the family had money. And as for pro bono, it was an old Latin phrase that loosely translated as "Okay, you get to do the work, but you don't get paid."

They spoke for twenty minutes, just long enough for Jaywalker to seriously doubt that the case was a plea to manslaughter or anything else, not with the way Jeremy was already talking about self-defense. So instead of being an appearance or two, it was just as likely to be a protracted negotiation or even a trial, which meant a year's worth of appearances and a ton of work.

And yet.

What was the *and yet* part?

Jaywalker would ask himself that very question a hundred times over the weeks and months to come. And each time he asked it, the best answer he could come up with was that the kid was so damn likeable, with his soft voice and guileless expression, and the way he looked directly at you with those big pale blue eyes of his. What was Jaywalker supposed to have told the judge? Sorry, I won't do it? Go get some other sucker?

No, McGillicuddy had known exactly what he was doing when he'd singled out Jaywalker from among the dozen lawyers sitting in the front row of his courtroom. He'd known full well that there was one among them who, no matter how easily he might mouth off to a judge in open court, simply didn't have it in his power to say no to a kid in deep trouble.

Talk about *bullshit*.

"So," the judge asked when the case was recalled. "Will you be representing Mr. Estrada?"

Jaywalker was standing at the defense table with Jeremy this time. Apparently McGillicuddy didn't intend to offer him the luxury of an off-the-record bench conference, where he might attempt to refuse in relative privacy. But the judge needn't have worried.

"Yes, sir."

"Now, would you like to approach with Ms. Darcy, to discuss a possible disposition of the charges?"

"Nothing personal, but no, sir."

"Very well. Fill out a notice of appearance. The case is assigned to Judge Wexler in Part 55. Three weeks for defense motions. Same bail conditions. Next case."

Back in the pen adjoining the courtroom—Jaywalker never left a courtroom without first explaining to his client what had just happened and what was likely to happen between now and the next court appearance—he told Jeremy that later in the week he'd have him brought over for a real visit. The young man smiled at the thought. No doubt he and Mr. Fudderman hadn't spent too much time together.

"Can you do me a favor?" Jeremy asked.

"I'll try."

"My mom's in the courtroom. Could you tell her I'm okay?"

"Sure."

"And…" And here Jeremy hesitated, as though embarrassed to ask.

"Yes?"

"Could you ask her to bring me some socks? It gets cold at night."

"Yes, I can do that."

They both stood, though they'd shortly be heading in very different directions. Jaywalker would be going back into the courtroom and then, once Johnny Cantalupo's sentencing was done, out into the fresh air of Centre Street. Okay, relatively fresh air. Jeremy would be moved to another pen, there to wait for the one o'clock bus back to Rikers Island.

Jaywalker extended a hand, and they shook. In the age of AIDS, hepatitis C and drug-resistant TB, his fellow defense lawyers had long abandoned the practice. For Jaywalker, that was just one more reason to adhere to it.

"Thank you for taking my case, Mr. Jaywalker," said Jeremy, reading the name with some difficulty from the business card Jaywalker had handed him earlier, the one with the home phone number on it. Another thing that distinguished Jaywalker from his colleagues.

"Call me Jay."

Jeremy smiled. "Jay Jaywalker?"

"Just Jay." It didn't seem necessary to explain that once upon a time he'd been Harrison J. Walker, and that he'd dropped the Harrison part as too pretentious and rejected Harry as too Lower East Side.

"Thank you, Mr. Jay."

Back in the courtroom, Jaywalker found Jeremy's mother and ushered her out to the hallway. She was a short, stout woman who answered to the name Carmen. He relayed her son's message about being okay. He didn't mention the socks.

"How does it look for him?" she asked in a gravelly voice, thick with an accent.

"It's too early to tell," said Jaywalker.

"Jew gotta do your best for him, Mr. Joewalker. Jew gotta promise." It would be her first of many attempts to get his name right. As for her mispronunciation of the word "you," he'd get over that, too, but it would take some doing.

Jaywalker promised. He'd won cases and lost cases, but no one—no one—had ever accused him of not doing his best.

She reached into her pocket and withdrew a handful of crumpled bills. "I brought this for Mr. Fudderman," she explained. "Am I supposed to give it to jew instead?"

"That's up to you," said Jaywalker. He would have loved to say no, that wasn't necessary. But he was a month and half behind with his rent, so he allowed her to hand him the money, and thanked her. He waited until after they'd spoken and she'd walked away before bothering to line up the bills and count them.

They added up to fifty-eight dollars, a pretty modest retainer even by Jaywalker's standards. Not even his rent was that low.

Johnny Cantalupo finally got his probation about 12:30 p.m., but Jaywalker still didn't leave the building. Instead he took the elevator down to the seventh floor and the district attorney's office, for a meeting with Katherine Darcy, the assistant who'd stepped up to the bench earlier that morning. It turned out it was her case, meaning she would stay with it, even try it, if it came to that.

Now, sitting across her desk, he decided she was older than he'd thought—maybe forty, he guessed—but every bit as pretty, if only she'd lighten up a bit. She could start, he almost suggested, by taking off the glasses; they made her look like a librarian, or a detention hall monitor. But he fought off the impulse to share his insights with her, pretty sure that voicing them could only get him into trouble and hurt his client at the same time.

"So," he asked her, "what do we have here?"

"What we have here is a couple of young macho studs and their girlfriends," she said. She said it easily, without having to look at the file. It was clear that she knew her case.

"One of them says, 'You lookin' at me?' and the other says, 'Yeah, I'm lookin' at you.' To tell you the truth, I don't know who started it. But it doesn't matter. A challenge is thrown down and accepted. They walk a few blocks, square off and duke it out."

Duke it out? Maybe she was older than she looked.

"It's a fair fight," she continued, "with fists. By all accounts, your guy wins it. Then, not satisfied, he pulls out a gun and shoots the victim, a twenty-year-old kid named Victor Quinones."

"Just like that?"

"Just like that."

"Witnesses?" Jaywalker asked her.

"Witnesses. Three of them, maybe four. The first wound isn't bad, a freaky in-and-out shot that grazes Victor's abdomen. He runs. Your guy catches up to him and, as Victor's lying on the pavement begging for mercy, grabs him by the hair and shoots him between the eyes at point-blank range. The next day, he takes off for Puerto Rico. Stays there six, seven months. Comes back, turns himself in. Must have gotten rid of the gun by then, and figured the witnesses would be long gone. Only they're not. They're all around and available. So, to answer your question as plainly and as simply as I possibly can, what we have here is an execution."

3

DUMB-ASSED QUESTIONS

"So I suppose, then," Jaywalker said to Katherine Darcy, "that a plea to disorderly conduct is pretty much out of the question."

"I'm glad you find the case so amusing," she said. But on the middle syllable of *amusing,* her voice broke just the tiniest bit. Jaywalker caught it, and raised both eyebrows— he'd tried to master raising just one at a time, but had given up some time ago—to let her know he hadn't missed it. But she refused to acknowledge his look, choosing instead to pretend that nothing had happened. And maybe nothing had. Maybe the poor woman had a speech defect, for all Jaywalker knew, or polyps in her throat, or a cold. He let it go.

"I try to find something amusing in all of my cases," he told her. "If I didn't, I'd have blown my brains out a long time ago."

She said nothing.

"So tell me," Jaywalker asked her. "What would you need on a Man One?" Unlike murder, on a plea to first-degree manslaughter a judge would have a broad sentencing range, from as much as twenty-five years all the way down to as little as five.

But Katherine Darcy wasn't biting. "Let me make myself clear," she said. "There's not going to *be* an offer in this case, not to Man One or anything else. I've run it by my bureau chief and presented it at a weekly meeting. Nobody gets too excited about the first shot. Heat of the moment, no serious injury, not such a big deal. But as soon as they hear about the last shot, the *coup de grace,* everyone agrees that's a deal-breaker. Or, like I said a little while ago, an execution. So it's a murder case, and it's going to stay a murder case. If some judge wants to give your guy the minimum on a plea to the charge, so be it. I have no control over that."

Not that she needed any control over that. The minimum sentence on murder was fifteen to life. "Sounds like you want to try the case," said Jaywalker.

She shrugged her shoulders. "If I don't try this one, I'll try another one. It honestly makes no difference to me."

Jaywalker stood up. It seemed as good a time as any to leave, before he started getting really pissed off at her. In his book, it was okay for a prosecutor to be tough, as long as he or she was reasonable about it and willing to be flexible when the situation called for it. It was quite another thing to treat all cases as fungible commodities, and to act as though defendants were readily interchangeable. They *weren't* interchangeable, at least not to Jaywalker's way of thinking. Each one was a human being, however imperfect and flawed. Each one was different, and the facts and circumstances of each case were different. It might not always seem that way from a distance, but if you got close enough, you could see it was true.

"How many murders have you tried?" he asked her, trying to make the question sound innocent and born out of nothing but idle curiosity. Small talk.

She hesitated for a moment, and he thought she might be counting in her head. But it turned out she wasn't. "This will actually be my first," she said. "But I've been in the appeals bureau for eight and a half years, and I bet I've briefed and argued at least fifteen or twenty."

"It's not quite the same," he suggested.

"I'm sure it's not," she said with what he took for a condescending smile. "But I'll manage. And in the process, it'll be a great honor to learn from the very best. I've heard a lot about you, Mr. Jaywalker, and—"

"Jay."

"—and I'm very much looking forward to the experience. I really am."

Riding down the elevator, Jaywalker told himself to breathe deeply, calm down and not take Ms. Darcy's attitude personally. Working in the appeals bureau was something like practicing in a law library. You dealt with statutes crafted in legalese, abstract principles of law and cold rules of evidence. You spent your time reading transcripts of trials hundreds of pages long, sometimes thousands. They might contain each word spoken from the witness stand and every comment made on the record. But what they didn't have, what they left out, was just as important: the stammering and sweating of the witnesses, their inability to make and maintain eye contact, the repetition of phrases or mispronunciations that, in real time and place, spoke volumes, volumes that never showed up on the printed page. The transcripts said nothing about the young man or broken woman sitting shaking in the defendant's chair, nothing about the mother sobbing softly back in the third row. To the appellate lawyer, sentences were numbers, governed by statutory minimums and maximums and measured against statistical means and averages. They told you nothing about the filthy cells those sentences would have to be served in, nothing about the rapes that would be almost as regular as the meals, nothing about the toddlers back home who'd be growing up without fathers or mothers, or sometimes both.

But even as he told himself these things and tried to excuse Katherine Darcy's ignorance as nothing more than the product of her cloistered career, Jaywalker wasn't quite ready to forgive her. He'd been around long enough to know how things worked in the D.A.'s office. When an assistant was ready to handle her first homicide case, they'd hand her an absolute winner, an open-and-shut felony murder, or a case with ten eyewitnesses and a full videotaped confession. Something along those lines. Evidently they considered Jeremy Estrada's case a perfect example. But instead of approaching it with a sense of humility over the fact that one young man was dead and another likely to grow old in prison, she was looking at it as a numbers game, in which she was determined to rack up as high a score as possible. To her, that meant no lesser plea. And if it went to trial, so much the better. Along the way, she might pick up a thing or two and hone her courtroom skills. If not, the next one would go to trial, or the one after that.

And Jaywalker's reaction to that?

As much as he hated rolling the dice with somebody's freedom at stake, already there was a part of him that wanted to try the case, just so to he could *beat* her, watch her face drop as she listened to some jury foreperson read off the words *Not guilty*. See if *that* didn't knock that smug little smile off her face, along with those library-issue glasses of hers. And not just because he wanted to see how pretty she might be without them, either.

Though that was surely part of it.

He had his first real sit-down meeting with Jeremy Estrada two days later, in an attorney visit room on the thirteenth floor. A lot of buildings don't even have thirteenth floors; they're generally considered bad luck and therefore undesirable. At 100 Centre Street, just about everyone had had bad luck and was considered an undesirable, so somebody must have decided that the number made no difference.

Jeremy showed up looking tired and wearing an orange jumpsuit, courtesy of the Department of Corrections, and a pair of old sneakers. Jaywalker, who had no cases of his own on this day, was decked out in his casual Friday finest, faded jeans and a denim work shirt with a frayed collar. It also served as his casual rest-of-the-week finest. A lot of things were important to Jaywalker, but clothes weren't one of them.

"What time did they wake you up?" he asked Jeremy, once they'd taken seats across from one another, separated by a wire-mesh partition.

Jeremy smiled. "About three o'clock," he said.

"Sorry." He knew the drill. Up at three, to be herded into the dayroom at four to wait a few hours. Onto the bus at seven or seven-fifteen. At the courthouse by eight, eight-thirty. Up to the pens at nine. After that, it all depended on when your lawyer showed up. That could mean as early as nine-thirty if you were lucky enough to have a Jaywalker, or as late as four in the afternoon if you weren't. If your case got called in the morning session, you made the one-o'clock bus and were back on Rikers by three. If you missed the one o'clock, you had to wait for the five o'clock, which never pulled out before six-thirty, and got you back to the Rock around ten or ten-thirty. Meaning you'd not only miss chow, but if you had to be back in court the next day, you'd get three hours of sleep if you were lucky. Jaywalker knew all this not only because he'd heard it from defendants, but because he'd been in the system himself more than once, whether serving an overnight contempt sentence after piss-ing off some judge, or something equally silly, like getting caught snooping around in the chief clerk's office in order to get a peek at the judicial courtroom assignment sheet for the following month, so he could engage in a little judge-shopping.

"So," he said, "how about telling me what happened."

"Where would you like me to start?" Jeremy asked in a voice so soft Jaywalker had to lean forward to hear it.

"I'd like you to start at the beginning. And take your time. I need details."

Jeremy took a deep breath and smiled. "It's kind of a long story," he said.

"I've got all day," Jaywalker told him.

"I guess it started," Jeremy said, "when I met this girl."

No shock there. Jaywalker had learned long ago that most murders were about money or drugs. But if they weren't, they were about girls. "What was her name?" he asked.

"Miranda. Her name was Miranda."

"And?"

"We, we became friends."

"Friends?" Jaywalker asked. "Or lovers, too?"

"No. We never got a chance."

"How did it go?" Jaywalker asked him. "The friend-ship."

"It went good, at first."

"And then?"

Already Jaywalker could see that getting information out of Jeremy was going to be a slow and painful process. Over time, he'd come to liken it to dental extraction. Not only did Jeremy speak in something between a whisper and a murmur, he summarized. A summary can be helpful if you want to get from the beginning of a story to the end of it in a hurry. On the other hand, if you're interested in finding out what really happened and *why,* a summary is the opposite of what you're looking for. Again Jaywalker told Jeremy to take his time, that it was detail he was after. But if Jeremy understood the word, he was for some reason unable to follow the direction.

"There was a problem," he said.

"What kind of a problem?"

"There were these guys," said Jeremy. "Seven or eight guys, actually, and one girl. One of the guys, the main one, kept going like Miranda belonged to him, even though she didn't. And they gave me a hard time because of that. You know."

"No, I don't. How did they give you a hard time?"

"They followed me. They called me names. They told me they were going to get me. That kinda stuff. You know."

"And?"

"And finally I had a face-off with one of them."

"A face-off?"

"Yeah."

"Why don't you tell me about it," said Jaywalker. His therapist used to say that, back when Jaywalker had gone into treatment following his wife's death, because he couldn't sleep at night, couldn't get out of bed in the morning, couldn't even remember why he was supposed to. *"Why don't you tell me about it?" "How does it make you feel?" "What do* you *think about it?"* The therapy hadn't lasted too long. But bit by bit, Jaywalker had begun sleeping at night again, and getting out of bed in the morning, and life had somehow gone on. So who was to say? Maybe the therapy had helped. Maybe the same sort of dumb-assed questions might work with Jeremy.

"We had a fight, him and me."

"A fight. With weapons?"

"No," said Jeremy. "With fists."

"Who won?"

A shrug. "I did, I guess."

"Then what?"

"He pulled a gun," said Jeremy. "We fought over it. It went off. I got it away from him."

"And then?"

"And then I shot it at him."

"Once?" Jaywalker asked him. "Or more than once?"

"More than once."

"How many times?"

Jeremy shrugged again. "I'm not sure," he said.

"But you killed him?"

Jeremy's answer was so soft Jaywalker couldn't hear it and had to say, "What?"

"I guess so."

"Shot him between the eyes?"

"If that's what they say."

"That's what they say," said Jaywalker.

"Then I guess it must be true."

"Why did you shoot him between the eyes?"

Jeremy seemed to think about that for a minute. Or maybe he was honestly trying to remember. Squinting through the wire mesh of the partition that separated them, it was hard for Jaywalker to tell.

"Self-defense?" But the way Jeremy said the words, they came out sounding more like a question than an answer or a recollection. No doubt he knew nothing about the nuances of justification, the body of law that allows one to use force—occasionally even deadly force—to protect one's self or someone else. But despite his ignorance, it was pretty obvious that even Jeremy knew it wasn't going to be much of a fit to the events he'd described.

Jaywalker figured it was as good a time as any to start finding out. "Was the guy armed at the moment you fired that shot?" he asked. "The one that hit him between the eyes?"

"No," said Jeremy. "Not then he wasn't."

"Was he coming at you?"

"No."

"Threatening you in any way?"

"No."

"What *was* he doing?"

Jeremy closed his eyes. Maybe he was trying to picture things as they'd happened that day, seven months ago. Maybe he was even trying to relive the incident, seeing if he somehow couldn't make it come out differently this time. After a long moment, he opened his eyes and, looking directly at Jaywalker, said, "I don't really remember."

So much for self-defense.

They talked for a while more before Jeremy asked what time it was. And even though Jaywalker told him it was barely noon, Jeremy repeated the question five minutes later.

"You want to make the one o'clock?" he asked.

Jeremy nodded sheepishly.

"Okay," said Jaywalker. They hadn't been talking all that long, but he sensed that still might amount to something of a record for Jeremy. And so far, all he'd been able to pull out of the kid was the most basic outline of the shooting and the events that had led up to it. But there'd be time, and Jeremy certainly wasn't going anywhere. In New York State the right to bail is pretty broad, but it stops at the door of the accused murderer's cell. And even before McGillicuddy had gotten a hold of the case, another judge had ordered Jeremy held in remand. Meaning there was no bail set at all. Not that Carmen Estrada and her fifty-eight dollars could have come up with it anyway.

But before they parted, Jaywalker had one more order of business with Jeremy. "Do me a favor," he told him, "and put these on." Taking two pairs of woolen socks from his briefcase, he slid them beneath the wire-mesh partition.

"Put them on here? Both pairs?"

"Yup," Jaywalker told him. "Otherwise the C.O.'s will take them away from you and have me arrested for smuggling contraband into the jail." The C.O.'s were the corrections officers, and the truth was, they never would have had him arrested. Others, yes, but not Jaywalker. To them, he was one of the good guys. Not only did he talk like them and ask about their wives and kids, he had a law enforcement background. And most of all, he did right by his clients, even the ones who were jammed up the worst. *Especially* the ones who were jammed up the worst. In other words, he was one of them. So Jaywalker wasn't worried about himself at all. He was looking out for the C.O.'s themselves, lest some captain spot Jeremy carrying in the socks and write up one of the C.O.'s for looking the other way and allowing them in.

Jeremy slipped off his sneakers and did as he was told. But when he tried to put his sneakers back on, he found it all but impossible. He ended up having to leave them spread wide open. Lacing them up was no issue; shoelaces weren't allowed on Rikers Island. They could too easily be used as a weapon, to strangle another inmate. Or to "hang up," as in committing suicide.

Jeremy stood up and tried walking a few paces. From the way he did it, it was clear he was going to need some practice.

But his feet sure were going to be warm at night.

4

A REAL NICE KID

He'd only been on the case three days, but already Jaywalker pretty much knew that the fact that Jeremy Estrada's feet would be warm was about all the good news he should expect.

Murder cases pretty much fell into two distinct groups, Jaywalker had long ago learned. There were the *whodunnits,* where the issue was whether the prosecution could prove that it was the defendant who'd committed the crime. And there were, for lack of a better term, what he called the *yesbuts.* That was his catchall category for all the other cases, where the identity of the killer was beyond serious dispute, and if the case was going to be won, it was going to be won with a "yesbut" defense. Yes, the defendant had killed the deceased, but it had been an accident, or he'd acted in self-defense, or had been too young or too retarded or too insane to make it murder, or—and this one you were unlikely to find in the statute books, unless maybe you were in Mississippi or Alabama or west Texas—the victim had needed killing.

Unfortunately, none of those defenses seemed to apply to Jeremy's case.

To begin with, not only did Jeremy readily admit that he was the killer, but Katherine Darcy, if she was to be believed, had a handful of witnesses ready to walk into court and prove it to a jury's satisfaction. So it wasn't a whodunnit. Which meant it didn't call for a SODDI defense, the letters referring to a highly technical principle of law which, spelled out in full, stood for Some Other Dude Did It.

But when Jaywalker turned to the question of what exactly had made Jeremy do it, things didn't get any more promising. The shot between the eyes at point-blank range could hardly be excused as an accident. And with Victor Quinones lying unarmed and helpless on the ground, self-defense was pretty much out of the question. Next, although Jeremy might look fifteen, it turned out he was actually seventeen, the same age he'd been at the time of the killing. And appearance didn't count; the fact was, he was old enough to be considered an adult under the murder statute. And if he seemed a bit on the slow and quiet side, he certainly didn't strike Jaywalker as being either not legally responsible for his acts or incompetent to stand trial. Under New York law, you were competent if you knew what you were charged with and could carry on a conversation with your lawyer. Hell, Jaywalker had come across *radishes* that passed that test. In terms of insanity, Jeremy had no psychiatric history that Jaywalker knew of, and his behavior seemed calculated and purposeful, hardly the product of a mental disease or defect, something an insanity defense required. Finally, they were in Manhattan, the enlightened heart of New York City, not the deep South; "deserving to die" simply didn't cut it here. And even if it had, giving someone a hard time by calling him names and then losing a fistfight to him hardly rose to the level of sufficient provocation.

The most that Jaywalker had to work with so far was the

fact that Jeremy had eventually turned himself in to face the music. And that he was soft-spoken, extremely good-looking and didn't seem capable of hurting a fly, much less blowing someone's brains out.

Which wasn't much help, seeing as that was exactly what he'd done.

So as much as a part of Jaywalker would have loved to try the case and teach Katherine Darcy a little humility, he knew he wasn't going to get his chance. Not on this case, anyway. To begin with, Jaywalker wasn't a gunslinger by nature, a cowboy who tried cases for the fun of it. Or for the fee of it, the extra money it brought in if you were on the clock and were interested in running up the hours. As good as he was at trial—and those who'd been up against him, alongside him or anywhere else in the courtroom would tell you there was no one better—Jaywalker *hated* trying cases. For one thing, he put so much of himself into the battle that each time out, it nearly killed him. He stopped eating, he lost weight, his hair fell out in clumps and he didn't sleep at night. But those things he regarded as minor inconveniences. More to the point, he recognized that a trial was nothing but a crapshoot, a roll of the dice. It ultimately left the defendant's fate in the hands of a judge or jury. And though Jaywalker's acquittal rate was up in the ninety-percent range, an unheard-of statistic, the fact remained that he lost cases. Not often, but occasionally. The only lawyers who didn't lose were television lawyers or were liars. And if Jaywalker were to lose this one, if the dice happened to come up wrong for Jeremy Estrada, it would mean a life sentence.

No, this wasn't a case that could be tried. It was one of the ninety percent that would have to be plea-bargained. And even though Katherine Darcy had talked tough, insisting that there would be no offer, that was now. Jaywalker's job, as he saw it, was to convince her otherwise, to over-come her resistance.

Just how would he go about doing that?

Well, time would be on his side, for one thing. Eight months had already passed since the death of Victor Quinones. By the time the case was trial-ready, Jaywalker would see that another year had gone by. He'd draw out the discovery process, do some serious investigating, file written motions, ask for pretrial hearings, and do everything else in his power to play the clock. Little by little, Katherine Darcy would get worn-out and distracted. She'd get assigned other cases and find herself fighting other battles. Witnesses would disappear, detectives would retire and move to Florida or Arizona, and family members of the victim would give up and go back to Puerto Rico. Who knew? With a little bit of luck, the rigid Ms. Darcy might even mellow a bit and develop a sense of proportion.

There was one small problem with that strategy, of course. It meant that Jaywalker had to get down to work.

One of the built-in advantages the prosecution enjoys over the defense is its head start. In a typical case, that head start may be as minimal as a day or two. A crime gets committed. A person gets arrested, processed at the station house of the local precinct and brought to the courthouse. There the arresting officer or detective sits down with an assistant district attorney, and together they draw up a complaint. Essential witnesses are interviewed while their recollections of events are fresh. If the case is a felony, particularly a serious one like murder, a grand jury presentation is quickly scheduled. The assistant district attorney conducts that presentation, both as prosecutor and "legal advisor" to the grand jurors. There's no judge present, and nobody to represent the defendant. The sole exception to the last part of that occurs when a defense lawyer insists that his client be permitted to testify. But even in the rare instance when that happens, the lawyer gets to ask no questions, raise no objections and make no statements; he's effectively gagged. Meanwhile, the assistant district attorney is free to cross-examine the defendant and pin him down at a point when he's barely had time to explain the events to his own lawyer.

Not that any of that had happened in Jeremy Estrada's case. By fleeing to Puerto Rico immediately following the shooting, Jeremy had forfeited his right to appear at the grand jury. And by staying away for seven months, he'd taken the prosecution's customary day-or-two head start and multiplied it by a factor of several hundred.

Normally Jaywalker's approach to catching up would have involved an extended sit-down with the prosecutor. There were plenty of assistant D.A.s who would have been willing to pretty much open their case files to him and supply him with copies of documents he wasn't even remotely entitled to at that point. But Katherine Darcy had already made it clear that she wasn't from that school. Getting information out of her, he knew, was going to be about as easy as getting it out of Jeremy. So Jaywalker wasn't ready to go back to her. Not yet, anyway.

Instead, he took a deep breath, told himself to be nice, and put in a call to Alan Fudderman, the civil lawyer who'd stood up for Jeremy at his arraignment. The guy who'd helped Carmen when they'd turned off her electricity, and then tried to plead Jeremy guilty to murder, hoping for probation.

They met at Fudderman's office, a cramped cubbyhole in a high-rise on lower Broadway. The walls were stained and peeling, and there was so much paper on top of the desk that separated them that Jaywalker had to sit up straight just to see over it. But Fudderman himself turned out to be as affable in person as he'd been adrift in criminal court. He didn't bother making copies of the documents in his file; he simply turned over all the originals to Jaywalker.

"I'm glad they've found someone who seems to know what he's doing," he said. "I was a little out of my element."

"Happens to the best of us," said Jaywalker. Though it never happened to him. But that was because he wouldn't have been caught dead in civil court, or housing court, or before the Taxi and Limousine Commission. He didn't write wills, handle divorces or do closings. There were even criminal cases he wouldn't touch, because they required some specialized knowledge he lacked. The list included prosecutions involving securities, wire fraud, stock transfers, money laundering and the like. Just about anything calling for a knowledge of how money worked. Money, Jaywalker had come to realize long ago, was something he was no good at, whether that meant understanding it, earning it, investing it or simply keeping it from evaporating into thin air.

"He seems like a real nice kid," said Fudderman.

"Yeah," Jaywalker agreed. "He does."

"I hope you can do something for him."

"Me, too."

Jaywalker thanked him for his time. At the door, Fudderman extended his hand. Jaywalker had to shift the file from one arm to the other in order to shake with him.

"Let me know," said Fudderman, "if there's anything else I can ever do for you."

"Thanks," said Jaywalker.

Come to think of it, he *was* two months behind with his electric bill.

* * *

That night, Jaywalker passed up watching a Yankee game. It actually wasn't that much of a sacrifice, as he thought about it. They were already so far out of contention for a playoff spot that he'd given up on them and was instead already looking forward to football season and the Giants.

His wife had accused him of being a fair-weather fan, and there was some truth to it. She'd never understood how he could turn off a game just because his team was a couple of runs or touchdowns behind, but could stay up past midnight to catch the final out of a blowout victory. He'd tried to explain to her that it was all about enjoyment; if it looked like his guys were going to win, every minute of it was fun, if it didn't, why would he want to torture himself?

"But suppose they make a comeback?" she'd asked him more than once.

"From fourteen down?"

"It could happen," she would say.

God, how he missed her. More than a decade had passed now since her death, and he still reached out for her in the dark of night.

"Enough," he said out loud.

He did that from time to time. Talked to himself in the privacy of his studio apartment. He'd worried about it at first, wondering if it was an early symptom of dementia. But then he'd convinced himself that it really wasn't so different from whistling in an empty elevator, or singing to himself in his car on the rare occasions when he drove it.

"Enough," he said again. And walked over to his desk/dining room table/laundry sorter/ironing board, where he'd placed the accordion file Alan Fudderman had given him that afternoon.

He untied the little stringy thing that kept it closed and

dumped the contents onto the table. There wasn't much. A
copy of the indictment; a warrant issued long ago for
Jeremy's arrest; his rap sheet, showing one prior for marijuana possession but no disposition for it; a paper copy of
what must have been a morgue photo of Victor Quinones,
too grainy to really show what he'd looked like; a sketch of
the crime scene, indicating where the fistfight had taken
place and where Quinones had been found by the first re-
sponders; the autopsy report and death certificate; a police
property voucher for two shell casings from a 9-mm pistol
and a small piece of deformed lead; and a few other mis-
cellaneous documents, none of which promised to give up
any secrets.

He spent the next two hours reading, rereading, making
notes and organizing the material into subfiles. Then he
made a list of things that *weren't* there, that Katherine Darcy
had notably declined to turn over to Alan Fudderman, and
that she'd no doubt resist turning over to Jaywalker. By the
time he was finished, the list dwarfed the items she'd
actually supplied.

He walked over to the TV set, turned it on and found the
Yankee game. A graphic at the top of the screen told him
they were down 7-3 in the bottom of the eighth. He watched
Derek Jeter strike out on a nasty slider in the dirt, clicked
it off and went to bed. Bed being a pullout sofa that he
hadn't bothered pulling out in three months, or whenever
the last time was that he'd had company of the sleepover
variety.

The next morning, when other lawyers were taking cabs
downtown to their offices, corporate clients or courthouses,
Jaywalker took three subways to the Upper East Side. Not
the Upper East Side of uniformed doormen, handsomely
groomed poodles and multimillion dollar apartments, but

the Upper East Side of housing projects, bodegas and car repair shops. The *upper* Upper East Side.

He could have hired a private investigator to do it, but there wasn't room in his fifty-eight dollar retainer to do that. Besides, Jaywalker had long been his own investigator. His background as a DEA agent equipped him for the task, and though he no longer carried a gun—it was somewhere in the bottom of his closet, probably, but he'd had no reason to dig it out for years now, and would no doubt shoot himself in the foot as soon as he did—he was no stranger to bad neighborhoods, having spent half his life in them. The secret was to dress the part, and then look and sound like you belonged, all talents that came easily to him.

Using the crime-scene sketch as a road map, he got off the train at 110th Street and walked east to Third Avenue. There he turned left and headed north. It was a little after eight o'clock, early afternoon by Jaywalker standards, and the sun was just beginning to clear the buildings to his right. He kept to the west side of the avenue, where he could feel its warmth. By afternoon, he knew, he'd be looking for shade.

He walked three blocks before crossing over and turning into the courtyard that would take him into the little pocket park carved out of the redbrick buildings of the housing project. He found the benches drawn in the sketch and marking the site of the fistfight, where back in September two young men had squared off. One of them had thought it was going to be a fair fight. The other had come "packing," "strapped" for the occasion, as they said on the street. From there, Jaywalker paced off the distance to the spot where Victor Quinones had found death in the form of a 9-mm bullet.

If there'd been blood on the pavement, or the chalked outline of a human body, it was long gone, washed clean by a hundred rains. If there'd been witnesses other than the ones Katherine Darcy promised were "around and available," they weren't showing their heads this morning. Jaywalker straightened up and looked around in all directions. It was almost as though he was hoping the crime scene would speak to him, reward him for his pilgrimage. All he needed was some clue, some tiny nugget that might help him understand just what had driven Jeremy Estrada to take the life of another young man. Something he could take away with him and bring to the office of a tough prosecutor who, when she looked at the case, saw only an execution. Or to a jury, if all else failed.

But there were no clues in sight this morning, no tiny nuggets.

The park was saying nothing.

He met again with Carmen Estrada, Jeremy's mother. She came to his office that afternoon. Or, technically, the office of a colleague, Jaywalker having given up his own space in the building back at the time of his suspension, some five years ago.

About the killing and the events that had led up to it, Carmen was short on specifics but long on loyalty.

"It wasn't Jeremy's fault, Mr. Johnnywalker. It was all on account of the problem he had with those guys," she explained. "On account of the girl, Miranda. The guys, they made him do it. It's all their fault, the accident that happened."

Over the weeks and months to follow, he wouldn't get much more than that out of her. It was easy to see where Jeremy had learned the habit of summarizing instead of going into factual detail. To Carmen, the harassment her son had been subjected to would always be "the problem," just as the deadly culmination of that problem would always be "the accident."

Before leaving, she reached down the front of her dress, and for a frightening moment Jaywalker thought she might be about to undress. Not that it would have been a first for him. But he'd already decided that Jeremy must have gotten his good looks from his father's side of the family. And loyalty, while surely a virtue, was hardly what Jaywalker looked for in a bed partner.

But when Carmen's hand reappeared from between her breasts, it was clutching an envelope, folded in half. "Here," she said. "It's for jew."

Inside, he would find five well-used twenty-dollar bills.

So if the going rate for a murder case was somewhere in the neighborhood of fifty thousand dollars, that meant he had only $49,842 to go.

With Carmen Estrada proving to be something less than a font of information, Jaywalker resigned himself to trying another visit with Jeremy. On their previous meeting, he'd found Jeremy so preoccupied with making the one-o'clock bus back to Rikers Island that he was incapable of going into the facts of the case in any really useful detail. So Jaywalker decided to do it the old-fashioned way. Rather than having his client brought over to 100 Centre Street for a counsel visit, he would make the trip out to Rikers himself. Sure, by the time he was back it would have cost him an entire day, what with subway rides back and forth, long waits for short hops on Department of Corrections buses, sign-ins and searches and more waiting. But, he figured, what else did he have to do with his time?

Following his reinstatement, he'd tried a murder case up in Rockland County and handled a few things that had come his way, such as Johnny Cantalupo's drug case. But he'd been slow to rebuild his practice, unsure that he wanted to keep lawyering for a living. He'd tried his hand at writing, figuring he had plenty of stories to tell. But writing took self-discipline, he'd soon discovered, and Jaywalker and self-discipline had always had something of a rocky relationship.

So out to Rikers it would be, to the grim little island plunked halfway between the Bronx and Queens. From afar it could fool you, its redbrick buildings looking pretty much like the public housing on the mainland. It was only when you got close that you noticed. On top of those buildings were guard towers manned by sharpshooters with automatic rifles and 12-gauge shotguns. And where there were openings for windows, in place of glass there were thick steel bars that held back the equivalent of a medium-sized city's entire population.

"Thanks for coming out," said Jeremy once they were seated across a table in the counsel visit room. There was no wire mesh partition separating them this time, only a uniformed corrections officer sitting thirty feet away. "None of the other lawyers ever come here," Jeremy added.

Jaywalker smiled. He liked nothing better than to be reminded that he was different from other lawyers. "You're welcome," he said. Then he explained his purpose in making the trip. "Last time we met, you gave me a pretty good idea of what happened, in general terms. It was very helpful, a good place to start. Today, I'm here for the details. Do you know what details are?"

"Sure," said Jeremy.

But his uncertain smile left Jaywalker less than convinced. "Do me a favor, will you?"

Jeremy nodded. As would always be the case, he was eager to please. The problem was that he often didn't know how to. He reminded Jaywalker of a not-too-bright puppy he'd gotten his daughter when she was five or six. Asked to sit, it would lie down. Told to lie down, it would roll over. Instructed to stay, it would come running. But it did everything with such unflagging energy and good humor that it was impossible to punish, and ended up getting more treats than a kid on Halloween.

"Describe me," said Jaywalker, "in as much detail as you possibly can."

"Describe you?" said an uncertain Jeremy.

"Yeah. Pretend you're describing me for somebody who's never met me and will have to pick me out from fifty people on a subway platform. Pretend your life depends on his being able to recognize me, just from what you tell him I look like."

"Can I look at you while I do it?" Jeremy asked.

"Absolutely."

Jeremy gave it his best shot, but as shots went, it fell far short of the rim. Jaywalker had to prompt him half a dozen times, reminding him to include clothing, height, weight, body build, hair color, absence or presence of facial hair, and age. With the prompting, Jeremy proved that he was a competent enough observer. In other words, if Jaywalker tried hard enough and long enough, he could extract accurate details. Well, except for age, anyway. When he got to that, Jeremy looked him up and down several times, then took a guess.

"Thirty-five?"

"Thank you," said Jaywalker, unable to hide a smile. It wasn't that he was flattered; Jaywalker didn't do flattered. No, he was remembering back when he himself had been in his teens, and anyone over thirty was so ancient that the numbers didn't matter.

"Was I close?" Jeremy asked.

"I'm actually fifty-two," Jaywalker confessed.

"Wow!" said Jeremy. "Don't die before my case is over, okay?"

Jaywalker assured him he'd try his best not to.

They spent the next two hours going over the events that had led up to the day of the shooting, with Jaywalker prodding for details and Jeremy doing his best to supply them. At first it went surprisingly well, with Jeremy's face lighting up from time to time, and his words, if not quite flowing, at least trickling out at a fairly steady pace.

He'd been walking to school one morning. It had to have been sometime in May, a little over a year ago. It was a new school he was going to, that he'd begun in January. He'd been going to Catholic school before then, but his mother had reached the point where she could no longer afford the tuition.

He'd started noticing this girl. This *young lady,* he called her. She worked in a flower shop on the avenue, and he'd see her out front sometimes, sweeping out the place before opening up. It had taken him a week to get up the courage to stop and talk to her, but finally he'd made himself do it. They'd told each other their names. Hers was Miranda.

"What did she look like?" Jaywalker asked, wondering if their exercise a few minutes earlier would pay dividends.

"She was pretty," said Jeremy. "Very, very, very pretty. Thin, real thin like. A couple inches shorter than me. I'm five-nine, five-ten. Reddish-brown hair, long and straight. And these great big brown eyes. Yeah, very pretty."

They'd begun seeing each other. "Not like going out, you know. Not really dating. We'd sit on a park bench and talk. We'd eat ice cream cones. We'd talk about TV shows, our families. Silly stuff like that. I know it's gonna sound dumb, but it was the happiest time of my life."

"Doesn't sound dumb at all," said Jaywalker. "Sounds wonderful." What he didn't say was that for the young man sitting across the table from him in the orange jumpsuit, the chances of his ever feeling that way again were just this side of nonexistent.

Up to that point, Jeremy had performed beyond Jaywalker's expectations. Sure, there'd been some interruptions and requests for specifics, but at one point Jeremy had spoken uninterrupted for a minute or more, which might have been a record for him. Then again, he'd been talking about Miranda and what he'd described as the best part of his life. Now he was about to begin talking about the worst part of his life, the "problem," as his mother called it. And even as Jeremy got ready to go on, Jaywalker could see an unmistakable tightening of the young man's facial muscles and sense a noticeable tensing of his entire body.

"Then these guys started coming around."

"How many?" Jaywalker asked.

"Usually there were about six or seven of them. Sometimes a few more, sometimes less. One was a girl. And one of them, sorta the leader, would go like Miranda was his lady."

"Was that true? I mean, had she been?"

"Nah. He was just runnin' his mouth, was all."

"How old were they?" Jaywalker asked. He knew from the death certificate that Victor Quinones had been twenty at the time of his death.

"My age, I guess. Or a little bit older."

At first it had just been taunts and name-calling, harmless enough stuff. But soon it began to escalate into more.

"What kind of more?"

"They'd follow us, or follow me if I was alone. They'd say they were going to get me. That kind of stuff. You know."

"No," said Jaywalker, "I don't know. You have to tell me. Just like you were able to tell me what Miranda looked like."

But as easy as it had been for Jeremy to describe Miranda, that was how hard it was for him to talk about the "stuff" he'd had to put up with at the hands of his tormentors. They got through it, Jaywalker and Jeremy, but it was tough slogging, and by the time they reached the day of the fight and the shooting, they'd been it at it for almost three hours, and Jaywalker decided to call it a day. He still had precious little in the way of real detail, but he'd learned a few things.

The group that had given Jeremy such a hard time that summer had called themselves the Raiders. Members had occasionally sported Oakland Raider football jerseys or caps, bearing the skull and crossbones of pirate lore. Several had matching tattoos, and a few had worn windowpanes, decorative coverings on their teeth. Their self-appointed leader, the one who'd acted as though Miranda belonged to him, had been a young man named Alesandro, whom the others had called Sandro. Among his followers had been Shorty, a guy who Jeremy guessed couldn't have been more than five-two, but who had a quick temper and a foul mouth. There'd been Diego, a tall, skinny kid with tattoos covering both arms, and a little guy called Mousey. The female member of the group had been Teresa, a name Jaywalker recognized from the papers Alan Fudderman had given him. If she was Teresa Morales, she'd been the girlfriend of Victor Quinones, and had been an eyewitness to the fight and the shooting.

Which, of course, created a problem.

Of the four people who'd been right there for that final shot, one—Victor—was dead. As for Miranda, Jeremy hadn't seen or heard from her in eight months, and had no idea where she might be. Jeremy himself was what the law referred to as an *interested witness,* which meant that his version of the events was likely to be devalued by a jury. There was even an instruction a judge was permitted to include in his charge to the jurors, specifying that in assessing the defendant's credibility, they could consider his stake in the outcome of the trial, a stake that was greater than that of any other witness.

So with Miranda missing and Jeremy's testimony likely to be viewed with skepticism, Teresa Morales promised to be a key witness. And the fact that she'd been Victor's girlfriend didn't exactly comfort Jaywalker. Was she going to agree that Victor and the others had harassed Jeremy in the weeks and months leading up to the fight? And was she likely to support Jeremy's account of the killing?

Not a chance.

So Jaywalker had made a point of pressing Jeremy to find out if there was anyone else who might be able to back up his version of things.

"No," said Jeremy. "Only me and Miranda."

He did describe one incident that had taken place about a week before the shooting. The group had tried to get at him, he said, while he was in a barbershop. But the shop had since closed, he'd heard, and the owner—who, except for Jeremy and Miranda, had been the only one around that day—had moved back to Puerto Rico.

Other than that, Jeremy couldn't come up with anybody who might be able to corroborate his account of anything.

Riding the subway back home, Jaywalker played back the meeting in his mind. One of the things that struck him was the contrast in Jeremy's moods. It almost seemed to him that there were two Jeremys. Early on in the visit—while talking about Miranda, for example—he'd been bright-eyed and forthcoming, capable of providing exactly the sort of specifics that would make him a pretty decent witness on the stand. But moments later he'd tightened up and reverted to the quiet Jeremy, the Jeremy of nods and grunts and one-word answers. And Jaywalker? He thought he understood the reason, figured it was attributable to a combination of Jeremy's natural shyness and slowness, along with the best-of-times/worst-of-times business. After all, who didn't prefer to talk about the good stuff and minimize the bad? Jaywalker himself was no exception to the rule. Ask him how a trial of his had turned out and he'd tell you, "We won," and launch into an unbidden twenty-minute mono-logue. But if it had gone badly, he would unconsciously remove himself and his ego from the equation and answer, "They convicted him," and let it go at that.

But looking back later at these early stages of his dialogue with Jeremy Estrada, Jaywalker would realize that he'd been missing something important. Despite all his probing and prompting, and notwithstanding his clever examples and constant reminders, when it came down to comprehending the real reason behind Jeremy's reticence and his own inability to pierce through it, he was making little progress. In time he'd come to understand that it hadn't simply been a matter of a young man's natural preference for focusing on good things rather than bad ones. No, the real reason for Jeremy's reluctance to talk about that summer ran much deeper than that, and would eventually take both lawyer and client into much darker territory.

5

JUST GETTING STARTED

That night, Jaywalker sat down at his computer. It actually had its own table, if you didn't want to get too picky about *table*. Its former life had been spent as a shipping crate. And not one of those cutesy things they sell at Pottery Barn or Eddie Bauer, either. This one was the real thing, complete with bent nails, rusted wire and fist-sized holes where shipboard mice had gnawed through the wood. It bore tags and stamps from faraway places like Singapore, Jakarta and someplace that looked like Hangcock but probably wasn't. And every inch of the thing's surface was covered with a thousand daggerlike splinters-in-waiting.

But as lovely as it was, it made for a pretty lousy desk. Its surface was uneven, it lacked both drawers and knee room, and the whole thing wobbled from side to side and vibrated in synch with the printer. All that said, the price had been right. He'd found it abandoned on a street corner eight or nine years ago. At least he'd assumed it had been abandoned. Still, he'd lapsed back into his DEA days and *conducted surveillance* on it for a while *with negative results*. Then he'd pounced, dragging the thing off as fast as he could. Two minutes into a five-block struggle, he'd noticed a couple of guys catching up to him from the rear. "Busted," he'd thought, and was already thinking up defenses like entrapment, lack of intent and temporary insanity. But the guys turned out to be neither cops nor crate owners, only day laborers on their way home from work. Assessing the situation without comment, they proceeded to hoist the thing up in the air and carry it four and a half blocks and then up three flights of stairs. All a grateful Jaywalker could do was to take their lunch pails and lead the way, thanking them more times than was seemly. And when he tried to force a twenty-dollar bill on them, they declined with broad smiles and *"No, gracias."* Was it possible that there was not only one god on duty that day, but two? And that both of them were likely to be undocumented aliens?

In any event, from that moment on the thing was more than just a crate; it was the embodiment of people at their best. And the sight of it would always bring a smile to Jaywalker's face.

So he sat at it now, composing a set of motion papers in Jeremy's case. He'd long ago developed a template of sorts, so it was pretty much a matter of filling in the blanks and fine-tuning what relief to ask the court for.

There was nothing he needed to suppress because of any Constitutional violation of his client's rights. Because Jeremy had surrendered seven months after the killing, no physical evidence had been seized from him. Because he'd been accompanied by an attorney, even one unschooled in criminal practice, the detectives hadn't questioned him. They'd arranged a lineup at which an unnamed witness had identified Jeremy. But according to papers Fudderman had received from the D.A.'s office, the ID had been merely "confirmatory," because the witness "had seen the defendant on a number of prior occasions." To Jaywalker, that careful wording almost certainly meant that the identifier had been Victor Quinones's girlfriend, Teresa Morales. Still, he included a motion to suppress her identification of Jeremy, figuring it might get him a pretrial hearing, or at least force Katherine Darcy to elaborate a bit on the *number of prior occasions*. If that number turned out to be substantial enough, it might work in Jeremy's favor, corroborating his claim that the group had been constantly harassing him.

Next Jaywalker moved to exclude any inquiry by the prosecution into Jeremy's prior arrest. It had been for marijuana possession, and Jaywalker still didn't know exactly what had happened with the case. But he already knew that if they were ever to go to trial, Jeremy would have to testify. And he didn't want some juror turning against him just because he'd smoked a joint back when he was sixteen.

He knocked out a Demand to Produce, asking the prosecution for all sorts of documents, reports, photographs and particulars relating to the case. Finally, he asked the court to dismiss the case altogether, or in the alternative to reduce the charge from murder to some level of manslaughter. This request, he knew full well, would be DOA. If Teresa Morales had testified before the grand jury, as Jaywalker was all but certain she had, she would have described the final point-blank shot between the eyes, and no judge on earth was going to dismiss or reduce anything. It had been, as Darcy had so delicately described it, an execution.

He printed out half a dozen copies of the papers. Jaywalker always made it a point to give his client a copy, whether he'd requested it or not. The D.A. got one, and the court clerk got one. The remaining three Jaywalker would place in separate files for safekeeping, obsessive-compulsive that he was.

With no business in court over the next few days, he thought about mailing the D.A. and the court clerk their copies. But it being a murder case, the motion papers were a bit more lengthy than usual, and Jaywalker was short on stamps and couldn't be sure how much postage would be required. He could have walked the dozen blocks to the post office and stood in line for twenty minutes, but the thought of doing either of those things was resistible. So he said "Fuck it," and went on to Plan C, which would mean taking the subway downtown to serve and file the things the old-fashioned way, by hand.

And then he had a sudden inspiration. Plan C, Variation 2, he would have called it, had he been talking to himself at that moment. Instead of simply serving the D.A.'s office by dropping a copy off at their seventh-floor reception desk and having them time-stamp the others, he decided he might as well peek in on his good friend Katherine Darcy and personally deliver her a courtesy copy. Just that morning there'd been an article in the *Times* on global warming. The polar ice caps, it seemed, were melting at an accelerated rate, far more rapidly than computer models had predicted just two years ago. So who was to say? Could the icy Ms. Darcy, too, have thawed just a bit over the past few days?

Apparently not.

"You could have just left this at the reception desk, you know."

Perhaps it was something he'd said or done, or not said or done. Maybe it was his faded jeans and work shirt, or the fact that he hadn't shaved in two days. Or his showing up without an appointment, announced only by a voice over the intercom at the front desk. But Jaywalker had the distinct feeling it was none of those things.

Back when he'd left the Legal Aid Society and gone into practice for himself, law schools were only beginning to turn out women graduates in significant numbers. As a result, women filled only a tiny minority of slots in the

Manhattan District Attorney's office. The early arrivals, or at least those whom Jaywalker encountered, struck him as uniformly young, bright and attractive. They also tended to be extremely guarded, as though afraid some slightly older male defense lawyer was going to somehow take advantage of them.

It took some doing, but over time Jaywalker managed to overcome that obstacle. It helped considerably that he soon developed a reputation as a good lawyer who could be trusted. But he learned some things along the way, too. Accustomed to calling male prosecutors by their first names without giving it a second thought, he discovered that if he did the same thing right off the bat with a female prosecutor, she was likely to take offense, thinking he was hitting on her. Or, worse yet, hitting on her to gain some edge in the courtroom. So he got smarter about that, and more careful in general.

As the ranks of women prosecutors gradually grew from a small minority to a virtual majority, the problem largely disappeared. It might simply have been a matter of Jaywalker's getting older and no longer being perceived as on the prowl. Because right around the same time, he'd noticed that the checkout girls at the supermarket had stopped smiling at him seductively; they were by that time much more interested in the young managers or the boys bagging groceries.

Katherine Darcy was no checkout girl, and no recent law-school graduate. At forty, or whatever she was, she had nothing to fear from the twenty-five and thirty-year-old defense lawyers. Them she could treat as schoolboys. But Jaywalker had turned fifty not too long ago. When he straightened up, he was an even six feet. He'd kept his hair, even though it was currently working its way from gray to white. And enough women had told him he was good-looking, at least in a craggy sort of a way, that he'd come to accept it as a fact. Was it possible that in Katherine Darcy's mind he posed a threat, much the same way he had to a younger generation of her officemates, twenty years ago? Was she perhaps afraid Jaywalker was approaching her not as a fellow lawyer sharing a case with her, albeit on opposite sides, but as a predator seeking to take advantage of her because he equated being a woman with weakness? Or, more simply put, maybe she thought he was trying to get into her pants so he could get into her files.

As if.

"That's how it's usually done," she was telling him now.

"How *what's* usually done?" Getting into her pants?

"Serving papers. At the reception desk."

"Right," said Jaywalker. "It's just that I had a couple of questions and thought if you weren't too busy…" He let the thought hang there, inviting her to say that of course she wasn't too busy.

"What kind of questions?" she asked, making a point of looking first at her watch and then at the clock on the wall.

"Well," he said, "for one thing, have you by any chance heard of the Raiders?"

"Aren't they a baseball team?"

"Close," he said without bothering to correct her. His wife had had the same problem. Football, baseball, basketball. To her, they'd all been "sports," and pretty much interchangeable. In her mind, and perhaps in Katherine Darcy's, too, each fall the players put their bats and gloves in storage and replaced them with helmets and shoulder pads. In wintertime, when the cold chased them indoors, they simply stripped down to shorts and undershirts. They were still the same players and teams; only the uniforms and equipment had changed.

"The Raiders are also a group of young thugs," said Jaywalker. "A loosely organized gang who made it their business to target my client."

"No," she said. "I've never heard of them."

"Why don't you ask Teresa Morales about them?" he suggested.

"What makes you think *she's* heard of them?"

"Because if my client's telling the truth, and I think he is, she was one of them."

"You're trying to tell me it was a *coed* gang?"

"Hey," said Jaywalker. "Welcome to the twenty-first century. No more stay-at-home moms or glass ceilings. If Mother Teresa were still with us, she might've traded in her rosary long ago and be packing a Ruger."

And in spite of herself, Katherine Darcy actually broke into something vaguely resembling a smile before quickly regaining control. "You said you had a couple of questions," she reminded Jaywalker. "What's the next one?"

"I see you gave Mr. Fudderman a copy of the autopsy protocol," he said. "But I didn't notice a serology or toxi-cology report." Both would show the presence of drugs or alcohol in Victor Quinones's system at the time of his death, the former in his blood, the latter in tissue samples removed from his body.

"Those take a little longer to come back."

"It's been eight months," said Jaywalker. He knew from experience that "a little longer to come back" generally meant two to three weeks at most.

"I'll look into it," said Katherine Darcy. "Anything else?"

"Yeah. Has the name Sandro come up at all? Or Alesan-dro?"

"Not that I can recall. Why?"

"Because," said Jaywalker, "he seems to have been the leader of the gang."

She shrugged.

"How about Shorty? Or Diego? Or Mousey?"

Three more shrugs.

"How about Man One and five years?"

That brought a real smile from Katherine Darcy. "You don't quit trying, do you?" she asked with what Jaywalker took to be a hint of grudging admiration.

"No, I don't," he said. "And what's more, before this case is over, I'm going to get you to like me, or at least to realize I'm not out to hurt you. And I'm going to get an offer out of you, too. Because as you begin to look into some of these questions, I think you're going to come to see that this isn't really a murder case after all."

"I like you just fine," she said, though it came out sounding like Barack Obama telling Hillary Clinton that she was *likeable enough.* "But you're never going to get an offer out of me. Never."

Two days later, Jeremy's mother met Jaywalker at the information booth of the courthouse. He would have preferred having her come to his office, but there was that little impediment of not having an office for her to come to. And he seriously doubted that she could survive climbing the three flights of stairs to his apartment.

"This is Julie," she said of a pretty young woman standing by her side. "Jeremy's sister."

"Nice to meet you," said Jaywalker, shaking hands with her. "Older or younger?" To a woman who looked to him to be anywhere between fifteen and twenty-five, he had no idea which the more tactful guess might be.

"Older," said Julie. "By ten minutes."

"Aha."

So Jeremy had a twin sister. Funny, he'd never mentioned her. Then again, Jeremy wasn't much of a mentioner. He volunteered little, revealing things only when absolutely forced to.

"So how does it look for my son, Mr. Jakewalker?"

Jaywalker turned back to Carmen. "We're just getting started," he told her. "But it's a very serious case, as you know."

"Those guys gave him a very hard time," said Julie.

"Did you see any of it?" Jaywalker asked her. Maybe she could be a witness, able to testify to some of the things they'd said or done.

"No," she said. "But it had to be real bad."

"How do you know?"

"Jeremy."

"Things he said?"

Even as he waited for Julie's answer, he braced himself for the disappointment it would bring. No matter how graphically Jeremy might have described what the Raiders had done to him, neither his mother nor his sister would be permitted to repeat his accounts in court. It would be hearsay, the secondhand account of someone who hadn't been there.

But Julie surprised him. "No," she told him. "It wasn't just the things he said. It was how he said them, and how he acted."

"Here," said Carmen, before slipping Jaywalker another of her folded envelopes. She did it so furtively that for an instant he feared it might contain drugs, instead of just money.

They spoke for about half an hour. Jaywalker had to break up the meeting. He actually had a case on that morning, a young couple accused of shoplifting thirty dollars' worth of baby food and formula for their hungry child. He had a little speech prepared that he was hoping would bring the judge to tears and the case to an end. He thanked Carmen and Julie, and headed to the bank of elevators to see if any of them might be working. As he waited to find out, he tore open the folded envelope and found two hundred dollars inside it.

But that was hardly the best news of the morning. Julie Estrada had supplied that. It turned out that both she and her mother could testify after all. Not to anything Jeremy had said to them, but to how he'd *acted* that summer. That wouldn't be secondhand words; it would be firsthand observations.

And there was more.

If Jeremy's torment had been so significant as to be readily visible at home, it must have been far more severe than Jeremy had so far let on. Surely Jaywalker had made it clear how important the details were, how essential to any possible defense they might mount. Jeremy had to have heard that. Yet he'd continued to summarize, to gloss over events without ever going into particulars.

Why?

What was Jaywalker missing here?

And all he could think was that it must be time for another trip out to Rikers Island.

If Jaywalker's earlier meetings with Jeremy had reminded him of dental extractions, Friday's session proved to be the equivalent of a root canal. Instead of picking up where they'd left off and moving forward into the day of the fight and the shooting, Jaywalker insisted on backtracking, on going over the same events they'd already covered. But this time he demanded far more detail and focused on something he'd failed to do earlier.

He forced Jeremy to not only describe the things that Sandro and his cohorts had done to him, but to talk about how those things had made him *feel*.

They made little progress at first, because Jeremy was such a stranger to his own emotions. He could use words like *nervous, scared* and *upset,* but more revealing terms like *embarrassed* and *humiliated* simply weren't part of his vocabulary. Finally Jaywalker decided to try a different tack. Instead of prodding his client for more and better descriptions of his inner reactions, he asked him if his everyday activities had changed, and if so, how.

And the ice broke.

Not all at once, of course; that would have been too much to expect from a young man as inarticulate as Jeremy. But while feelings were almost impossible for him to describe, activities were something else.

In order to avoid the Raiders, Jeremy had been forced to alter his entire schedule. Having helped his mother out with after-school and weekend earnings since the age of fourteen, Jeremy lost three jobs over the course of that summer. He dropped out of school. He became a virtual prisoner, afraid to leave the apartment for days at a time. He was unable to eat or sleep, and lost so much weight that his clothes no longer fit him. He got blinding headaches and stomach cramps that doubled him over in pain, prompting his mother to threaten more than once to take him to the doctor. That would have meant the emergency room of the local hospital, which served the medical needs not only of the Estradas, but thousands of others who knew what it was like to have their electricity cut off.

"Good!" exclaimed Jaywalker after one such revelation, causing Jeremy to look at him so strangely that he had to add, "Good you could tell me that, I mean."

From there they moved forward to the final day, and for the first time Jaywalker learned how seamless the transition had been, how Jeremy's four months of anguish had all but dictated the ending. The fistfight with Victor Quinones hadn't been some *"You lookin' at me?" "Yeah, I'm lookin' at you"* exchange between a couple of macho teenagers at all. It had been the predictable, almost inevitable explosion of everything that had preceded it. And the shooting that had followed it? Well, it would be Jaywalker's job to show that it, too, had been just as predictable—and just as inevitable.

He came away from Rikers Island with a whole new understanding of the case. Throughout his previous conversations with Jeremy, he'd completely failed to grasp the impact of everything that had happened to him. He hadn't been harassed by Sandro and the others; he'd been *tortured.* He hadn't just been embarrassed in front of his new girlfriend; he'd been *devastated,* over and over again, right up to and past the breaking point. And it had been the degree of that torture, and the depth of that devastation, that had combined to make it so painful for Jeremy to talk about. Pushed to the wall, he'd finally had it. And only then had Jaywalker come to appreciate the extent of what the young man had lived through, and what it had done to him.

Riding the subway back to Manhattan, Jaywalker knew that his trip had been more than worth the effort. Because out of the ashes of that very same torture, up from the embers of that utter devastation, would rise his defense of Jeremy Estrada.

6

WELCOME TO TOMBSTONE

Under New York State law, the crime of murder is defined as intentionally causing the death of another person. Gone are such archaic considerations as motive, premeditation and malice aforethought. It is sufficient that the defendant intends to cause the death of another and succeeds. It isn't even necessary that his victim be the one he meant to kill.

But there's a defense written into the statute, too. If the jury can be persuaded that the defendant acted under the influence of "extreme emotional disturbance," it may return a verdict of not guilty on a murder charge.

If those words applied to anyone, Jaywalker decided, they had to apply to Jeremy Estrada. The cumulative effect of his torment at the hands of Sandro, Shorty, Diego, Victor and the rest of the Raiders had surely disturbed Jeremy, not only emotionally, but physically, as well. Could there possibly be any doubt that that disturbance had been "extreme"? It would take a closer reading of the statute to make sure, and an exhaustive study of the case law, but already Jaywalker knew he had the raw materials to make a good argument that the words fit Jeremy like a glove.

There was one hitch, however, and it was a big one. The same statute that spoke of extreme emotional disturbance made it abundantly clear that it was a defense only to murder, not to manslaughter. In other words, it was a *partial defense,* permitting a jury to knock the crime down a notch, but not to forgive it altogether.

Not that it wasn't a start. A murder conviction would mean a mandatory life sentence, with the minimum to be set by the judge at anywhere from fifteen to twenty-five years. A sentence for first-degree manslaughter, on the other hand, had to be a *determinate*—or fixed—one, and could range from as little as five years to as many as twenty-five, again depending on the judge's discretion.

So in his mind, Jaywalker had already figured out a way to avoid a life sentence for Jeremy, even if a term of twenty-five years still loomed as a very real possibility. But he'd accomplished something else, too. He'd found the key with which he might just be able to unlock Katherine Darcy's stranglehold on the case. She could talk all she wanted to about the case being an execution, and how she'd never offer a Man One on it. But Jaywalker no longer needed her to do that; a jury could do it on its own, without her blessing and even over her objection.

Which, of course, Jaywalker would be sure to point out to her, next time they met. But he felt no particular need to rush back to see her. He might not exactly be in the driver's seat yet, but at least he was no longer being dragged along bodily, clinging to the back bumper.

The following Wednesday they appeared in Part 55 before the man who, for better or for worse, was to be their trial judge. Unlike Judge McGillicuddy, who worked in an "up front" part and sent cases out after a single appearance, Harold Wexler would hold on to the case forever. *Forever* being a relative term, but not all *that* relative. In Jeremy Estrada's case, it would include all pretrial proceedings and hearings, the trial itself, if there was to be one, and the sentencing in the event the prosecution prevailed, which was about eighty percent of the time generally, though only about ten percent of the time if Jaywalker happened to be representing the defendant. Only after all that would the case finally leave Part 55 to begin its climb through appellate courts manned by other judges.

Actually, to say, "They appeared in Part 55," while technically true, would be pregnant with omission. A more instructive way of phrasing it would be, "Jaywalker appeared in Part 55 before Katherine Darcy did."

Jaywalker had been knocking around 100 Centre Street for more than twenty years. It was his *home court,* as he liked to call it, and he knew the players. He especially knew the judges, because it was his business to. Not that he socialized with them; Jaywalker didn't socialize with anybody if he could help it. But he'd known a lot of the judges from back when they'd been colleagues of his at Legal Aid or adversaries in the D.A.'s office. Together they'd grown up in the system, often battling, sometimes brutally, but never personally. Jaywalker's occasional antics might drive some of them crazy, but not one among them doubted that if the police were ever to come banging on the door after midnight, his would be the number they'd call.

Jaywalker had known Harold Wexler as an angry young civil rights lawyer, long before he'd become an angry middle-aged judge. As bright as anyone on the bench and as well-read in the law, he too often fell victim to his own impatience and his inability to suffer fools, be they defendants, defenders, prosecutors or innocent bystanders. He appreciated good lawyering when he saw it in his courtroom, and he saw it unfailingly in Jaywalker. Those he didn't see it in, he attacked with a biting wit, his sarcasm projecting to the farthest row of the audience. A lawyer who hadn't done his homework could expect to be told, "I see you've avoided the dangers of over-preparation, Mr. Jacobs." Another, forced to answer "No" when asked if she was ready for trial, might hear, "Well, at least that has the virtue of clarity."

Generally, Jaywalker had learned, you got a fair trial from Harold Wexler. But he tended to get emotionally involved in his cases. If your client was truly sympathetic, Wexler could be your best friend. But if he decided your client was a total slimebag who deserved to be locked up for the remainder of the century, you were in for a long week or two.

It mattered.

And because it mattered, Jaywalker had made it a point to arrive at Part 55 that morning neurotically early, so early that the doors hadn't even been unlocked by the court officers. Jaywalker knew them, too, and the clerks and interpreters and stenographers and corrections officers. They knew him and liked him, and it made his job easier in a hundred little ways.

So once the doors had been unlocked and the other early arrivals had begun trickling in, the clerk mentioned to Judge Wexler that Mr. Jaywalker was there on Jeremy Estrada's case.

"Why don't you come up and tell me about it?" said the judge.

Which, of course, was the whole idea.

Katherine Darcy, meanwhile, was nowhere in sight. So a younger assistant joined Jaywalker at the bench, an assistant who had a file but knew absolutely nothing about the case. He kept glancing toward the front door, hoping Ms. Darcy would show up and rescue him.

"What do we have here?" the judge wanted to know.

"What we have," said Jaywalker, "is a seventeen-year-old kid who makes the mistake of falling in love. A local gang of thugs rewards him by tormenting him for three months, placing him under virtual house arrest. Finally, he sees one of them alone. They have a fistfight, which by all accounts the defendant wins. But the other guy turns out to be a poor loser. According to my guy, he pulls a gun, they struggle over it, my guy gets it away from him and shoots him. Unfortunately, his aim happens to be very good."

Wexler looked to the young A.D.A., but the poor guy was busy leafing through the file, trying his best to decipher handwritten notes.

"It's Katherine Darcy's case," said Jaywalker. "She's going to tell you it's a no-plea case, an execution."

"And you? What are you going to tell me?"

"I'm going to tell you that if it's not justification, it's certainly extreme emotional disturbance. To me it's a Man One, five years."

"Here comes Ms. Darcy now," said the young assistant. All eyes turned to see her hurrying up the aisle like a bride late for her own wedding.

"Looks like I missed something," she said.

"Feel free to arrive in my courtroom at nine-thirty," Judge Wexler told her, "and I assure you you'll miss nothing."

"Sorry."

Not that the judge didn't give Katherine Darcy a chance to explain her view of the case. He did, and she placed the gun in Jeremy's hand, not Victor's, and described how he'd delivered the final shot to a victim who lay helpless on the ground, begging for mercy.

At that Wexler turned to Jaywalker and said, "There goes your justification defense."

"That's why I told you Man One and five years."

"No way," said Darcy.

The judge gave her a hard look. "You really see this as a no-lesser-plea case?"

"Absolutely," she said, trying to trump his skepticism with complete certainty.

Jaywalker said nothing. But he did look up at the ceiling, his not-so-subtle substitute for rolling his eyes in exasperation.

"I see cases like this all the time," said Wexler. "Two guys, one girl, much too much testosterone. I'd split the difference. I agree it's a first-degree manslaughter, but I think it's worth the maximum, twenty-five years. Talk to your client, Mr. Jaywalker. And you go meet with your supervisors, Ms. Darcy. Only this time?"

"Yes?"

"I suggest you don't show up late."

She didn't call him until the following afternoon. He was sitting at his computer at the time, trying to write. He'd been trying to write for several years now, *trying* being the operative word. Still, he had this fantasy of getting out, of running from the law and becoming a bestselling author, the next John Grisham or Scott Turow. Because the thing was, he had all these incredible stories from his years in the trenches, and he thought he knew how to write well enough to tell them. Hell, he'd been an English major once. Which was why he'd had to go off to law school after college, to learn a trade. But he really *could* write, no small feat for a lawyer. The problem seemed to lie elsewhere. His old therapist had suggested that perhaps Jaywalker didn't want to get out at all, that in fact he preferred to spend the rest of his days down at 100 Centre Street, trying cases until they carried him out in a box.

He answered the phone on the third ring with his customary, "Jaywalker."

"Hi," said a woman's voice he didn't recognize. "This is Katie Darcy. From the D.A.'s office. Jeremy Estrada's case?"

"Sure," said Jaywalker. "Right." His silence wasn't the result of his not knowing who she was, or who employed her, or what case they had together. It was the first name that had caught him. Just when had she ceased to be *Katherine* and become *Katie?* And whenever it had been, wasn't it, as Martha Stuart might have put it, a good thing?

"Is this a bad time?" she asked.

"No, no. It's a fine time."

For a moment neither of them said anything. As curious as he was about the reason for her call, Jaywalker wasn't about to ask. As they used to say back in the old days, before double-digit inflation, it was her dime.

"I truly believe," she finally said, "that Judge Wexler is dead wrong. I think the case *is* a murder case. But I've got to tell you. After spending fifteen minutes with him, I have no desire to be his punching bag for two weeks. If your client wants the Man One, he can have it."

"With five years?"

"No," she laughed. Actually *laughed*. "With twenty-five years, and not a day less."

If the "it" wasn't quite ice in the wintertime, it was pretty close. Nonetheless, Jaywalker didn't want to be rude. Not when Katherine had become Katie and made them an offer of any sort, all in one conversation. "I'll talk to Jeremy," he said. He could have said "my client," but he preferred to personalize him. He wanted to begin the process of getting *Katie* to think of Jeremy Estrada as a kid, instead of as a case.

Obviously that Katherine-to-Katie switch had gotten to him. So much so that it seemed silly to ignore it. "So," he asked her, "when did you become Katie?"

"I've always been Katie," she deadpanned. "My middle initial is T. So I'm really K. T. Darcy."

"What's the T stand for?"

"Ahhh," she said. "That's for me to know."

He had Jeremy brought over two days later for a counsel visit. The two trips to Rikers Island had worn Jaywalker out. He figured it was Jeremy's turn to travel.

"What's up?" Jeremy asked, his eyes puffy from the 3:00 a.m. wake-up.

"The D.A.'s willing to give you a manslaughter plea," Jaywalker told him. "But only if we agree to a twenty-five year sentence."

"How much do I do on that?"

"Around twenty." A dozen years back, truth-in-labeling had come to sentencing. Gone were the days when a judge could sentence a defendant to a public-pleasing thirty-year prison term, confident the parole board would quietly let him go home in six months.

"Do I have to take it?" Jeremy asked.

"Of course not."

"Will you be mad at me if I don't?"

"Jeremy, this isn't my case. It's yours."

"And you'll still fight your hardest for me, even if I don't take it?"

"Absolutely."

Jeremy's mother was somewhat more empathetic.

"That's too much time, Mr. Walkerjay. He was only a boy. They made him do it."

Jaywalker tried to explain that he was simply the messenger. But the distinction seemed totally lost on Carmen Estrada. "Jew gotta do better for him," she insisted. "I'm paying jew a lotta money here. Jew gotta get him less time, a lot less." And she handed him another envelope, this one with seventy-five dollars in it.

A lotta money indeed.

They went back before Judge Wexler in mid-October. He ruled on Jaywalker's motions, predictably refusing to dismiss the murder charge or reduce it to manslaughter. He postponed until just before trial any decision on whether the prosecution would be entitled to ask Jeremy Estrada about his prior arrest if he were to take the stand. When it came to the issue of the fairness of the lineup at which Teresa Morales had picked Jeremy out, the judge turned to Ms. Darcy.

"You're saying the identification was purely confirmatory?"

"That's correct."

"They knew each other?" the judge asked.

"So to speak."

"What she's trying to tell you," said Jaywalker, "is that Teresa Morales is one of the gang members who stalked the defendant for three months."

"Gang members?" said Wexler and Darcy in unison.

Jaywalker let out a snort, a hybrid somewhere between a laugh and a grunt. The existence of gangs in the five boroughs had long been one of the city's dirty little secrets. Gangs were a phenomenon supposedly restricted to other places, like the Watts area of Los Angeles, the South Side of Chicago, and pretty much all of Newark and Camden, New Jersey. New York City might have a colorful history of Irish Westies and Italian Mafiosi, but when it came to modern counterparts with names like Bloods and Crips and Latin Kings, the official word of the day was *denial.* So Jaywalker's use of the term had bordered on burn-him-at-the-stake heresy.

"Please forgive me," he said. "The last thing I want to do is to disparage the emperor's new clothes."

"You'll have to excuse Mr. Jaywalker," said Wexler to Ms. Darcy. "From time to time he mistakes my constant smile and jovial good humor as an invitation to make bad jokes."

"Let me withdraw the term *gang*," said Jaywalker. "How about *marauding band of drug-dealing thugs?*"

"How about instead we get to the point?" suggested the judge. "How many times, Ms. Darcy, had your witness encountered the defendant prior to the incident?"

Which, of course, was precisely what Jaywalker had wanted to hear all along. If her answer were to be "just once or twice," then the lineup *hadn't* been merely confirmatory, and the defense would be entitled to a pretrial hearing on its admissibility. If, on the other hand, she were to say "a dozen or more," that fact would play nicely into Jeremy's claim of constant, continued harassment at the hands of the Raiders.

Ms. Darcy's hesitation to answer suggested she recognized the trap. "I don't know the precise number," she said.

"Perhaps," said Wexler, "you could give us a ballpark figure. Like more than five, ten to twenty, less than a thousand."

"Less than a thousand," she said, apparently taking the judge literally.

"She likes to play things close to the breast." As soon as the words were out of Jaywalker's mouth, he knew they didn't sound quite right. He hoped the other two had missed it. But Harold Wexler never missed anything.

"I believe," he said, "that the expression is *close to the vest.*"

"That, too."

"Once again, Ms. Darcy, you'll have to forgive Mr. Jaywalker. If only a small fraction of recent rumors are to be credited, his competence before the court is rivaled only by his legendary exploits between the sheets."

Jaywalker could only wince, while Katherine Darcy actually blushed, something Jaywalker thought had gone extinct around 1940, along with fainting couches and lace handkerchiefs.

"Listen," said the judge. "Can't we resolve this case? Is there still no offer here?"

"As a matter of fact, there is an offer," said Ms. Darcy, happy to move on. "I've told counsel that Mr. Estrada can have the first-degree manslaughter plea if he wants it."

"With twenty-five years," added Jaywalker.

"Fair enough," said Wexler. "Mr. Jaywalker?"

"We're not even close. He'd take five, *maybe* six or seven, though I'd probably have to break his arm. But *twenty-five?* That's way—"

"Let me make my own position clear," said the judge. "I'm strongly inclined to agree with Ms. Darcy's assessment of this case. The first shot doesn't disturb me too much. But the second one, the one at point-blank range between the eyes, as the victim lies on the ground begging for his life? I think *execution* is an appropriate description of that. So the defendant can have the twenty-five years and be out in twenty. Or he can go to trial, get convicted of murder, and have the exact same twenty-five years, but as his minimum, with life as his maximum. His choice. I could care less. Next case."

If you happen to be a devotee of old black-and-white Westerns, as Jaywalker had been in his youth, you soon learn that long before the arrival of Technicolor, things were already pretty much color-coded. The good guy almost invariably sported a white hat and rode a white horse, or perhaps a palomino, if white horses happened to be in short supply. The bad guys just as uniformly wore black and rode black.

Just three weeks ago, Katherine Darcy had been the villain in Part 55 for the sin of refusing to offer a manslaughter plea. She'd quickly discovered it was a role she didn't enjoy playing. So she'd done something about it. She'd offered Jeremy Estrada the plea, but only on the condition that he accept the maximum allowable sentence of twenty-five years. Now the judge had not only agreed with her and adopted her position as his own, he'd threatened to impose the maximum sentence for murder if the defendant rejected the offer and the jury were to convict him of the top count.

Or, put another way, in the short space of three weeks, Jaywalker had gone from good guy to bad guy. He would ride into trial wearing the black hat, astride the black horse. The judge would do everything in his power to make sure there was a guilty verdict on the murder count. Not that he would be obvious about it. Harold Wexler was much too smart to be heavy-handed in dispensing biased justice. No, he'd do it in small and subtle ways, all but unnoticeable to both a jury and an appellate court reviewing a transcript. But the cumulative effect would be absolutely devastating.

Welcome to Tombstone.

7

BRICKS AND BOOKS

Exempt as they are from New York's speedy trial rules, murder trials tend to travel through the system more slowly than other cases. Jeremy Estrada had been arrested only seven weeks ago, a fact that normally would have put him at the very end of the line. But in court time, Jeremy's case had actually begun with his indictment seven months earlier and was therefore now approaching its first birthday. That fact alone immediately caused it to jump half the cases ahead of it. By Jaywalker's calculation—and he considered it his business to be able to predict such things with accuracy—they were looking at a trial sometime around the middle of next year.

That might have seemed like an awful lot of time to somebody else, but not to Jaywalker. He was firmly convinced that of the acquittals he'd gotten—and he got more acquittals than most lawyers allow themselves to *dream* of—a good half of them were won before the trial had ever begun. Other lawyers prepared for trial. Jaywalker over-prepared; he *ultra-super-hyper*-over-prepared. He organized, interviewed, investigated, interrogated, subpoenaed, photographed, recorded and visited the crime scene. And then he did all those things over again, three or four times. He totally obsessed over every single case, no matter the simplicity or complexity of the charges, or the length of the potential sentence, and he did it to a degree that was arguably pathological. His therapist had suggested that he was engaged in a struggle to the death with his father, in order to win his mother's affection.

"They're both dead," Jaywalker had commented dryly from the couch. Okay, the big leather chair.

"Ahaaa!"

Make that his *former* therapist.

So the time clock Jaywalker now envisioned in Jeremy Estrada's case was anything but a generous one. In Jeremy he had a defendant who gave up information only grudgingly, and who would take endless hours to prepare. Then there were the other witnesses to hunt down and interview. There was research to conduct, cases to read on justification, deadly force and extreme emotional disturbance. There was the autopsy report to reread, break down and comb for clues. There were the ballistics report and the crime-scene sketch. Not only did the list go on, the *list of lists* went on. And as Jaywalker thought about it, the sheer amount of work that lay ahead of him was enough to trigger a migraine.

Nor did he have the usual comfort of knowing that his adversary would be in pretty much the same bind. Katherine Darcy had been working on the case from day one, or at least day two or three, when it had first been assigned to her. That fact had given her a significant head start, a head start that no matter how hard he worked, Jaywalker would never be able to erase.

So it was time to get down to work. And work would begin with hitting the bricks.

* * *

The first thing he wanted to do was to locate and nail down defense witnesses. Jeremy's mother and twin sister could testify to the changes they'd observed in Jeremy as a result of his torment at the hands of the Raiders. But their value as witnesses would be limited. For one thing, they hadn't actually seen any of the gang members or directly observed any of the events that had occurred. And even if they had, their relationship with Jeremy, and their under-standable loyalty toward him, would immediately render their testimony suspect. But the good news was that neither Carmen nor Julie was going anywhere. They'd be right there for Jaywalker to interview indepth and prepare to testify, whenever he got around to it.

He was much more concerned with locating the two people who'd actually witnessed the harassment. The first of these, and by far the more important, was Miranda. For starters, she'd been the catalyst who'd set off the entire chain of events; she was the case's Helen of Troy. Next, ac-cording to Jeremy, she'd been present on a number of oc-casions when Sandro and the others had confronted Jeremy and bullied him. Finally, she'd been right there at the fight between Jeremy and Victor Quinones, and at the shooting itself. Whatever Victor's girlfriend Teresa Morales could say about those events, Miranda could contradict and hopefully neutralize. So in every sense of the word, she was indispens-able.

But neither Jeremy nor his family had seen or heard from Miranda since the days following the shooting. And as Jaywalker pondered that fact, he realized that he didn't even know her last name. It was a sobering thought, and it reminded him once again of how much work he had ahead of him.

The other witness he needed to find was the owner of the

barbershop where the gang had tried to get at Jeremy. Jaywalker had already been told that the shop had since closed and the owner had returned to Puerto Rico. On top of that, in this instance Jaywalker didn't even have a first name to work with, let alone a last.

He walked to the bathroom, opened the medicine cabinet and searched for something strong. But most of the pill bottles were either empty or bore expiration dates from the previous millennium. He settled on a couple of Motrin. *Motrin?* Perhaps some overnight guest had left them behind. Then again, headaches were sort of like brain cramps, weren't they? Next he brewed himself a pot of strong caffeinated coffee and downed two cups, black and bitter.

No migraine was going to get in his way.

An hour later, Jaywalker found himself standing on the corner of 112th Street and Third Avenue, where, according to Jeremy, there'd once been a barbershop. He stopped everyone who looked like they might speak English, and asked them if they remembered one. To those who answered him with a blank stare and a *"No comprendo,"* he tried *"Barberio"* and pointed to his own hair, just to make sure they wouldn't mistake him for a barbarian. Finally an old man with no teeth shook his head and said, *"No más."*

"Sí, sí," said Jaywalker. "But *donde* was it?"

Like an idiot, he'd taken French and Latin.

"Come with me," said the man, in perfect English. And took him a half a block east, where he pointed out a small shop with the word *Botanica* printed above it.

Inside were rows upon rows of shelves overflowing with dusty jars and amber bottles of vitamins, supplements and herbal remedies. Bilingual hand-lettered signs explained which were good for stomach ailments, which immediately improved eyesight or hearing, and which promised to cure cancer or SIDA, the Spanish equivalent of AIDS. There were cloves for toothaches, mercury compounds for gout, and dried chicken heads for use in Santeria rituals.

Jaywalker was not tempted.

The proprietor, a small woman with a ready smile, spoke no English. *"Momentito,"* she said, and ducked beneath a curtain and into a back room. When she returned a *momentito* later, she was accompanied by a girl of seven or eight, presumably her daughter and translator.

Jaywalker explained his business. Did they know if the place had ever been a barbershop? Yes. By any chance, had they bought out the lease from the owner of the barbershop? Yes, exactly. Did they happen to remember his name? No, but if he cared to wait a few minutes, they had papers.

As Jaywalker's former therapist might have said, *"Ahaaa!"*

Twenty minutes later, Jaywalker reemerged into the sunlight. In his left pocket, as a result of his appreciation and a twenty-dollar bill, was a small bottle containing a scary fetal-like object labeled Black Toadwort and unconditionally guaranteed to cure him of migraines forever. But even were it to fail to live up to its claim, it would be well worth the investment. For in his right pocket was a piece of paper bearing the careful, practiced lettering of a third grader.

Francisco Zapata
Frankie and Friends
Barbershop

It wasn't all that far, so from the botanica Jaywalker walked north to 115th Street and the projects, where he found the building that matched the address Jeremy had listed at the time of his arrest. He slipped the lock of the outer door with a credit card and found the tenant board. There were two Estradas listed, one for 3G and the other for 8F. He pressed the buzzer for 3G, hoping it would be the right one. He knew from experience that the chances of either of the elevators working were slim, and the prospect of climbing seven floors was somewhat less than appealing.

"Quit pressing the buzzer, you fuckin' junkie bastards!"

He tried 8F.

"Who are jew?" came the familiar gravelly voice of a woman.

He spent the first half hour in Carmen's apartment trying to catch his breath, the next half hour declining her offers of food, and the final half hour quizzing her on what she knew about Miranda.

"Very, very pretty."

There seemed to be something of a consensus on that point.

"Miranda Raven."

A last name.

"'Cause her father was like a Indian, a real Indian. From Florida. Her mother told me that, when Jeremy was in Puerto Rico. The Semaphore tribe, I think she said."

Or perhaps the Seminoles. But whichever it was, she'd fled the city immediately after the shooting, afraid for her daughter. "To Baltimore," said Carmen. "That's in Marilyn." She still had a phone number for them, though. She'd saved it for Jeremy, so that when the problem was finally over, he could call Miranda up if he wanted to and go looking for her.

"Very, very pretty," she repeated, as though that was explanation enough. And maybe it was.

She dug out the number and let Jaywalker copy it down. "Jew going to call her?" she asked.

"No," said Jaywalker, who didn't want to frighten

Miranda off with a call from a total stranger. "You're going to call her mother and ask her to have Miranda call me."

"Okay. But are jew sure you don't want something to eat?"

Funny, she didn't *look* Jewish.

The following day Jaywalker checked with the licensing division of the Department of State. Francisco Zapata had indeed been the sole proprietor of the barbershop where the *botanica* now was, and he'd done business under the name "Frankie and Friends." If he'd employed anyone, it had been strictly off the books. Officially, at least, his "friends" appeared to have been his customers. And a little over seven months ago, Zapata had indeed sold his shop and requested that his licensing status be changed from active to retired. Despite a requirement that he furnish a forwarding address for tax purposes and service of process, he'd failed to do so, and the appropriate blank on the form listed his current whereabouts as "unknown" and his next of kin as "none."

Now most other investigators, and just about all other lawyers, would have quit right there, writing off the notion of the barbershop owner being a witness as a dead end. But Jaywalker was stubborn to a fault. To him there *were* no dead ends, just detours. So he made a note in his To Do file, which had by that time grown to a dozen pages. He'd reached the age in life where he no longer trusted his memory to serve him. If something was worth remembering, it was worth putting down on paper. That way, he could save his diminishing brain cells for the important stuff, like remembering to eat at least once a day, shaving every other day and calling his daughter once a week. Back when his wife had been alive, one of her jobs had been to serve as his constant reminder. He'd been ambivalent about it at the time, and had even accused her of being a nag when she got pushy about it. Only with her death had he come to realize just how many hats she'd worn during their marriage, and how utterly lost he was without her.

Katherine Darcy called the following day. Evidently Jaywalker's "close to the breast" slip had caused her to take a step back from being Katie. Once again, she was all business on the phone.

"The toxicology and serology reports have come in," she said. Not "I found them," or "I've decided to let you in on what they say." No, they'd *come in*. Almost a year late. Which, to Jaywalker, could only mean there had to be something in them that was good for him and bad for her.

"Do you want me to send you copies of them?" she asked. "Or fax them to you?"

"You can send them," he said. "My fax is down at the moment." As it no doubt would have been, if he'd had one. "So what do they show?" he asked her, knowing it would make her squirm to read off anything that might give him an advantage, however small.

"The usual," she said. "Ethanol and opiates in blood, bile and brain."

Unless Victor Quinones had been tanking up on gasoline additives, the presence of ethanol meant he'd been drinking. And opiates would be heroin.

"How much ethanol?" he asked.

"Let me see. Point one one."

"And the opiates?"

"Not quantified," she said.

"Didn't this thing happen in the morning?" Jaywalker asked. He knew the answer, of course. The witnesses had placed the shooting at a few minutes after 11:00 a.m.

"The victim was pronounced at twelve-fifteen in the afternoon. And they didn't take samples until the autopsy, which was conducted the next day."

She was right, technically. According to the death certificate, which Jaywalker had also committed to memory some time ago, Quinones hadn't been officially pronounced dead until an hour after the shooting, at the hospital. And the autopsy hadn't been performed until the following afternoon. But none of that mattered. Death had a funny way of bringing the body's metabolism to a screeching halt. If Victor had had a .11 reading lying on the morgue table, he'd had the same exact reading when he'd taken a bullet between the eyes some thirty hours earlier. A .11 meant eleven hundredths of a percentage point of alcohol in his system, by weight. It might not have sounded like much to a layman, but to Jaywalker it translated out to roughly five drinks, all of them knocked back well before noon. Enough to place him over the limit for driving and into the category of legally intoxicated. And that was before you even started talking about the undetermined amount of heroin he'd had in his system.

"Nice breakfast," said Jaywalker.

Over the weeks that followed, he spent three full days rereading the crime-scene reports, the ballistics findings and the autopsy protocol. When the serology and toxicology reports showed up in the mail, he read those, too, even though he'd already had Katherine Darcy read them to him over the phone two days earlier. He revisited the crime scene, taking more measurements and snapping more photos than he had the last time he'd been there.

He had Jeremy brought over to 100 Centre Street for a dozen more counsel visits, each time probing for greater detail about both the months leading up to the fatal day and the events of that day itself. The process continued to feel like dentistry, but over time Jeremy gradually became a more cooperative patient. Where he'd once dug in and resisted every inch of the way, he now finally began to let go of his secrets. Not happily, and certainly not easily. But with Jaywalker constantly reminding him how important it was to their chances at trial, Jeremy finally demonstrated that he got it, that he made the connection between his providing sufficient detail and a jury believing what he was telling them. Still, it continued to be a painstaking process, as well as one that promised to continue right up to the minute the young man would finally take the witness stand.

Jaywalker met twice more with Jeremy's mother and his twin sister, Julie, pushing them to tell him again about the changes they'd noticed in Jeremy over the course of the summer of the "problem." After the second session, he was already on his feet, gathering up his papers and stuffing them back into his briefcase, having politely but firmly resisted Carmen's insistence that he take home some pork, rice and beans in a "dog bag," when she stopped him.

"Oh," she said. "I almost forgot to tell jew."

"Forgot what?"

"She called."

"She?"

"The girl," said Carmen. "The girl, Miranda. She called, just like I told her mother she had to do."

Jaywalker sat back down. His instructions had actually been for Miranda to call *him*. But this was a start, at least. "And?" he said.

"And they're coming to New Jork. In January they're coming."

"To stay?"

"No," said Carmen. "Just for a weekend. There's a wedding. A uncle of the girl's is getting married. Her mother's brother, I think. So I told her she gotta talk to jew."

"And?"

"And that's it. I told her she gotta talk to jew. That means she gotta talk to jew. Right?"

And all Jaywalker could think to say in return was, "Right."

And finally, when he'd run out of other things to do, he hit the books. Doing legal research had never been Jaywalker's favorite pastime, but as much as he tended to put it off, he knew it was an indispensable part of his job.

He started with the Penal Law and the Criminal Procedure Law, the twin bibles of the New York criminal law practitioner. He read and reread the relevant sections on justification, physical force, deadly physical force and extreme emotional disturbance until he knew them by heart. From there he moved on to the case law, the written opinions of appellate judges in which they'd interpreted the statutes and measured them against specific fact patterns presented by actual cases. He searched for key words and phrases that might apply to the facts of his own case.

Suppose the jury were to find that Jeremy, and not Victor Quinones, had been the initial aggressor? Did that finding strip the defense of its claim of justification? Had Jeremy been under a duty to retreat, to run from Victor? Did justification end at the point when Victor lay on his back, begging for mercy? Did Jeremy's perception that his life was in immediate danger have to be a reasonable appraisal of the facts? If so, was the test of reasonableness an objective one or a subjective one? In other words, were Jeremy's actions to be measured against the standard of what a reasonable person should have done under the circumstances, or of a person who'd been through everything Jeremy had been through? Suppose, for example, that Jeremy's perception had been severely distorted by the events of the summer and of the day of the fight? Could that distortion be considered? Were the jurors to act as cold, detached, impassionate judges of the facts? Or were they supposed to somehow place themselves in Jeremy's shoes and try to see things as he'd seen them?

And who had to prove what? Justification, it turned out, was defined as a defense, so once it was raised, the prosecution bore the burden of proving its *absence*. But extreme emotional disturbance was an affirmative defense, meaning Jaywalker would have to prove its *existence*.

But prove to what standard? While the lack of justification had to be proved by the prosecution *beyond a reasonable doubt,* the presence of extreme emotional disturbance could be proved by the defense with a mere *preponderance of the evidence.*

But offsetting that important advantage for the defense was the far more significant one that favored the prosecution. Justification was a *complete* defense, requiring a jury to acquit a defendant altogether. Extreme emotional disturbance, on the other hand, was only a *partial* defense, reducing the offense from murder to first-degree manslaughter. It still left a defendant exposed to a twenty-five year sentence, a twenty-five year sentence that Harold Wexler had promised in no uncertain terms to Jeremy Estrada, even if Jaywalker were to succeed in knocking out the murder count.

He went to bed dizzy and exhausted, with statutes and cases spinning wildly in his head, knowing that with sleep would come nightmares of being shot between the eyes and left to bleed out on the pavement. Seven nights in a row he went to bed like that. But by the end of the week there was no one in the universe who understood the principles, permutations and nuances of justification and extreme emotional disturbance half as well as Jaywalker did.

With the possible exception of Harold Wexler.

8

DUTCH TREAT

They went back to court just before Thanksgiving. When Jaywalker indicated that Jeremy still had no interest in a manslaughter plea and a twenty-five year sentence, Harold Wexler could barely conceal his irritation.

"You want a trial, Mr. Estrada? Then a trial you shall get. How soon can the People be ready?"

By *the People,* he meant the prosecutor, who technically represented the People of the State of New York. It was a designation that Jaywalker hated and refused to use. To his way of thinking, its sole purpose was to suggest to the jury that the assistant district attorney was one of them, while the defendant and his lawyer were outsiders. *Non-people.*

"The People can be ready in two weeks," said Katherine Darcy.

"Mr. Jaywalker?"

Two weeks would take them pretty close to the holidays, a time when almost no trials started, especially murder trials, which tended to last a couple of weeks at a minimum. Jaywalker would have loved to bluff, just to unsettle Ms. Darcy a bit, but even were he to answer that the defense was ready now, he knew full well that as a practical matter, *now* would end up meaning sometime in January at the very earliest. But the truth was, he was nowhere near ready. Miranda Raven wasn't due to return to the city for another six weeks, and Frankie the Barber was somewhere in Puerto Rico, a pretty big place. On top of that, he still had an awful lot of preparation to do with Jeremy, and a lot of other stuff, as well.

"I think February or March is realistic," he said. "I've got a couple of witnesses to locate. One is out of state, and the other is out of the country."

"This case is already fourteen months old," said Wexler. The implication was clear.

"So it is," said Jaywalker. "And that's exactly how much time Ms. Darcy has had to prepare. I've had three months."

"February first," said the judge. "For trial."

"That's a Sunday," observed the court clerk.

"Terrific. February second."

And that was Harold Wexler on a *good* day.

"What witnesses?" Katherine Darcy asked Jaywalker as soon as they were outside the courtroom.

He could have told her it was none of her business. Under New York rules, neither side was under an obligation to reveal the names of its witnesses at this point, and with a few specific exceptions like alibis and psychiatrists, the defense was never required to do so. But Jaywalker was a horse trader at heart, and he immediately sized up the question as an opportunity to learn something.

"Who wants to know?" he asked in mock seriousness.

"Never mind," she said. All serious, no mock.

"Don't you ever lighten up?"

"Of course I do," she insisted. "Only this is a murder case, and a bad one." And with that, she began walking away, toward the elevator bank.

"Got any good ones?" he asked, lengthening his stride to catch up to her without making it too obvious.

"You know what I mean."

"Let me guess," he said. "You mean it's an execution."

"Don't make fun of me."

"Listen," said Jaywalker. "Do you have anything else on?"

Her response was to glance down at her dress, then to look back up at him with a mixture of confusion and panic. Had it been a *New Yorker* cartoon contest calling for a caption, his entry would have been, "*What do you have, X-ray eyes?*"

He decided some clarification was in order. "In court, I mean. Do you have anything else on in court? Like other cases?"

"Oh," she said, her face instantly turning red. It was the same blush she'd displayed at an earlier court appearance, back when Judge Wexler had made a reference to Jaywalker's reputation for indiscretion. Now, as then, her steely exterior had cracked just a bit, allowing the Katie in her to emerge.

"No," she said. "I have no other cases on this morning."

"Good," said Jaywalker. "I need a cup of coffee, and I'd love you to join me."

She looked around. He couldn't tell if she was checking to see if any of her supervisors were in the area, or hoping to find an excuse to turn him down. But there were no supervisors or excuses in sight. Just defendants, family members, court officers, and other lawyers waiting around for an elevator to show up.

"Okay," she said. "But it's got to be Dutch treat. You understand I can't allow you to pay for me. It would be—"

"Perish the thought," said Jaywalker.

* * *

At Jaywalker's insistence, they bypassed the first-floor luncheonette and found a place a block west, on Lafayette Street. In-house loyalty was one thing, but ptomaine poisoning was quite another.

She ordered coffee and a bagel, he tea with lemon.

"You should eat something," she said. For some reason, women were always telling him that. Maybe it was the combination of his being six feet tall and weighing a hundred and fifty pounds. Okay, a hundred and forty-eight.

"I try to make it a point to avoid eating before five o'clock," he said.

"That's terrible. Don't you like food?"

"I *love* food," he explained. "But I'm a binge eater. So I put off eating till the end of the day. Postponed gratification."

"That's really, really bad for you." Then again, maybe something about him brought out the mothering instinct in them.

"I'm sure you're right," he agreed. "And it's not like I'm recommending it or anything. I was just answering your question."

"Which makes you one for two."

"Excuse me?"

"I actually asked you two questions," she said. "You only answered one of them."

And here he thought he'd been paying close attention to her. He stared at her for a moment from across the booth that separated them, and in the process managed to lose track of the conversation. He'd forgotten how pretty she was, glasses and all. But suggesting she try contacts would be way over the line, wouldn't it? Particularly if it turned out she had some terrible condition that prevented her from wearing them.

"You only answered one of my questions," she said again.

"What was the other one again?" He truly had no idea.

"I asked you, 'What witnesses?'"

"Ahhhh." He laughed at her segue back to business. "*That* question. All right, but you still haven't answered one of mine."

"Don't change the subject." Only this time, the *mock* clearly overtook the *serious*. Somehow, in less than an hour's time, she'd gone from Ms. Darcy to Katherine, and now she was threatening to morph all the way into the elusive Katie. He thought of *The Three Faces of Eve* but decided against mentioning it.

"I'm not changing the subject," he said instead. "You were supposed to let me know how many times Teresa Morales had seen my client before she picked him out at a lineup."

"So I was," she admitted.

"So you tell me that," he said, "and I'll tell you who my witnesses are."

"Sorta like, I'll show you mine, you show me yours?"

"Sorta like," he echoed.

No blush in sight this time. Too bad.

"Okay," she said. "Teresa Morales says she knew your client from the neighborhood, that she'd seen him at least a dozen times, at least half of those for extended periods of time. I meant to put that on the record this morning. I will next time."

So the lineup had indeed been confirmatory, meaning Jaywalker wouldn't get a hearing into how it had been conducted. On the plus side, Teresa's testimony that there'd been as many as a dozen pre-shooting encounters between Jeremy and the Raiders would corroborate Jeremy's account of being constantly harassed by them.

Jeremy and the Raiders. Wasn't that a rock group?

"Your turn," said K. T. Darcy.

"Fair enough. The first witness I'm looking for is a former barber named Frankie something." It wasn't *exactly* a lie. He *was* named Frankie something, even if Jaywalker happened to know what the something was. He didn't want Darcy's investigators getting to his witnesses before he did. He was willing to play this show-me game, but only up to a point. And that point was located right before revealing so much that it might hurt his client.

"What's this Frankie going to say?" she asked.

"Frankie says he witnessed an encounter between my client and the gang. I'm sorry, the *Christian youth group*. Only now Frankie's retired, and all I know is he's supposed to be somewhere in Puerto Rico. Probably the rain forest."

"And?"

"And the other witness," said Jaywalker, "is a young lady who goes by the name Miranda."

"Might that be Miranda Raven?"

"It might be." Jaywalker nodded. Actually, he'd intended to fudge on her last name, too, and was surprised to learn that Darcy not only knew it but had it on the tip of her tongue.

"We're looking for her, too," she said.

"Oh?"

"Yes," said Darcy. "Have you spoken with her yet?"

"Uh, not exactly."

"Well, we have," said Darcy. "And she corroborates our other witnesses' accounts of the fight and the shooting."

"Including the shot between the eyes?" Jaywalker asked, his voice audibly catching on the word *eyes*.

"Including the shot between the eyes," said Darcy. "The one where the victim's lying on his back, begging for his life. And your client calmly takes it away from him."

"*Calmly?* Miranda said *calmly?*"

"Okay," said Darcy. "Maybe that wasn't precisely the word she used. But find her if you can, and talk to her. Then get back to me, and we'll compare what she tells you with the statement she wrote out and signed for the detectives."

For a moment Jaywalker was speechless. When he recovered, it was to ask, "How about showing me her statement now, so I can confront her with it?"

"Were you going to tell me her last name?"

"No," said Jaywalker. "No, I wasn't. *Mea culpa.*"

"How about Frankie the Former Barber?"

"His last name I honestly don't know," he lied.

"You talk with Miranda," said Katherine Darcy. "And then we'll take a look at her statement together."

God, she was *good.*

The check came to $5.75, and after protesting that her having had a bagel meant she should pay most of it, she relented and agreed to split it down the middle. Outside on the street, Jaywalker thanked her for having joined him. "Too bad the stakes of this case are so high," he told her. "Otherwise, it would be fun."

"You're right," she said. "Maybe some other time."

Afterwards, he played those last four words over in his head fifty times before coming to the conclusion that they'd been nothing but a polite rejoinder, her way of agreeing that trying a shoplifting case, say, or an auto theft, would likely prove a more pleasant experience than going up against each other in a murder trial.

But, being Jaywalker, at the time she'd said it, he hadn't taken it that way at all. No, he'd heard the words *Maybe some other time* as a direct response to his comment about having *fun* together. And immediately invited his imagination to take over from there. Thus emboldened, he proceeded to do exactly what his upper brain, the one located between his ears, had managed to keep him from doing not half an hour earlier.

"Have you ever tried wearing contacts?" he distinctly heard his lower brain say.

"Why would I?" Suspiciously.

"Oh, you know. They don't break or fog up. Less glare. Much easier on your ears and the bridge of your nose. Then there's all that pocket space they free up. Lots of reasons." All, of course, except the real one. But he couldn't very well come out and say, "Because your glasses hide that pretty face of yours." People got fired, even went to jail, these days for saying stuff like that, didn't they?

"It wouldn't make much sense," she said.

Now he'd done it. Here comes the part about cancer of the cornea, he decided, or *retinitis fatalis*.

"They're nothing but plain glass," she told him. "My eyes are fine. I wear these to look older, and so people will take me more seriously. Here." And with that she removed them and simultaneously shook her head so that her hair came free of whatever had been holding it back.

All the usually glib Jaywalker could do was gulp. And not silently, or even softly. No, this was a full-throated gulp, one that would have done a bullfrog in mating season proud.

"What *was* that?" she asked.

"Nothing," said Jaywalker, pretending to be absorbed in looking through the glasses. She was right; they were definitely nothing but plain glass.

"Are you sure you're okay?"

"I'm fine," he assured her. "Just releasing a bit of excess testosterone into the atmosphere. I belong to a cap-and-trade program, actually."

"You'll have to excuse me," said Katherine Darcy, standing up. "I've got to get back to work."

* * *

Well, he'd certainly managed to screw *that* up, hadn't he? He was reminded of an airline commercial he'd seen on TV not too long ago. This guy's at a big office meeting, and he nods off. He starts dreaming about his dog, petting him and calling him "good boy" over and over again. He wakes up to realize he's been saying that out loud and stroking the hair of the woman sitting next to him, while everyone else in the room is staring at him like he's totally lost it.

"Wanna get away?" the announcer asks.

9

Jaywalker wasn't exactly a white-knuckle flyer. The fact was, the prospect of dying didn't bother him all that much. It was something he knew he'd get around to sooner or later, so he didn't spend much time worrying about it. That said, traveling by plane didn't come easily to him. Days before his scheduled departure, he'd begin making exhaustive lists of everything he'd need to bring and do. The night before, he'd lay everything out on the floor and then pack obsessively in the smallest bag that could possibly hold his things. If that bag were to prove insufficient, he would move up a size, and he'd been known to go through three or four in the process. The next morning—he booked only early flights, because the *equipment* was always there, rather than being expected momentarily from Boston or Philadelphia— he'd set out for the airport neurotically early. He liked to allow enough time to get lost on the way, suffer not one but two blowouts, have trouble finding an empty spot in the long-term parking lot, discover that the shuttle bus wasn't running, encounter record-breaking lines at the security checkpoint, and be pulled out, grilled and strip-searched as a suspected terrorist.

The result, of course, was that he invariably ended up

sitting for long hours at the gate as earlier flights arrived, unloaded, refueled, reloaded and departed. But that, too, Jaywalker had planned for, having brought along the morning's *New York Times,* the latest unread issue of the *New Yorker,* the most recent *Sunday Magazine* section crossword puzzle, and—should all those diversions prove insufficient—a paperback book or two for good measure.

Today, finally, he settled into his window seat, arranged his reading material and belted himself in. Outside, a thin freezing rain was falling, a mid-December harbinger of the coming winter. He smiled at his good fortune in having picked a good day to be leaving. Just then the loudspeaker system crackled, and he looked up, afraid he might miss some safety equipment demonstration or announcement of great importance. Like he was on the wrong plane, for example, or he'd left his headlights on in the parking lot.

"Good morning, ladies and gentlemen, and welcome aboard Southwest Airlines flight 562, nonstop from Newark to sunny San Juan, Puerto Rico."

Wanna get away?

Most arriving visitors to the island make their first stop whatever hotel they're staying at. A few melanomaphiles head directly to the beach. Still, others make a detour into Old San Juan for a picturesque lunch or dinner, depending on the time of day, or a bit of shopping.

Jaywalker, unsurprisingly enough, did none of those things. Instead, he took a cab downtown to the large white government building that housed the Commonwealth's division of the United States Department of Education, which he knew from his Internet search had jurisdiction over the licensing of barbers and cosmeticians. According to Jeremy's best estimate, Frankie the Barber was in his fifties. And having once been given a ride home by Frankie,

Jeremy distinctly remembered the vehicle, a beat-up old minivan. Even allowing for a significant margin of error in the age-guessing game, those two pieces of information suggested to Jaywalker that Francisco Zapata was too young to retire and spend the rest of his days sitting by the pool. And if he had to keep working to support himself and perhaps a family, as well, what better place was there for him to have started than the one where they issued barbers' licenses?

So Jaywalker started there, too.

And immediately hit pay dirt.

An hour later he had the name of a shop opened just two months earlier, a street address, the number of a provisional license, and a high level of confidence that he was hot on the trail of the very same Francisco Zapata he'd come looking for. The name of the shop? *Frankie y Amigos.*

By seven-thirty that evening, he'd found Frankie, interviewed him, handed him a subpoena of dubious legitimacy and extracted from him a solemn promise to honor it. From there Jaywalker took a cab to his hotel, checked in and made it down to the beach. To be sure, it was getting seriously dark by that time, and all of the *turistas* had long since departed for happy hour, dinner, dancing or other activities. The only remaining signs of life were the seagulls, the sand crabs, a toothless old man drinking *cerveza* out of a bottle and from time to time casting a line into the surf, and a couple of giggling teenagers making out furiously under a blanket.

Perfect.

10

Jaywalker arrived back home four days later, a bit more rested, a trifle tanner and considerably poorer than before. It was a good thing that Frankie the Barber had decided to move no farther away than Puerto Rico. The low coach airfare had made the trip financially possible, if only barely, and not needing a passport had proven critical, seeing as he'd let his expire years ago, following his wife's death. His days of transatlantic travel were behind him, he figured, unless they should suddenly decide to reinstate the draft and begin recalling guys in their fifties.

Anyway, if Frankie proved true to his word, it meant Jaywalker had lined up his first witness, not counting Jeremy and his immediate family.

A week later, the second one phoned him.

"Mr. Jaywalker?" said a voice so hesitant and childlike that for a moment Jaywalker thought it might be his six-year-old granddaughter, playing a joke on him. But he was just uncertain enough to say "Yes?"

"This is Miranda. Miranda Raven."

Jaywalker bolted upright and tried to say, "Hello," "Thanks for calling" and "Where are you?" all at once. Then he caught himself and slowed down, but just a little.

"I'm in Baltimore," said Miranda. She sounded more grown-up now, at least twelve. How old had Jeremy said she was? Sixteen? Seventeen? Or hadn't he said at all?

"Carmen told me you're coming to New York," he said. "Is that right?" He realized he was overenunciating, the way one might speak to a foreigner or a hearing-impaired person or, yes, a small child.

"That's right," she said. "We'll be there a week from today."

"I need to see you," said Jaywalker. "It's very, very important for Jeremy."

"My mother's afraid for me."

"Tell her not to be," said Jaywalker, before realizing how stupid that sounded. "It'll be okay." As though that was any better.

"How's Jeremy?" Miranda asked.

"He's okay. He misses you."

"Can I see him?"

He wanted to say yes, sure. But already a warning light was flashing. If Katherine Darcy really had a written statement from Miranda putting her account of the shooting at odds with Jeremy's—and Jaywalker had no reason to doubt Darcy's word on that—it meant Miranda was already a compromised witness. Allowing her to go out to Rikers Island to talk with Jeremy, and having her story suddenly line up with his, would smack of collusion. But he was afraid to tell Miranda that, afraid that suggesting she couldn't see Jeremy might keep her away altogether.

"Yes," he heard himself telling her. "Yes, you can see him. But only after you and I meet. That way, it won't look like you and Jeremy got together and decided what you should say."

Was it a lie? Maybe. He'd have to see how things shaped up. But all that could wait. As grateful as he was for

Miranda's having called him, his loyalty didn't belong to her; it belonged to Jeremy. The defense lawyer's path was full of conflicts of interest, laid out like land mines along the way. Over the years Jaywalker had developed a pretty simple way of looking at the problem. He worked for one person and one person only, and that person was his client. Not that client's parents, not his boss, not his friends, and certainly not his witnesses. If Jaywalker had just lied to Miranda Raven, so be it. She was a big girl, and she'd get over it. Come on, she had to be at least sixteen. Didn't she?

The next day, Katherine Darcy phoned.

"So how was Puerto Rico?" she asked.

"Fine," said Jaywalker, trying his hardest not to miss a beat. How on earth did she know he'd been there? Was he on some kind of combined terrorist-and-defense-lawyer watch list? But as much as he wanted to know, he'd be damned if he was going to give her the satisfaction of asking.

"Did you find her?" she asked.

"Her."

"Miranda."

"No," said Jaywalker. "No, actually I didn't. But I'm working on—"

"That's because she's in Maryland."

"Is that so?"

"Yup."

Jaywalker said nothing. He could be pretty good at playing dumb when he wanted to. And sometimes even when he didn't.

"Don't you want to know how I knew you were in Puerto Rico?" she asked.

"Only if you want to tell me."

He read her silence as disappointment over his reaction.

"I've got some more photos," she said after a moment. "And some additional discovery material. Reports and stuff."

"Want to send me copies?"

"I could," she said. "But I've also got something you might want to see in person."

"What's that?" he asked.

"We think we may have found the murder weapon."

He made it to her office a little after four o'clock. The first thing he noticed, being Jaywalker, was that she looked different—and terrific. The second thing was that she wasn't wearing her glasses.

"Where'd they go?" he asked her.

"Where did *who* go?"

"The prop." By way of clarification, he raised an index finger to the outer corner of his eye.

"Oh," she said. "I had a birthday."

It didn't strike him as much of an explanation, but he said "Happy birthday" anyway, and then followed up with "Can I buy you a drink?"

"No, thanks," she said. "It was a big one," she added with exaggerated gloominess.

"Thirty?" He'd been around women long enough to know you took your lowest guess and then subtracted at least ten years. Fifteen, if you really wanted to play it safe.

"Forty."

He raised both eyebrows in mock surprise. "You're kidding," he said.

"Thanks. Anyway, as soon as it happened, I developed this sudden urge to look younger."

It couldn't be easy, being a woman.

"And you," she said, looking him over. "How come you're not tan?"

He shrugged. "It's the price one pays for hitting the beach just before sunset."

"So aren't you even a little bit curious as to how I knew you were there?"

"No," he lied, knowing that she was itching to tell him and would get around to it sooner or later.

She located a folder of papers on her desk and extended it toward him. "A lot of this stuff you may already have," she said, "but some of it's new."

He took the folder. From the lack of heft, he decided there couldn't be too much inside, old or new. "What about this gun you mentioned?" he asked.

She got up, walked over to a metal filing cabinet, unlocked it, pulled the top drawer open and reached in. When her hand emerged, it was holding a good-sized silver semiautomatic. He knew from the ballistics report that the weapon had been a 9 mm or a .380. Either one was capable of firing the ammunition and discharging the spent shell casings that had been recovered.

"Ballistics?" he asked.

"Inconclusive."

That was a nonanswer if ever he'd heard one. Test-firing either established that this was the gun that had fired the re-covered rounds or that it wasn't. Without coming right out and saying it, Darcy was conceding that there was no match.

"Prints?" he asked.

"Not by the time we got it," she said. "Some kid found it in an alley off 113th Street, took it home, played with it for a day and a half. Lucky for him, it was empty. His mother saw it finally, phoned the precinct. Patrol picked it up, didn't know it might be a murder weapon."

"May I?"

She extended the gun to him delicately, the way one might offer up a dead bird or mouse. He took it and held it by the grips. It felt good, pleasantly heavy but nicely balanced. Even without looking for the maker's name, he recognized it as a Browning. He'd owned one back in his DEA days. Bought it for undercover work. You couldn't very well show up to buy drugs packing a six-shot .38 Smith & Wesson Detective Special.

Katherine Darcy had said they'd found the thing empty, and presumably it still was. But rule number one was that you always assumed the opposite. He jacked the slide back to clear the chamber. Nothing ejected. Applying gentle pressure to the trigger, he eased the hammer back in place. Then he depressed the magazine release, and the clip dropped easily into his palm. It, too, was empty. He visually checked the chamber, the safety and the firing pin, then jacked the slide back again to cock the gun. Taking aim at the on button of the air conditioner unit in the window, he dry-fired.

"Bang!" he shouted, and smiled as Darcy lifted a full inch off the floor.

Gripping the gun by the barrel, he handed it back to her. "It's not the murder weapon," he told her.

"How do you know?"

He said nothing.

"I'll tell you how I know you were in Puerto Rico," she said. *I'll show you mine if you show me yours.*

He shrugged.

"I'll be your best friend."

"Getting warmer now," he told her.

"I'll let you buy me that drink."

"You're on," he told her.

"One of my girlfriends from appeals happened to spot you at the airport. She knows I have a case with you, and she thought I ought to know. Also…"

"Yes?"

"She said you were awfully early for your flight."

"That would be me," Jaywalker conceded.

"So why isn't this the murder weapon?"

"Because," said Jaywalker, "there *was* no murder. If it was anything, it was manslaughter."

Which was arguably true, if you wanted to factor in extreme emotional disturbance, but was sneaky at best. What Jaywalker *hadn't* told Katherine Darcy was that the Browning's firing pin was just slightly off-center, a hair toward eight o'clock. From the ballistics photos of the re-covered spent shell casings, he already knew that the gun that had killed Victor Quinones had a dead-center firing pin, and therefore almost certainly had to have been a Glock or a Tech Nine.

That *drink* turned out to be nothing more exciting than a hot chocolate at a small coffee shop down by the federal courthouse. True to her word, Katherine Darcy actually let Jaywalker pick up the tab this time. And she waited until they were finishing and he was paying to bring up the case again.

"So," she said, "if you're so confident this is nothing but a manslaughter case at worst, what's your guy looking for?"

"Five years," said Jaywalker. He had absolutely no idea what, if anything, Jeremy might be willing to take. But five years was rock bottom for first-degree manslaughter and would be an absolute steal, especially for an *execution*. So it seemed to Jaywalker like a pretty good place to start.

"Get serious," she said.

"What would be serious? Ten?"

"Twenty," she said. "*Maybe* eighteen or nineteen. But don't count on it."

"Tell me ten," said Jaywalker, "and I'll ask him."

"Never. Absolutely never."

And that was how the discussion ended.

* * *

But the thing was, not only had Katherine Darcy earlier backed off from her insistence that it was a murder case with no lesser plea, now she'd indicated a willingness to consider something less than the twenty-five-year maximum on a manslaughter plea. In other words, for the second time, the prosecution had blinked.

Why?

He met with Jeremy two days later.

"Suppose I could get you twelve years," he said. He figured if Darcy had already blinked and offered eighteen or twenty to his five, sooner or later he might be able to talk her into splitting the difference. "Would you be interested?"

"How much of that would I have to do?"

"On twelve? A dime." He figured Jeremy had been in long enough by now to have picked up the language of state time. A *dime* was ten, of course, just like a *deuce* was two, a *trey* three, and a *nickel* or a *pound* five.

Slowly Jeremy shook his head from side to side. There was nothing arrogant to the gesture, nothing the least bit defiant. Had Jaywalker been forced to come up with a word to describe it, the best he would have managed was *sad*.

"I feel like, you know, like I put up with a lot from those guys," said Jeremy. As he spoke, his eyes locked onto Jaywalker's own. They were as blue-gray as ever, even in the poorly lit visiting area of 100 Centre Street, but there seemed to be some sort of film coating them. Jaywalker had never seen Jeremy cry, and had decided he never would. He wondered if the young man had shed more than his share of tears during the long summer of his torment, and if this slight watery look was all he had left. Or maybe Jeremy just wasn't a crier.

"You did," Jaywalker agreed. "You put up with a lot." He

paused for a few seconds before following up with the caveat. "But the law doesn't always look at it that way."

"Not even if I was trying to save my life?"

"As long as you were trying to save your life," explained Jaywalker, "what you did was absolutely justified. No question about that. But once you get the gun away from Victor, and once he's lying on the ground unarmed and helpless…" He let his voice trail off from soft to silent. This wasn't an argument they were having, after all, or a lecture he was delivering. It was more like a commiseration. In the short space of four months, Jaywalker had grown surprisingly fond of this young man, had come to care deeply about the impossible predicament in which he now found himself. But personal feelings were one thing, and being a criminal defense lawyer was another. The fact was, he owed Jeremy more than empathy, more than compassion, more than caring. In addition to all those things, he owed Jeremy the benefit of his twenty-some years in the trenches, and whatever wisdom might have come along during them. And leading a client valiantly into a battle they were sure to lose was no way to satisfy those debts.

"The law says," he told Jeremy, "that self-defense ends once the threat ends. From that moment on, no matter what you've been through, you can't pull the trigger. You're allowed to defend yourself, but you're not allowed to get even. That's what the judge is going to tell the jury, in so many words. He has no choice. The law requires him to do that. And it's very hard for me to imagine twelve ordinary people getting together and agreeing to blow him off and do the opposite of what he's told them."

"They weren't there," said Jeremy.

"No, they weren't," Jaywalker agreed. "And that will make it even harder for them to understand how you felt. It will make it just about impossible, in fact."

"Can't you explain it to them?"

The question was so utterly simple, and yet so disarmingly naive, that it completely broke the spell and forced Jaywalker to smile broadly. "Sure," he said, "I can try. But I'm going to need an awful lot of help from you."

"You won't be mad at me?"

"Mad at you? For what?"

"For making you go to trial."

"Hey," said Jaywalker. "Going to trial is what I do."

For a week and a half there was no word from Miranda. From what she'd told Jaywalker over the phone, he figured she should have been in New York at least three or four days by now. He called Jeremy's mother half a dozen times. Half a dozen times she told him pretty much the same story, though it was hard not to detect a trend in the way she phrased it.

"Be patient. She's gonna call me. Jew gonna see."

"What can I say, Mr. Jackwalker? She told me she'd call me as soon as she get here."

"I still don't hear from her. So, how does the case look? Jew got to get him less time, Mr. Jakewalker. I know the other boy, he passed away. But still, an accident is an accident, and that's the truth. Right? I hope she calls."

"If it's God's will, she'll call."

"The wedding was yesterday, I found out. And still she don't call me. That's not right."

"I don't hear nothing from the little tramp."

* * *

The packet of additional discovery material Katherine Darcy had given Jaywalker turned out to contain nothing new, with a single exception. That exception was a photograph of Victor Quinones, evidently taken at the time of the autopsy. It was a black-and-white head shot, not too gory, but it showed the entrance wound of the fatal gunshot, squarely between the eyes. It also revealed what a scary dude Victor had been in life. In addition to scraggly chin whiskers and shiny windowpaning that covered several of his front teeth, he had pockmarks on both cheeks, which Jaywalker took to be old acne scars. He slipped the photo into a subfile entitled *M.E.*, for Medical Examiner, resolving to figure out some way to get it in front of the jurors, just in case Katherine Darcy didn't bother. Like so many things, it was something of a double-edged sword. The almost surgical precision of the wound was compelling evidence that Jeremy had aimed and fired deliberately and at close range. But if you were to factor in the windowpaning and Victor's overall menacing appearance, it was a plus for the defense. Now, was it relevant that the guy Jeremy had killed happened to have been exceedingly ugly? Technically, no, of course not. But in the real world, you bet it was. In the eyes of a juror sitting on a close case, it mattered hugely.

Now all Jaywalker had to do was figure out how to make it a close case.

So why had Katherine Darcy gone to the trouble of inviting him over to pick up the additional packet of discovery when she just as easily could have mailed it to him or waited until the next court appearance to hand it over? It certainly hadn't been to show him the gun, which she must have known she wasn't going to be able to introduce as the murder weapon, even if she thought it was.

So it had to have been the offer—the twenty years, maybe eighteen or nineteen—that she'd wanted to make but hadn't gotten around to actually offering until he was ready to pay for their hot chocolates.

The Blink.

Interesting.

"She's here."

The clock by the bed told him it was 6:14 a.m. For Jaywalker, that would have been late to still be lying in bed had it been summertime, or even late spring or early fall. But it was the last week of January and still pitch dark outside, not to mention cold. Hibernating season. He rubbed his eyes and shifted the phone receiver from his left ear to his right, the one that heard better. And tried to place the gravelly voice.

"Who's *she?*" he managed to ask.

"She. The girl, Miranda. She's here, with me."

"That's good," said Jaywalker, suddenly awake. "That's *great.* What time can you bring her to the office?" The "office" was the conference room of a suite where he'd once rented a room. For an occasional contribution of copy paper, toner or fax machine cartridges, they still let him meet the occasional client there.

"Any time jew like," said Carmen.

"How about ten?" Most of the lawyers would be in court by then, he knew. They might even be able to use one of the empty private offices.

"Too early," said Carmen. "She's jung. They like to sleep late in the morning, the jung people."

"Eleven? Twelve?"

"How about two?"

"Two it is."

So much for *any time you like.*

* * *

They showed up at a quarter of three, Carmen literally leading Miranda by the hand into the conference room.

Very pretty didn't even begin to describe her.

Try *stunning. Breathtaking. Exquisite. Gorgeous.* And *delicate,* thin to the point of looking almost breakable. Long, straight hair, somewhere between red and auburn. Whether it was from nature's palette or something poured out of a bottle, Jaywalker couldn't tell. But then, he never could. Skin a shade too dark for an Anglo but a bit too light for a Latina. A perfect nose, a mouth just a trifle too full, and high cheekbones that might or might not have had something to do with her "Semaphore" blood.

And then you got to the eyes.

As blue-gray as Jeremy's were, that was how brown Miranda's were. And they were huge, disproportionly huge, making her look almost like one of those waifs that artist guy used to paint. Klee? Maybe. But his subjects ended up slightly freaky-looking, and Miranda was anything but that.

"This is Miranda," said Carmen, perhaps sensing that Jaywalker was too busy staring to introduce himself. "And this is the lawyer, Mr. Jameswalker."

They shook hands. Hers was impossibly thin. Again the word *delicate* came to Jaywalker's mind.

"Pleased to meetcha," said Miranda.

And immediately the spell was broken.

It wasn't just the *meetcha,* though certainly that was a big part of it. It was that as soon as she opened her mouth, she sounded just like any other teenager. And that threw him, the total and totally unexpected disconnect between her extraordinary looks and her very ordinary voice. And in some strange way, that disconnect comforted Jaywalker and allowed him to visualize Miranda and Jeremy as an item. Had she sounded like the goddess Jaywalker had fully expected her to once he'd seen her, he would have been incapable of putting the two of them together. But suddenly it made sense. Jeremy himself was exceedingly good-looking, but at the same time he was shy and introverted to a fault. *Slow,* to put it charitably. Now, Jaywalker realized one sentence into their meeting, so was Miranda. And he got it. In this beautiful but limited young lady, Jeremy had finally found himself, just as she'd found herself in him.

He asked Carmen to go out to the waiting room so he could talk with Miranda in privacy.

"But I'm Jeremy's mother," she protested.

"That's the point," he explained. "I plan on calling both of you as witnesses. I don't want the D.A. to be able to say we discussed the facts of the case together."

She grumbled, but she went.

Still, it was impossible. As Miranda and he sat there at the conference table, lawyers who had rooms in the suite kept popping in and out, going to and from the copy room, the secretaries' area, the restrooms or the conference room itself, which doubled as a library and was lined with stacks of law books that on any other day did nothing but collect dust and serve as decoration. But on this particular day, it seemed they'd all become instant, must-read bestsellers.

Everyone wanted to get a look at Miranda.

Or better yet, two or three or four looks.

He finally found them an empty room and retreated to it, and they were able to speak for the better part of an hour. That was the good news. The bad news was that fifteen minutes into that hour, Jaywalker realized that Miranda wasn't going to be able to help Jeremy.

It wasn't that she didn't want to; she did. But in the days following the shooting, the detectives had quickly identified her, located her and picked her up. They'd brought her to the precinct, whether voluntarily on her part or not. But legally, it made no difference. A criminal defendant gets to complain about violations of his rights, and if those violations are serious enough, evidence gathered as a result of them can be suppressed and kept out of his trial. But when the violations are of other people's rights—Miranda's, for example—the defendant lacks what lawyers call *standing* to object.

According to Miranda, the detectives had threatened to arrest her as an accomplice to murder and as an "accessory after the fact," a layman's term that doesn't even appear in the pages of the Penal Law. But they'd succeeded in frightening her sufficiently to get her to write out and sign a statement. In it she'd said she didn't know whether it had been Victor Quinones who'd first pulled the gun or Jeremy, even though she now assured Jaywalker it had been Victor. And she'd described the final shot the same way the other witnesses had, putting the gun in Jeremy's hand as he stood over his fallen victim, who lay helplessly on the pavement, looking up and begging for mercy.

Miranda Raven was a poisoned witness.

That meant whichever side called her would suffer the consequences. When a lawyer puts a person on the stand, whether to testify as a fact witness, an expert or a character witness, the jury anticipates that that person is going to help the side that's called him. Sure, there may be some inroads made on cross-examination, but the natural expectation is that on balance, the witness will end up helping the side that called him. After all, that was why he was called in the first place, to help.

If Jaywalker were to call Miranda, Katherine Darcy would have a field day attacking her with her signed statement. Even if Miranda were to disown it as the product of intimidation, her value to the defense would be so diminished that she'd end up hurting far more than helping. Conversely, if Katherine Darcy called her, no matter how many times she reminded Miranda of what she'd said in the statement, her repudiation of those things at trial would seriously undercut the prosecution's chances. In other words, it mattered greatly which side chose to call Miranda, because in doing so, that side implicitly vouched for her credibility and stood to lose significantly in the eyes of the jury once she was neutralized on cross.

So it wasn't just a matter of Miranda being a mixed bag, a witness who would both help and hurt each side at the same time. In immediately sizing her up as a poisoned witness, Jaywalker was grasping a more fundamental and critical truth about her: that whichever side made the mistake of touching her first would be the one infected, and the results could well prove fatal.

He didn't tell her any of that, of course. To do so would have been nothing short of cruel. It would have been tantamount to saying, "You screwed up so badly by writing out and signing that statement that now you're of no use to Jeremy, and as a result, he's probably going to be convicted." No, he couldn't do that. All he could tell her was that they'd see how things played out, then ask her to keep in touch.

"Can I see Jeremy?" was all she wanted to know.

There was a part of Jaywalker that still wanted to say no. But as he thought about it, he realized that to do so would be to succumb to his anger at her. Why anger? Because she'd been so easily intimidated by the detectives. Because she'd been stupid enough to believe they could really charge her with a crime just for the accident of being present when one had been committed. He wanted to ask her how she possibly could have thought that and tell her how shallow her loyalty to Jeremy had been. He wanted to yell at her, to grab her by the shoulders and shake some sense into her. But it was too late for all that, he knew. All he would succeed in doing would be to make her cry.

So he said, "Sure. Sure, you can see Jeremy." And even described the steps she'd have to go through in order to do it.

But it hurt. It hurt terribly. Of the four people who'd been in the immediate vicinity of the shooting, one was dead and another was severely compromised, first because he was the defendant, and second because he was so withdrawn and in-articulate. Now a third, whom Jaywalker had considered his greatest hope, had been rendered totally useless. That left only the fourth, Teresa Morales.

Teresa Morales was anything but disinterested. She'd not only been a member of the Raiders gang herself, she'd been Victor Quinones's girlfriend. Yet the way the trial was suddenly shaping up, it was beginning to look as though she was going to have the definitive word as to what had happened.

Which was bad news indeed for Jeremy Estrada.

11

GETTING ANGRY

If you've been lucky enough to have spent any significant time driving across the lower forty-eight, or even watching it go by from the window of a train—and Jaywalker had done both in younger days—you've learned not to look for city skyscrapers before you've first passed through outlying towns and suburbs; that on your way to the banks of the mightiest of rivers you'll first have to cross a series of creeks, brooks and streams; and that mountains almost invariably have foothills.

Trials have postponements.

Though, for some reason, lawyers prefer to think of them as adjournments. Perhaps the bias has something to do with the differing implications inherent in the words themselves. To *postpone* is to put off, to avoid for the present an unpleasant task or event. It carries a distinctly negative connotation. To *adjourn,* on the other hand, is an act of continuance, a forward-looking promise to reconvene and readdress the matter on another day. It somehow manages to suggest that progress is being made, that the journey goes on.

And just as the foothills grow taller as the mountain is approached, the density of homes increases as the city looms larger on the horizon, and the streams deepen and broaden as the river nears, so, too, do adjournments change. Their intervals become increasingly shorter. They take on new designations of purpose: "for discovery," "for control purposes," "for hearing," and, finally, "for trial." Warning labels begin popping up: "People to be ready," "final versus defendant," "no further adjournments," "final versus both sides," and eventually "date absolutely certain for trial."

Jaywalker was more than just fluent in the language; he loved the journey itself. He'd learned long ago that every case had a built-in clock of its own, an inner circadian rhythm to guide it as it ripened and readied itself toward maturity. He knew that with rare exception prosecutors could rush cases to trial only so much, defense lawyers could dodge the day of reckoning only so long, and even judges—yes, even the Harold Wexlers of the system—were pretty much powerless to significantly speed things up or slow them down. To succeed in doing so would be tantamount to hastening the sunrise or holding back the tide.

Jaywalker hardly spent the intervening months sitting back and enjoying the passage of time. In the buildup to a trial, sitting back became all but constitutionally impossible for him. To be sure, he didn't focus on Jeremy's case to the exclusion of everything else. There were other cases to attend to, and even a couple of trials. But they were *lesser* trials. One was a bench trial, a non-jury affair over whether a client named Adam Williams had known that the suitcase he'd found in an alley and decided to claim as his own had been stolen property. It had indeed been stolen, as Jaywalker readily conceded, but Adam had had no way of knowing that; to him it appeared to have been discarded, abandoned. A judge reluctantly agreed, but not before delivering a stern lecture to Adam on how foolish he'd been to pick the thing up and carry it off, and how lucky he'd been to find a good lawyer. The other case Jaywalker tried to a jury, but a jury of six, not twelve. That was all you were entitled to on a misdemeanor, and drunk driving was a misdemeanor. The officers claimed that Tammy Cuccinotta had blown a .15 on the station house breathalyzer test, nearly double the .08 required for a conviction. Jaywalker put her on the stand, where she claimed the cops had fabricated the result after she'd threatened to sue them for false arrest. The jurors didn't actually buy that, they confided to Jaywalker afterwards; their acquittal actually had more to do with liking Tammy, a single working mother of three young children, and also liking the short skirts she wore to court each day. This time Jaywalker delivered the lecture.

But he learned from those trials, just as he took something home from every case he tried. From Adam Williams he was reminded anew that reality wasn't everything; it was sometimes the defendant's *perception* of reality that mattered. And from Tammy Cuccinotta he received a refresher course in just how absolutely crucial it was that jurors found a defendant *likeable*. Now, if he could just find a short skirt in a men's medium....

And, of course, Jaywalker continued to work on Jeremy's case. He reported back to Katherine Darcy that there would be no manslaughter plea. He spent more hours over more visits with Jeremy than he could count. He mined Carmen's and Julie's memories for details of how Jeremy had acted during the summer of his ordeal. He had a pathologist friend of his go over the autopsy report line by line in case he himself had missed something (he hadn't), and coaxed an old chemistry major friend into attempting to quantify the exact amount of opiates present in a sample of Victor Quinones's blood (he couldn't). He tapped a private investigator who owed him a favor, and sent him out to find and interview Teresa Morales. But after a month of searching, the guy reported back that Teresa was nowhere to be found.

"She's not in jail and she's not in the neighborhood," he told Jaywalker. "She doesn't have a driver's license, a Social Security number, a Medicaid card or a credit card. She doesn't work on the books, vote at election time or own a cell phone. And she doesn't have a criminal record. Are you sure she exists?"

"She exists," said Jaywalker, and sent the investigator back out to find her. But he never did.

Jaywalker checked in so regularly with Frankie the Barber in Puerto Rico that the phone company threatened to cut off his long-distance service. "You do that," Jaywalker warned the representative, "and I'll sic Alan Fudderman on you."

"Who?"

He met once more with Miranda, to help her with the documents she needed to get her onto Rikers Island to visit Jeremy. But he charged her for the service, after a fashion. Before allowing her to leave, he snapped a half dozen photos of her. "Just in case the jury never gets to meet you in person," he explained, "I want them to see the face that launched a thousand ships." If he'd thought for a moment there was any chance they still read Homer in high school, her blank stare was answer enough.

And each time they went back to court, Harold Wexler would warn Jeremy that he was making a big mistake in turning down the manslaughter plea. "Your lawyer's good," he'd say, "but he's not *that* good."

And each time Jeremy would smile sheepishly, shake his head slowly from side to side and say softly, "I'd like a trial."

"Wonderful," Wexler told him on the last such occasion. "You just keep on taking advice from all those jailhouse lawyers on Rikers Island. Don't stop to ask yourself why, if they're all so smart, they're still there."

"I'd like a trial," said Jeremy.

"Then a trial you shall have. February second. That's a date absolutely certain for trial. Do I make myself clear?"

Both lawyers assured him he had. But as Jaywalker left the courtroom to visit once more with Jeremy in the pens, the word *clear* kept echoing in his head. It was the same word he'd heard shouted back when his wife's heart had stopped beating toward the very end and they'd called a code. A dozen hospital personnel had rushed into the room, pushing him aside and reducing him to a bystander. They'd ripped her gown open, slammed the paddles onto her chest and shouted "Clear!" They'd managed to save her that time, but the experience had taught Jaywalker that there would be no second time, or third or fourth.

Goddamn you, Harold Wexler, he thought, for having yanked him back in time to a memory he'd done his best to keep buried for a dozen years. But if ever there'd been a judge who knew how to push Jaywalker's buttons, Wexler was the one. There were others who were tougher and plenty who were meaner, but their heavy-handedness invariably gave them away on the printed page and got them reversed on appeal. Wexler was smart enough to cover himself, to get away with tilting the playing field in whatever direction he wanted. And from his long-running commentary, it was pretty clear that what he wanted in Jeremy's case was going to make it a steep climb for the defense. But that was okay. As much as he preferred working with a judge who had no agenda, Jaywalker relished the occasional street brawl. It got his adrenaline pumping, his juices flowing. It got him *angry.*

And right then and there, standing in front of an eleventh-floor feeder pen at 100 Centre Street, he looked upward toward the heavens—which on this particular day bore a striking resemblance to peeling yellow paint—and silently vowed to his wife that even if it turned out to be the last case he ever tried, he was going to win it, not just for Jeremy, but for her.

Then he broke out laughing at the absurdity of it.

Well, he still had a whole week to get angry again.

12

"**J**urors entering!"

With those two words the trial of the People of the State of New York versus Jeremy Estrada got under way. No *"Hear ye, hear ye, hear ye."* No *"Draw nigh, give your attention, and you shall be heard."* Not in Harold Wexler's court. About the only concession to ritual that Wexler made was the black robe he wore from time to time. Other judges circulated detailed written rules of decorum, banged their gavels, raised their voices and threatened to clear their courtrooms at the slightest disruption. Wexler simply peered out over rimless reading glasses, his shoulders hunched slightly forward, his jaw set tightly in a withering stare. Rumor had it that back in his Legal Aid days he'd punched out his immediate supervisor, a guy who'd outweighed him by fifty pounds and stood five inches taller than he did. Jaywalker happened to have been there at the time and knew it was no rumor.

As soon as the last of the seventy-five prospective jurors had found seats, they were directed to stand up again so they could be sworn in. A couple of them declined to take an oath and were permitted to repeat the word "affirm" in place of "swear." There was no real difference, of course. Except to

Jaywalker. He looked for jurors who were willing to stand
up for their beliefs—or their *non-beliefs*—even if that put
them in a distinct and perhaps uncomfortable minority. And
he was especially looking for them in Jeremy's case, which
he'd long ago decided was going to be an uphill battle at
best. On the rare occasion when he was the favorite going
into trial, Jaywalker wanted normal, mainstream jurors.
When he was a long shot he wanted misfits, weirdos, people
who liked to swim against the current. And he was definitely
a long shot in this one. So he jotted down descriptions of
the two affirmers and what they were wearing, since he
didn't yet have names to attach to them.

Then Jaywalker turned to Jeremy, seated at the defense
table alongside him. He'd dressed Jeremy up for the trial,
but only a little. No jacket or tie; that would have been
phony. But khakis and a white shirt. Jeremy had wanted to
wear his reading glasses, and Jaywalker had said okay, but
told him to keep them off most of the time. They were
rimless and made him look studious, which was good. But,
perhaps influenced by Katherine Darcy's example, Jaywalker felt they made Jeremy look older. And he wanted the
jurors to think of him as young. Hell, he wanted them to
think of him as a baby. Now, putting one hand on the young
man's shoulder and using the other to gesture toward the
jurors, he explained the significance of what had just
happened. Jaywalker liked to keep his client informed of everything. He was forever reminding Jeremy that it was *his*
case, not Jaywalker's. Except for tactical decisions, that
was, like what their defense would be and whether Jeremy
would take the stand or not. Autonomy was sweet, democ-
racy noble, discussion fine. But they had no place at the trial
table. There, such lofty notions gave way. There, winning
trumped everything.

There was quite another reason Jaywalker had gone to

the trouble of explaining to Jeremy the difference between swearing and affirming. He wanted the jurors to see the interaction between the two of them, wanted them to see that hand of his resting on Jeremy's shoulder. In short order those jurors would hear from the judge and the lawyers, but it would be days, perhaps weeks, before they'd hear from Jeremy. So Jaywalker needed to immediately establish what the case was about. It wasn't about Victor Quinones or Teresa Morales. It wasn't about justification or extreme emotional disturbance. It wasn't even about murder as opposed to manslaughter. It was about Jeremy. So the explaining and the hand on the shoulder were about personalizing Jeremy, showing the jurors right off the bat that he was not only approachable and touchable, but he was concerned, he was interested. And above all, he was *important*.

One by one, the court clerk pulled eighteen slips of paper from a wooden drum and read off eighteen names, mispronouncing as many of them as she possibly could. One by one, eighteen prospective jurors gathered up their belongings, rose from their seats, made their way to the jury box and took the seats that corresponded to the order in which their names had been called. Harold Wexler spent the next hour and a half talking to them, first as a group, then individually. By the time he turned things over to Katherine Darcy, he'd told the eighteen a little bit about the case, but *only* a little bit; introduced the lawyers and the defendant to them; found out what each of the jurors did, the general neighborhood where they lived, whether they were married or single, and whether they'd ever been convicted of a crime. Those jurors who succeeded in persuading him that they either couldn't be impartial or had something far more important to do than sit on a murder trial, he excused with a sarcastic comment and a promise to send them across the street to a boring civil trial.

Katherine Darcy rose, gathered her notes and stepped to the lectern. She, too, was wearing her glasses for the occasion, apparently having opted for looking serious at the expense of looking older. Why did Jaywalker dwell on such things? Because they mattered, that was why. If his adversary was going to try to impress the jurors with her seriousness, that meant Jaywalker would need to adjust his game plan. He'd need to both out-serious her at times, while every once in a while undercutting her by injecting a little humor into the proceedings. The idea was to outflank her on both sides.

But as soon as Darcy began to address the panel, he realized it wasn't going to be easy. She had a nice conversational way of interacting with the jurors. Not that she was entirely comfortable on her feet; a slight quiver in her voice and a bit of fumbling through her notes gave her away from time to time. But Jaywalker knew that those lapses were anything but deal-breakers: a little nervousness often went over well with jurors. He himself had profited from that bit of knowledge in his younger days, when he'd played the role of the new kid on the block. But as he'd aged he'd had to adjust, much the way a veteran pitcher learns to add changeups and sliders to compensate for a fading fastball. By now he'd settled into the role of the experienced, confident defender who'd been around long enough to recognize a bogus prosecution when he saw one. And if it wasn't as much fun as his former incarnations, it seemed to serve him pretty well.

What Darcy *hadn't* learned was what type of questions to ask the jurors. She spent far too much time on their interests and hobbies, what kind of TV shows they watched or magazines they read, and whether they'd ever been crime victims. Jaywalker knew where she was going with that stuff, of course. She was trying to find mainstream, conservative jurors more likely to identify with the People of the State of New York than with a defendant accused of murder. The problem was that every bit of information she learned, Jaywalker learned, too. So even as she succeeded in identifying jurors she wanted, Jaywalker knew to challenge them.

Still, she was good, and by the time she sat down it was clear that the jurors liked her. And Jaywalker knew not to underestimate the importance of that. A prosecutor who comes off as likeable has accomplished something significant. In liking her, the jurors would tend to trust her and believe in the legitimacy of her case, and would be prone to find her witnesses credible. For Jaywalker, the job would be a little trickier. Not only would he have to get the jurors to overcome the affection they'd developed for Katherine Darcy and come to like him and trust him more, he'd also have to get them to like his client, that very same accused murderer.

Only he wasn't going to get his chance yet, not with Harold Wexler declaring a recess for lunch. So at the moment, all Jaywalker could do was sit at the defense table as close as he possibly could to Jeremy, while fifty-eight jurors—down from the original seventy-five—filed out of the courtroom. Only when the last of them had left and the door had been closed would a court officer lead Jeremy out. But they would use a side door, one that led into the pens instead of out to the corridor. Rather than being free to choose from among the restaurants and coffee shops in the area, Jeremy would spend the next hour and a quarter in a five-by-ten cell. And instead of getting to order the curried chicken salad or the sushi, he'd dine on a bologna or cheese sandwich, washed down with the lukewarm brown water they called coffee. Jaywalker knew; he'd had more than a few of those meals himself over the years. But he'd never been facing twenty-five years of them, as Jeremy was.

That said, his lunch this day would consist of a container of iced tea, sipped as he sat on a windowsill on the eleventh floor. The liquid would keep his kidneys from shutting down, the sugar would get him through the afternoon session, and the lemon would protect him against scurvy. And don't think you can't get scurvy at 100 Centre Street, along with just about every other malady known to Western civilization.

When jury selection resumed that afternoon, Jaywalker lost no time in asking the kind of questions that had become his trademark. They weren't the information-seeking questions that Harold Wexler and Katherine Darcy had asked, and the answers they elicited were of almost no consequence. Instead it was the questions themselves, and the information contained in them, that were important. And like everything Jaywalker did when he was on trial, this was no accident.

He began by reminding the jurors that this was a murder case in which one young man had taken another's life. He added the fact that the fatal shot had been fired at extremely close range and had struck the victim between the eyes. Then, just before drawing an objection from Darcy that he was testifying—an objection that Wexler no doubt would have sustained—he turned the information into a question.

"Now, Ms. Leach, does hearing any of that make you feel that perhaps this isn't the kind of case you should sit in on?"

Even before Ms. Leach had finished assuring him that she was perfectly capable of judging such a case, Jaywalker was moving on. "Suppose I were to tell you, Mr. Lowden, that my client is in fact the young man who fired that fatal shot? Does that end the case for you? Or do you want to know more? Do you want to know what led up to that shot?"

Of course Mr. Lowden wanted to know more. And so did the other fifty-seven jurors in the room, who now—not because of any answer from Mr. Lowden, but by the very asking of the question itself—knew that the case was no longer about who had killed Victor Quinones, but about the events that had preceded the killing. Just like that, Jaywalker had changed it from a *whodunnit* to a *yesbut*.

Still in the guise of asking questions, he told them about Jeremy's prior marijuana case, which the judge had ruled Ms. Darcy could ask about. It turned out Jeremy had pleaded guilty to the charge in exchange for doing two days of community service. Some lawyer, perhaps Alan Fudderman, had done him no favor there. He told them about Jeremy's having gotten rid of the gun, having fled the city, and having spent seven months hiding out in Puerto Rico. He told them about Miranda and how, as Jeremy's girl-friend, she'd witnessed the incident from start to finish. But, he told them, her whereabouts were now unknown, and neither side would be calling her as a witness.

"Are you going to hold that against my client, Mrs. Fisher?"

Mrs. Fisher assured him that she wouldn't.

What he *didn't* tell them was that the reason Miranda's whereabouts were unknown was that Jaywalker had decided not only that he didn't want to call her as a witness, but that he didn't want Katherine Darcy calling her, either. So he'd struck a deal with her. He'd fulfilled his part of the bargain by making good on his earlier promise to get her into Rikers Island to see Jeremy. It had required a bit of an identity switch, arming her with identification belonging to Jeremy's twin sister, Julie. But it had worked. Which was good, because had it not, both Miranda and Jaywalker would have been looking at serious felony time. Miranda's part of the bargain was that after seeing Jeremy and returning Julie's identification, she was to disappear, to vanish. And she had.

Finally Jaywalker told them about one witness he *was* going to call. "And the name of that witness—" and here he paused just a beat for effect, being careful not to overdo it "—is Jeremy Estrada." He asked them if they could listen to him with their minds open despite his prior brush with the law, despite his quiet voice, his habit of speaking slowly, and his perhaps not being the smartest kid they'd ever come across. In the run-up to a presidential debate they might have called all of that *lowering expectations,* and the phrase could be applied pretty well to trials, as well.

One by one the jurors assured Jaywalker that they could still be open-minded, just as they did when he told them they would witness sobbing from the victim's grieving parents, see gruesome photos of the deceased, learn grisly details from the medical examiner, and hear the word *execution* from the prosecutor's lips. The jurors' assurances, once again, were hardly the point. The idea was to get these things out in the open now, to strip away from them as much of their shock value as Jaywalker possibly could. And to get the jurors to remember, as each of the things would in turn come up during the course of the trial, that they already knew that and had promised not to be influenced by it. So implicitly, without even being aware of what they were doing, the jurors were agreeing to *discount* the prosecution's evidence—not in the sense of ignoring it altogether, but in the other, more literal meaning of the word: to *devalue* it, to mark it down drastically even before Katherine Darcy had had a chance to call a single witness to the stand.

Of such little things are trials won or lost.

This was Monday. It would take them until late Thursday

afternoon to complete the process. It was a murder trial, after all, a class A felony that carried a mandatory life sentence, and each side had the full complement of twenty peremptory challenges to use. And the thing was, there wasn't that much daylight between the type of jury Jaywalker was looking for and the one Katherine Darcy wanted. Sure, Jaywalker preferred renegades, loners, anti-establishment types, while Darcy was seeking people more compliant and less likely to question the government's case. But notwithstanding that difference, their concerns were remarkably similar. Both the defendant and the victim were Latin Americans; both had been young at the time of the incident; both had had prior encounters with the law that included drug arrests; and both had sympathetic family members who would testify at the trial. Those similarities made for less-than-obvious choices when it came time to either challenge or accept a particular juror, and for the better part of four days the lawyers engaged in something of a cat-and-mouse game, trying to shape the final product in sometimes subtle ways.

Throughout the process, Jaywalker was struck by how controlled Darcy was. Not just conservative in her choices, but careful about how she played. Her guiding principle seemed to be retaining a numerical edge over Jaywalker at all times. The challenges were exercised in rounds, meaning that both sides were presented with eighteen prospective jurors at a time and forced to strike those they didn't want, right then and there. Faced with such a now-or-never dilemma, Jaywalker felt compelled to challenge jurors about whom he was on the fence. He couldn't afford to let someone slip by who might turn out to be a closet law-and-order type who couldn't wait to take over deliberations and engineer a conviction. Darcy, on the other hand, seemed more preoccupied in guarding her challenges so that when the end game came, as it finally did on Thursday afternoon, she would have a greater say in the last few jurors selected.

That said, they ended up with a jury that, had you woken Jaywalker up during the middle of the night and asked him for his opinion, he would have had to admit that while he wasn't in love with any of them individually, as a group they weren't all that bad. There was William Craig, 53, white, an electrical engineer, and by virtue of having been the first juror called to be selected, the foreman; Lucille Hendricks, 67, black, a retired elementary school teacher; Gladys Leach, 44, white, a homemaker; George Gonsalves, 38, Hispanic, a Wall Street trader; Miriam Goldring, 51, white, a registered nurse; Sanford Washington, 60, black, a probation officer; Lillian Koppelman, 58, white, a sales clerk; Vincent Tartaglia, 33, white, unemployed; Consuela Marrero, 24, Hispanic, an administrative assistant and college student; Desiree Smith-Hammond, 32, black, a waitress and aspiring actress; Walter van der Kaamp, 72, white, a retired history professor; and Jennifer Wang, 28, Asian, a Web site master. Five men, seven women. Six white, three black, two Hispanic, one Asian. Average age, 45. All things considered, they could have been a lot worse. Jaywalker had had juries that were all white; juries stacked with government employees, bankers and actuaries; juries so timid or fearful that their responses to questions were all but inaudible; and juries whose average age was deceased. Against that sort of standard, Jeremy Estrada's jury struck him as pretty good.

But if Jaywalker was satisfied with the result of four days' work, Harold Wexler wasn't. Ignoring the fact that it was already after five o'clock, he directed the clerk to call the names of twenty more jurors—they were by that time on their fourth panel of seventy-five each—from which they would select four alternates. The clerk sighed, the court officers grumbled, and the stenographer called for someone to relieve her. But Wexler pushed on. He'd promised the lawyers they would have a jury by the close of business that day, and he wasn't about to let the time or a little grumbling stand in his way.

It was almost nine o'clock by the time Jaywalker got home, time to change his clothes, wash his face, make himself something to eat and grab four hours of sleep. He set his alarm for 3:00 a.m. But he needn't have; he knew full well he'd be up anyway. Tomorrow was Friday, and he'd have the weekend to recuperate.

Some cases, Jaywalker had long ago learned, were won during pretrial investigation and preparation, which was why he obsessed over those endeavors like no one else. Others cases were won by tactics and strategy, the way a chess match was won, by outplotting your opponent. And some were won by brilliant questioning of the witnesses, whether on direct examination or cross. But this case, Jaywalker was firmly convinced, wasn't going to be won by any of those things. This case was going to be won by whichever side succeeded in telling the better story. The facts that underpinned that story, to be sure, would come from the mouths of witnesses. But to Jaywalker's way of thinking, not one of those witnesses—not Teresa Morales, not the medical examiner, not Jeremy's mother or sister, not even Jeremy himself—would be able to dictate the jury's verdict. When the evidence was finally in, the winning side wasn't going to be the one with more witnesses or better exhibits. It was going to be the side whose lawyer had put it all together and told the better story.

For the defense, that story would be divided into two parts. Jaywalker liked to think of them as bookends at the far opposite ends of a shelf. In between them would be everything else: the prosecution's case, the defense case, the competing accounts of the various witnesses, the physical exhibits, the objections sustained or overruled. But all of that stuff was pretty much predetermined, fixed long ago by what people had seen and heard and photographed and drawn and written down and committed to memory, accurately or not. It might contain a surprise here or there, and an effective direct or cross-examination might enhance or undermine it a bit. But only a bit. Because all that stuff was static, in the sense that it was history. What was different, what was still to be written, was how each lawyer took that raw material and shaped it into a narrative that provided the jurors with a lens to view the case through, until they had a meaningful understanding of not only *what* had happened, but *why* it had happened. And with that understanding, they would ultimately either convict Jeremy or acquit him. That was the dynamic part of the case, and that was where Jaywalker was going to win it, if ever he was going to. And Friday would bring with it his first real chance to set his plan in motion. Friday would be the day of his opening statement, the first of the two bookends.

13

I HAD A SON

The sixteen jurors—twelve regulars and four alternates—were led into the courtroom and seated in the order they'd been selected. Judge Wexler addressed them for twenty minutes, outlining what they should expect over the coming week or two, instructing them on several basic principles of law, and describing both his role in the trial and theirs. Then he called upon Katherine Darcy to open on behalf of the People.

As Jaywalker had by that time fully expected she would, Darcy delivered a coherent, competent opening statement. Barely glancing at her notes, she demonstrated a comfortable command of the facts. She made the obligatory comparison between her opening and the table of contents of a book. She read the indictment, word for word. She outlined what witnesses she would call and, in broad strokes, what each of them would say. Then she told them that once all the evidence was in, she would have another opportunity to address them, at which time she would ask them to find the defendant guilty of murder. With that she sat down, barely fifteen minutes after she'd begun. It was an effective, if understated, opening.

Jaywalker's would be different.

* * *

"It is May," he began.

Years ago, he'd decided to dispense with the traditional "May it please the court." And not too long after that, he'd gotten rid of "Ladies and gentlemen of the jury." The last to go had been "Good morning" and "Good afternoon." By the time Jeremy Estrada's trial came around, Jaywalker had settled on launching directly into what had happened from his client's perspective. What he liked to think of as the narrative opening.

The story.

He began the telling of it with those three little words, "It is May," speaking them so softly that the jurors were not only forced into immediate and total silence, but were literally compelled to lean forward in their seats in order to hear him. And by standing directly in front of them, without so much as an index card in his hands, he demanded their visual attention, as well. Katherine Darcy had delivered her opening statement behind a lectern, a podium with a slanted top, perfect for placing documents or concealing notes. She'd ventured out from behind it once or twice, but had each time quickly retreated to its safety.

Jaywalker's distaste for tradition was matched by his disdain of safety. He was about to tell the jurors a story, a story that he knew so well by then that he could have recited it backwards, had he been called upon to do so. He needed no notes, and he wanted no barrier.

Perhaps it was his ego at work, but Jaywalker was convinced that he could tell Jeremy's story better even than Jeremy himself could. Jeremy's turn would come, but it wouldn't come for the better part of two weeks, after all the other witnesses for both sides had had their say. And when it came, it would come in Jeremy's halting, hesitant way, constantly interrupted by objections and exceptions, sidebar conferences, rulings and recesses. Jaywalker simply couldn't afford to wait that long for what might prove to be a fractured, fragmented account of the events. He'd decided instead to tell the story from start to finish now, in his own voice. That way, when the jurors eventually heard Jeremy's account, they would not only have a framework, an overview of what had happened, they'd even be able to fill in the blanks Jeremy would invariably leave with details Jaywalker had already provided them.

"It is May. Perhaps it is even two years ago to this very day. Jeremy Estrada wakes up and gets ready for school. He's all of seventeen years old. Seventeen. He's a student, though not a very good one. Part of that is because Jeremy has learning disabilities, and things don't come easily to him. And part of it is because he also works several part-time jobs after school and on weekends, as he has since the age of fourteen, in order to help out his mother and his sister. There is no father in the home.

"It's a bright, sun-drenched morning as Jeremy walks down the avenue, his book bag slung over one shoulder. The stores on the avenue are just beginning to open for business. As he passes one of them, a flower shop, some slight movement off to his right catches his attention, and he glances inside. There he sees a young lady, a girl, really, also seventeen years old. And in that moment, in that split second, their eyes meet. And this case begins."

Right at that point, Jaywalker suddenly and unexpectedly felt the full impact of the case come crashing down on him. For the first time he could feel—*truly* feel, way down deep in his gut—the terrible, undeserved plight of this boy, this child, sitting behind him in a huge courtroom built for and filled up with grown-ups. A boy whose only sin had been the unpardonable act of falling in love.

Jaywalker's voice had cracked on the second syllable of

the word *begins,* and his lower lip had begun to quiver un-
controllably. He knew better than to continue, realizing that
whatever he might try to say next would bring him to tears.
Even as he turned away from the jury to hide his embarrassment from them, he knew they couldn't have missed it;
he'd made it impossible for them to miss anything. Yet all
he could do was to stand there, his back to the jurors, and
breathe in and out deeply, deliberately. Once, twice, a third
time. He was a wuss by nature, Jaywalker was, a grown man
easily brought to tears by a bad movie or a good commercial. But never before had anything quite like this happened
to him in front of a jury.

After what seemed to him like minutes but was no doubt
only seconds, he forced himself to turn back to the jury box,
telling himself he could continue, telling himself he *had* to
continue. And somehow he managed. Each word he spoke
got him to the next one, and to the one after that, and gradually he regained control. And as he did, he became aware
that something had changed. If possible, the jurors were
paying even more attention now. It was as if his succumb-
ing to his emotions, and his obvious embarrassment at doing
so, had opened a window for them, a window into just how
deeply Jeremy's story had come to affect him.

One of the most valuable assets a successful trial lawyer
can possess is his credibility in the eyes of the jury. *Believe
me,* he urges them in a thousand tiny ways, *and it follows
from there that you'll believe what I believe.* Now, by the
pure accident of having being blindsided by the sudden rec-
ognition of his own feelings, Jaywalker had stumbled upon
an equally authentic corollary to that proposition. *Trust me,*
his meltdown had invited the jurors, *and it follows from
there that you'll come to feel as I feel.* And though he hadn't
meant for the incident to occur in the first place, he now
fully intended to take advantage of it.

By the time he sat down, he'd been on his feet for exactly an hour, making the opening statement his longest ever. Hell, he'd *summed up* in less time than that in plenty of cases. And during that hour, not once had he lost his train of thought or looked at a note. Although he'd planned on spending the entire time standing directly in front of the jurors, he hadn't. Several times, as he'd described Jeremy's torment at the hands of the Raiders, he'd made his way over to the defense table. There he'd taken up a position directly behind his seated client, placed his hands on Jeremy's shoulders and continued to face the jurors as he spoke. *These are my words,* he'd been telling them, *but this is what this young man actually lived through.*

He'd described for them the fateful events that had left Victor Quinones dead and Jeremy himself thinking he'd been shot, as well. He'd told them about Jeremy's fear of retaliation at the hands of Sandro and his gang, his panic that they could reach out and get him even in prison, especially in prison. He'd described Jeremy's flight from the scene to his home, from his home to the Bronx, and from the Bronx all the way to the hills of Puerto Rico.

He'd paused, much as Jeremy must have paused at the notion of staying in those hills forever. But he'd chosen not to stay there, Jaywalker had told them. He'd made the conscious, deliberate decision to come back and face whatever awaited him.

"The day after his return to New York, he walks into the police station. He holds out his wrists so that handcuffs may be placed around them and locked shut. He goes to jail. He learns to call Rikers Island his home, and to surrender his name for a ten-digit inmate number. He's brought to this building, where he listens as he's charged with murder. He speaks the words *Not guilty* and asks for a trial, a trial in front of twelve ordinary men and women plucked from all walks of life. Twelve men and women who've set aside their jobs, their families—indeed, their very lives. Twelve men and women who've promised to be fair, to be impartial, to be open-minded. And all he asks of them is that they to listen to his story.

"Because this isn't my story or Ms. Darcy's story or Judge Wexler's story. This isn't even Victor Quinones's story. Yes, he's the victim. But as much as we mourn for him and feel for his family, and we do, this story isn't really about him or his family.

"This is Jeremy's story."

With that, he'd turned from them, walked to the defense table and sat down. Just as he'd forgone opening pleasantries when he'd begun speaking to the jurors, so did he bypass thanking them for their attention or asking them— as Ms. Darcy had made a point of doing—to deliver a particular verdict at the end of the trial.

Harold Wexler immediately declared a recess.

To be sure, they were by that time two hours into the morning session, and judges tend to be mindful of jurors' limited attention spans and bladders. But Jaywalker strongly suspected that Wexler's real interest was in breaking the spell that Jaywalker had created. For in the sixty minutes he'd been on his feet, he'd succeeded in turning the trial completely on its head, taking Jeremy Estrada from a prohibitive long shot to an odds-on favorite. And as Jaywalker sat at the defense table watching the jurors file out of the courtroom, he knew that he'd never been better and might never be. And he knew also that there was only one thing that could possibly undo the magic he'd just performed.

Unfortunately, that one thing was the evidence, and it would begin as soon as the recess ended.

* * *

"The People call César Quinones," Katherine Darcy announced when they resumed, adding that the witness would need the assistance of an English-Spanish interpreter. César was the father of Victor Quinones. The ostensible purpose for which he was called was to tell the jury that he'd identified his son's body at the medical examiner's office the day after the shooting. Jaywalker had offered to stipulate to his testimony, to concede that it was indeed Victor Quinones who'd been killed. But Darcy wanted this little bit of drama played out in front of the jury, and he was powerless to prevent it. Knowing that, he'd brought it up during jury selection, warning the jurors that they would see and hear from a distraught member of the deceased's family, in spite of the fact that the identity of the victim wasn't in issue. Then, in order to avoid an objection, he'd turned the matter into a question, asking the jurors if they could remain fair and impartial nonetheless. For what it was worth, they'd assured him they could.

Now, as he watched this frail, broken man limp to the witness stand, Jaywalker had no way of knowing just how powerful his appearance would be to the jurors. Would they recognize it for what it was, a shameless theatrical stunt intended to prejudice them, right down to the black clothes the man wore, almost two full years after his son's death? Or would they instead adopt the father's grief as their own and hate Jeremy all the more for having caused it?

DARCY: Do you have children?

QUINONES: I used to. I had a son.

DARCY: What was his name?

QUINONES: Victor.

The witness removed a handkerchief from his back pocket and dabbed at his eyes. Jaywalker took the opportunity to rise and once again offer to stipulate to the identity of the deceased. Doing so in front of the jury, after his offer had already been refused, was highly improper, and Judge Wexler angrily overruled him and told him to sit down. Still, he'd made his point.

DARCY: How old was Victor when he died?

QUINONES: Twenty.

The absolute silence of the courtroom told Jaywalker all he needed to know about the impact the witness was having upon the jury. When it came his turn for cross-examination, he said he had no questions. He tried to say it in a tone and with a shrug that implied "Why would I?" without being too heavy-handed about it, but it was a fine line to dance.

At one point he'd thought about asking Mr. Quinones a series of questions about his son, like whether he'd known he belonged to a gang, had half a dozen arrests and got a special kick out of terrorizing people. He'd given the idea some serious consideration for about five seconds before abandoning it. He could see Darcy jumping to her feet, Wexler not only sustaining her objection before she could make it but also warning Jaywalker he was seriously out of line, and the jurors nodding in agreement.

Quite apart from having no legitimate questions to ask César Quinones, Jaywalker wanted him out of there as quickly as possible. But the man wouldn't go away. Instead of leaving, he made his way from the witness stand to the spectator section, where he took a seat next to his wife.

Together they would sit there for the remainder of the trial, these two destroyed people, dressed all in black. Their English was virtually nonexistent, and they would understand little of the proceedings. But their silent vigil would continue, their very presence a powerful witness for the prosecution.

The jurors, having followed Mr. Quinones's every step as he limped to his seat, now tried to look away from him and back to the judge, but Jaywalker could see they were finding it almost impossible. At the table next to him, he felt Jeremy slip away from him just an inch, just that much closer to spending the rest of his life in prison. He wondered if Jeremy felt it, too.

Katherine Darcy hadn't counted on Jaywalker's summation to eat up an entire hour. She'd let him know in advance that she intended to call one of the eyewitnesses to the shooting next. But with only fifteen minutes left to the one-o'clock lunch recess, she decided to shift gears and put on a short witness, in more ways than one.

Adalberto Garcia was the detective who'd originally been assigned to the investigation into the death of Victor Quinones. He stood barely five feet, a height that once would have disqualified him from becoming a police officer. And his entire testimony, direct and cross, would take barely five minutes.

DARCY: Did there come a time when you identified a suspect in connection with the shooting?

GARCIA: Yes, there did.

DARCY: Can you tell us the name of that suspect?

GARCIA: Jeremy Estrada.

DARCY: And what, if anything, did you do with
        respect to him?

GARCIA: I began to look for him, to arrest him.

DARCY: Do you happen to know when he was even-
        tually arrested?

GARCIA: *[Referring to notes]* Yes. That was on
         May 14th of last year.

Jaywalker's only interest on cross-examination was in
amplifying the term *arrest* for the jurors.

JAYWALKER: Did you ever find Jeremy Estrada?

GARCIA: No.

JAYWALKER: Ever arrest him?

GARCIA: Me personally? No.

JAYWALKER: In fact, the arrest in this case was an
            arrest only in the technical sense.
            Correct?

GARCIA: I'm not sure what you mean.

JAYWALKER: What I mean is, on May 14th of last
            year, Jeremy Estrada walked into a
            police station voluntarily and gave
            himself up, knowing full well he'd

be arrested. And he was. Isn't that in
fact what happened?

GARCIA: Yes.

It was a much better note to go to lunch on than César
Quinones's testimony. Not that Jaywalker had any plans of
going to lunch; he never did when he was on trial. Which
didn't sit well with Jeremy's mother.

"Jew gotta eat," said Carmen. "Jew gotta be strong."

Jaywalker tried explaining that habits were habits, and
that he needed to spend the hour preparing for the afternoon's witnesses. Never mind that he'd been prepared for
them for months now.

"That's no good," Carmen told him, shaking her head
sadly, like the concerned mother she was. But she let it go,
walking off with her daughter, Julie, in tow. Both had been
in the audience all morning, but on the defendant's side of
the courtroom, as opposed to prosecution's side, where the
parents of Victor Quinones had sat. Trials are a little like
weddings in that respect, where guests of the bride often sit
across the aisle from those of the groom.

It had actually taken some doing on Jaywalker's part, as
well as some generosity on Katherine Darcy's, to seat
Carmen and Julie Estrada anywhere in the courtroom.
Either side may ask that potential witnesses be excluded
prior to testifying, and such requests are routinely granted.
But Jaywalker had felt that the rule worked a special
hardship in this case. Though he intended to call both
Jeremy's mother and sister, neither of them would be testifying to the same events the prosecution's witnesses would
be describing—the fistfight and the shooting—and their
presence during the testimony of those witnesses would
give them no advantage. Jaywalker had taken his concern
to Darcy, who'd agreed to give it some thought.

"I'll tell you what," he'd added, "I'll agree to call them at the very beginning of the defense case."

"And keep whoever you're calling second outside while the first one's on the stand?"

"You got it," Jaywalker had said, and they'd had a deal.

That afternoon Darcy called Magdalena Lopez to the stand. She was an eyewitness, one of the people who'd observed the fight and the shooting. She was a middle-aged, dark-skinned woman employed as an outreach worker at a cancer center for women. On the morning of the incident, she'd been walking through the projects with a friend when she'd noticed two young males arguing. As she'd watched, they'd begun fighting.

DARCY: What did you see?

LOPEZ: I seen them hitting each other.

DARCY: With what?

LOPEZ: Their fists.

DARCY: What happened next?

LOPEZ: One of them reached down the front of his pants. And when I looked at him, he had a gun in his hand. He started shooting at the other one, from very close to him. I heard one shot, then another. I got scared, and I started running toward the building. My friend grabbed me, pulled me back. There was a stray bullet coming our way. It passed me so close I could hear it as it went by. I seen it hit the building we was running to, cracked a piece of the brick. I looked back and I heard one more shot. They were in a different spot now, but I could still see good. And I seen the person down on the ground, the other one.

DARCY: The man who did the shooting. Do you see him in the courtroom?

LOPEZ: Yes, I do.

DARCY: Can you point him out for us?

LOPEZ: *[Pointing]* He's over there.

Over there was Jeremy.

Jaywalker had a loose rule of thumb that went something like this. When he was going to put his client on the stand to dispute the testimony of an eyewitness who was pretty much telling the truth, he wanted to get that eyewitness off the stand quickly. He'd found over the years that too many lawyers spent too much time cross-examining such witnesses. They rarely made much headway, and their efforts often served only to reinforce the witness's testimony in the minds of the jurors.

Still, he couldn't resist asking Magdalena Lopez about the bullet she'd heard whiz by her and then seen strike the building. To have actually observed either of those things was a long shot up there with winning the lottery. To have observed both of them was flat-out impossible, the stuff of grade B Westerns or video games. Yet Ms. Lopez stuck to her story, insisting that her memory of what she'd heard and seen was still vivid.

JAYWALKER: How about the friend you were
                        with? What can you tell us about
                        her? Or him?

LOPEZ: Her.

JAYWALKER: Okay, her. What's her name?

LOPEZ: I don't know.

Jaywalker had known that would be her answer. A month
ago he'd asked Katherine Darcy for the name of Ms.
Lopez's friend so he could try to find her on his own and
see what she'd seen and heard. A week later Darcy had
reported back that Lopez had never supplied the name and
could no longer recall it.

JAYWALKER: Well, did you ever know her name?

LOPEZ: Yes, sure, back then. But that was a long
                time ago, like a whole year or more.

JAYWALKER: So let me get this straight. Today
                        you're telling us you can no longer
                        remember the name of your own
                        friend who was with you that day?

LOPEZ: That's right.

JAYWALKER: Not even her first name?

LOPEZ: No.

JAYWALKER: A nickname?

LOPEZ: No.

It wasn't much, but he figured it was as good a place to quit as he was going to get. Come summation time, he'd point out to the jurors that if Magdalena Lopez's memory was so faulty, they should discount her account of the incident itself, which had actually taken place a year and a half ago. Or, in the alternative, if they disbelieved her testimony that she couldn't remember her friend's name, they might want to wonder why she'd lied about that. Had she been afraid, perhaps, that if identified, located and called to testify, her friend might have described the events in quite different terms?

Katherine Darcy followed up Lopez's testimony by calling Wallace Porter to the stand. Porter was the second of the prosecution's three eyewitnesses, and in some ways he would prove to be the most damaging to the defense.

Porter hadn't come to court alone. Rather than being summoned from the witness room or the hallway, he was led in through a side door and escorted to the witness stand by a pair of uniformed court officers. Accompanying him was a young man whom the judge introduced to the jury as Mr. Porter's lawyer. The reason for all this special attention would soon become obvious. Wallace Porter was, like Jeremy Estrada, a guest of the state. Several weeks earlier he'd pleaded guilty to a low-level sale of drugs, and he was awaiting sentencing.

Porter was a slender, dark-skinned African-American, dressed in a gaudy red satin warm-up suit. Both his appearance and his demeanor suggested something slick and evasive, and Jaywalker eyed the jurors to see if they were responding to him the same way he was. That said, Jaywalker knew better than to sit back and relax. He'd learned over the years that the same juror who's tough on crime is at the same time fascinated by criminals. Having already pleaded guilty to the charges against him, Porter had nothing to lose by admitting that he was a drug seller. And Katherine Darcy would have worked long and hard with him to make sure he did just that. His willingness to do so, and to go into the details of his own crimes, would end up earning him points for candor. "Look at how honest he was in talking about his past," Darcy would argue to the jury. "That shows he's telling you the truth about what he saw."

It didn't, of course, not for a minute. Still, there was a logic of sorts to the argument. And Jaywalker knew that if he chose to underestimate either it or Wallace Porter, he'd be doing so at his peril and, more importantly, at Jeremy's.

Darcy wasted no time in bringing out Porter's criminal record. In addition to the case he was awaiting sentencing on, Porter admitted to two prior arrests, a larceny bust in Massachusetts back in 1999, and a drug possession in Brooklyn in 2005. Both were misdemeanors, minor crimes. From there Darcy moved on to the day of the shooting.

DARCY: Do you recall that day?

PORTER: Yup.

DARCY: Where were you about five o'clock that afternoon?

PORTER: I was playing cards in a little park area in the projects, the Jefferson Houses.

DARCY: How many people were playing cards?

PORTER: It was four of us, and two others on the side.

DARCY: Other than playing cards, what were you doing?

PORTER: We was barbecuing. We had chicken, franks and burgers. Stuff like that.

DARCY: As you were playing cards and barbecuing, did something happen?

PORTER: Yeah. We was sitting there, we was playing cards. And I seen this girl and this dude walk by, and this guy running behind them, and another girl following him. And they started fighting, the two guys. The one was pretty good, and he beat up the other one pretty bad. He was bleeding a little from his nose and his mouth. He reached into his socks. He had like two or three pairs of sweat socks on. I thought he was pulling out a knife, but he had a gun, he pulled out a gun. And he just shot the guy, he shot him. Then he chased him and shot him like three more times. When he fell to the ground, he picked him up by the collar and he shot one or two more times at him.

Katherine Darcy had to back up and have her witness clarify who was who. It was the guy who'd won the fight,

Porter explained, who'd pulled the gun and done all the chasing and shooting.

DARCY: Do you think you'd recognize him if you
             saw him again today?

PORTER: Yup.

DARCY: Would you look around the courtroom and
             see if you see him?

PORTER: I see him right there.

And he pointed directly at Jeremy.

It got worse. Porter described seeing the shooter pull back the slide of the gun just before firing it. He recounted how the victim had begged for his life before the final shot, asking, "Why you gotta shoot me?" He recalled looking at the victim close-up following the shooting, seeing the police arrive and telling them that he'd witnessed the incident. He concluded by saying he knew neither the shooter nor the victim, nor the two girls who'd been with them, nor a woman named Magdalena Lopez, the witness who'd preceded him.

During the short span of twenty-five minutes, Wallace Porter had transformed himself from a sleazy-looking drug dealer to an astute, impartial observer. An observer who, if believed, had described a scenario in which Jeremy Estrada was nothing but a cold-blooded murderer. As Jaywalker rose from behind the defense table, he knew he had to go after Porter. Ridiculing him for claiming he'd ducked a bullet whizzing by his head, as he'd been able to do with Magdalena Lopez, wasn't an option and wouldn't have been good enough, anyway.

JAYWALKER: It was hot that day, wasn't it?

PORTER: In more ways than one.

JAYWALKER: Well, let's stick with the weather for a moment, okay?

PORTER: Okay.

JAYWALKER: It was hot?

PORTER: Yup.

JAYWALKER: So in addition to the burgers and franks you were barbecuing, you and your group were having something to drink, right?

PORTER: No, we wasn't drinking at all. We just had food and beers. Not beers, soda and stuff.

JAYWALKER: Didn't you just say food and beer?

PORTER: You confused me.

JAYWALKER: How did I confuse you?

PORTER: By mentioning beer.

Jaywalker had the court reporter read the exchange back from her stenotype notes. Then he got Porter to agree that he himself had made the first mention of beer. He'd made an honest mistake, Porter then explained.

JAYWALKER: No beer?

PORTER: No beer.

JAYWALKER: Just soda and stuff.

PORTER: Yup.

JAYWALKER: The kind of stuff you smoke? Or the kind you might sniff through a straw?

PORTER: No, man. None of that kind of stuff.

JAYWALKER: What did you mean by "stuff," then?

PORTER: Just soda.

JAYWALKER: So when you said "just soda and stuff," you really meant "soda and soda." Is that right?

PORTER: You messin' wid me, man.

JAYWALKER: Sorry.

It wasn't much, but at least it restored some of Porter's slipperiness. From there, Jaywalker moved on to an inconsistency he'd noticed between Porter's testimony and something he'd told the detectives at the scene, shortly after the incident.

JAYWALKER: Did you hear the shooter and the victim arguing about money?

PORTER: No.

JAYWALKER: Did you tell the detectives you had?

PORTER: I mighta.

JAYWALKER: Did you tell them *[reading]*, "Right
before the shooting, I could hear the
two of them arguing about money?"
Were those your words to the detectives, just minutes after the incident?

PORTER: Yeah, I said that to the detectives. But it
was a mistake.

JAYWALKER: Can you tell us how it is that you
made that mistake?

PORTER: I don't know. It just came out.

JAYWALKER: You just said it, even though there
was absolutely no truth to it?

PORTER: Yeah.

JAYWALKER: Did you ever correct it?

PORTER: They never asked me again.

JAYWALKER: Did you ever take it upon yourself to
say, "Hey, I made a mistake back
there. I said I heard them arguing
about money, but I didn't. I just de-

cided to make that part up"? Did you
ever say anything like that?

PORTER: No.

Jaywalker had done a little amateur boxing back in his
youth. Right now he felt like he was seriously behind in the
last round and needed a knockout in order to win the fight.
But all he seemed capable of doing was scoring a few points
here and there on jabs. He knew it wasn't going to get the
job done.

He moved on to Porter's criminal record. Katherine
Darcy had done her best to preempt the subject by bringing
it out herself. But that didn't mean Jaywalker couldn't take
a shot at it.

JAYWALKER: How many times have you been
locked up, Mr. Porter?

DARCY: Objection.

THE COURT: Sustained.

JAYWALKER: May we approach?

Up at the bench, Judge Wexler reminded Jaywalker that
only convictions, not arrests, were relevant to the witness's
credibility.

"I know that," said Jaywalker. "But Ms. Darcy asked
about prior arrests. By doing so, she opened the door. I
have a right to ask if there've been more arrests than the two
the witness admitted to. If there are, he lied, and that goes
to credibility, too."

It wasn't often that Harold Wexler was forced to reverse

himself on a ruling, but when Darcy nodded meekly at Jaywalker's account of her direct examination, Wexler did just that. But in order to make it look otherwise, he directed Jaywalker to rephrase the question, without using the objectionable words *locked up*.

JAYWALKER: How many times, in total, have you been arrested, Mr. Porter?

PORTER: No more than five or six.

JAYWALKER: I see. The 1999 Massachusetts larceny, right?

PORTER: Right.

JAYWALKER: What did you steal?

PORTER: Nothing.

JAYWALKER: What did they say you stole?

PORTER: A TV set.

JAYWALKER: The Brooklyn drug possession in 2005.

PORTER: Right.

JAYWALKER: What drug?

PORTER: Cocaine.

JAYWALKER: Powder?

PORTER: No.

JAYWALKER: Crack?

PORTER: Yeah.

JAYWALKER: What else?

PORTER: A coupla loiterings, a disorderly conduct kinda thing. That's all. Nothing big.

JAYWALKER: And the sale case you're awaiting sentencing on.

PORTER: Yeah.

JAYWALKER: What are you looking at on that?

PORTER: Two to six.

JAYWALKER: Years?

PORTER: Yeah.

JAYWALKER: The original charge carried eight and a third to twenty-five, right?

PORTER: Yeah.

JAYWALKER: Do you expect to get two to six?

PORTER: I *hope* to get time served.

JAYWALKER: In other words, you might walk on it, do no more time at all?

PORTER: Yup.

JAYWALKER: And why might that happen, do you think?

PORTER: In consideration of my testimony.

JAYWALKER: Your testimony where?

PORTER: Here.

JAYWALKER: In other words, if Ms. Darcy is pleased with your testimony in this trial, she's going to go to bat for you and try to get you less time, or no additional time at all, on your case. Is that your understanding?

PORTER: Yeah, something like that.

JAYWALKER: Well, am I wrong, the way I just described your understanding?

PORTER: No, you ain't wrong.

JAYWALKER: Tell me, Mr. Porter. Have you discussed this case with anyone?

PORTER: No.

JAYWALKER: No one at all?

PORTER: No one at all.

JAYWALKER: How about your lawyer here? Haven't you discussed it with him?

PORTER: My lawyer? Sure.

JAYWALKER: How about Ms. Darcy? Discussed it with her?

PORTER: Yeah.

JAYWALKER: Discussed it with the detectives?

PORTER: Yeah.

There were two factual areas Jaywalker would have liked to question Porter about. The first was the business about the shooter's having pulled the gun out from his socks, and the second was his having jacked the slide back before firing. He decided to let the first one go, fearing all he would accomplish was to reinforce Porter's version. But he took a stab at the second.

JAYWALKER: Now you know a little something about guns, right?

DARCY: Objection.

THE COURT: Sustained.

JAYWALKER: You say you saw the shooter pull
back the slide of the gun. Is that
right?

PORTER: Yup.

JAYWALKER: How many times do you claim you
saw him do that?

PORTER: Just once.

Jaywalker did his best to hide his disappointment. He'd
been hoping Porter would say "each time he fired." That
would have made no sense at all. The signature feature of
a semiautomatic weapon was that each squeeze of the
trigger not only fired off a round, but at the same time it
caused the slide to move back and forth, first ejecting the
spent shell, then chambering the next bullet in the magazine.
Either Porter had been telling the truth when he'd said "just
once," or he knew enough about guns to spot Jaywalker's
trap and steer clear of it. Still, his "just once" left the obvious
question, "When?"

Logically, the shooter would have had a good reason to
jack the slide back before firing the first shot, if the chamber
had been empty up to that point. To have jacked the slide
at any other point would have accomplished nothing but
ejecting one live bullet just to replace it with the next one.
Jaywalker was toying with idea of trying to get Porter to say
the "just once" had been right before the final shot. He was
thinking if he loaded the question up enough—by using
words like *deadly, fatal* or *coup de grace*—he might appeal
to Porter's ego and get him to bite. But would Porter even
understand *coup de grace?* And as Jaywalker was search-

ing his mind for a suitable street synonym, he noticed that
Porter was looking directly into his eyes from the witness
stand, a tiny but unmistakable smirk on his face.

I dare you, he was saying.

"No further questions," said Jaywalker.

They broke for the day.

Though he was tired and hungry, having slept little the
night before and eaten nothing all day, Jaywalker didn't
leave the courtroom by walking out the front door with just
about everyone else. Instead he fell in behind Jeremy as a
couple of uniformed court officers led them through a side
door and into the pens, where a corrections officer locked
lawyer and client into a holding cell.

It was one of the many things that endeared the courthouse staff to Jaywalker. It went beyond their identifying
with him because of his law-enforcement background, or
admiring him for being willing to piss off judges when he
had a point to make, or feeling a kinship with him because
in any given year he didn't make any more money than they
did. No, it was how he treated his clients. Here it was,
already after five o'clock on a Friday afternoon, and even
if the stories were true and the guy didn't have much of a
life outside the courthouse, surely he could've found something better to do than spend the next hour behind bars with
an accused murderer.

And though he'd never admit it out loud, Jaywalker delighted in their allegiance to him. On a practical level, it
brought him a certain amount of perks, everything from
little kindnesses extended to his clients to crucial tips about
what was going on in the jury room during deliberations.
But even beyond that, it was gratifying to know that the
crew, the working stiffs, were on his side. In many ways he
felt more at ease with them than with the judges, other de-

fenders and prosecutors he spent time with. They were civil servants, these regular guys and gals. To Jaywalker, they represented the closest approximation to a practice jury in the building. If he could win them over, didn't it follow that he could just as easily win over those dozen men and women sitting in the real jury box?

But all of that could wait. Right now he needed to talk with Jeremy about what the day's witnesses had brought, and what lay in store for them next week.

"Why does Porter have you picking up Quinones by the collar before firing the final shot?" he asked. "Unless it happened that way."

By way of answer, Jeremy shook his head slowly from side to side, before answering, "I don't remember it that way."

It was how he always dealt with the issue. Not "He's lying" or "It didn't happen that way" or "He must be mistaken." Simply that he, Jeremy, didn't remember it that way. It was the great paradox of the case. The prosecution witnesses would describe the last shot just as Katherine Darcy herself had, as an execution. And the best Jeremy could offer to counter that characterization was a lack of recollection.

"It's going to get worse Monday," Jaywalker said.

"What happens Monday?"

"Victor's girlfriend, Teresa Morales." It wasn't just a guess on Jaywalker's part, though it certainly would have been a logical one. He'd asked Katherine Darcy, and she'd told him. "Is she going to say the same thing?" Jaywalker asked.

Jeremy smiled his sheepish smile and looked directly at Jaywalker with those pale blue eyes of his. "I guess so," he said.

God, it was hard to dislike this kid.

"She's going to bury you," Jaywalker warned him. Trying to get a denial out of him, a contradiction, a bit of outrage, *something*.

Instead, a shrug, another smile and a refrain that Jaywalker was getting much too accustomed to hearing: "I don't remember it that way."

14

STUBBORN AND SELF-DESTRUCTIVE

The ringing of the phone jarred him out of a fitful half sleep. He looked around to get his bearings, realized he was on his back on his un-pulled-out sofa bed, a stack of Teresa Morales discovery material piled on his chest. He reached around for the phone, picked it up, and said "Jaywalker."

"They chased her and threatened her," said an excited voice with a vaguely familiar gravelly quality.

"Who?" was the best Jaywalker could come up with.

"Julie, my daughter. The guys, the same guys. They ran after her, saying bad things. They going to beat her up, or worse. Jew gotta do something."

Jaywalker sat up, spilling reports onto the floor. "Is she okay?"

"No, a course she's not okay," said Carmen. "Would jew be?"

"Is she there?"

"Yes."

"Can I talk to her?"

"Not now. I give her a pill, make her sleep. But I can't let her be a witness. Not after this. Jew unnerstand?"

Jaywalker said nothing. He was still trying to digest what had happened.

"I got only two kids, Mr. Jakewalker. They already take my son away. I'm not going to let anything happen to my daughter. Jew hear me?"

"I hear you," said Jaywalker. "But I need to talk to Julie. Tomorrow. Okay?"

"No, no, no. It's not okay. Tomorrow I gonna take her to the Bronx, hide her. I gotta protect her from those guys."

"Good," said Jaywalker.

There was a click, then silence. He cradled the phone. The clock next to it told him it was 1:42, and though he couldn't be entirely certain, he was pretty sure it meant a.m. Either that or there was a total eclipse going on outside. He stood up, stretched and walked over to his two-burner stove. There was a pot of something on one of the burners, either thick coffee or thin, black bean soup. He lit the flame beneath it.

There was work to be done.

He called Katherine Darcy later that morning. He waited until nine, which he figured was late enough for a Saturday morning.

"How did you get my home number?" she wanted to know. It was unlisted, as were those of all her colleagues. The district attorney apparently didn't think it would be a good idea to have defendants and their families calling his assistants at home.

"You gave it to me."

"No, I didn't."

"Well," said Jaywalker, "someone who looked like you and sounded a lot like you did."

"When was that?"

"Over coffee," he said, "and a bagel. You had a bagel. I had tea with lemon. You scolded me for not eating."

That seemed to convince her, or at least quiet her. The

part about the coffee and bagel and tea with lemon were true, of course. Even the part about the scolding. It was a technique Jaywalker had adopted and perfected back in his undercover days at the DEA, learning to sandwich his lies in between highly detailed demonstrable truths. And it had been right around the same time that he'd learned how to tease unlisted numbers from the directory assistance operators.

"And just *why* did I give you my number?" Darcy asked him.

"For emergency purposes."

"I see," she said, a bit of doubt still lingering in her voice. "So what's the emergency?"

He explained what had happened to Julie Estrada, how she'd been chased five blocks by a half-dozen young Hispanic males, shouting curses at her and telling her that her life was over if she showed up in court again. Not that he'd had a chance to speak with Julie directly; Carmen still wouldn't let him. But he'd had Carmen spell it out to him as best as she understood it. Now, just in case she'd missed anything or left anything out, he added a few embellishments of his own, like a knife and a couple of Oakland Raiders jackets.

"I'll look into it," said Darcy.

"That's *it*? You'll *look into it*?"

"What would you like me to do?" she pleaded. "Go out and round up every kid in the city who roots for the Raiders during baseball season?"

"Football," he corrected her. "And no, just the ones who intimidated my witness and are trying to deny my client a fair trial."

"And how would you suggest I go about that?"

"How about a sting operation?" Jaywalker suggested on

the fly. "Get a couple of your detectives assigned, and we'll follow her at a distance, see what happens."

"We?"

"Sure. Where's your sense of adventure?"

"Mr. Jaywalker, it's nine-fifteen on a Saturday morning. In order to fulfill my sense of adventure, I'll be spending my weekend preparing to call witnesses in a trial we shouldn't be having. And *wouldn't* be having, if you and your client weren't so damn stubborn and self-destructive."

Which was pretty much where the conversation ended.

He spent the weekend getting ready for Teresa Morales and the rest of the week's witnesses, both prosecution and defense. He worked on requests to charge, things he wanted Judge Wexler to instruct the jury about. He reviewed his summation notes file. In between, he left half a dozen messages for Carmen Estrada, asking her to call him so he could at least talk to Julie. When Carmen finally got back to him Sunday evening, it was to tell him there was no way she was going to let her daughter testify.

"Jew gotta unnerstand," she explained. "I'm not going to scarface my daughter on account of to save my son." Her English might have used some work, but her logic was pretty hard to argue with.

And as he lay in bed that night, trying to get a decent night's sleep before the week ahead, Jaywalker kept hearing Katherine Darcy's characterization of him and his client.

Stubborn and self-destructive.

What hurt about her words was that she might just be right. Here she'd blinked and come off the murder count. Not only had she offered them a plea to manslaughter, but she'd said she was willing to take less time on it than Harold Wexler had promised to give Jeremy if the jury were to acquit him of murder and instead convict him on the very same manslaughter count. In other words, she'd offered them a win-win proposition. Because the chances of an outright, across-the-board acquittal on all charges were diminishing to the point of disappearing altogether, what with the testimony of Magdalena Lopez and Wallace Porter already in, and that of Teresa Morales still to come.

So she certainly had a point. They *were* being stubborn and self-destructive. Jaywalker won more of his trials than anyone he knew, but even he was human, and he lost from time to time. On the occasions when he did, the experience was excruciatingly painful. And if he were to lose this one— as it was looking more and more certain he would—it would be in large part because he'd allowed his client to insist upon going to trial in a case they couldn't possibly win.

It was thoughts like that that kept Jaywalker awake, leaving his average night's sleep hovering somewhere between three and four hours. And that was on *weekends,* when he tried to catch up.

Stubborn. Stubborn and self-destructive.

Damn Katherine Darcy.

Damn her for being right.

15

A TWO-BIT PUNK

First thing Monday morning, Katherine Darcy called her star witness to the stand. It was a move that even Jaywalker, who considered tactics and strategy key components in his trial arsenal, had to admit deserved a solid 10. Sure, she'd given Jaywalker all weekend to prepare his cross-examination, but that was something he'd done weeks ago, months ago. As Darcy no doubt knew. But by calling her most important witness—and clearly her most vulnerable one—at ten o'clock in the morning of a brand-new week, she could be assured of not only getting through her own direct examination by eleven or eleven-thirty, but of forcing Jaywalker to begin his cross without the benefit of a lunch break, and to complete it in the afternoon, without going overnight. It was little things like that, Jaywalker knew only too well, that could make the difference in a closely con-tested trial.

When Teresa Morales walked into the courtroom, it marked Jaywalker's first glimpse of her. He'd had Jeremy describe her, but as was so often the case, Jeremy's words had painted something less than a complete picture. He'd used adjectives like *dark-haired, attractive* and *kind of pretty.* And to be fair to Jeremy, none of those characterizations had been wrong, Jaywalker realized now, at least not in a technical sense. There was, for example, no disputing that Teresa had dark hair. And he would have been hard-pressed to deny that there was something attractive about her. *Kind of pretty,* however, was a stretch, and a rather long one if your idea of prettiness was Jeremy's twin sister, Julie, or even Jeremy himself, if you were secure enough to attach the word to a young man. If, on the other hand, you wanted to use Miranda Raven as your gold standard, Teresa was immediately disqualified. Then again, so was just about everyone else on the planet.

The problem was that, to Jaywalker at least, there was something *tough* about Teresa. Or if not quite tough, then certainly *hard,* in the sense that she appeared just a bit too streetwise. Maybe he was being unfair, Jaywalker conceded. Maybe he knew too much about her. Where the jurors were seeing her white blouse, dark gray skirt and inch-and-a-half black heels, he was picturing her in a black leather Raiders jacket, skin-tight jeans and motorcycle boots. Where they were thinking *manicured,* he was remembering *menacing.*

All of these thoughts, understand, flashed through Jaywalker's semiconscious mind during the five seconds or so it took Teresa to walk the thirty feet from the side door to the witness stand. And at the same time he was processing them, he was also busy arranging the contents of his cross-examination file on the table in front of him, locating a pad of paper on which to take notes, testing a couple of pens to see which of them wrote more fluidly, and leaning his body toward Jeremy's to signal how comfortable he was with him, all the while projecting an air of quiet confidence that when his turn came he'd be able to expose this witness as something entirely different than what she might seem.

Trying cases was like that. At least, trying them the Jaywalker way was. Which was funny, because in any other venue he was a perfect example of the guy who couldn't walk and chew gum at the same time. Stick him in front of a TV set, for example, and he'd have trouble eating a sandwich, let alone talking on the phone, reading a newspaper or conducting a conversation. But toss him into a courtroom with a thousand little things going on at once, and he suddenly became a world-class multitasker. Go figure.

Katherine Darcy began her direct examination by bringing out the fact that Teresa Morales was now married. A couple of months ago she'd become Teresa Rodriguez, or Teresa Rodriguez Morales, if you wanted to arrange the names the way Latinos do. Jaywalker wondered if the marriage had had something to do with his investigator's inability to locate her and try to interview her prior to trial. That thought was quickly replaced with his marveling at Teresa's resilience. She had, after all, been Victor Quinones's girlfriend just over a year and a half ago. But if Victor's parents, sitting silently in the second row of the audience, were destined to spend the rest of their lives grieving over the loss of their son, Teresa's period of mourning had apparently been somewhat briefer.

From Teresa's marriage, Darcy jumped unexpectedly to the day of the shooting. Unexpectedly, because Jaywalker found it hard to believe that she'd leave it to him to go into Teresa's—and the rest of the Raiders'—past contacts with Jeremy. Was it possible he'd overestimated his adversary's trial skills? He sure hoped so.

DARCY: Do you remember the day Victor died?

TERESA: Yes.

DARCY: Were you there?

TERESA: Yes.

DARCY: Did you see the man who shot him?

TERESA: Yes.

DARCY: Would you recognize him if you saw him today?

TERESA: Yes.

DARCY: Would you look around the courtroom and tell us if you see him?

And, of course, Teresa pointed directly at Jeremy.

At that point, Katherine Darcy surprised Jaywalker again. Rather than going into the details of the shooting, she backed up. But not to the fistfight that had immediately preceded the gunfire, nor to the first of the series of encounters Teresa and her friends had had with Jeremy. Instead she took her witness back a week, to the day of the barbershop incident, and had her describe how Victor and several others had stood in front of the shop, calling Jeremy to come out.

DARCY: How many people were telling him to come out?

TERESA: Just Victor and his friends.

DARCY: Do you know the names of his friends? Any of them?

TERESA: One was Sandro. Shorty. Diego, maybe.
         But I don't remember everybody's name.

DARCY: What happened outside the barbershop?

TERESA: The guys were calling him out and, you
         know, playing with their fingers, going
         like this to him *[indicating]*, trying to get
         him to come out. But he wouldn't.

Jaywalker jumped to his feet. Teresa had formed her
fingers into the shape of a gun, complete with a trigger-
pulling motion. He wanted the gesture made part of the
record, lest some appellate court judge two years down the
line tried to fob it off as a harmless wave.

JAYWALKER: Could we describe the motion?

THE COURT: Yes, describe it.

    Darcy tried her best to put a neutral spin on it.

DARCY: For the record, indicating like a finger
        pointing.

But for once Judge Wexler came to the rescue of the
defense. He, too, had seen the motion.

THE COURT: She has a thumb up and the index
            finger fully extended, and the index
            finger keeps moving back and forth.

Jaywalker sat down. He couldn't have described it any
better if he'd wanted to.

Teresa went on to describe how Victor and his friends had tried to get Jeremy to come out and fight, until finally an older man from the barbershop had come out and gotten the group to leave. From there Darcy returned to the day of the shooting. This struck Jaywalker as something of a mistake on her part. He'd been the one who'd told her about the barbershop incident in the first place. Obviously Darcy had questioned Teresa about it, and when Teresa had confirmed that it had taken place, Darcy had preemptively made it part of her direct examination, trying her best to play it down. But at the same time she'd apparently chosen to ignore the other occasions—and over coffee she'd stated that there'd been at least a dozen of them—on which Teresa, and presumably her friends, had encountered Jeremy.

Jaywalker, needless to say, had no intention of ignoring them. To the extent that he had one, the sum of those encounters—including but by no means limited to the barbershop incident—was his defense.

As Teresa returned to day of the shooting, she described how things had begun casually enough. She and Victor had been on 110th Street, walking toward Third Avenue, when they'd almost bumped into Jeremy and his "lady." There'd been two girls with them, one a good bit younger than the other.

DARCY: The person you described as his lady. Do you know her name?

TERESA: I heard her name was Miranda. But I don't really know her.

DARCY: Do you know what she looks like?

TERESA: She's got reddish hair. She's slim.

DARCY: Tell us what happened.

TERESA: Victor told him, "Come on, tough guy. I
         heard you want to fight me." And they
         were calling each other names. "Punk."
         "Chicken." Stuff like that.

She described how she and Victor had walked north to
113th Street, when she noticed that Jeremy and his lady had
followed them.

DARCY: Then what happened?

TERESA: When I noticed he was behind us, I tried
         to get Victor to walk faster. But it hap-
         pened so quickly. They just started fight-
         ing, hitting each other.

DARCY: Tell us what you saw.

TERESA: The guy, he punched Victor in the lip. Vic-
         tor took off his sweatshirt, and they kept
         on fighting. After a minute or two they
         backed off, and the guy just pulled out a
         gun from his waist. I told Victor, "Run,
         run!" And when he ran, the guy shot him,
         and Victor like went down on the ground.
         Then he got up, and the guy shot again,
         and it hit the street. Then Victor ran again,
         inside the park, around a bench. But he
         tripped. And then the guy just walked
         over, grabbed him and killed him.

She recounted how, following the shooting, Jeremy and his lady had run from the scene, toward Third Avenue and out of sight.

DARCY: What did you do?

TERESA: I was screaming for help.

DARCY: What else?

TERESA: I was laying down, holding his neck.

DARCY: Why?

TERESA: I was putting my fingers on the hole at the back of his neck where he was bleeding from.

DARCY: What happened then?

TERESA: After a while, the cops came, and then an ambulance. We went to the hospital, to the emergency room, and they wheeled him away.

DARCY: Did you ever see Victor alive again?

TERESA: No.

Cross-examining a sympathetic witness could be tricky business, as Jaywalker well knew. Even if she'd gone and gotten married to another man not too long after the incident, Teresa Morales had seen her boyfriend gunned down in front of her, and he'd all but died in her arms. To top that off, in the eyes of the jury she'd come off as a pretty straightforward witness. Jeremy insisted that it had been Victor, not he, who'd first pulled the gun, and he continued to deny any recollection of firing the last shot as Victor lay helpless on the ground. Jaywalker's own internal jury was still out on both those questions. But the jurors had now heard three accounts of the incident, and while they varied from version to version, all three put the gun in Jeremy's hands first and pretty much agreed about the final shot.

The execution.

What was more, Teresa hadn't even appeared to stretch things. Her account of the barbershop incident had been pretty much as Jeremy had described it. Her graphic demonstration of the way in which Victor and his friends had mimed shooting had, Jaywalker strongly suspected, taken Katherine Darcy by surprise. And it had been Darcy, rather than Teresa, who'd tried to gloss it over as nothing but an innocent pointing gesture. So Jaywalker knew he had to proceed cautiously, lest he run the risk of antagonizing the jurors. Still, he couldn't tread all that carefully; Teresa had been too damaging a witness for him to leave alone.

He began gently, asking her about her relationship with Victor, trying to establish her loyalty to him and, consequently, her natural bias against the man who'd killed him. He asked her what Victor had done for a living, and when the best she could come up with was "odd jobs," Jaywalker decided to let her off the hook. He figured there was little to be gained from attacking the victim's reputation with not only his former girlfriend on the witness stand, but his grieving parents present, as well. Besides, Jaywalker had a surrogate to attack, another member of the gang who had no supporters in the courtroom.

JAYWALKER: Tell me about Alesandro.

TERESA: Who?

JAYWALKER: Maybe you knew him as Sandro?

TERESA: I knew him. Not well, though.

JAYWALKER: How long had you known him for?

TERESA: Not long. Three or four years.

JAYWALKER: What was his last name?

TERESA: I don't know.

JAYWALKER: You knew him three or four years, yet you never learned his last name?

TERESA: Yeah. It's like that on the street. You know people by their first names, or maybe their nicknames.

JAYWALKER: I see. What were some of the other first names or nicknames of the members of the gang?

DARCY: Objection to the term "gang." There's been absolutely no testimony—

THE COURT: Sustained. Rephrase the question.

JAYWALKER: Sure. Ms. Morales, it's true that you

used to hang out with Victor and
Sandro and some other guys, right?

TERESA: Sort of.

JAYWALKER: And that's what you were doing the
day the guys were going like this
[demonstrating] outside the barbershop? Not doing anything illegal,
just hanging out like a gang of
friends. Right?

TERESA: Yes.

DARCY: Objection, again, to the word "gang."

THE COURT: Well, the witness seems to have
agreed with Mr. Jaywalker's termi-
nology. So your objection is overruled.

JAYWALKER: Was Victor there that day?

TERESA: Yes.

JAYWALKER: Sandro?

TERESA: Yes.

JAYWALKER: Who else?

TERESA: Shorty. Diego. Mousey. Maybe a couple
of others. I don't remember.

JAYWALKER: How many of them were wearing
their Raiders jackets that day?

TERESA: Excuse me?

By sneaking the question in unexpectedly, Jaywalker had hoped to camouflage its importance from Teresa and get not only a number out of her, but an acknowledgment that the group referred to themselves as the Raiders. But she hadn't bitten. He asked her a few innocuous questions before taking another stab at it.

JAYWALKER: Whose idea was it to call the group
the Raiders?

Not "Did the group have a name?" or "Was the group called the Raiders?" or even "Wasn't the group called the Raiders?" Put any of those ways, the question not only telegraphed its own significance but could be answered with a simple "no." But by phrasing it in such a way as to *assume* that the group was called the Raiders, asking instead the completely irrelevant question of whose idea that had been, Jaywalker hoped to slide it by Teresa and get her to identify the person. In so doing, of course, she'd be agreeing with the assumption.

He also needed to slide it past Katherine Darcy. A question that contains an assumption not established by the evidence is improper. The oft-cited example is "When did you stop beating your wife?" But Jaywalker had burned Darcy a few minutes earlier over his inclusion of the word *gang* in several of his questions. Granted, her initial objection had been sustained, but a moment later he'd gotten Teresa to concede that she and her friends had been just that. Darcy had won the skirmish but lost the battle, and Jay-

walker guessed that this time she'd be gun-shy and let the
question be answered without objecting. And in fact, she
did.

But Teresa didn't.

TERESA: We didn't call ourselves anything.

JAYWALKER: Well, weren't you aware that other
                          people called you the Raiders?

TERESA: I wouldn't know.

JAYWALKER: But members of the gang—I'm
                          sorry, the group—did wear Raiders
                          jackets, didn't they?

TERESA: Not that I'm aware of.

Twice burned, Jaywalker gave up on the Raiders and got
back to Sandro. He asked Teresa if she knew what he did
for a living. She said she didn't, that she hadn't been aware
that he'd had a job of any sort.

JAYWALKER: In all of the three or four years you
                          knew him, he never once went to
                          work?

TERESA: Not that I remember.

JAYWALKER: Never talked about working?

TERESA: No.

JAYWALKER: And that's because Sandro supported himself by selling drugs, didn't he?

TERESA: I don't know.

Jaywalker stared at her, letting her words hang in the air for a few seconds.

JAYWALKER: Were you ever aware of a relation-ship between Sandro and Miranda, the young woman who was with Jer-emy the day of the shooting?

TERESA: Sandro once told me he was seeing her.

JAYWALKER: Did you ever see the two of them together, Sandro and Miranda?

TERESA: What do you mean, together?

JAYWALKER: Well, not when the group was chasing Jeremy, or pretending their fingers were guns and—

DARCY: Objection.

THE COURT: Sustained.

JAYWALKER: I mean "together" like man and woman, like you and Victor. Did you ever see Sandro and Miranda like that?

TERESA: No.

JAYWALKER: Never?

TERESA: Never.

He took her through the barbershop incident, making her
repeat some of the names the group had called Jeremy by,
and some of the taunts they'd hurled his way. He had her
describe how the owner had come out and finally gotten
them to leave.

JAYWALKER: Even as they were leaving, they said
            things to Jeremy, didn't they?

TERESA: Yes.

JAYWALKER: What did they say?

TERESA: "We'll get you next time."

JAYWALKER: Excuse me?

TERESA: "We'll see you next time."

JAYWALKER: Well which was it, "We'll see you"
            or "We'll get you"?

TERESA: "We'll see you."

Jaywalker had heard her correctly the first time, of
course. He just wanted to make sure the jurors had.

JAYWALKER: And that day at the barbershop, that
            wasn't the first time the group had

chased Jeremy and threatened to get
him, was it?

TERESA: No.

JAYWALKER: It had happened a number of times
that summer, hadn't it?

TERESA: A few times.

JAYWALKER: A few times? How about seventeen
times, not counting the barbershop?

He'd made up the number on the spot. He'd learned over
the years that if you were specific enough with numbers or
pretended to be reading from some official-looking piece
of paper, people tended to get intimidated and ended up
agreeing with you.

TERESA: I don't know. I wasn't really keeping
count.

Jaywalker decided to leave it there, figuring it was about
as good as he was going to get before he began to draw
denials from Teresa and yawns from the jury box. He knew
that when it came time for him to put Jeremy on the stand,
he'd be able to go into the earlier confrontations in depth
and breadth. And all he'd be up against would be Teresa's
lame *I don't know, I wasn't counting* as the prosecution's
version.

Now he took a look at the clock, saw it was ten minutes
to one. He was about to move forward to the day of the fight
and the shooting, but he didn't want to do so only to have
to stop ten minutes in. So rather than ask a question, he

caught Judge Wexler's eye. Wexler, who'd tried a few cases in his day as a defense lawyer, got the message.

"This might be a good time," he announced, "to break for lunch."

Once the jurors had been led out one door and Jeremy had been escorted through a very different one, Jaywalker sat back down and began gathering up his notes and files. As always, he intended to find a bench or a windowsill where he could spend the next hour refining the rest of his cross-examination. But suddenly Jeremy's mother was hovering over him, extending a brown paper bag his way.

"What's that?" he asked.

"Lunch," she said. "Jew gotta eat somesing."

Jaywalker stared at the bag. There was a large grease spot on one side of it, and a strong smell emanating from it. Cumin, perhaps? Garlic? He looked away, forcing himself to breathe through his mouth. Had he eaten breakfast, he would have been in serious danger of losing it right then and there.

"It's good," Carmen assured him. "I make it myself. Pork, rice and beans. Very good for jew. Give jew energy, Mr. Jailwalker."

He looked around for help, but the only court officer in sight, an old friend who was quite familiar with Jaywalker's trial diet, was trying his hardest not to burst out laughing at the scene. Everyone else had left, like rats fleeing a doomed ship. Next thing he knew, Jaywalker found himself not only accepting the bag—grease spot, aroma and all—but thanking Carmen for her thoughtfulness. He'd learned over time that you didn't reject heartfelt offerings from people of modest means. When the court-appointed client with no roof over his head extended a twenty-dollar bill your way after a hard-earned acquittal, you explained that the rules prohibited you from accepting it, that the city would be sending you a check to cover your hours. But when the guy insisted and said, "Please, you saved my life," you took the twenty and you pocketed it. To refuse a second time would be nothing less than a slap in the face, a rejection of a kindness. And if the disciplinary judges wanted to disbar him for that, so be it, they could have his ticket.

He thanked Carmen again and took the bag with him to the fifteenth floor, where he opened it, gagged from an overwhelming whiff of its contents and left it on a bench. Someone, he told himself, would be thrilled to discover it. Someone with a stomach far stronger and even emptier than his own.

When they resumed that afternoon, Jaywalker had the sense that the jurors were looking at Teresa Morales a little differently from the way they'd regarded her first thing that morning. In their eyes, she'd begun the day as not just a witness but a victim of sorts. Her boyfriend had been beaten up in front of her, then shot, chased and murdered. She'd tried to stop him from bleeding to death and had been unable to. The last she'd seen of him had been when he'd been wheeled away from her at the emergency room.

But as the morning wore on, the jurors had learned other things about Teresa. She'd gotten married to another man within a year, for one. She'd been forced to admit that she'd been part of a group that had followed Jeremy, called him names, taunted him, promised to "get" him, and finally backed up their words with gestures that could only be construed—unless you happened to be Katherine Darcy—as mimicking gunfire. So by the time the afternoon session began, the average defense lawyer would have concluded that Teresa had been softened up to the point where she was now ripe for the kill, and would have pounced on her.

Jaywalker, however, was anything but your average

defense lawyer. Never was, never would be. As strong as the temptation was to attack a wounded witness, he knew better than to try. For one thing, he considered it entirely plausible that Teresa Morales had told the truth that morning and would continue to do so that afternoon. With very few exceptions—the Raiders jackets and which boy had first pulled the gun—nothing Jeremy had ever told Jaywalker contradicted Teresa's testimony in general and her account of the day of the shooting in particular. So a full-bore attack ran the risk of accomplishing nothing more than getting her to repeat herself, only in more—and more convincing— detail than before. Again Jaywalker reminded himself that Jeremy would have his turn on the witness stand. Any blanks in the story left by Teresa meant more room for Jeremy to fill in as he recalled things.

In other words, less could actually be more. A proposition that sounded so alien and counterintuitive to most lawyers that they rejected it out of hand.

JAYWALKER: Do you remember who threw the first punch, Victor or Jeremy?

TERESA: No.

JAYWALKER: But after a while it became apparent that Jeremy was winning the fight. Right?

TERESA: Right.

JAYWALKER: And at some point Victor stopped to take off his sweatshirt. Right?

TERESA: Right.

JAYWALKER: In order to do that, did he have to pull it up over his head?

TERESA: Yes.

JAYWALKER: Did Jeremy attack him while Victor was busy doing that, while—

TERESA: No.

JAYWALKER: —he was blind and defenseless?

TERESA: No, not that I remember.

JAYWALKER: And then they resumed fighting?

TERESA: Yes.

JAYWALKER: Victor was now wearing just a T-shirt, a long T-shirt. Right?

This was actually an important point. According to Jeremy, the first he'd seen of the gun had been when Victor had pulled it from his waistband. That meant it must still have been hidden by something after Victor had removed his sweatshirt.

TERESA: I don't remember.

JAYWALKER: Well, he wasn't bare-chested, was he?

TERESA: I don't remember.

Jaywalker decided that was good enough. Jeremy would testify that Victor still had on a shirt of some sort. Teresa claimed she couldn't remember, and neither of the other eyewitnesses, Magdalena Lopez and Wallace Porter, had ever described Victor as being shirtless at any point. In his summation, Jaywalker would argue that had that been so, surely at least one of them would have recalled it and mentioned it, if only to differentiate between the two young men who'd been nameless strangers to them.

JAYWALKER: How about Jeremy? He had a shirt on the whole time, too. Didn't he?

TERESA: Yes.

JAYWALKER: Did you ever notice what Jeremy had on his feet?

TERESA: No, not really.

JAYWALKER: Do you have any recollection that he had two or three pairs of sweat socks on?

That, of course, had been Wallace Porter's version, along with his claim that he'd seen Jeremy pull the gun from his socks.

TERESA: No.

JAYWALKER: No recollection whatsoever. Right?

TERESA: Right.

JAYWALKER: So who finally won the fight?

TERESA: Him, I guess *[pointing]*.

JAYWALKER: Jeremy?

TERESA: Yeah.

JAYWALKER: Victor kind of gave up?

TERESA: Kind of.

JAYWALKER: And that's when you say you saw Jeremy pull the gun. Right?

TERESA: Right.

JAYWALKER: From his waist.

TERESA: Yeah.

JAYWALKER: Not his socks?

TERESA: No.

JAYWALKER: Did you ever see him do something like this with the gun *[gesturing]*, pulling something back on the top of it with his other hand?

TERESA: No.

Teresa couldn't say how many shots she'd heard, but Jaywalker got her to agree that everything had occurred "very fast" at that point, with Jeremy "just shooting like crazy."

Which, Jaywalker decided, was as good a place as any to quit. Whoever had first pulled the gun, it was agreed that Jeremy had ended up with it and done the shooting. And the image of things happening very quickly, with Jeremy momentarily out of control, dovetailed nicely with Jaywalker's theory of the case. As for Victor's getting up, running, stumbling and being shot again as he lay defenseless on the pavement, there was no way Jaywalker was going to get Teresa to retreat from those assertions. So the less said about them, the better.

"I have no further questions of the witness," he said.

Trials are something like trains, to the extent that neither of them tend to run too closely on schedule. One of the jurors had developed a toothache overnight and had that morning asked Judge Wexler's permission to visit her dentist that afternoon, explaining that the dentist could squeeze her in as an emergency at four-thirty. Now Wexler announced that her request would be granted, and that the trial would be in recess until the following morning. Then, as soon as the jurors had filed out of the courtroom, he summoned the lawyers up to the bench. "You know what they call a lawyer who asks about everything but the crime?" he asked.

Jaywalker was willing to take a stab at it. "A genius?"

It drew a muffled laugh from Katherine Darcy but seemed to do nothing for Wexler's disposition. "Not in my book," he said. "How about a *loser?*"

Jaywalker figured that particular question was a rhetorical one, and except for a shrug, he let it go unanswered. Wexler turned his attention to Darcy. "Are you still willing to consider offering the manslaughter plea?" he asked her. "With twenty years?"

"I suppose so," she answered. "I'd have to talk to my bureau chief."

"I suggest you do so. In the meantime, you talk to your client, Jaywalker. If the jury convicts him of murder, you can tell him I'm going to give him twenty-five to life. You may think you're going to be able to fool them into returning a manslaughter verdict, but I don't. And I'll promise you this much—there's no way you're walking out of here with an acquittal, not once I've finished charging them on when the right to use deadly force ends. To me, Jaywalker, your client's nothing but a two-bit punk who killed another punk, and if our legislature had any balls, he'd get the same sentence the victim got. So why don't you do us all a favor and stop trying to be a hero for once in your life, and start kicking some sense into this kid, will you?"

"I'll do my best," said Jaywalker.

And then, in spite of the fact that he'd planned on going into the pens and spending a few minutes with Jeremy, he made it a point of turning around, picking up his things as quickly as possible and walking not into the pens at all, but out the front doors. And for good measure, muttering "Fuck you" under his breath.

Okay, not exactly under his breath.

As pissed off as Jaywalker had been at the time by Judge Wexler's appraisal of the case, he'd calmed down by that evening. Food and the simple passage of time had a way of doing that. Not that a few hits from a joint hadn't helped.

And the truth was, he had to admit, Wexler did have a point. Here Jaywalker had thought he'd had a pretty good day with Teresa Morales. Even on direct examination, she'd described the barbershop incident pretty much the way Jeremy would in turn, complete with taunting, name-calling, simulating guns and threatening to get him next time. On cross, she'd admitted there'd been earlier encounters, though she'd been vague on the numbers. And if he hadn't quite gotten her to concede that the group called themselves the Raiders and favored Oakland Raiders leather jackets, her "Not that I'm aware of" demurrer had come off as pretty lame. As far as the fight was concerned, she'd not only agreed that Jeremy had been winning it, but portrayed him as too gentlemanly to go after his opponent while Victor had been taking off his sweatshirt and had been momentarily defenseless.

On the issue of where Jeremy had supposedly pulled the gun from, Teresa's recollection that it had been from his waist contradicted Wallace Porter's version that it had been from his socks. But Jaywalker wasn't sure if that was good news or bad. Porter had obviously lied as to several other points. First there'd been his insistence that he and his friends hadn't been drinking beer, only seconds after he himself had slipped and mentioned that they had been. Then there'd been his statement to the detectives that he'd heard the two young men arguing over money just before they began fighting. Porter had been forced to admit that while that statement had had no truth to it, he'd never attempted to correct it. In fact, he now said he didn't even know why he'd said it in the first place.

But Jaywalker did. Porter had simply been drawing on his own personal experience. Two young guys fighting to the death could mean only one thing to Wallace Porter: drugs. And drugs equalled money. So he'd simply embellished the tale with some details of his own. Why did Jaywalker see this so clearly? Because it was the kind of thing he himself did from time to time.

So if indeed it had been Jeremy who'd pulled the gun—and despite Jeremy's denials, Jaywalker considered that a distinct possibility—Teresa Morales's waistband version was much more likely than Wallace Porter's sweat-sock story. Still, the contradiction was a major one, and there was no way the jurors could have missed it. And just in case they had, Jaywalker would hammer the point in his summation. So all things considered, Jaywalker felt he'd survived the testimony of the three eyewitnesses in pretty fair shape. Yet here was Harold Wexler telling him in so many words that he was dead in the water.

It's often been said that because the prosecutor gets to sum up after the defense lawyer does, he or she has the last word in a trial. But Jaywalker knew that wasn't really the case. Following the summations, it's the judge who gets to speak last, often for an hour or more, while he charges the jury, lecturing them in detail on the various principles of law they're required to follow during their deliberations and in arriving at a verdict. When Harold Wexler had warned Jaywalker up at the bench that Jeremy's chances of being acquitted would vanish the moment the jury heard the charge on the limits of deadly force, he had a point. Even if the jurors were to remain as undecided as Jaywalker was on the issue of who'd begun the day with the gun, even if they felt Jeremy had been defending himself the first time he'd fired—or arguably the second or third time—once Victor had been lying helpless on the ground, there was no way that Jeremy's shooting him a final time between the eyes could be deemed justified. Wexler intended to make that point to the jury, and to make it as loudly and clearly as he possibly could. His message to Jaywalker had been direct and to the point: you can talk about justification and extreme emotional disturbance all you want, but there's no way you're getting around that final shot, not in my courtroom.

And if you chose to combine Harold Wexler's words with those of Katherine Darcy, uttered the very first time Jaywalker had met her, you had the case distilled right down to its essence. It was all about that stumble Victor had taken, that moment when he'd fallen to the ground and been reduced to begging for his life. That marked the precise instant when self-defense and sympathy ended, and the execution began.

He would talk to Jeremy tomorrow. Tonight he would sleep.

Or at least try to.

16

SLIM AND NONE

When Jaywalker went into the pens and talked with Jeremy before court the following morning, he found his client as resolute as ever.

"I think it's going pretty well, Jay."

Jaywalker tried to explain for the third time in fifteen minutes that no matter how well things seemed to be going, there was still the problem of the final point-blank shot between the eyes. The one that had been fired at a point when Victor had no longer posed a threat of any sort.

"I don't remember it that way," said Jeremy for the umpteenth time. "And I'd rather take my chances."

Jaywalker had once listened to an interview with Bill Russell, a long-ago basketball star for the Boston Celtics. Asked about the prospects of some other team beating them in the championship series, Russell had said, "They got two chances. Slim and none." Despite the fact that Jaywalker had been trying his best to explain that those words described their own chances of an acquittal to a T, the choice to continue the trial or not was still Jeremy's. When it came to tactics and strategy, Jaywalker took over, never allowing a client to tell him how to try a case, lest the advice interfere with his winning it. But on the fundamental question of whether to take a plea or go to trial—or in this case, continue with a trial—that decision was the defendant's, and the defendant's alone. Jaywalker could and did give advice on the matter. He often weighed in heavily on one side or the other, with a good ninety percent of his recommendations being to cop-out. If he felt strongly enough—and Jaywalker had never been a stranger to strong feelings—he'd resort to arm-twisting and head-banging. But when he was done with the twisting and the banging, he'd move on and redirect his efforts to winning. Other lawyers he knew admitted to taking a measure of satisfaction from telling a client, "I told you so," after losing a case. Jaywalker delighted in hearing those very same words *from* a client, after he'd *won* a case he'd called unwinnable. And hear those words he had. Not always, but a lot.

Though he knew he probably never would from Jeremy.

Katherine Darcy called Police Officer Joseph Campanella to the stand. Campanella had been the first officer to respond to the scene of the shooting. Checking his memobook entries from time to time, he recalled how he'd found someone identified later as V. Quinones lying on the pavement in a semiconscious state, apparently the victim of multiple gunshot wounds. He'd also encountered a young woman named Teresa Morales, who'd been attempting to aid Mr. Quinones.

DARCY: You say "semiconscious." Was he talking?

CAMPANELLA: No, ma'am. He was breathing, but he didn't respond to any verbal requests I made of him. He wasn't making any motions. His eyes were closed, and it was—it appeared as though he was sleeping.

Officer Campanella had called for an ambulance. While waiting for it to arrive, he'd done chest compressions on the victim, while someone else had performed mouth-to-mouth breathing. Then the ambulance had arrived and EMTs had placed the victim inside it. Miss Morales and Officer Campanella had also gotten in.

DARCY: What happened in the ambulance?

CAMPANELLA: They were rendering whatever aid they could give him.

DARCY: What was Mr. Quinones's condition as time went on?

CAMPANELLA: It was progressively worsening.

DARCY: Tell us how.

CAMPANELLA: He never regained consciousness. He never spoke or opened his eyes. From what I observed, his vital signs were diminishing. He was becoming paler as the minutes were passing. And he was just generally deteriorating.

DARCY: What happened at the hospital?

CAMPANELLA: Shortly after our arrival, he was

> pronounced dead by the emergency room doctor.

Officer Campanella had completed some paperwork, checked in with his precinct commander, and then returned to East 113th Street to help secure the crime scene. Darcy asked him if he'd noticed any sort of evidence upon his return.

CAMPANELLA: Yes, I did. There was a sweatshirt. And if I'm not mistaken, there were two shell casings and two spent rounds lying on the walkway. I'd also recovered another spent round in the ambulance.

DARCY: What was done with those items, if you know?

CAMPANELLA: They were all vouchered and removed as evidence.

DARCY: Were you able to draw any conclusions about the type of weapon or weapons that had been involved in the shooting?

CAMPANELLA: Only that there'd been an automatic involved.

Asked to clarify, he explained that while a revolver retained its spent shells in its cylinder after firing, an automatic or semiautomatic discharged each empty shell as it was fired. As for the "spent rounds" he'd referred to, those were the slugs or projectiles that were fired from the shells.

DARCY: Did you do something else in connection
with this case several days later?

CAMPANELLA: Yes, I did.

DARCY: What was that?

CAMPANELLA: I went to the city morgue and
identified the body of Mr.
Quinones.

Jaywalker asked the officer no questions. Campanella
had been a good witness. He'd managed to avoid lapsing
into *copspeak,* a strange dialect that for some reason
compels its ranks to favor "At that point in time I did
proceed to take exit of my vehicle" over "Then I got out of
my car." He'd been clear, concise and direct. That said, he
hadn't really said anything that hurt Jeremy, and Jaywalker
saw no particular reason to give him a chance. Multiple
shots had in fact been fired from a semiautomatic weapon.
Victor Quinones had been shot, and had died of his wounds
not too long afterward. Ballistics evidence and a sweatshirt
had been recovered at the scene.

Jaywalker was a lot of things, but one thing he wasn't
was a showman. He never questioned witnesses for the sake
of questioning them, or to show off his cross-examination
skills. And for the life of him, he failed to understand why
so many of his colleagues seemed compelled to do so.

Although it was only eleven o'clock, Judge Wexler
decided to take his midmorning recess early, and he excused
the jurors for fifteen minutes. The reason soon became

apparent: the arrival of a dignitary of sorts, a justice from the appellate division.

Jaywalker couldn't quite place the man at first, though he looked very familiar. And then it came to him. He was Miles Sternbridge, the presiding member of the three-judge disciplinary committee that had suspended Jaywalker from practice some years back. Sternbridge had actually treated Jaywalker fairly, first by grudgingly allowing him to finish up ten of his pending cases before the suspension had kicked in, and later by terminating it early in order to appease a Rockland County judge anxious to move along the case of a defendant who wanted to hire Jaywalker. Still, Jaywalker found it hard to feel all warm and fuzzy about the man. To begin with, what kind of a guy went around calling himself *Miles Sternbridge?* Not that he'd named himself, of course. But had Jaywalker been tagged with a handle like that, he would have done something about it, just as he had with Harrison J. Walker. Then there'd been the bit about that "sexual gratuity" Jaywalker had been accused of accepting. Sternbridge had to have known that hadn't been his idea, and the stairwell security video had even backed him up, showing him trying to resist the efforts of his overly appreciative client. But in the absence of a sound track of any sort, Sternbridge had claimed to be able to divine that Jaywalker's opening-and-closing of his mouth signified *moaning,* rather than protestations of "No, no!"

Okay, so maybe it had been a combination of the two. But even if it had been, was it really so different from accepting the twenty-dollar bill from the insistent guy you'd just won an acquittal for? Wouldn't both clients have been equally offended by outright rejection of their expressions of gratitude?

"Come up, Mr. Jaywalker." It was Harold Wexler's voice,

summoning Jaywalker up to the bench, where the two judges had been huddling for several minutes.

Jaywalker approached cautiously, wondering what it was he'd done this time. Going to trial instead of taking a plea couldn't possibly be grounds for disciplinary action, could it? He looked around the courtroom, wondering if he was going to need a lawyer, but didn't see anyone he would be interested in hiring even if he'd had the money.

"Nice to see you again," said Sternbridge.

"Likewise, I'm sure." He'd heard John Malkovich say that once in a movie, one of those things where everyone was wearing powdered wigs and pirate shirts.

"Harold here tells me you've been behaving yourself." Said with obvious astonishment, and perhaps even a tinge of disappointment.

"I've been trying," said Jaywalker.

"Good," said Sternbridge. "Good."

Jaywalker said nothing.

"Well, then," said Sternbridge, "carry on, gentlemen." And shaking hands with Wexler—and only Wexler—he turned and left.

"Friend of yours?" Wexler asked with a smile, once Sternbridge was out the door.

"Oh, yeah," said Jaywalker, and they exchanged smiles. Wexler knew all about Jaywalker's run-in with the committee; everyone did. Now he motioned Katherine Darcy to come up and join them at the bench. Once she had, he assured her that they hadn't been discussing the case, only Jaywalker's criminal record. Darcy answered with a knowing smile.

"So," Wexler asked her, "have you talked to your bureau chief?"

"I have."

"And are you authorized to agree to twenty years on a manslaughter plea?"

"Yes."

Even before the judge turned his way, Jaywalker was shaking his head from side to side. "He doesn't want it," he explained.

"Big mistake," was all Wexler would say, his jaw set tightly. Then he stood up and walked out of the room, leaving the two lawyers standing there. He could be like that, Jaywalker knew. Putting in a good word for you one minute, then turning on you the next. But the thing of it was, come sentencing time, it wouldn't be the smiling Harold Wexler who'd be sentencing Jeremy Estrada. It would be the other one, the angry, vindictive Harold Wexler.

Just one more example of how the words *I told you so* always seemed to come into play down at 100 Centre Street.

Katherine Darcy called Detective Regina Fortune. A member of the Crime Scene Unit, Detective Fortune would succeed in demonstrating, by the time she stepped down from the witness stand, that her name was far and away the best thing about her.

Darcy began her examination by asking about the duties of her unit.

FORTUNE: CSU responds to certain crimes within the five boroughs. All homicides, assaults where a person is likely to die, sex crimes—rape, sodomy, child abuse—and what we call pattern robberies or pattern burglaries. We respond in order to preserve the crime scene, and we do that through taking photos, making notes and drawing sketches and

diagrams. And when we recover any
type of evidence at a scene, we photograph it and note it in our sketches and
diagrams.

Darcy drew Detective Fortune's attention to September
6th. Referring to her notes, she testified that she'd arrived
at 113th Street and Third Avenue shortly after four o'clock
that afternoon. She'd found the scene already secured and
evidence preserved by uniformed patrol officers who'd
arrived earlier. She'd noted a sweatshirt, two .380 shell
casings and a spent round, which she more accurately described as "a piece of deformed lead." She'd made notes,
taken measurements and photographs, and drawn a rough
sketch of the area. Back at her office, she'd created a large
diagram of the scene, drawn to scale and showing the
relative location of the various items she'd spotted. Without
objection from Jaywalker—he had no interest in making it
seem worth fighting over—the diagram was received in
evidence and published to the jurors. For some reason that
Jaywalker had never understood, lawyers seem to prefer
using words like *publish* when mundane ones like *show*
would do just fine.

Up to that point, Regina Fortune had been a model
witness, and perhaps it was that fact that led Katherine
Darcy to get greedy. As Harold Wexler might have put it, it
was a big mistake. But prosecutors are lawyers, too, and
they occasionally succumb to the temptation to ask too
many questions of a witness.

DARCY: You mentioned a .380 shell.

FORTUNE: Yes.

DARCY: What is a .380 shell?

FORTUNE: The number signifies the size of the caliber. Guns come in all sizes—.38s, 9 mms, .45s. A .380 is a middle-range gun. It's bigger than a .38, smaller than a 9 mm, much smaller than a .45. Those are all caliber sizes.

DARCY: Have you seen .38s and .380s?

FORTUNE: Yes, I have.

DARCY: And are you able to approximate the size of a .380?

FORTUNE: A .380 would probably be the size of my hand. It's an automatic. It's stream-lined, kind of thin. But it would probably be the size of my hand.

It suddenly dawned on Jaywalker where Darcy was going with this line of questioning. Wallace Porter had claimed to have seen Jeremy pulling the gun from beneath two or three pairs of sweat socks. Despite the unlikelihood of that having happened—Teresa Morales's waistband version had struck Jaywalker as far more plausible—Darcy was now casting her lot with Porter and trying to get Detective Fortune to say that it could have happened the way he'd testified. And sure enough...

DARCY: Anything about a .380 that would be incon-sistent with its being carried in somebody's sock?

FORTUNE: No, it could be carried in somebody's
sock.

DARCY: Are you familiar with ankle holsters?

FORTUNE: Yes.

DARCY: If somebody were to pull sweat socks over
an ankle holster, would that conceal the
holster?

FORTUNE: Yes, it would.

Sooner or later, there came a moment in most trials
when Jaywalker woke up. Not that he'd been asleep up to
this point. But knowing that he would eventually be putting
Jeremy on the stand, he'd pretty much sat back and let the
early witnesses have their say. He hadn't even gone after
the eyewitnesses too hard—Magdalena Lopez, Wallace
Porter and Teresa Morales—preferring to get them off the
stand fairly quickly. But for some reason, Katherine
Darcy's last line of questioning with Detective Fortune
pissed him off. Perhaps it was no more than his frustration
over not being able to dent the consensus that it had been
Jeremy who'd pulled the gun and murdered a defenseless
victim. Or perhaps it had been Harold Wexler's certainty
that there was going to be a conviction and that he was
going to bang Jeremy out at sentencing time. Maybe it had
even had something to do with Miles Sternbridge's cameo
appearance that morning, and his snide remark about being
glad to hear that Jaywalker had been *behaving himself.*
Whatever it was, the juices were suddenly boiling within
Jaywalker's belly. That was something that didn't happen

all that often, but when it did, it made him an exceedingly dangerous cross-examiner, as Regina Fortune was about to find out.

JAYWALKER: Detective Fortune, have you ever owned a .380 automatic?

FORTUNE: Me? No.

But Jaywalker had, back in his DEA days. A nickel-plated one, with genuine walnut grips. It had been big, the exact size of a .45, and had taken one round in the chamber and eleven in the clip, and you could go to war with it if you had to.

JAYWALKER: Are you by any chance familiar with the Browning .380?

FORTUNE: I've seen it. It's about the size of my hand.

JAYWALKER: Is the Browning .380 a very common .380?

FORTUNE: I wouldn't know.

JAYWALKER: What are some other makes of .380s?

FORTUNE: I see so many guns, I wouldn't know.

JAYWALKER: Tell me one other.

FORTUNE: I can't remember right now.

JAYWALKER: I'll give you a few minutes.

FORTUNE: I don't know makes of guns, really.

JAYWALKER: Do you know the difference between
           a .380 and a 9 mm?

FORTUNE: The size of the gun. Because the caliber
           is a little bigger?

From the way she raised her voice at the end, turning her
answer into question, it was clear that not even Detective
Fortune believed that one. But before Jaywalker could
continue, Judge Wexler came to her rescue.

THE COURT: You're not a ballistics expert, are
           you?

FORTUNE: No, I'm not.

But by asking her about guns on direct examination,
Katherine Darcy had opened the door to Jaywalker's line
of questioning, and Wexler was obviously smart enough to
know he had no choice but to let things continue.

JAYWALKER: Detective, when we talk about mil-
           limeters, a 9 mm versus a .380, say,
           what are we referring to?

FORTUNE: It's the size of the caliber of the gun.

JAYWALKER: What does that mean?

FORTUNE: It's the size of the bullet.

JAYWALKER: Is that in length? Diameter? Radius?
Or circumference?

FORTUNE: It's measured by weight.

That one took even Jaywalker surprise. Here he'd been
nice enough to make things easy for the witness by asking
her a multiple-choice question. And she'd decided to go
with "none of the above."

JAYWALKER: The millimeter is a unit of weight?

FORTUNE: That's how they determine it.

JAYWALKER: How about a meter? Is that a unit of
weight?

FORTUNE: No, it's not.

JAYWALKER: Isn't a millimeter a fraction of a
meter?

FORTUNE: Yes.

JAYWALKER: What fraction would that be?

FORTUNE: A hundredth?

JAYWALKER: Close. How about a thousandth?

FORTUNE: Okay.

JAYWALKER: Does that perhaps cause you to

change your previous answer that a
millimeter is a unit of weight?

FORTUNE: Yes.

JAYWALKER: Good. So do millimeters refer to the
diameter of the bullet, the radius of
the bullet, the circumference of the
bullet, or the length of the bullet?
Now that we've ruled out weight.

FORTUNE: I believe it's lengthwise, the length of
the shell.

This from a detective, mind you. A detective assigned to
the Crime Scene Unit.

JAYWALKER: Ever heard of a .22?

FORTUNE: Yes.

JAYWALKER: Is there such a thing as a .22 long?

FORTUNE: Yes, there is.

JAYWALKER: Such a thing as a .22 short? Sometimes called a .22 corto?

FORTUNE: The .22 short I know. Yes.

JAYWALKER: Yet they're all .22's, in spite of the
fact that they have different lengths.
Aren't they?

FORTUNE: Yes.

JAYWALKER: Does that by any chance cause you to change your previous answer that the term *millimeters* refers to length? To think that it refers instead to the diameter of the bullet?

FORTUNE: I guess so. I'm not an expert.

At least that much was clear. But Jaywalker still needed to undermine the detective's claim that the discovery of .380 shell casings told her something about the size of the gun they'd come from.

JAYWALKER: Now you told us that a .380 automatic is smaller than a 9 mm. Right?

FORTUNE: Right.

JAYWALKER: Yet they can both fire .380 ammunition, can't they?

FORTUNE: Yes, I guess so.

JAYWALKER: And either one can be as big as a .45 automatic. Right?

FORTUNE: Right.

JAYWALKER: Which would make it considerably bigger than your hand. Right again?

FORTUNE: Right.

JAYWALKER: So the fact that .380 shell casings were found at the scene really tells us just about nothing in terms of the overall size of the gun they came from. Isn't that true?

FORTUNE: Yes.

From there, Jaywalker moved on to the subject of ankle holsters.

JAYWALKER: You've seen lots of ankle holsters, haven't you?

FORTUNE: Yes.

JAYWALKER: And is it fair to say that whenever you've seen one, it was for a two-inch, snub-nosed .38 revolver?

FORTUNE: Yes.

JAYWALKER: You've never, ever seen one for a .380 automatic, have you?

FORTUNE: No.

JAYWALKER: Or a 9 mm?

FORTUNE: No.

JAYWALKER: In fact, neither of those guns would fit into an ankle holster made for a two-inch .38 revolver? Would they?

FORTUNE: No.

JAYWALKER: What would be likely to happen if you tried to wear one of them in such an ankle holster?

FORTUNE: It's too big. It would probably fall out.

JAYWALKER: Kind of like if you tried to wear it in just your socks, without a holster?

FORTUNE: Kind of like that.

JAYWALKER: Probably fall out?

FORTUNE: Yes.

JAYWALKER: Same thing even if you wore extra pairs of socks?

FORTUNE: Same thing.

At some point during the morning, Jaywalker's daughter had slipped into the courtroom. She'd been in the neighborhood, having had to pick up some document at the Board of Health a few blocks away. As soon as Jaywalker finished his cross-examination of Detective Fortune, Judge Wexler recessed for lunch. At that point Jaywalker's daughter walked over to him, hugged him and said, "You shredded her, Dad."

And it was true. Regina Fortune had been a terrible witness, far too ready to testify to things about which she knew little or nothing. And Katherine Darcy had been complicit in unmasking the detective by asking her questions she didn't need to and never should have.

But Jaywalker knew something his daughter didn't. From Detective Fortune's scale-drawn diagram of the crime scene, the jurors would be able to determine the precise distance between the area where Jeremy Estrada and Victor Quinones had fought to the spot where Victor had ultimately sustained the fatal shot and bled out onto the pavement. That distance, Jaywalker also knew, would form the cornerstone of Katherine Darcy's summation argument that Victor had indeed attempted to flee from Jeremy after being shot the first time, and that Jeremy in turn had run him down and executed him.

That distance had been forty-five feet.

As Jaywalker was busy explaining that little detail to his daughter, Jeremy's mother sidled up to them, another greasy paper bag in her hands.

"She's your daughter," said Carmen.

Not "Is she your daughter?" or "This must be your daughter." No, the way Carmen stated it left absolutely no room for doubt. She might just as easily have been presenting a newborn baby to a mother in the delivery room, or announcing the results of a DNA test excluding any other possibility by a factor of a billion to one. And while it was true that there was a certain resemblance between Jaywalker and his daughter, it wasn't like they were mirror images of each other. Which made Carmen's pronouncement seem all the more like something straight from the mouth of a clairvoyant or a Gypsy fortune-teller.

Jaywalker introduced the two of them, and they traded a "Pleased to meet jew" for an "I hope things work out for your son." Then Carmen turned back to Jaywalker, and the dreaded moment came.

"Chicken," she said. "I made jew chicken with brown graven."

Jaywalker took the bag and thanked her. They spoke for a few more seconds before a court officer anxious to clear the courtroom ushered Carmen out. Jaywalker and his daughter he left alone, knowing they'd know to use the side door.

"Thanks for stopping by," said Jaywalker, who saw little of his daughter these days, now that she was living in New Jersey with her husband and children of her own. "I miss you. And do me a favor, will you?"

"What's that?"

He extended the bag in her direction. She laughed at the offer, but immediately put her hands behind her back. Family resemblances were one thing, and blood might indeed be thicker than water. But when it came to chicken and brown graven, it seemed Jaywalker was still pretty much on his own.

That afternoon Katherine Darcy called Dr. Seymour Kaplan to the stand as her eighth and final witness. Dr. Kaplan was an assistant to the chief medical examiner of the City of New York, and he would prove to be as good a witness as Detective Fortune had been a bad one.

Darcy began by having Dr. Kaplan run through his credentials and qualifications, and they were truly impressive. After graduating from Harvard, he'd earned a doctorate in neuroanatomy, and taught anatomy and histology at Albert Einstein Medical School, before enrolling there himself. Following graduation and an internship, he'd completed a three-year residency in pathology at Massachusetts General Hospital. From there he'd returned to New York to accept a teaching fellowship in forensic pathology at Mount Sinai. He was board certified in both anatomical pathology and forensic pathology, which he described as the interaction between the science of the medical cause of death and the legal world of the criminal justice system. He'd worked as an assistant medical examiner in New York for eleven years, during which time he'd performed over two thousand autopsies himself, as well as assisting at more than three times that number.

Twice during the recital Jaywalker offered to stipulate that Dr. Kaplan was qualified as an expert in forensic pathology. But Katherine Darcy could evidently sense the jury's reaction to her witness's résumé and intended to play it for all it was worth. Finally, on the third attempt, Jaywalker's offer was accepted. At that point Judge Wexler took a moment to explain to the jurors that having been qualified as an expert, Dr. Kaplan would be permitted to offer his medical and scientific opinion within the field of his particular expertise.

Darcy had him describe what an autopsy was, and how he'd performed one on the body of Victor Quinones. In response to her questions, he stated that he'd found two gunshot wounds, a non-fatal one to the torso, and a fatal one to the head, both complete with telltale entrance and exit holes. He was careful to say that from his examination he had no way of telling which wound had been sustained first.

DARCY: Would you describe for us the shot to the torso?

KAPLAN: Yes. That shot was actually a bit unusual, out of the ordinary in terms of its geometry. It was a shot through the body wall. It entered just below the ribs on the left side, and the bullet stayed within the soft tissue of the body wall. It came out the body wall without ever entering the abdomen or causing internal damage. It formed a very nice linear streak, which is visible on the body. I probed the line, opened it up. And found there was no injury at all from it.

What also made it unique was that after the bullet left the body, there was a gap of a few inches where the skin was perfectly normal. And then there was an extension of that same line on the hip, indicating what appeared to me to be the continuation of the path of that bullet. It caused a grazing wound, a contusion. There was a bruise of the hip without the skin being broken. In other words, a bruising injury in a perfect line with the streak on the body wall that I described earlier.

Because I didn't think these injuries were fatal, I didn't include them on the death certificate as contributing in any way to the cause of death.

Darcy asked him to describe the other wound, the one that had proved fatal.

KAPLAN: There was a small, well-circumscribed wound just above the bridge of the nose, equidistant from the eyes. By "well-circumscribed," I mean it was almost a complete circle in shape. I deemed it to be an entrance wound of a projectile, almost certainly a bullet. Following its trajectory with a thin metal probe, I discovered that it went through the skull, breaking off several small fragments as it did so. From there it entered the left cerebral hemisphere of the brain, just slightly off the midline that divides the two hemispheres. At that point the projectile began to "wander" somewhat in what appeared to me to be a tumbling motion. As it did so, it caused massive damage to both hemispheres. There was significant evidence of herniation, or swelling of the brain itself within the skull. That would have happened as a result of bleeding, most of which would have taken place in the minutes following the impact.

After passing through the brain, the projectile again encountered the skull, this time from the inside, as it exited through the back of the head, the upper portion of the neck. Unlike the entrance wound, this exit wound was large and irregular, further evidence that the projectile had tumbled in the brain and had picked up both skull fragments and brain matter as it did so.

I deemed that shot to have been the fatal one.

A polite way, if Jaywalker understood correctly, of saying that Victor Quinones had died as a result of having a combination of metal and bone churn through his brain.

Not too different from having had the Roto-Rooter man clean an ever-widening path through his skull, from front to back. But if that wasn't bad enough, the worst was still to come. Darcy wanted to know if Dr. Kaplan was able to say how close the gun had been to the victim's head when the fatal shot had been fired.

KAPLAN: I'm able to say it was quite close.

DARCY: What evidence did you see that supports that conclusion?

KAPLAN: The scalp was lifted off the skull enough so as to cause radial tearing around the edge of the wound.

DARCY: You used the words "quite close." Are you able to give us a medical opinion as to just how close that shot was fired from the front of Victor Quinones's head?

KAPLAN: Yes. What I found was consistent with a distance of anywhere from maybe a quarter of an inch to four or five inches.

Jaywalker had known for months that that detail was coming, not only from his own reading of the autopsy report, but from picking the brain of a friend who happened to be a pathologist. Still, as prepared as he was for it, and as ready as he ever would be to cross-examine on it, he knew he wouldn't be able to seriously challenge Dr. Kaplan's conclusion. Sometimes the truth is just that, and when delivered from the mouth of a bright, articulate witness with no interest in the outcome of the case, it tends to sparkle.

Which on most days Jaywalker would agree was a wonderful thing.

Just not right now.

Because this particular bit of truth, that Jeremy Estrada had delivered the *coup de grace* at point-blank range, was every bit as devastating in its way as the fact that Victor Quinones had run forty-five feet before stumbling, looking up and seeing the gun pointed squarely between his eyes. It took only a furtive glance in the direction of the jurors to tell Jaywalker that their rapt attention and grim faces added up to no good for the defense.

And Darcy still wasn't finished with Dr. Kaplan. She got him to agree that the nonfatal wound could have been sustained while the victim was in a crouched position, bent forward, with the shooter firing at him from directly in front of him. Finally Darcy asked her witness if, following the fatal shot—the one to the head—Victor Quinones would have been able to run or walk a distance of forty-five feet.

KAPLAN: In my opinion, that would have been virtually impossible. In all likelihood, the victim would have lost consciousness immediately or almost immediately.

DARCY: Would he have been able to talk? Specifically, to beg for his life?

KAPLAN: In my opinion, no and no. Given the damage to the left hemisphere of the brain, which controls speech, the shot would have made it all but impossible for him to speak. And I would go so far as say that given the extent of the injuries, it would have been equally impossible

for him to have formed the thought of
begging, convert that thought into words,
and utter those words. It's my opinion
that once the victim sustained that
wound, he wouldn't have been able to do
much of anything other than to collapse
and die shortly afterward.

Or, as Bill Russell might have put it, the chances that
Victor had sustained the fatal wound where he and Jeremy
had struggled over the gun, and then had either walked or
run forty-five feet before collapsing—as Jeremy seemed to
be telling Jaywalker—were slim and none.

From there Darcy drew Dr. Kaplan's attention to a minor
injury he'd noted in the autopsy report, a fresh cut Victor
Quinones had sustained to the inside of his mouth.

DARCY: In your opinion, was that cut consistent
            with the victim's having bitten his lip when
            his head was dropped to pavement?

KAPLAN: Yes, it was.

And with that last little tidbit, Katherine Darcy thanked
her witness and sat down.

If the cross-examiner is smart enough to ask no questions
of the witness who hasn't hurt his client, what does he do
with the witness who's absolutely demolished him? That
was the question on Jaywalker's mind as he stood up now.
Complicating his problem was the nature of Dr. Kaplan
himself: not only had his testimony been devastating and
his credentials impeccable, but his manner had been absolutely engaging. He'd instructed the jury without speaking

down to them, had demonstrated an expertise uninfected by ego, and had restricted his opinions to those areas where he felt qualified to draw conclusions. As a result, he'd not only come off as objective and informative; he'd also ended up being thoroughly likeable.

So Jaywalker knew there was no way he could go after Dr. Kaplan the way, say, that he'd laid into Detective Fortune. At the same time, he knew he had to question the man. To leave him alone would have been tantamount to an admission of defeat, given how devastating the doctor's testimony had been. But understanding that the most he could hope to accomplish was to score a point here or establish a fact there, Jaywalker knew he needed to lower his sights. In other words, rather than attacking Kaplan, he needed to adopt him as his own witness. Sometimes cross-examination can be a little bit like playground politics: if another kid looks too big to beat up, try getting him to join your side.

He began with the issue of the position of Victor Quinones's body at the moment he'd sustained the first, nonlethal wound. Jaywalker felt it was the weakest part of Dr. Kaplan's testimony, not because Kaplan himself had overreached, but because Katherine Darcy had tried to get too much out of him by asking him if Victor "could have sustained" the wound while bent forward in a crouched position.

JAYWALKER: Would you agree that it's every bit as likely that this wound was sustained while Mr. Quinones was standing up straight and struggling over the gun, which was chest high and pointed straight downward?

KAPLAN: Yes, I would.

JAYWALKER: That could just as easily explain the entrance wound just below the chest, the shallow trajectory, the exit wound on the abdominal wall, and even the hip wound?

KAPLAN: Yes, sir. That is correct.

JAYWALKER: And the gun could have been quite close to the entrance wound?

KAPLAN: It could have been. Yes, sir.

JAYWALKER: Nothing in your findings rules that out. Correct?

KAPLAN: That is correct.

From there Jaywalker moved on to the victim's physical appearance. He wanted the jury to hear that Victor had been physically fit and presumably an equal match with Jeremy in a fistfight. Also that he'd been menacing-looking, and as ugly as Jeremy was handsome. While that fact might have lacked relevance in a technical sense, Jaywalker was nevertheless banking on it to affect the jurors. When you were fighting to keep someone out of prison for the rest of his life or pretty close to it, you looked for every advantage you could find, and you didn't let the technical stuff get in your way.

JAYWALKER: I see from the autopsy report that you described Mr. Quinones as about five-nine, well developed and fairly muscular? Is that your recollection?

KAPLAN: Yes, it is.

JAYWALKER: Any facial hair?

KAPLAN: A thin, wispy mustache and chin whiskers.

Jaywalker walked over to the prosecution table and asked Katherine Darcy for the autopsy photos. From the half dozen she handed him, he picked out one taken of the victim's face in which the entrance wound showed the least. Victor had had rather heavy eyebrows, and the wound was right between them, where they met just above his nose. His eyes were closed in the photo, and if you didn't know better, you might have thought he was sleeping. But his mouth was open, and the "windowpanes" were visible on his teeth, and his cheeks were pockmarked from what looked like old acne scars.

Jaywalker had the photo marked for identification, then handed it to the witness.

JAYWALKER: Is that a fair representation of what Mr. Quinones looked like?

KAPLAN: Yes, it is.

JAYWALKER: I offer the photo into evidence as Defendant's Exhibit A.

DARCY: No objection.

THE COURT: Received.

Which meant that the jurors would be able to look at the exhibit themselves. Whiskers, windowpanes, pockmarks and all.

JAYWALKER: Can you tell us what those things are on Mr. Quinones's teeth?

KAPLAN: Those are called windowpanes.

JAYWALKER: What are windowpanes?

KAPLAN: They're decorative coverings that are placed over the teeth, with a cutout vignette. Sometimes the cutout is a box or a circle, sometimes a heart or a star. It's my understanding that they're purely decorative, rather than for any dental necessity. And they covered three of Mr. Quinones's teeth.

JAYWALKER: And in this particular case, what kind of finish was on the windowpanes?

KAPLAN: They were gold.

Jaywalker turned to the toxicology and serology reports, and brought out the fact that Victor Quinones had had both ethanol and opiates in his system. From the .11 blood-alcohol reading, he was able to get Dr. Kaplan to estimate the number of drinks Victor had consumed at five or six.

And it had still been morning when he died. But the doctor had no way of quantifying the amount of opiates he'd taken.

> JAYWALKER: And when we say opiates, what drug is the first one that comes to your mind?

> KAPLAN: Heroin. Although it could have been di-laudid, or something like that. But heroin would be the most likely candidate.

It was time to get down to the most devastating area of Dr. Kaplan's testimony, his opinion that the fatal shot had been fired at a distance of no more than four or five inches from Victor's head. Jaywalker knew he wasn't going to be able to get the witness to reverse himself on that conclusion, but he wanted to at least show that the basis for it was a fairly narrow one.

> JAYWALKER: Are you familiar with the term "muzzle stamp"?

> KAPLAN: Yes, I am.

> JAYWALKER: What's a muzzle stamp?

> KAPLAN: A muzzle stamp occurs if the gun is placed against the skin when it's fired, and the pressure and heat of the gasses coming out with the bullet cause an impression. That impression will show up on the skin as a contusion, a black-and-blue mark. And in size and shape it will be identical to the muzzle, the end of the

barrel of the gun. Again, it occurs only when the gun is held against the skin, particularly if it's held against it tightly.

JAYWALKER: Did you find any evidence of a muzzle stamp in this case?

KAPLAN: No. But I wouldn't have expected to, because the point of entry was largely covered by the hair of his eyebrows.

JAYWALKER: Hair singes rather easily, doesn't it?

KAPLAN: It can, yes.

JAYWALKER: Any singing of the eyebrows in this case?

KAPLAN: No, sir.

JAYWALKER: What is "stippling"?

KAPLAN: *Stippling* is the term for little dots caused by tiny blood vessels—known as capillaries—breaking. It, too, is an indication that the shot was fired at close range.

JAYWALKER: Any stippling around the head wound?

KAPLAN: No, sir.

JAYWALKER: What is "fouling"?

KAPLAN: *Fouling* is the unburned powder that comes out of the muzzle. It would leave a grayish discoloration, if you were within close range. Though it could be washed off at the hospital, in the emergency room.

JAYWALKER: Any evidence of fouling in this case?

KAPLAN: No, sir.

JAYWALKER: So just to recap. With respect to the fatal wound, you found absolutely no evidence of a muzzle stamp, no singed hair, no stippling and no fouling. Do I have that right?

KAPLAN: You do.

There was one last area Jaywalker wanted to explore with the witness. Katherine Darcy had made a point of having Dr. Kaplan testify that a cut he'd noticed inside the victim's mouth had been consistent with his having bitten his lip when his head had been dropped to the ground, presumably after Jeremy had shot him between the eyes.

JAYWALKER: Let's talk about this term "consistent with" for a moment.

KAPLAN: Okay.

JAYWALKER: All that "consistent with" means is you can't rule it out. Right?

KAPLAN: That is correct.

JAYWALKER: In other words, it's one of perhaps any number of possibilities that you can't eliminate.

KAPLAN: True.

JAYWALKER: Is there anything at all in the findings you saw that tells you Mr. Quinones's head was ever picked up and dropped?

KAPLAN: No.

JAYWALKER: Were you ever informed that Mr. Quinones had been in a fistfight immediately prior to his death?

KAPLAN: I don't believe I was.

JAYWALKER: Is this cut to his mouth every bit as consistent with his having taken a good right-handed punch to that area of the mouth as it is with anything else?

KAPLAN: Yes, sir. It's consistent with absolutely anything that would have caused the tooth to bite through the lip.

JAYWALKER: Thank you.

And with that Jaywalker let him go. Despite his having been able to score a few points on cross, he knew that

Dr. Kaplan had been a pivotal witness for the prosecution. And the fact that Katherine Darcy didn't feel any need to get up and rehabilitate him on redirect examination underscored what Jaywalker already knew: the witness's conclusion that the head shot had been fired from inches away—or even less—wasn't really in doubt and was something the jurors would be hearing much more of during Darcy's summation.

Between direct and cross, Seymour Kaplan's testimony had taken over two hours, and by the time he stepped down from the witness stand it was nearly five o'clock. Judge Wexler recessed for the day. "And I know you'll be disappointed to hear this," he told the jurors, "but tomorrow is my calendar day. That means I'll be spending the morning dealing with other cases, ones that aren't on trial. As a result, your presence won't be required until two-fifteen in the afternoon. But don't let my generosity lull you into being late. I'm told by the Department of Corrections that there are plenty of vacancies on Rikers Island."

Vintage Wexler, taking what promised to be a beautiful free morning in mid-May and turning it into a threat of jail time.

Even with the next day's late start, that evening was a busy one for Jaywalker. Not that they all weren't when he was on trial. But once they resumed Wednesday afternoon, Katherine Darcy would announce that the People were resting their case. That meant it would be the defense's turn.

In exchange for Darcy's agreement to permit Jeremy's mother and sister to remain in the courtroom during the testimony of the prosecution witnesses, Jaywalker had promised to call them first, and it was a promise he intended to keep. Carmen had been steadfast in her refusal to allow her daughter to testify, and Jaywalker had neither seen Julie nor spoken with her since she'd been chased and threatened by the Raiders. As a result, following Carmen's testimony he would be putting Francisco Zapata on the stand. True to his word, Frankie the Barber had flown in from Puerto Rico over the weekend, and Jaywalker now arranged to meet both Carmen and him at the courthouse at noon, to go over their testimony one last time.

After them, of course, would be Jeremy. And it was only fitting that he should be the trial's final witness. In a very real sense, all those who preceded him on the stand—the grieving father, the three eyewitnesses, the police officers, the crime-scene detective and the medical examiner, and even the defense's own witnesses—were nothing but a preface to the main act. The case wasn't about Victor Quinones or his father, or Teresa Morales or Regina Fortune or Seymour Kaplan. No, it was about Jeremy, about his falling in love, paying a terrible price for having done so, and finally fighting back. Tomorrow afternoon his mother and his barber would set the stage for him. And then, most likely Thursday morning, the jurors would hear what this case was really about.

They would hear Jeremy's story.

17

THE PROBLEM AND THE ACCIDENT

As things turned out on Wednesday, Judge Wexler's calendar spilled over into the afternoon session, and it was after three o'clock before the trial resumed. Jaywalker regarded the delay as a minor blessing. For one thing, it gave him an additional hour to make sure that Carmen and Frankie the Barber were fully prepared to testify. Not that that they wouldn't have been without it; he'd already spent hours with each of them. But there was prepared, and then there was Jaywalker prepared.

Beyond that, the delay made it all but certain that Jeremy wouldn't be taking the stand until Thursday morning. That was good for several reasons. It would give Jaywalker an opportunity to reconcile Jeremy's version of the facts with anything unexpected his mother or Frankie might say. And it would mean that in all likelihood Jeremy's testimony would begin and end on a single day, rather than being broken up and spread out over two days. Not only would that enhance his story, at the same time it would deprive Katherine Darcy of the luxury of an overnight between Jaywalker's direct examination and her cross.

It was little things like that, Jaywalker knew, that could affect the outcome of a close case. What worried him right now, however, were those last three words: *a close case*. Because as prepared as his witnesses were, not one of them was going to be able to tell the jury much of anything about the fatal shot. Carmen and Frankie because they hadn't been there, and Jeremy because even though he *had* been and didn't dispute the fact that he'd fired it, it seemed he had no real recollection of doing so.

Carmen Estrada didn't so much walk to the witness stand as waddle. She promised to tell the truth, the whole truth, and nothing but the truth in a voice so low and gravelly that Jaywalker abandoned the lectern in favor of standing back by the wooden rail that separated the front of the courtroom from the spectator section. Years of experience had taught him that the farther he stood from the witness, the more that witness would be forced to raise his or her voice. If that didn't work, he'd try cupping a hand behind one ear, in an exaggerated parody of deafness. And if all else failed, he'd badger and bully his witness into speaking more loudly. That last technique usually did the trick and often created an extra measure of sympathy for the poor witness.

Little things.

JAYWALKER: Do you know the defendant, Jeremy Estrada?

CARMEN: Sure, I know him. He's my son.

Jaywalker took her back two years. She'd been living on the Upper East Side with Jeremy and his twin sister, Julie, their father having left some ten years earlier. That May, Jeremy had been seventeen. He'd been attending Catholic school at All Hallows High. But Carmen had reached a point where she could no longer afford the tuition, so

Jeremy had transferred to public school and was by that time attending Park East, on 105th Street between Second and Third Avenues.

JAYWALKER: In addition to going to school, was Jeremy doing anything else?

CARMEN: Yes, sure. After school and on weekends he was working.

JAYWALKER: Where was he working?

CARMEN: At a bodega, and a dry-cleaning store, and later a hardware store. Lots of places.

JAYWALKER: Did something happen, some change with respect to Jeremy, that May or June, that you became aware of?

CARMEN: Yeah.

JAYWALKER: Tell us about it, please.

CARMEN: Well, before he was normal, regular. You know, like any other seventeen-year-old boy.

JAYWALKER: And then?

CARMEN: After a while he became very nervous-like. I see him walking back and forth in the house, looking out the window through the venetian blinds. He stop eating, stop talking. I ask him what happen to him. He say, "Nothing." He don't want to tell me.

JAYWALKER: Anything else you remember?

CARMEN: Sometime he be shaking or crying in the nighttime, while he's sleeping. I try to wake him up. I say, "What happen, what's the matter?" And he say, "Nothing, nothing." Finally, one day in June, a letter had arrived from school.

JAYWALKER: Did you open the letter?

CARMEN: Yes.

JAYWALKER: What did it say?

CARMEN: That he was absent from school.

JAYWALKER: After you read the letter, did you do anything?

CARMEN: Yeah, sure. I spoke with Jeremy.

JAYWALKER: And what did he say?

CARMEN: In the beginning, he don't want to say anything. But I make him tell me what the problem is. He say he's afraid to go to school because they follow him and threat him.

JAYWALKER: They?

CARMEN: These guys. This gang.

JAYWALKER: What did you say?

CARMEN: I say, "We gotta go to the police." He say
no, he was scared for his life. A gang was
following him, and they was going to
kill him.

Carmen described how she'd pulled Jeremy out of school
at that point. By that time it was too late to put him in
another school, so he'd just stopped going. Her son's life,
she said, was more important than anything they could teach
him at school.

Jaywalker tried to draw Carmen out as to the changes
she'd noticed in Jeremy, but despite all his hours of preparation, she used conclusive words when descriptive ones
would have been more compelling. He was "panic," she
recalled, "nervous," "hysteric." But she did manage to say
that he'd lost one job after another because he was scared
he was being followed.

Jaywalker moved to the very end of August and the day
of the barbershop incident.

JAYWALKER: Do you know a man by the name of
Francisco Zapata?

CARMEN: That's Frankie, the man from the barbershop.

JAYWALKER: Did there come a time when something happened just before Labor Day, involving Frankie?

CARMEN: Yeah.

JAYWALKER: Tell us what you remember.

CARMEN: I was in my kitchen cooking when they knocked on the door. It was about six-o'clock. When I opened the door I get scared. I see my son all white, like pale.

JAYWALKER: Was anyone with him?

CARMEN: The girl, Miranda. And Frankie from the barbershop.

JAYWALKER: How was Jeremy acting?

CARMEN: He was very nervous. He can't even talk. He was panic, crying. I asked him what happened, he can't answer me. The man, Frankie, he told me to keep him home, don't let him go downstairs.

JAYWALKER: Did Frankie say why?

CARMEN: No. But I could tell it must have been very, very bad.

It was time to bring Carmen to the day of the shooting.

JAYWALKER: Do you remember a day about five or six days later, in the very begin-

ning of September? Do you remember something happening then?

CARMEN: You mean the accident?

There it was again: the *accident*. Jaywalker had warned
her at least a dozen times not to use the term. He realized
now she simply couldn't help herself, that she would go to
her grave thinking of it as just that.

JAYWALKER: The shooting. Tell us the first thing
you remember about that day.

CARMEN: I remember when Jeremy came home.

JAYWALKER: Was he alone, or was he with someone else?

CARMEN: He was with the girl, Miranda.

JAYWALKER: What did you see when they came
in?

CARMEN: I see Jeremy very, very nervous, walking
back and forth. He can't talk. There was
blood on his face, his mouth. And his
shirt was all like burn, with like a little
hole in it. And under it, right under it, his
skin was red.

She found a spot on her own midsection, and began
rubbing it. Even as she answered the next few questions, re-

calling that Jeremy had been so nervous he couldn't talk, she continued to massage her belly.

It had finally fallen to Miranda to describe what had happened.

JAYWALKER: After that conversation, did you do something with Jeremy?

CARMEN: Yeah. I took him and Miranda out of the apartment.

JAYWALKER: Why did you do that?

CARMEN: Because when he could talk again, he told me he was too scared to stay there.

JAYWALKER: Did he say who he was scared of?

CARMEN: Yeah. He told me that the gang, the gang was going to kill him.

JAYWALKER: Where did you take him?

CARMEN: I took them to the Bronx.

JAYWALKER: What was in the Bronx?

CARMEN: My sister.

JAYWALKER: Did Jeremy stay in the Bronx for a long time?

CARMEN: No, just one night.

JAYWALKER: Where did he go from there?

CARMEN: I send him to Puerto Rico.

Jaywalker paused. He figured seven months was certainly worth a pause.

JAYWALKER: Did there come a time when Jeremy
came back to New York?

CARMEN: Yes.

JAYWALKER: Did you and he go somewhere then?

CARMEN: Yes.

JAYWALKER: Where did you go?

CARMEN: To a lawyer.

JAYWALKER: And did you and the lawyer and
Jeremy do something?

CARMEN: Yeah.

JAYWALKER: What did you do?

CARMEN: We took him to the police.

JAYWALKER: And did Jeremy give himself up?

CARMEN: Yeah.

Jaywalker thanked Carmen and sat down. Despite hours of preparation, she'd earned no better than a C in his book.

Her nervousness had caused her to leave out most of the details she'd been able to recall at the office, her home, and even in the courthouse as recently as an hour before she'd taken the stand. And whose fault was that? Jaywalker's, of course. Because Carmen was his witness, he'd been barred from asking her leading questions in which he could have suggested the answers to her, such as "Did Jeremy suffer from nightmares?" Nor could he have asked her to repeat conversations she'd had with Miranda; those would have been hearsay. Still, he knew, when a witness underperformed, as Jeremy's mother had, it was rarely the fault of the witness and almost always that of the examiner. Whatever shortcomings Carmen had, it had been Jaywalker's job to identify them and overcome them. In failing to do so, he'd failed her and, more importantly, Jeremy.

And that had only been on direct. With cross-examination about to begin, Jaywalker shuddered at the thought of Carmen trying to answer questions she was even less prepared for. And it didn't take long for his fears to be realized.

Katherine Darcy began by getting Carmen to concede that she herself had never been a witness to anyone following her son, chasing him or threatening him. That she'd never seen a weapon of any sort either displayed or mimicked. And that she'd never encountered a gang member, and knew nothing about the Oakland Raiders or the jackets their fans wore. Then she asked about Jeremy's attendance record at All Hallows High School, before he'd ever met Miranda. It had been very good back then, Carmen assured him.

But Darcy had done her homework. She'd subpoenaed records from All Hallows, and now she handed them to the witness.

CARMEN: I don't have my glasses.

DARCY: Do you have them in the courthouse?

CARMEN: No.

THE COURT: Here, try mine. They're reading glasses, magnifiers.

CARMEN: Thank you. *[Puts on glasses.]* No, these are no good. I don't see this. I got, what you call it, a stigmatoid.

THE COURT: And you never thought to bring your reading glasses with you?

CARMEN: I thought I was going to have to talk, not read.

She did have a point there.

Darcy moved on, evidently figuring she'd have a crack at Jeremy on the subject of his attendance, once he took the stand. And perhaps unconsciously, Jeremy took that moment to take off his glasses and slip them into his shirt pocket.

Darcy wanted to know about Miranda's current whereabouts. Jaywalker had long anticipated her interest in the matter. If she could show that Carmen knew where Miranda was, she could suggest that the defense had deliberately decided against calling her as a witness, and might even succeed in getting the judge to give a *missing witness charge,* an instruction to the jury that they could infer that Miranda's testimony would not have supported the rest of the defense's case.

DARCY: When was the last time you saw her?

CARMEN: Miranda?

DARCY: Yes.

CARMEN: Last time I saw her was exactly the day
        I brought her to Mr. Jackwalker's office.

DARCY: A few months ago?

CARMEN: Yeah. She disappear after that.

Darcy moved on to Carmen's contacts with the police while Jeremy had been in Puerto Rico. The detectives' reports strongly suggested that she'd withheld her son's whereabouts from them, and Jaywalker had told her it was absolutely essential that she admit she'd lied to them.

DARCY: Did the police come visit you shortly after
        the shooting?

CARMEN: Yes.

DARCY: Did they ask you where Jeremy was?

CARMEN: Yes.

DARCY: Did you tell them you didn't know where
        he was?

CARMEN: Yeah. I lied to the police.

For once, Carmen came through perfectly.

DARCY: Did you tell them you'd try to find out
where Jeremy was, and let them know?

CARMEN: Yeah. That was a lie. I lied to the police.
I did.

Apparently she was determined to admit it every chance
she got.

DARCY: In fact, you knew at the time that he was in
Puerto Rico. Didn't you?

CARMEN: Of course I know. I send him to Puerto
Rico because he told me his life is in
danger because of the gang, the same
gang.

DARCY: And because the police were looking for
him, right?

CARMEN: No, not right. He wasn't scared of the
police. He was scared of the guys from
the gang. They said he go to jail, they
was going to kill him in jail.

Darcy asked her about the last job Jeremy had held, at a
hardware store. Jaywalker noticed that again she was
working from a document in her hand.

DARCY: Isn't it a fact that your son only worked
there for two weeks?

CARMEN: Yes. He stopped working there.

DARCY: He was fired. Isn't that correct?

CARMEN: They fired him because he had to stop going. Because the guys, they followed him there.

Katherine Darcy gave up at that point. Carmen Estrada had proved to be a difficult witness for both sides. If anything, Jaywalker felt she'd helped her son more on cross-examination than on direct. Still, he needed to clarify one point.

JAYWALKER: Miss Darcy asked you when it was that you brought Miranda to my office.

CARMEN: Yes.

JAYWALKER: How many times did that happen?

CARMEN: Just one time.

JAYWALKER: Do you remember exactly when that one time was?

Of course she didn't. But Jaywalker had brought his last year's calendar book with him. It was the kind of thing you did when you were driven to prepare for every conceivable contingency. He asked permission to approach the witness, intending to show her the entry he'd made of the meeting, in order to refresh her recollection of the date. Then he remembered that without her glasses, Carmen wouldn't be able to see it. He caught himself halfway to the witness stand, pivoted and showed the book instead to Katherine

Darcy, who agreed to stipulate that the meeting had taken place on January 26th.

Four months ago.

JAYWALKER: Have you seen Miranda since that day?

CARMEN: No.

JAYWALKER: Spoken with her?

CARMEN: No.

JAYWALKER: Do you know where she is?

CARMEN: No.

He thanked her and sat down.

Later that afternoon, when they would break for the day, Carmen would come up to Jaywalker and ask him how she'd done. The truth was, she'd made up some ground on cross-examination and then redirect, to offset her disappointing performance on direct. To Jaywalker, she'd ended up as an okay witness. The problem was, Jeremy didn't need okay witnesses; he needed nothing less than *dynamite* witnesses.

"You were terrific," he would tell her, just as he would have had she been unable to remember her son's name on the stand, or her own. What was he supposed to say, that because of her testimony Jeremy was more likely than ever to go to prison?

Jaywalker called Francisco Zapata to the stand. Zapata was a good-looking man in his mid-fifties, with a thick head of black hair turning gray at the temples. A full mustache failed to hide his ready smile. Jaywalker had spent far less time with him than he had with Carmen, and only a small fraction of the many hours he'd devoted to preparing Jeremy. Still, there was something about the man that inspired confidence and prompted Jaywalker to feel the jurors would not only like him but would believe what he had to say. It had been Zapata, after all, who'd stood up to the Raiders that day outside his barbershop, with nothing but his words and his wits.

JAYWALKER: Mr. Zapata, where do you live?

ZAPATA: I live in Baldaria, Puerto Rico.

JAYWALKER: What are you doing here in New York?

ZAPATA: I'm here because you asked me to come, to describe some things that happened a while ago.

JAYWALKER: Who paid for your trip?

ZAPATA: Me. I paid for it.

JAYWALKER: Do you work?

ZAPATA: Yes, I cut hair. I am a barber.

Jaywalker took him back to the end of August, nearly two years ago. Zapata had been living in Queens at the time, and working at a barbershop in Manhattan, at 112th Street, between Second and Third Avenue.

JAYWALKER: What was the name of that barbershop?

ZAPATA: Frankie and Friends.

JAYWALKER: And who was Frankie?

ZAPATA: Me. I'm Frankie.

Jaywalker walked over to the defense table, where
Jeremy sat. Standing behind him, he placed his hands on his
client's shoulders.

JAYWALKER: Do you know this young man here?

ZAPATA: Yes. He was a customer of mine. I used to
cut his hair, ever since he was a small boy.

JAYWALKER: What do you call him?

ZAPATA: I call him Jerry.

JAYWALKER: Do you know his last name?

ZAPATA: No, I'm afraid I don't. Sorry.

Jaywalker directed Frankie's attention back to the very
last day of that August, and asked him if he remembered an
incident that had occurred at his shop. He replied that he did.
Jerry had come in around five o'clock in the afternoon, and
asked if he could wait there for his girlfriend.

JAYWALKER: And what did you say?

ZAPATA: I teased him at first. I still thought of him
              as a boy, and here he was telling me he had
              a girlfriend. But then I told him sure, he
              could wait there.

JAYWALKER: What happened next?

ZAPATA: When the girlfriend came, Jerry opened
              the door for her, and she came in. He said,
              "Close the door!" because some guys be-
              hind her wanted to come in and get him.

JAYWALKER: Who were these guys?

ZAPATA: I don't know their names, but I had seen
              them hanging around on the street all the
              time. I'm pretty sure they were drug deal-
              ers.

DARCY: Objection. Move to strike.

THE COURT: Yes. The last part of the answer, what
                  the witness thought, is stricken. The
                  jury will disregard it.

Although the admonition was meant for the jurors, it was
Jaywalker whom Wexler glared at while delivering it. Both
men knew full well that despite the judge's words, disre-
garding the suggestion that the Raiders were drug dealers
was impossible. In fact, when Frankie had mentioned it to
him months ago, down in Puerto Rico, Jaywalker had explained that the judge probably wouldn't let him ask about
it. "Then again," Jaywalker had said at the time, "if you
happen to say it without my asking you..." And Frankie, as

quick a study as Carmen was a slow one, had picked it up, tucked it away, and now come out with it at the perfect moment.

Once the witness was off the stand and the jury excused, Harold Wexler would castigate Jaywalker, accusing him of planting the objectionable testimony. Jaywalker would deny it, naturally, and there would be little the judge could do beyond issue a stern warning. But stern warnings scared Jaywalker about the same way that sharp cliffs scared mountain goats. The jury had heard that the Raiders were drug dealers; there was simply nothing Wexler could do to unring that bell. And in Jaywalker's book, that was precisely as it should be. Sometimes the rules of evidence worked just fine. But occasionally you had to fine-tune them on the fly.

JAYWALKER: Did the guys come inside?

ZAPATA: No. I locked the door. But they kept shouting through the window and threatening Jerry.

JAYWALKER: What did you see?

His answer was to point his index finger to his temple, his thumb pointed upward. Jaywalker described the demonstration for the record. Then he asked the witness if he'd been able to hear any of the things the guys had shouted.

ZAPATA: They were saying they were going to get him, to kill him. They were saying bad things, using bad language, in English and in Spanish. Very bad.

JAYWALKER: Please tell us exactly what they said.

ZAPATA: They called him a son of a bitch.

JAYWALKER: Was that the worst?

Frankie smiled nervously and looked down at his feet. Just two hours earlier, he'd told Jaywalker much worse. But now he was clearly too embarrassed to repeat the words in open court.

JAYWALKER: Would your honor direct the witness to answer.

THE COURT: Yes. Use the actual language you heard.

Frankie leaned over to the court reporter and repeated the words. But the courtroom had grown stone-cold quiet, and despite his whispering, no one could have missed his answer.

ZAPATA: They called him *maricon*. That's how we say faggot in Spanish. They called him pussy and...

JAYWALKER: And?

ZAPATA: And cunt-face.

JAYWALKER: How many of them were there?

ZAPATA: Six or seven. I'm not sure.

JAYWALKER: How old did they look?

ZAPATA: A few years older than Jerry. Nineteen, twenty. Something like that.

JAYWALKER: Were they all guys?

ZAPATA: There was one girl.

Frankie described how finally he'd gone outside, shutting the door behind him, and tried to talk to them. They'd quieted down after a minute or two and assured the barber they had no problem with him. "But we're going to get him," they'd said, pointing.

JAYWALKER: Who did they point at?

ZAPATA: At Jerry.

JAYWALKER: Did there come a time when they left?

ZAPATA: Finally. I had a van parked around the corner. I went and got it, and pulled in front of the shop. I put Jerry and his girlfriend in my van, and I took them to his house.

JAYWALKER: How did Jerry seem on the way to his house?

ZAPATA: He was very, very nervous, shaking. His face was white. His eyes, he was like he wanted to cry. But I guess he was ashamed to cry in front of his girlfriend.

THE COURT: The part about what the witness

> guesses is stricken. The jury will
> disregard it.

JAYWALKER: Mr. Zapata, you can only tell us what
             you saw, what you heard and what
             you did. Okay?

ZAPATA: Okay. Sorry.

The remark hadn't been for the witness, of course. It had
been for the contempt citation, in case Harold Wexler were
to decide that Jaywalker had planted that little nugget of objectionable testimony, too. Although that one Wexler would
forget.

JAYWALKER: When you got to Jerry's building,
             did you leave him and his girlfriend
             downstairs?

ZAPATA: No, I was too scared for Jerry. I took them
          upstairs, and I told his mother to keep him
          there in the house, not let him go out.

Katherine Darcy spent only a few minutes cross-
examining Zapata. Jaywalker sensed that she knew his
testimony had been truthful, and that probing for incon-
sistencies or more detail could only get her into trouble. Or
perhaps she was trying to take a page from Jaywalker's
playbook and send a message to the jurors that Zapata really
hadn't hurt her case.

DARCY: Did you see any guns that day?

ZAPATA: Real guns?

DARCY: Yes, real guns.

ZAPATA: No.

DARCY: Any knives?

ZAPATA: No.

DARCY: Did the shop have a large storefront window?

ZAPATA: Not so large.

DARCY: Did they break it?

ZAPATA: No.

DARCY: Did they try?

ZAPATA: No.

DARCY: When you went outside to talk to them, did they harm you?

ZAPATA: No.

DARCY: And they left, didn't they?

ZAPATA: Not right away.

DARCY: But after a few minutes?

ZAPATA: Yes. After a few minutes, they left.

Francisco Zapata stepped down from the stand, and Judge Wexler excused the jury for the day. The following morning, Frankie the Barber would board a plane and fly back to Puerto Rico. Although he'd been able to testify to less than an hour of Jeremy Estrada's torment, Jaywalker felt that Zapata's had been a powerful presence at the trial. The simple fact was that he'd traveled some fifteen hundred miles at his own expense in order to answer questions about an incident that had taken place some twenty months earlier, involving a young man whose last name he didn't even know. To Jaywalker, that said an awful lot about Frankie right there. Perhaps, to the jurors, it might say something about Jeremy, too.

After sitting through his warning from Judge Wexler, Jaywalker retreated to the pens to spend one last hour preparing Jeremy for his testimony the following day. Had this been a court-appointed case, Jaywalker would have been expected to keep track of his time and how he'd spent it. But even in those situations, he'd ended up seriously under-reporting when it had come time to enter a number alongside *Trial Preparation*. While most of his colleagues padded their hours, some flagrantly, Jaywalker had known better than to submit an honest accounting of the sessions he'd devoted to readying his witnesses. How, for example, could he submit a voucher asserting that he'd spent over a hundred hours with Jeremy alone, when he knew lawyers who routinely put their clients on the stand after interviewing them for forty-five minutes? So he always ended up cutting his hours by more than half, fully expecting trial judges to do the same again before signing off on them.

The unreimbursed hours? He'd tended to think of them as taxes withheld by the government, and he liked to think he'd compensated for the lost income by cheating on his

1040 Form as much as he possibly could. But even if he hadn't, he still would have gone into the pens to spend one last hour getting his client ready. He told himself it was for Jeremy, because of how much he liked the kid and what a raw deal life had given him. But that was only part of the story, of course. The rest was that he was Jaywalker, and being Jaywalker, he simply couldn't help himself.

18

THE WITNESS IN THE HALLWAY

Thursday.

Jeremy's day.

Jaywalker had characteristically slept little. To him, the day had long loomed as no less nerve-wracking than a summation day or an argument before the Court of Appeals in Albany. Perhaps Jeremy's case was unwinnable, one of those one-in-ten trials that no matter what he were to do, an outright acquittal would remain forever out of reach. But Jaywalker wasn't ready to admit that. Not yet, anyway. What he did understand, what was absolutely clear, was that for them to win it, Jeremy would have to come off as a near-perfect witness. He would have to be able to describe his first—and perhaps last—encounter with love in a way that would make the jurors ache with memories of their own. He would have to be willing to go into the painful details of his torment at the hands of the Raiders, and describe the effects that torment had had on his body and his psyche. And he would somehow have to convince twelve strangers that in shooting another young man between the eyes from a distance of no more than five inches, he'd acted not as an executioner but as a blinded man trying to save his own life.

And all the while, he would have to make those jurors like him—indeed, love him—enough to want to forgive him and set him free.

It was a tall order, made even taller by Jeremy's lifelong shyness and natural reticence to talk about himself, by his limited education and intellect, and by a lot of extremely inconvenient facts. Still, Jaywalker felt that if ever he himself would be prepared to tackle the challenge, it was now. He could only hope that Jeremy was ready, too.

But as ready as he was, Jaywalker was about to discover that the vagaries that invariably accompany a trial had one of their surprises in store for him that morning. The messenger in this particular instance wore a court officer's blue uniform and approached Jaywalker just seconds before the jurors were about to enter the courtroom.

"You've got a witness waiting for you," the officer told him. "Out in the hallway."

And since Jeremy was his only remaining witness, Jaywalker's knee-jerk reaction was that his client had somehow managed to escape or post bail. But there *was* no bail; Jeremy had been held in remand status since his surrender a year ago, and not even Jaywalker had deluded himself into thinking some judge might set bail. And if his client had escaped, why wasn't the court officer out in the hallway himself, trying to wrestle Jeremy to the floor and handcuff him?

The bewildered expression on Jaywalker's face was enough to prompt a bit of information from the officer. "It's a young woman," he said. "Pretty. Eighteen, nineteen."

Miranda.

This could be disastrous, Jaywalker realized. Here he'd taken pains to make sure she was nowhere around, knowing that the statement she'd written out for the detectives hurt Jeremy far more than her testimony could possibly help him. And now she'd shown up on her own? What was he supposed to do? Put her on the stand at Jeremy's peril? Turn her over to the prosecution? Or accept a missing witness charge that her testimony would have conflicted with the rest of his case's? Whichever one of those three doors he chose to open promised nothing but disaster.

He got Judge Wexler's permission to step outside for a moment and fell in behind the court officer, who led Jaywalker up the aisle, pushed against the courtroom door and held it open for him. As Jaywalker stepped out into the hallway, he was still trying to figure out what he would say to Miranda. Could he tell her to get lost, to dart into the nearest stairwell and disappear? Would the court officer give him up, or support his claim that by the time they got out there, Miranda was nowhere to be found?

Which actually seemed to be the case.

Because as he looked all around him, Jaywalker saw absolutely no sign of her. Not her auburn hair, not her almost-too-thin body, not her arresting brown eyes.

"I'm here," she said, standing right in front of him, so close he almost jumped.

Once, as a young boy, Jaywalker—back then Harrison J. Walker—had sneaked out to the kitchen late one night to raid the refrigerator. But even before he'd opened it, he'd noticed a generous dollop of chocolate sauce on the countertop. He'd gleefully scooped it up with his index finger and deposited it onto the tip of his tongue, savoring its forbidden richness. And the truth was that for a second or two, it really had tasted like chocolate. Then his senses had registered the fact that it wasn't. It had actually been thick grease that had dripped from the electric meter directly above the counter.

It was that way now. So convinced had Jaywalker been that he would encounter Miranda in the hallway, that even as he stood in front of the young woman, his mind continued to compel him to believe that she'd not only dyed her hair blonde, but had put on fifteen or twenty pounds, as well, and somehow changed the color of her eyes from brown to blue-gray. And had she not spoken her name aloud at that point, he no doubt would have persisted in trying to reconcile the discrepancies between how he remembered her and how she looked today, just four months later.

"Julie," she said.

But it didn't register.

"Julie," she repeated, before adding, "Jeremy's sister?" Her voice rising on the last word, the way teenagers can turn a simple declarative statement into a question.

"Julie!" Jaywalker half shouted, loudly enough to turn heads in the hallway. "You're supposed to be hiding out in, in—"

"The Bronx."

"Right," said Jaywalker, before realizing that some of the turning heads might be attached to the jurors back in the courtroom. Dropping his voice to a whisper, he herded her into the nearest stairwell and closed the door behind them. "What are you doing here?" he asked.

"I'm going to testify," she said.

"What?"

Not a incredulous "What?" as in "What, are you crazy?" More like the "What?" of a middle-aged man with mediocre hearing, two descriptives that actually fit Jaywalker pretty well. But it wasn't just that. The truth was, he'd been so busy looking around for surveillance cameras that he'd allowed his attention to wander, and if he'd heard Julie's answer, it hadn't quite registered.

So she repeated it.

"I'm going to testify," she said, looking Jaywalker squarely in the eye.

"But your mother—"

"I don't care about my mother," she said. "Jeremy is my twin brother. I'll spend the rest of my life blaming myself if I hide out somewhere and they find him guilty. I can't do that."

Jaywalker thought about it for a moment, but only a moment. Had he himself had a twin brother or sister facing a murder charge, he would no doubt have spoken pretty much the same words as Julie had, and he wouldn't have let anyone talk him out of it. Still, Carmen was Jeremy and Julie's mother. She'd hired Jaywalker, at least after a fashion, and was paying his fee, slowly if not so surely. Over a year's time, she'd given him a little over two thousand dollars. If she were to continue making payments at that rate—a statistical rarity, given that, win or lose, the end of a trial almost always brought with it the end of payments— she would have the balance paid off sometime around 2025.

But none of that mattered.

It wasn't Carmen's case any more than it was Jaywalker's. It was Jeremy's case. Julie was nineteen, old enough to vote and enlist and get married without her mother's permission. If she wanted to testify, it was going to be her decision, hers and her brother's.

Jaywalker had her wait in the stairwell while he headed back into the courtroom to deal with a confused client, an impatient judge and a mother he at least owed an explanation. Then again, what could she do about it? Threaten to cut off his fee payments a few days early? Stop bringing him lunch, please God?

In the end, she did neither of those things, and Jaywalker thought he even detected a bit of motherly pride over her daughter's decision. As for Jeremy, he was willing, if Jaywalker thought it might help. And Harold Wexler displayed both his generosity and its limits by granting Jaywalker ten minutes to prepare what would now be his next-to-last witness.

It would be enough.

JAYWALKER: The defense calls Julie Estrada.

The jurors watched intently as she made her way forward to the witness stand. If she wasn't quite as pretty as Jeremy was handsome, she was still good to look at, with the same surprising blond hair and blue-gray eyes as her brother. And there was a hint of defiance in the way she walked and held herself, a hint that Jaywalker hoped wasn't lost on the jurors, or misread by them.

JAYWALKER: Are you related to the defendant?

JULIE: Yes. He's my brother.

JAYWALKER: Are you older than he is, or younger?

JULIE: I'm older, by about five minutes.

Jaywalker's peripheral vision picked up a handful of smiles and nods in the jury box. This was going to work, he told himself. *It better,* came the response.

He had Julie describe the brother she'd once had, back before the summer of Miranda and the Raiders. Jeremy had been almost perfect, she recalled. He'd never been the smartest kid at school. He was, well, a little slow, according to his teachers. And he was shy. But he was polite and considerate, and he worked to bring home money to help his mother. And he was always fun to be around.

JAYWALKER: Anything else?

JULIE: *[Inaudible.]*

JAYWALKER: I'm sorry. I didn't hear that.

JULIE: Nothing.

JAYWALKER: What was it you said?

JULIE: I said, "I want him back."

As the tears ran down her face, she made no attempt to hide them. And Jaywalker, who knew how to be a gentleman and where they kept the tissues for just such moments, didn't go to her rescue. Instead, he moved forward into June and July, and asked her if she'd begun to observe a different Jeremy.

JULIE: Yes, very different.

JAYWALKER: In what ways?

JULIE: He started seeming afraid of everything all the time. He thought he was being followed. He couldn't sleep. He stopped eating. He'd move the food around on his plate, but he wouldn't eat it. He jumped at loud noises. He couldn't look me in the eye anymore. He began to stutter, and he developed these funny movements in the muscles of his face, uh—

JAYWALKER: Tics?

JULIE: Yes, tics.

JAYWALKER: As the weeks went on, did he seem
to get better, or worse?

JULIE: Worse, much worse.

JAYWALKER: How so?

JULIE: He lost weight. He got these dark circles
around his eyes. He would cry for no reason,
or at least no reason he would talk about.
And he, he—

JAYWALKER: What?

JULIE: He began…he began to wet his bed. He
didn't think we knew, my mother and I. And
we pretended we didn't. But we did, we
knew.

Jaywalker let that one hang there for a few beats. He tried
to imagine something more devastating to a seventeen-year-
old boy than regressing into bed-wetting. The only thing he
could come up with was having his mother and twin sister
aware of it. And as Jaywalker opened his mouth to ask his
next question, he heard a muffled sound behind him. When
he turned to look, he saw that Jeremy had slumped forward
and laid his head on the defense table. For a horrified
second, Jaywalker thought the young man might have
passed out or, worse yet, fallen asleep. But then the heaving
of Jeremy's shoulders gave him away, and Jaywalker could
tell he was sobbing. And he realized that until that moment,
the poor kid had thought he'd gotten away with stripping

the wet sheets off, secretly washing and drying them, and then remaking his bed before nightfall. Even as Jaywalker winced at having added yet another layer of humiliation to his own client's anguish, he caught himself wondering if the jurors had understood what had just happened, and found himself hoping they had.

Judge Wexler declared a brief recess.

Jaywalker had fully intended to ask Julie about how she'd been chased and threatened by a group of the Raiders five or six days ago. He knew he would be on shaky ground, because technically, that incident had no relevance to the murder charge against her brother. But if he could get it in, it at least showed that there had been, and still was, a bunch of thugs who went around wearing Oakland Raiders jackets and intimidating people.

But Julie's testimony, and her brother's reaction to it, had created a powerful moment right before the recess, a moment in which the depth of Jeremy's suffering had been revealed in full measure. Jaywalker had no desire to water that down now with a new line of questions that had more to do with Julie than with Jeremy. He also secretly hoped that Katherine Darcy, in cross-examining Julie, would blunder into opening the door to the recent incident. So when they resumed and the jury was brought back in, with the witness once again on the stand, Jaywalker rose and announced he had no further questions of her.

Which, he knew, created a dilemma for Darcy.

He watched her closely now as she stood and walked slowly to the lectern, saw from her hesitation that she recognized immediately the trap Jaywalker had set for her. And as she began her examination, he grudgingly gave her credit for not falling into it, as much as he would have liked her to. Still, he wondered if at some point she might not get careless.

DARCY: You are the defendant's sister, aren't you?

JULIE: Yes.

DARCY: His twin sister, in fact.

JULIE: Yes.

DARCY: Is it fair to say you love your brother?

JULIE: Yes.

DARCY: Very much?

JULIE: Yes.

DARCY: If he were in serious trouble, would you help him out if you could?

JULIE: Of course.

DARCY: Would you lie for him?

It was one of those questions prosecutors loved to death. If the witness were to say no, the jury would disbelieve her. What sister wouldn't lie for a brother in serious trouble? Yet if the witness were to say yes, that she would lie, then her own answer would brand her as a perjurer unworthy of belief on the rest of her testimony. In other words, for the questioner it was one of those absolutely irresistible win-win questions, and the problem for the witness was that there seemed no way out of it.

The problem for Katherine Darcy, on the other hand, was that Jaywalker knew all that stuff, too. So he always—*always*—made it a habit to prepare his witnesses for the question. However, in the ten minutes the judge had allowed him this morning, he'd neglected to remind Julie Estrada to expect it. Was there any chance she might remember his advice from weeks or months ago? He bit deeply into the inside of his cheek as he listened to Darcy repeat the question.

DARCY: Would you lie for your twin brother?

JULIE: You know, I'm pretty sure I would, if it came down to that. But so far, I haven't had to find out. Everything I've said is a hundred percent true, and even you know that.

Jaywalker had to hold on to the arms of his chair to keep from jumping to his feet and applauding. He couldn't have come up with as good an answer himself. Though evidently he had, some weeks ago.

Darcy understandably refused to quit on that note. She asked five or six more questions, but none of them, or the answers they drew, amounted to much. When finally she succeeded in scoring a tiny point by getting Julie to admit she couldn't remember the exact time frame of the bedwetting, she quit. That said, Jaywalker had to admire her for her discipline. While he'd burned her on the lying-for-your-twin-brother business, Darcy had continued to steer clear of the even more dangerous territory Jaywalker had hoped she would stumble into. All she would have had to do was ask Julie the same innocuous question she'd put to

Carmen—whether she herself had ever witnessed anyone in a Raiders jacket chasing Jeremy—and Julie could have answered, "No, but they chased *me* last week!" And even if Harold Wexler had let only the first word of the answer stand, Jaywalker's Jewish half would have smiled and said *Dayenu.*

It would have been enough.

"Call your next witness," said the judge.

Jaywalker stood, let a second or two click off the clock, and said, "The defense calls Jeremy Estrada."

19

JEREMY'S STORY

Even though the jurors had known for a full week that Jeremy would be taking the stand, every one of them locked eyes on the young man as he rose from his seat and began making his way toward the witness stand. There are few moments in a trial that rival the drama that accompanies the announcement that the defendant is about to testify. The delivering of the verdict, certainly, and perhaps the summations of the lawyers. But short of those events, which in this case wouldn't take place until the following week, Jeremy Estrada taking his place in the witness box was unquestionably the high point of the trial.

From an early age, we're conditioned to resolve disputes by hearing from both sides. Try to visualize a scene in which a mother hears a crash coming from the kitchen. Upon investigating, she finds the cookie jar in a hundred pieces on the floor, her two young sons standing equidistant from its remains.

"Did you do that?" she asks one of them.

"No," he says. "Not me."

Turning to the other one, she asks, "Did you?"

Son number two decides to invoke his privilege against

self-incrimination, and says nothing. Though only four, he's read up on constitutional law and knows that his silence may not be used against him.

So who broke the cookie jar?

If you say the second boy, the one who refused to deny it, you're being nothing more nor less than human. We've grown to expect that someone accused of a transgression will either admit his guilt or deny it, and that—and here's the interesting part—*for some reason we think that simply by listening to him we'll be able to judge whether or not he's telling the truth.*

So Jeremy taking the stand in his own defense promised to be a defining moment for the jurors, most likely *the* defining moment. They would listen to him as he tried to explain away the evidence that had built up against him over the past five days, and from his answers they would know whether to walk him out the door or ship him off to state prison for the next twenty-five years or more of his life.

Telling the truth or lying.

Guilty or not guilty.

Black or white.

They could forget about reasonable doubt, ignore which side had the burden of proof, and stop looking for shades of gray. By putting the defendant on the stand, Jaywalker was making it easy for them. Once they heard from Jeremy, they would *know*.

Jaywalker, too, knew that was what they were thinking, of course. But long ago, perhaps as long ago as he'd set eyes on Jeremy and heard him say that when he'd shot Victor Quinones he'd been defending himself, he'd known it was a strategy he was going to have to adopt. Carmen hadn't been there at the fight and the shooting. Frankie the Barber had come all the way from Puerto Rico on his own dime, but he hadn't been there, either. Nor had Julie, with all her unexpected eloquence. Miranda had been there, but by writing out a statement for the detectives, she'd poisoned herself as a witness.

Which left only Jeremy.

So for better or worse, it would be left to him to tell his story, and it would indeed come down to how persuasively he could and would tell it. And now, as he placed one hand on a Bible, raised the other and swore to tell the truth, the whole truth and nothing but the truth, Jaywalker held his breath and prayed for the best. The hundreds of hours of prying Jeremy's story from him were a thing of the past. The mock examinations and cross-examinations were history. Even Jaywalker's last piece of advice delivered an hour ago would be forgotten. "Details," he'd told Jeremy. "We need details. And relax. You can't hurt yourself up there. You can only help yourself." It was a lie, of course. But to Jaywalker it was no worse a lie than a doctor prescribing a placebo for his patient and saying, "Take one of these for your headaches, but only one, because they're extra-strength."

Jaywalker started off gently with Jeremy, asking him short, easy questions that wouldn't require any real thought on his part. He wanted to give him a chance to warm up, to get his voice going, to get a feel for the process. He established that Jeremy was nineteen now, but had been barely seventeen two years ago; that he'd been living with his mother and twin sister; and that he'd recently transferred to a new high school, Park East, at 105th Street, which he walked to and from.

JAYWALKER: How were you doing in school?

JEREMY: Not so good.

JAYWALKER: Why is that?

JEREMY: I have a learning disability. I'm not good with numbers or writing. Also comprehension. School was actually pretty hard for me.

JAYWALKER: Did you hear Ms. Darcy asking your mother yesterday about your attendance?

JEREMY: Yes, sir.

JAYWALKER: And is it true that at times your attendance was poor?

JEREMY: Yes.

JAYWALKER: Even before that May?

JEREMY: Yes.

JAYWALKER: In addition to going to school, were you doing anything else?

JEREMY: Yes, I was working.

JAYWALKER: How old were you when you first started working?

JEREMY: I'd just turned fourteen.

Jaywalker had Jeremy describe the jobs he'd held up to that time. He'd worked part-time after school and full-time each summer. The jobs had been in the neighborhood, and he'd been paid in cash, off the books.

The preliminaries having been dispensed with, it was time to introduce the jurors to Miranda.

> JAYWALKER: Did there come a time that May, Jeremy, when you met somebody?

> JEREMY: Yes, I met this young lady.

> JAYWALKER: Tell us how that happened.

> JEREMY: Well, as I was walking to school one morning along Third Avenue, I passed this flower shop. And I saw her right inside. And even though neither of us said anything, we, like, made eye contact, you know?

> JAYWALKER: What did she look like?

> JEREMY: She was very, very beautiful.

The day Miranda had been at Jaywalker's office, he'd thought to take several photographs of her. He wasn't quite sure why at the time, had even suspected himself of wanting to keep them, so striking-looking she was. Now he drew the best of them from a file, had it marked for identification and handed it Jeremy.

> JAYWALKER: Do you recognize the person in this photograph?

For a split second all Jeremy could do was stare at it. Jaywalker hadn't shown it to him before this moment, hadn't told him he was going to. Sometimes, he felt, you got the best stuff out of your clients by surprising them. Finally Jeremy managed to pry his eyes away from the image and look up. But when he tried to speak, his voice failed him, and he looked as though he was about to cry. But then, Jeremy had these pale blue-gray eyes and often looked like he was close to tears.

JEREMY: Yes. That's her.

JAYWALKER: Did there come a time when you actually met her?

JEREMY: Yes. It took me a few days, but finally I get up the courage to go inside the shop. I pretend I'm looking to buy some flowers. And someone comes up behind me and says, "Can I help you?" And I turn around and I see her. So I start blushing, I guess, 'cause I'm nervous, kind of like I am now. She asks me if I want some flowers, and I go, "Yes, for my little niece. She's having a birthday party." And she says, "Am I invited?" So I say, "Sure."

Jaywalker sneaked a look at the jurors, saw they were enthralled. It was as if Jeremy's embarrassment at telling the story was providing them with a lens through which they could share his nervousness two years ago.

JAYWALKER: What happened next?

JEREMY: We talked for a minute. I introduced

myself. I said, "My name is Jeremy." And she said, "Pleased to meet you. I'm Miranda."

Jeremy had arranged to meet her at the shop at six o'clock, when she would be getting off from work. Then he'd turned to leave, only to have Miranda stop him and remind him that he'd forgotten to buy flowers for the party. But Jeremy hadn't had enough money to pay for them, and had been forced to confess that there was no party after all. "I just said it to meet you," he'd admitted. And she'd told him he hadn't needed to lie to her and should never do it again. But, she'd said, she would still meet him.

So Jeremy had picked her up after work. He described how they'd gone for ice cream, walked around and talked. And in the weeks that had followed, they'd seen each other often. They'd done everyday things, going for pizza or to McDonald's, or for ice cream. There was a little park where they'd sit and talk. Or they'd walk east to the river and look out across the water, watching the boats go by.

Jaywalker paused briefly before asking his next question. Having woven the spell of the young couple falling in love for the very first time, the moment had come to move on, to break that spell.

JAYWALKER: Did all go well in your relationship with Miranda, or did it not go well?

JEREMY: It went well up to a point.

JAYWALKER: And what happened at that point?

JEREMY: I noticed this guy who always seemed to be hanging around Miranda.

JAYWALKER: Can you describe him for us?

JEREMY: He was kinda dark-skinned. Muscular. And to me he seemed very mean-looking.

JAYWALKER: Did you ever learn his name?

JEREMY: Yes, Miranda told me. She said his name was Sandro.

JAYWALKER: What else did she say about him?

JEREMY: That he always wanted to go out with her, but that she didn't want to have anything to do with him or his friends.

According to Jeremy, Sandro was always surrounded by a gang of six or eight guys who looked to be in their late teens or early twenties. None of them seemed to work or go to school. Several of them sported crude, hand-done tattoos, and a few had "gold decorations" on their front teeth. And even though it was late spring and hot on the avenue, a couple of them still wore black leather jackets with "pictures of stuff" on them.

JAYWALKER: What kind of stuff?

JEREMY: They were Oakland Raiders jackets, and they had the face of a man on them, with crossed swords behind it. And the man has like a patch over one eye. It looks kind of like the face you'd see on a pirate flag. It's meant to be scary, I think.

JAYWALKER: What would happen when you'd see Sandro and his gang?

DARCY: Objection to the word "gang."

JAYWALKER: It's the word the witness himself—

THE COURT: Overruled. The witness did use the term. That said, it will be up to the jurors to determine whether it was a gang or not, should they feel the need to resolve the issue.

JAYWALKER: Could we have the question read back, please?

He listened as the court reporter began to reread the question from her stenotype machine. He wanted the jurors to hear the word *gang* again, but this time from a different, neutral voice that would serve to put an official-sounding imprimatur on it. A little thing? Sure. But Jaywalker deemed it crucial that by the time the jurors began their deliberations, whenever they'd think of Sandro and his group, the word *gang* would reflexively come to their minds. There was a world of difference, after all, between being harassed by a young man and his friends, and being harassed by a gang. And to Jaywalker's way of thinking, if you took enough little things just like that and added them all up, they could take a conviction and transform it into an acquittal.

REPORTER: Question: "What would happen when you would see Sandro and his gang?"

JEREMY: I'd be walking along, and Sandro would
say, "There go that white boy, that—"

JAYWALKER: Who were they referring to?

JEREMY: Me.

JAYWALKER: Did they call you names?

JEREMY: Yeah, you know.

JAYWALKER: No, we don't know. You have to tell
us.

JEREMY: Punk. Cocksucker. *Maricon*. Mother-
fucker. Stuff like that.

JAYWALKER: What does *maricon* mean?

JEREMY: It's like, "You fucking fag."

Jaywalker had him describe some of the things the gang
had done. Jeremy described hand motions imitating guns
being fired and knives being drawn across throats. He'd
been told to "get the fuck out of here," to "get lost if you
know what's good for you." And he'd been chased, often at
full speed.

JAYWALKER: Did this pattern continue for a period
of time?

JEREMY: Yes.

JAYWALKER: As it continued, what was your reaction? What were some of the things
you experienced?

This would be the hard part for Jeremy. Talking about Miranda had been easy. Even talking about what the gang had done or threatened to do had been manageable. But as Jaywalker moved from those areas into the subject of Jeremy's reactions, he found himself holding his breath between each question he posed and Jeremy's answer. Because this was the stuff that he'd had such difficulty over so many months prying loose. And despite all the hours lawyer and client had devoted to the process, as he waited for each response, Jaywalker had no real idea what to expect. Would Jeremy recite in riveting detail what he'd gone through that summer, or would he instinctively bend forward and go into a crouch, in order to protect himself from yet more humiliation?

JEREMY: I tried to keep going on like normal, but it was hard. I'd keep getting like paranoid, you know.

JAYWALKER: Tell us what happened to you physically.

JEREMY: I would cry all of a sudden, for like no reason. I had trouble eating. And when I did eat, sometimes I'd vomit, or get diarrhea. I lost weight. I had trouble sleeping. I—I—I—

JAYWALKER: What would happen when you did sleep?

JEREMY: I'd be getting nightmares, and wetting the bed sometimes.

Jaywalker asked about school attendance, and Jeremy admitted it had gotten even worse than before, because he'd grown afraid to walk down Third Avenue. As a result, he began getting "cut slips," warning him that he was in danger of failing his classes.

JAYWALKER: Did there come a time when your mother confronted you about your attendance?

JEREMY: Yes.

JAYWALKER: What happened?

JEREMY: She got a letter in the mail.

JAYWALKER: What happened as a result of that letter and that confrontation with your mother?

JEREMY: I told her everything, and she pulled me out of school.

JAYWALKER: Did you continue to work?

JEREMY: For a while.

JAYWALKER: And then what?

JEREMY: I got fired.

JAYWALKER: Why?

JEREMY: 'Cause I stopped going to work.

JAYWALKER: Why did you stop going to work?

JEREMY: 'Cause they'd follow me to my jobs and
          come inside and make trouble. Or follow
          me home. One time I had to hide in the
          bushes in front of my building 'cause they
          wouldn't leave.

JAYWALKER: What happened?

JEREMY: After an hour or so I urinated in my pants.
          And then after another hour or so I—I—
          I—

And as much as Jaywalker would have liked to rescue
the young man, to have spared him from continuing with
his answer, he stood there silently, listening to the stutter-
ing, watching the tears flow, waiting for the rest of it.

JEREMY: *[Continuing]* I couldn't hold it any longer.
          I—I defecated in my pants.

As much as the jurors, raised on a steady diet of politi-
cal debates and in-depth interviews, might have grown accustomed to that great American institution, the Follow-up
Question, Jaywalker sensed that this was one time when
none was required. If wetting one's bed had represented the
ultimate in shame for a seventeen-year-old boy, soiling
one's pants had to have been in the next universe of humiliation. And describing it in front of a roomful of strangers
would only have multiplied the agony.

So far, Jeremy had done what he'd had to do.

Jaywalker glanced at the clock and saw it was a few
minutes before one. Catching Harold Wexler's eye, he

raised his eyebrows ever so slightly, just enough to signal that he'd reached a good stopping point. The judge nodded, then recessed for lunch.

As the jury filed out, a friendly court officer sidled over to Jaywalker and offered the opinion that perhaps it hadn't been the most appetizing note on which to send the jury off for lunch.

"Good," said Jaywalker. "I want them to gag on it. I want them to choke on every last bite."

Even Carmen backed off without argument when Jaywalker looked down at her latest grease-stained, paper-bagged offering, thanked her, but assured her and Julie that he wouldn't be having lunch on this particular day. Then, once he'd made sure the last of the jurors was out of the courtroom, he reached past Carmen, grabbed Julie and hugged her tightly. "You were terrific," he told her. "And you be careful."

"Don't jew worry," said Carmen. "She be with me."

When they resumed that afternoon, Jaywalker lost no time in reintroducing the jurors to someone whose name they'd barely heard mentioned for nearly two days.

JAYWALKER: All right. Up until this time, it was Sandro who was the main person who was bothering you. Is that correct?

JEREMY: Yes.

JAYWALKER: Did there come a time in August when somebody else began bothering you?

JEREMY: Yes.

JAYWALKER: At the time, did you know the name
            of this other person?

JEREMY: No.

JAYWALKER: Have you since learned his name?

JEREMY: Yes, Victor. Victor Quinones.

JAYWALKER: Did you ever learn where Victor
            Quinones had been during the
            months of May, June and July?

Katherine Darcy rose to object, but for once Jeremy was
uncharacteristically quick with his response. His "In prison"
beat her "Objection, calls for hearsay" by a full second—
precisely as Jaywalker had coached him. And the judge's
"Sustained, disregard the answer" was pretty much beside
the point.

Jaywalker had Jeremy describe his first encounter with
Victor. Jeremy had been in the flower shop with Miranda,
and a few of the gang members had spotted him from
outside. One of them, a newcomer, had made a move to
come inside, but his girlfriend had stopped him.

JAYWALKER: Was his girlfriend the same young
            lady who testified earlier this week?

JEREMY: Yes, she was.

JAYWALKER: Do you now know her name to be
            Teresa Morales?

JEREMY: Yes.

Jeremy described several subsequent incidents in which Victor had played an increasingly central role. These included chasing Jeremy, spitting on him, and twice threatening him with a straight razor. And he seemed to have gradually taken over from Sandro in the name-calling department, as well.

JAYWALKER: What were some of the names he called you?

JEREMY: Cunt. Pussy. Pussy ass. You smell like pussy.

JAYWALKER: What did you do on these occasions?

JEREMY: Nothing.

Although the room was quiet, his voice could barely be heard.

JAYWALKER: How did you feel?

JEREMY: Like dirt. Ashamed. Embarrassed.

THE COURT: Angry?

Here was Harold Wexler, stepping in not only to break the flow of Jaywalker's examination, but to suggest that perhaps the shooting had been motivated by something other than self-defense. And while Jaywalker was tempted to object to the interruption, he knew better. For one thing, Wexler had what it took to get even: a black robe. More to the point, Jaywalker had known for months that this moment would come, in some fashion or another, and he'd warned Jeremy to expect it and not be intimidated.

JEREMY: Angry?

THE COURT: Yes, angry. Didn't all this make you feel terribly angry?

JEREMY: I honestly don't remember feeling angry. I do remember feeling scared, terrified. Paranoid.

JAYWALKER: When you say you felt paranoid, what do you mean by that?

JEREMY: I was always looking back to see if I was being followed. Or looking out the window to see if they were waiting for me downstairs.

JAYWALKER: And were you being followed?

JEREMY: Sometimes, yes.

JAYWALKER: And were they waiting for you downstairs?

JEREMY: Yes.

JAYWALKER: All the time?

JEREMY: A lot of the time.

It was time to move on. Not because Jeremy had folded under Harold Wexler's questioning—he hadn't—but because Jaywalker didn't want to run the risk of overdoing things and desensitizing the jurors to Jeremy's plight.

JAYWALKER: Where did you used to get your hair cut, Jeremy?

JEREMY: At Frankie's. At 112th Street, off Third Avenue.

JAYWALKER: Is Frankie the witness who testified yesterday?

JEREMY: Yes.

Jeremy described the barbershop incident as he recalled it. It pretty much dovetailed with Francisco Zapata's account. But where the group of tormenters had been anonymous to the barber, Jeremy was able to supply names. Sandro had been there, and Victor, as well as Shorty and Diego and three or four others. And the young lady Frankie had mentioned was Victor's girlfriend, Teresa Morales.

Following the barbershop incident, it had been six full days before Jeremy had dared to venture out of his apartment again. Jaywalker made a point of having Jeremy recite the two dates and calculate the exact number of days between them. Not only did it show just how terrified the boy had been, it meant—if Jeremy was to be believed—that he'd had no opportunity to go out and get hold of a gun.

JAYWALKER: Why was it, Jeremy, that having been afraid to go out for six days, you eventually did go out again?

JEREMY: Well, Miranda called my house to say she'd be going to the Labor Day carnival with her little sister and her cousin. And I thought at the carnival there'd be a whole bunch of people, and I'd be safe.

>   And I was tired of staying upstairs, you
>   know? I wanted to get out. I just thought
>   it would be okay.

And for a while, it had been. Jeremy had met Miranda and the girls right where'd they'd arranged. They'd gone on the Ferris wheel, played games, eaten popcorn and cotton candy. And for a little while the events of the summer had receded and Jeremy had even dared to believe that they might have been nothing but a long bad dream.

Until Victor had appeared.

They'd talked about fighting, Jeremy recalled, about having it out right there. Jeremy had surprised himself by saying he was willing. It had been Victor who'd said no. He'd said Jeremy was lucky that Teresa and Miranda and the little girls were there, that he didn't want to embarrass him in front of all of them.

JAYWALKER: What happened next?

JEREMY: He sucker punched me.

JAYWALKER: What's a sucker punch?

JEREMY: It's when somebody catches you off
          guard.

JAYWALKER: And does what?

JEREMY: Hits you out of nowhere.

JAYWALKER: Where did Victor hit you?

JEREMY: Alongside my right eye *[indicating]*.

JAYWALKER: What did he hit you with?

JEREMY: His fist.

JAYWALKER: What happened?

JEREMY: He caught me good. I went down to my knees. I think I stayed down a couple of seconds.

JAYWALKER: What happened next?

JEREMY: I got up and ran after him.

He'd chased Victor and Teresa up Third Avenue. Miranda had sent the girls home and followed Jeremy. At 113th Street, Jeremy had finally caught up with Victor.

JAYWALKER: Were you that fast, or was Victor that slow?

JEREMY: He didn't run that fast. It seemed like he wanted me to catch up to him.

JAYWALKER: What happened when you did?

JEREMY: He turned and said, "You want some more of that?" And we started fighting, right there.

JAYWALKER: What kind of fight was it?

JEREMY: It was a regular fistfight.

JAYWALKER: Do you remember what you were wearing?

JEREMY: Jeans, a shirt. Sneakers. It was hot.

JAYWALKER: You heard one of the witnesses from last week testify that you were wearing two or three pairs of socks. Was that true?

JEREMY: No. I hardly ever wear socks in the summer. If I'm going to wear them, I'm going to wear one pair.

JAYWALKER: Do you recall if you were wearing socks that day?

JEREMY: I honestly don't.

JAYWALKER: Did you have a gun in your waistband?

JEREMY: No.

JAYWALKER: In your socks?

JEREMY: No.

JAYWALKER: In an ankle holster?

JEREMY: No.

JAYWALKER: Anywhere?

JEREMY: No, absolutely not.

He had Jeremy describe the fight, how they'd traded punches until Victor had called a time-out to rest and take off his sweatshirt. Jeremy demonstrated pulling something over his own head. He remembered that underneath, Victor still had a long T-shirt on.

JAYWALKER: What did you do while Victor was pulling his sweatshirt up over his head to take it off?

JEREMY: I waited for him.

JAYWALKER: And what did you do after that?

JEREMY: We started fighting again.

Jeremy described how he'd hit Victor a couple of times, hard enough to hurt his own fist. He thought his punches had landed in the area of Victor's eyes and mouth. Jeremy himself had been hit on his lip and nose.

JAYWALKER: Who won the fight, Jeremy, if you can tell us?

JEREMY: I did.

JAYWALKER: What makes you say that?

JEREMY: He was more bruised up than I was.

JAYWALKER: How did the fight end?

JEREMY: He put his hands up, like this.

And Jeremy raised both his hands to shoulder height, palms facing forward, fingers slightly spread. Victor had surrendered.

Jeremy had just stood there at that point, bent over slightly with his hands on his knees, trying to catch his breath. He'd noticed blood, his own blood, dripping to the pavement from his mouth or nose, or both.

JAYWALKER: What happened next?

JEREMY: I heard a scream.

JAYWALKER: What did you do?

JEREMY: I looked up, and I saw Victor pulling out
              a gun.

JAYWALKER: Where was he pulling it from?

JEREMY: From his—from right here.

He pointed to his midsection, just above his waistband and slightly off to one side.

JAYWALKER: What did you do?

JEREMY: For a second, nothing. Then I charged
              him.

Jaywalker asked how far apart the two of them had been when Jeremy had first seen the gun. Jeremy pointed to the portion of the jury box closest to him, a distance of maybe eight or ten feet.

JAYWALKER: What happened?

JEREMY: I got to him before he could fire it, and we started wrestling over it. I was trying to stop him from pointing it at me. And he was trying to bring it up high, toward my body.

He stood up and demonstrated by clasping both hands against his chest.

JAYWALKER: Then what happened?

JEREMY: The gun went off, real loud. And I thought he shot me.

JAYWALKER: Why did you think that?

JEREMY: The bang was so loud, and as soon as it happened I felt a burning sensation right here, in my stomach *[pointing]*.

JAYWALKER: What happened next?

JEREMY: I thought I was falling down, but it was him, Victor, who was leaning to one side like.

JAYWALKER: And as he was doing that, what, if anything, did you do?

JEREMY: I grabbed the gun away from him, got my finger on the trigger, and I fired.

JAYWALKER: How many shots did you fire?

JEREMY: I don't know. I just kept pulling the trigger and hearing bangs.

JAYWALKER: Who was firing the gun?

JEREMY: I was. Me.

JAYWALKER: Did any of the bullets you fired hit Victor?

JEREMY: Yes.

JAYWALKER: How do you know?

JEREMY: Because he's dead.

Jaywalker let the last answer echo in the courtroom for just a second or two. So far, Jeremy had done as well as Jaywalker could have hoped for. But *so far* had been the easy part. Now came the hard part.

JAYWALKER: Jeremy, you've sat in this courtroom for a week now. And you've heard people take the same witness stand as you, and say that at some point after the first shot or shots, Victor ran quite a distance and fell. And that you ran after him and shot him one last time. Did you hear them say that?

JEREMY: I heard them say that.

JAYWALKER: Is that what happened?

JEREMY: I don't know. I can only tell you what I remember, and I don't remember anything like that. To me, it all happened fast, and it all happened at once. The first shot goes off. I think I'm shot. Victor leans away. I grab the gun, point it at him and start firing. So maybe those other people are right. But honestly, I don't remember it happening that way. I just remember shooting at him until he was on the ground and not moving anymore.

JAYWALKER: And then?

JEREMY: And then I must have stopped. And I looked and saw this gun in my hand. And I remember feeling like I was in a dream. And Miranda and me, we began walking away.

JAYWALKER: Did you walk, or did you run?

JEREMY: I tried to run, but I couldn't.

JAYWALKER: Why not?

JEREMY: I don't know. It felt like my legs wouldn't work right.

They'd walked uptown, Jeremy still holding the gun in his hand. At some point Miranda had told him to put it away. He'd tried to put it in his waistband, but it was too heavy and started slipping down his jeans. So he'd thrown it into the sewer. Then they'd kept walking to Jeremy's building.

JAYWALKER: Did you stay at home that night?

JEREMY: No.

JAYWALKER: Where did you stay?

JEREMY: Up in the Bronx.

JAYWALKER: And did you continue to stay in the Bronx?

JEREMY: No. I just stayed there that one night.

JAYWALKER: Where did you go from there?

JEREMY: To Puerto Rico.

JAYWALKER: Why did you go to Puerto Rico?

JEREMY: I was scared they were going to kill me.

JAYWALKER: Who?

JEREMY: Sandro and them.

Jaywalker established that Jeremy had spent seven months in Puerto Rico and could have stayed there indefinitely, but instead had returned to New York in late April.

JAYWALKER: What did you do when you got back?

JEREMY: I told my mother I was going to go to the
police and give myself up.

JAYWALKER: And did you in fact do that?

JEREMY: Yes, I did.

Jaywalker asked him when he had last seen Miranda. He
replied that it had been half a year ago, when she'd come
out to Rikers Island to visit him one time. Since that day,
he hadn't seen her or heard from her. Nor did he know
where she was now.

And finally…

JAYWALKER: Jeremy, you say you killed Victor
Quinones.

JEREMY: Yes, I did.

JAYWALKER: Can you tell us why you killed him?

JEREMY: I can only tell you what was in my mind
at the time.

JAYWALKER: And what was that?

JEREMY: In my mind, I was trying to save my life.

It had been a long and emotional direct examination, and
Judge Wexler granted Katherine Darcy a recess before requiring her to begin her cross.

To Jaywalker's way of thinking, Jeremy had come through with flying colors, far exceeding expectations. And it had been powerful stuff, which had to have moved the jurors. But direct examination often turns out to be the easy part, where sufficient preparation is almost guaranteed to pay dividends. Even Jeremy's final series of responses had been all but rehearsed, right down to the "in my mind," a phrase that, come summation time, Jaywalker would argue were the three most important words of the entire trial.

Cross-examination was different. On cross, instead of being a friendly teammate, the examiner was suddenly a hostile opponent. And the questions, far from being softballs lobbed over the middle of the plate, are fastballs, curves and nasty sliders aimed at the corners. But Jaywalker knew that, and he'd literally spent dozens of hours playing the role of prosecutor, trying to anticipate every conceivable pitch Darcy might try to throw at Jeremy. So the problem wouldn't be the unexpected question; Jaywalker had seen to that. The problem would be that there simply was no best answer to Dr. Seymour Kaplan's conclusion that the fatal shot between the eyes had been fired from a distance of no more than five inches, or to Detective Regina Fortune's assertion that Jeremy must have chased Victor Quinones some forty-five feet before delivering that shot. Those were facts that weren't going to go away, no matter how thorough Jaywalker's preparation had been, or how well Jeremy were to testify.

After the recess, Katherine Darcy showed just how smart she was. Instead of working chronologically, as Jaywalker had on direct, beginning with school and jobs and first meeting Miranda, Darcy moved right in for the kill.

DARCY: Mr. Estrada, did I hear you say you killed Victor Quinones in order to save your life?

JEREMY: That's how it felt to me at the time.

DARCY: How many guns did Victor have?

JEREMY: One.

DARCY: When you shot him between the eyes, who had the gun?

JEREMY: I did.

DARCY: What was Victor doing at that point?

JEREMY: I'm not sure. Falling, I think.

DARCY: Falling on you, or falling away from you?

JEREMY: Falling down. Sort of away from me, I guess.

DARCY: You hadn't been shot, had you?

JEREMY: I thought I had.

DARCY: But the truth is, you hadn't been. Isn't that right?

JEREMY: Yes.

Not the best answer.

And whenever that happened, Jaywalker blamed himself for having failed to anticipate the question. Better by far would have been, "The truth is, I thought I had been shot. Today, a year and half later, I know I wasn't." And then let Darcy wrestle with that one. But it was too late now. Not that Jaywalker wouldn't lose an hour of sleep over it that night, kicking himself for having let Jeremy—and himself—down.

Darcy backed up and spent a few minutes questioning Jeremy about his shoddy school attendance even before he'd met Miranda. She asked him about his marijuana conviction, which he readily admitted. Taking Harold Wexler's cue, she next tried to get Jeremy to admit that the taunts of Sandro and his friends had made him angry. But Jeremy refused to take the bait. He'd been scared, humiliated, even felt paranoid at times. But he didn't remember feeling anger.

DARCY: How about when Victor sucker punched you in the face? That made you angry, didn't it?

JEREMY: Yes, that did.

DARCY: So you chased him, right?

JEREMY: After I got up, yes.

DARCY: Weren't you afraid he might have some kind of a weapon? A knife, a razor or something like that?

JEREMY: I don't remember thinking about that.

DARCY: You weren't afraid?

JEREMY: I don't remember being afraid at that time.

DARCY: In fact, you had a very good reason not to be afraid. Didn't you?

JEREMY: *[No response.]*

DARCY: And that good reason was that you had your gun. You had a loaded gun, didn't you?

JEREMY: No, not at that point.

DARCY: Oh, right. You say Victor had it first. So when was the first time you saw it?

JEREMY: After the fight, right after somebody screamed. I looked up and I saw it in Victor's hand.

DARCY: Did you run away?

JEREMY: No.

DARCY: Why not?

JEREMY: I'm not sure. I guess 'cause I was too close to him to run. If I'd turned and tried to run, he would have shot me in the back. Or maybe shot Miranda. I don't know.

Darcy tried to pin Jeremy down about the number of times he'd fired, but he said he was unsure. He didn't know if he'd emptied the gun or not, or how many rounds it held. And he claimed to have absolutely no recollection of having chased Victor some forty-five feet while holding the gun in his hand.

Jaywalker bit his lip, knowing the worst was about to come. But knowing also that there was nothing he could do about it.

DARCY: Did you hear Detective Fortune say it was forty-five feet from where the fight was to where Victor was found?

JEREMY: Yes.

DARCY: And did you hear Dr. Kaplan say there's no way Victor could have walked or run those forty-five feet after being shot in the head?

JEREMY: Yes.

DARCY: So how do you explain how Victor got there, unless the true answer is that you chased him and shot him there?

JEREMY: I—I can't explain it.

DARCY: Do you think Detective Fortune was lying about the forty-five feet, or Dr. Kaplan was lying about Victor's not having been able to run after he'd been shot in the head?

Jaywalker could have objected, not only because it was two questions in one, but because it called for an opinion as to other witnesses' testimony. But he decided to let it go.

They'd been over this part a lot, the two of them, and he was pretty sure Jeremy could handle it.

JEREMY: I'm not saying they're lying. I'm just saying I honestly don't remember chasing him once I had the gun. I only remember getting it away from him and shooting at him until he was on the ground.

DARCY: How about holding the gun no more than four or five inches from him while you shot him between the eyes? Are you telling us you don't remember that, either?

JEREMY: I know we were close. I don't know exactly how close.

DARCY: How about Victor's begging for his life right before you shot him between the eyes? Remember that?

JEREMY: No. No, I don't.

DARCY: Or picking him up a little bit off the ground before shooting him between the eyes and letting him fall back down on the pavement? Remember that?

JEREMY: No.

DARCY: Could those things have happened?

JEREMY: I guess they could have. They must have. But I honestly don't remember them.

DARCY: How about your being the one who had the gun in the first place? Could that have happened, too?

JEREMY: No, that didn't happen. I'd know that.

DARCY: Yet you heard Magdalena Lopez say it happened, didn't you?

JEREMY: Yes.

DARCY: And you heard Wallace Porter say it happened, didn't you?

JEREMY: Yes.

DARCY: And you heard Teresa Morales say it happened, didn't you?

JEREMY: Yes.

DARCY: And she was standing right there, wasn't she?

JEREMY: Yes.

It was devastating stuff.

Jaywalker spent ten minutes on redirect, trying to rehabilitate Jeremy as best as he could. But he knew he wasn't fooling anybody, not even himself. With Katherine Darcy's last line of questions, the entire momentum of the trial had abruptly shifted. During direct examination and even up to a point on cross, the case had been up for grabs and the jury might even have been leaning to the defense's side. Then Darcy had systematically pointed out that in order for Jeremy's claim to be believed—that he'd still been trying to save his life when he'd fired the final shot—the jurors were going to have to flatly reject the testimony of a detective, an impartial medical examiner, and not one, but all three of the prosecution's eyewitnesses.

That was asking an awful lot of them.

Once Jeremy made his way back to the defense table, Jaywalker rose and announced that the defense was resting. Katherine Darcy stated that the prosecution was resting, too, though she referred to her side as "the People," as prosecutors love to do.

The next day was Friday, and not wanting to give the case to the jury with a weekend coming up, the judge excused the jurors until first thing Monday morning, when they would hear the lawyers' summations. "The court officers," he told them, "will explain what procedures you'll need to follow." Meaning: bring a toothbrush and a change of clothes, because you won't be going home Monday night unless you've reached a verdict.

The lawyers, on the other hand, would be due back in the morning, in order to meet with the judge and go over the instructions he'd be including in his charge to the jury.

"Do you want your client here tomorrow?" the judge asked Jaywalker, once the jurors had left the courtroom. "For the charge conference?"

Jaywalker put the question to Jeremy, who opted not to be woken up at three o'clock in the morning just to be brought over from Rikers Island for an hour of legal wrangling. A friendly court officer then allowed him to sit across the railing from his mother and then his sister for a few minutes, before leading him back into the pens.

"So how does it look, Mr. Jailworker?"

"I don't know," he told Carmen as they waited for an elevator.

"They still want to give him so much time?"

"Yup."

"Jew gotta get him less," said Carmen. "After all, it was only a accident."

20

THE LOST WEEKEND

Heading to Judge Wexler's courtroom the following morning for the charge conference, Jaywalker ran into his old client Johnny Cantalupo, who was in the building to check in with his probation officer. And because Jaywalker was characteristically a half an hour early, he stopped to catch up with Johnny.

"You staying out of trouble?" he asked.

"Yeah, yeah," said Johnny. "Pretty much."

"What does *pretty much* mean?"

"I missed a 'pointment," Johnny confessed. "And there was this…" His voice trailed off into an almost inaudible mumble.

"What for?" asked Jaywalker, who was actually quite fluent in mumble.

"Nuthin'. Disorderly conduct for smokin' reefer in a subway station. No biggie. Howbowchoo? You keepin' your nose clean?"

Jaywalker smiled. Johnny always seemed to get a big kick out of the fact that his lawyer got into trouble almost as often as he did.

"I've got to," said Jaywalker. "I'm on trial."

"Fronta McGillicuddy?"

"No. Wexler."

"I've hoid he's tough," said Johnny.

"You've heard right."

"What kinda case?" Johnny wanted to know.

"Murder."

"No shit?"

Jaywalker spent a few minutes describing the case. When he got to the part about the Raiders, Johnny stopped him. "Those punks? Buncha greasy spics who hang out up over on Toid Avenue?"

"Yeah," said Jaywalker. "Only this is the twenty-first century, Johnny, and we refer to them as American citizens of Latino extraction."

"I got your *Latino extraction,*" Johnny mimicked, grabbing his crotch for emphasis. "Buncha losers, is what they are."

"You want to hear about the case or not?"

Johnny nodded, and managed to listen without interrupting again while Jaywalker finished telling him about the trial. But as soon as he had, Johnny jumped in with another, "No shit? Your guy popped him? Just like that?"

"Seems so," said Jaywalker, glancing down at his watch. He still had fifteen minutes to get up to the eleventh floor.

"Stupid fuck," was Johnny's appraisal of Jeremy's conduct. And when Jaywalker nodded in agreement, Johnny seemed to take that as an invitation to amplify. "I mean," he said, "those guys are nuthin' but hot air. They never woulda done nuthin' to him."

Jaywalker looked around to make sure there were no stray jurors within earshot before remembering that they'd been excused for the day. "Do me a big favor," he told Johnny. "Don't go around repeating that."

"You got it," said Johnny. "But lissen. Anythin' I can do for you, you just say the word. I owe you, man."

Jaywalker promised he'd keep that in mind, though he had a bit of difficulty imagining exactly how Johnny Cantalupo could help out Jeremy Estrada. But once again, it was one of those heartfelt offers from a client that he hated to reject outright.

The charge conference was pretty uninspiring. Judge Wexler indicated what counts he intended to submit to the jury, starting with murder, following up with first-degree manslaughter and continuing all the way down to the unauthorized discharge of an unlicensed firearm within city limits. He agreed to instruct the jurors on both justification and extreme emotional disturbance, the former as a complete defense to all charges, the latter as a partial defense to the murder count only.

"How long do you expect your summations to take?" he asked. "Ballpark."

"Less than three days," said Jaywalker, who honestly had no idea, and certainly had no intention of committing himself. He knew Wexler well enough not to put it past the judge to interrupt him after an hour and say, "You told me you were going to be forty-five minutes."

"An hour" was Katherine Darcy's estimate.

Ask people what the term *lost weekend* means to them, and anyone old enough is apt to recall an ancient black-and-white movie of the same title, in which William Holden does his level best to drink himself into oblivion. Even those too young to have seen or heard of the movie are likely to associate the expression with a protracted bout with the bottle, a phenomenon commonly referred to these days as "binge drinking."

Jaywalker's drinking days were behind him by several years, but that fact didn't prevent him from occasionally experiencing his own version of the lost weekend. Only he called his *Getting Ready to Sum Up.*

Not that he couldn't have gotten up and delivered a competent summation that same Friday morning on a moment's notice. The truth was, he could have done it six months ago, and he could have done it without benefit of notes. He knew the case so well that he could have done it in his sleep, if he'd had to, and he did precisely that on a fairly regular basis.

But there was competent, and there was Jaywalker. And being the uncompromising obsessive-compulsive that he was, that particular distinction meant that for Harrison J. Walker, the next seventy hours would become an agonizing exercise in reading, rereading and reviewing every last word of the twelve-hundred-plus pages of the trial transcript; combing every inch of the miles of handwritten notes he'd scribbled over the past two weeks; and examining and reexamining every single shred of paper the case had generated over its two-year life. And the thing was, doing all that would be merely preliminary. Only once he'd dispensed with those tasks would he turn his attention to structuring what he wanted to say and how he wanted to say it. After that he would get down to the business of refining it into language designed not just to inform and persuade the jurors, but to move them emotionally to a place where it would become all but impossible for them to find Jeremy Estrada guilty of anything. In other words, all Jaywalker was striving for was absolute, one hundred percent pure perfection. And he wouldn't quit until he got there, along the way ignoring such niceties as sleep, nourishment, sunlight, human companionship and personal hygiene. Think Ray Milland if you're old enough to, or sophomore year of college if you're not.

Either way, as one might readily imagine, the recipe was pretty much guaranteed to make for a very lost weekend indeed.

21

BUTTERFLIES

Monday.

Told to be in court by ten o'clock, Jaywalker showed up at nine-fifteen and had to be let in a side door by a sympathetic court officer, the captain in charge of the part. Although he was as ready to sum up as he would ever be, that fact provided Jaywalker with not an ounce of comfort. He found it impossible to sit, excruciating to make small talk with the court personnel. He walked out of the courtroom, visited the pay phone down the hall, the men's room, the windowsill by the elevator bank.

His old friends the butterflies were back.

Another lawyer, a good one, wandered over and was about to say something. Noticing Jaywalker's blue suit, ironed white shirt and unwillingness to make eye contact, he caught himself, mumbled, "Good luck," and walked off. Having been there himself, he could tell, just like that.

Back in the courtroom, Jaywalker forced himself to sit down at the defense table and arrange his notes, notes he would never so much as glance at once he began. Jeremy was brought in and seated next to him, and they hugged. Katherine Darcy showed up, and spectators—many of them Jaywalker groupies—began filling up the front rows of the audience section. A Jaywalker summation had come to be regarded as something of an *event* at 100 Centre Street, something not to be missed.

Without fanfare, Harold Wexler entered by a side door and took the bench. "Are you ready, counsel?" he asked.

Darcy and Jaywalker answered that they were. The butterflies added their agreement by increasing the beating of their wings to a level somewhere beyond excruciating.

"Bring in the jury," Wexler told the captain.

They entered a moment later, the twelve regular jurors and four alternates. Earlier they'd stowed their travel bags in the jury room, just in case their deliberations should go overnight, and given their lunch orders to a court officer. Despite the fact that those with young children, old parents or needy pets had had a full weekend to make arrangements, they looked worried to Jaywalker. No doubt the thought of a night in "jail" was weighing heavily on their minds. Then again, Jeremy Estrada had by that time spent something like the past three hundred and eighty nights in a real jail, and was likely to spend the next twenty-five years in state prison. Even as the judge was telling the jurors they were about to hear the lawyers' summations and explaining that summations weren't evidence, Jaywalker found himself idiotically trying to do the math, twenty-five times three hundred and sixty-five, when he became aware of a disturbance coming from the audience section of the courtroom, behind him. He turned around in time to see a court officer talking with a group of five or six young men standing in the aisle and trying to find seats.

Harold Wexler was on his feet, banging his gavel and ordering other officers to remove the jurors from the courtroom. But the officers, evidently mishearing or misunderstanding him, must have thought he meant for them to remove the young men instead. As a result, two officers rushed to join their colleague, one of them dramatically vaulting over the wooden rail that separated the front of the room from the audience section. And sixteen jurors, quite naturally, turned as one to see what was going on.

What they saw were three uniformed court officers trying their best to usher half a dozen uniformed young men out the door. Uniformed, to the extent that every one of the young men wore either a black jacket, sweatshirt or T-shirt with an identical motif. Specifically, the menacing one-eyed, crossed-sword likeness of an Oakland Raider. Nor were the young men leaving willingly, with several of them loudly and pointedly objecting that it was a public court-room and they had every right to be there. One of them added, "What? You gonna throw us out just 'cause we're Latino?"

Judge Wexler finally succeeded in getting the jury removed and the Raiders brought before him in handcuffs. He had each of them identify himself by name and nick-name, under threat of an immediate thirty-day contempt citation.

"Alesandro Comacho," said the first. "They call me Sandro."

"Esteban Izquierdo. Shorty."

"Diego Herrera. I don't got no nickname."

"Wilfredo Rivera. Me neetha."

"Jorge Santana. Just Santana."

"Who put you up to this?" Wexler demanded to know.

"Nobody put us up to nussing," said Just Santana.

"Do you know this man here?" the judge asked, pointing at Jaywalker.

"No."

"Ever seen him before?"

"No."

"Spoken to him?"

"No."

To the court clerk, Wexler said, "Get me Judge Stern-bridge." Then, turning back to the five in handcuffs, he asked them what they thought they were doing there.

"Exercisin' our constitutional right to assemblify," said Shorty. "Jus' like cops do when wunna them gets murdered. Nobody stops them from showin' up at the trial, do they?"

He actually had a point there.

"Showin' support for a fallen brotha," chimed in Sandro.

"Get them out of here," Wexler ordered the captain. "Now."

"Maricon," muttered one of the Raiders, but no one could say exactly which one.

Too bad the jurors missed that, thought Jaywalker, smiling ever so slightly, but apparently not so slightly that Wexler missed it. "Mr. Jaywalker!" boomed the judge. "If I find out you had anything to do with this, anything at all, you'll think that three-year suspension of yours was nothing but a hiccup. We'll be in recess for fifteen minutes."

And all Jaywalker could think was that somehow, in all the excitement, the butterflies had vanished. Well, that and one other thought.

Johnny Cantalupo.

22

THE LAST WORD

"It is twenty months ago," Jaywalker told the jurors once they'd reassembled in the courtroom. "September. Labor Day, in fact. You and I are waking up to a beautiful morning with temperatures promised in the low eighties. Perhaps it's a family gathering we're looking forward to this day, a picnic or a barbecue.

"Up on 115th Street, in the tiny apartment he shares with his mother and twin sister, Jeremy Estrada wakes up, too. Has it been one of those nights of little or no sleep, of vivid nightmares? Has he been up with stomach cramps or diarrhea? Is it one of those mornings when he has to take his sheets, roll them into a ball and hide them in the bottom of his closet because he's wet his bed and doesn't want his mother and sister to know? Even though you and I now understand that they did know, and were just too kind to let on."

The image of Jeremy and his urine-drenched sheets blindsided Jaywalker for a moment, just as, during his opening statement a week and a half ago, the first encounter between Jeremy and Miranda had blindsided him. But this time Jaywalker refused to let it stop him, and he managed to continue without interruption. Still, he could tell that the jurors hadn't missed it, could sense that they were every bit as affected by Jeremy's plight as he himself was.

He reminded them how it had been six days since the barbershop incident, six days during which Jeremy hadn't once left the apartment. And there would no doubt have been a seventh such day, and more to follow, had not Miranda called to say she was taking her little sister and niece to the carnival.

"And Jeremy? Jeremy dares to think that in the midst of the carnival there'll be safety. With all those hundreds of people, with dozens of police officers mingling with the crowd, what can possibly go wrong?

"We watch as he dresses for the warm weather. Jeans, a shirt, sneakers. There are no two or three pairs of sweat socks, no ankle holster tucked into them. To this day, Jeremy honestly can't tell us if he put on a single pair of socks or not that morning. And why *would* he remember?

"We follow him downstairs and out onto the avenue as he walks to meet Miranda and the girls. We imagine them greeting each other, smiling, holding hands. We enjoy the rides, the games, the music, the food, the aromas. And we, too, dare to think that maybe, just maybe, things will be all right today.

"We're wrong, of course. Things will not be all right this day. By nightfall, Victor Quinones will be dead, and Jeremy Estrada will be transformed from a seventeen-year-old boy to a haunted young man fleeing retaliation and facing life in prison. But like Jeremy, we don't know any of that yet."

Jaywalker paused for just a moment. Barely ten minutes into his summation, he knew already that he had them, just as he'd known the same thing during his opening statement. The case was his to win or lose, he told himself. If he did it right, if he did it absolutely perfectly, he could walk

Jeremy out of the courtroom. Never mind the fact that extreme emotional disturbance was a defense to murder but not to manslaughter. Never mind that justification ended when the threat to one's life no longer existed. Never mind Katherine Darcy's ability to show just how far Jeremy had chased Victor before taking final aim at him, or just how close he'd held the gun to him before squeezing the trigger. And never mind Harold Wexler and his guarantee of not only a conviction, but a maximum sentence. No, this wasn't Darcy's case, wasn't Wexler's case. It never had been. This wasn't even Jeremy's case anymore.

Right now, this was *Jaywalker's* case.

"Suddenly," he told them, "we see Victor. And worse yet, Victor has seen us. There's no place to hide, and it's too late to run. Victor approaches, his girlfriend Teresa in tow. There's a confrontation, a conversation and a challenge. Although Jeremy's no fighter, the thought of a fistfight somehow strikes him as acceptable. Win or lose, it holds out the promise of bringing to an end a summer's worth of torture. So he says okay, he accepts the challenge."

Jaywalker turned from the jury box, walked over to the defense table and placed his hands on Jeremy's shoulders. "This poor kid is so naive, and so stupid, that he really thinks it's going to be a fair fight. What does it cost him?" Jaywalker asked. "A sucker punch, hard enough to put him on the pavement. Right after Victor had pretended to be a gentleman and refused to fight with the girls present.

"Does Jeremy stay down? After all, he's spent the entire summer staying down. What difference could one more humiliation possibly make? But something in Jeremy says no, not this time. Something in Jeremy causes him to get back up off the pavement and give chase."

Jaywalker spent a few minutes describing how Jeremy had run after Victor, fast enough to catch up with him. He pointed out how difficult that would have been if he'd had a gun in his waistband or his socks. And if he'd had a gun, what better time would there ever be to use it than right now? "But that doesn't happen, does it? It doesn't happen for one simple reason. It doesn't happen because Jeremy doesn't have a gun."

He described the fight, dwelling on the time-out Victor called to pull his sweatshirt over his head. Again a perfect opportunity for Jeremy to have pulled a gun and shot him. "Only Jeremy doesn't have a gun," Jaywalker repeated. "Instead he waits, waits like an idiot for the fight to resume. And he *wins* the fight, Jeremy does. Victor raises his hands and surrenders. And Jeremy, still playing by the rules, stops fighting.

"Who wants to get even after a fight?" Jaywalker asked the jurors. He waited just long enough to see several understanding nods and even hear one "The loser" from the second row.

"That's right—it's the *loser* who wants to get even. Jeremy's won. He's thinking his torment may finally be over. He's shown Victor and Teresa and the rest of the Raiders that he's willing and able to take a punch and fight back. He's not a pussy after all, not a cunt-face, not a *maricon*. Finally, in his moment of triumph, his humiliation may be over.

"So who's humiliated?" Jaywalker asked, and it seemed as though sixteen mouths in front of him formed the name *Victor.* "Who's issued a challenge, fought dirty and *still* lost?" Sixteen more silent *Victor*s.

"Forget what Teresa Morales told you. She's one of *them.* She was Victor's girlfriend, for God's sake. Forget Magdalena Lopez and her ability to hear bullets whiz by her head and then turn in time to see them hit buildings. And forget Wallace Porter and his lies about not drinking beer, having heard an argument about money, having seen a gun pulled from two or three pairs of sweat socks, and everything else he said in an attempt to lower his own sentence. Forget them and use your own, everyday common sense. You win a fight, you're on top of the world. You lose, and you're humiliated. Jeremy and humiliation were no strangers. Hell, he'd spent an entire summer being humiliated. But Victor? Victor had just been beaten up in a fair fight by the pussy, the cunt-face, the *maricon*. How was he ever going to live *that* down?

"The answer is, he wasn't. So he pulled his gun.

"Jeremy reacts instinctively. Too close to turn and run, he lunges at Victor and grabs for the gun. When it goes off, the sound of the explosion and the burning sensation to his abdomen convince him he's been shot in the gut. Still, he manages to wrestle the gun away from Victor and turn it on him.

"Does Jeremy shoot Victor at that point? You bet he does, and he's never once denied it. He shoots him, and he keeps shooting him until Victor's motionless, until the nightmare's over. And he tells you that."

Now came the hard part, Jaywalker knew, the part about the forty-five feet and the no more than four or five inches. Up till now, everything had been easy. Right now was when he would win the case—or lose it.

"Much has been said about Jeremy's having chased Victor down after the first shot, and having fired the final shot at a point when Victor was defenseless. Maybe those things happened. Witnesses have said they did, or must have. Ms. Darcy will tell you that if they're right, it was an execution. Here's what I tell you—it doesn't matter.

"Not one bit.

"And here's why. In order for you to decide this case, to truly decide it, you have to stop being William Craig and

Lucille Hendricks and Gladys Leach and George Gonsalves and Miriam Goldring and Sanford Washington. You have to forget you're Lillian Koppelman and Vincent Tartaglia and Consuela Marrero and Desiree Smith-Hammond and Walter van der Kaamp and Jennifer Wang. And instead, you have to become Jeremy Estrada. Because in a very real sense, that's precisely what the law requires you to do in this case.

"Here's what you may *not* do. You may not ask yourselves what a reasonable person would have done standing in Jeremy's shoes. Nor may you ask yourselves what you yourselves would have done. Because you didn't fall in love with Miranda. You didn't spend your seventeenth summer wetting your bed and defecating in your pants. You weren't reduced to the status of a prisoner in your own apartment because you were too afraid of a gang of thugs to go outside. You didn't live with that kind of pain and panic and paranoia.

"Jeremy did."

Jaywalker turned again, this time to face his client directly. "But you know? You were mistaken about something, Jeremy. You used the wrong word when you said you felt paranoid. When you're *really* being followed, when you're *actually* being chased, we don't call that *paranoid*. We call it *terrorized*."

He told the jurors that although the shooting of Victor Quinones had played out in slow motion during the testimony, to Jeremy it had taken place in real time, and taken only seconds. All of the witnesses had described it as having happened very fast, so fast that they disagreed on something as basic as the number of shots fired. "To Jeremy," he told them, "it must have been nothing but a blur. So when he's confronted twenty months later in the sterile confines of a courtroom and asked about the forty-five feet and the precise geometry of the fatal shot, all he's able to say is that he honestly doesn't remember it happening that way. That's his truth. And that's the only truth that matters.

"You want to know how to decide this case the right way?" he asked the jurors. "Here's how you do it. You listen to Jeremy's own words. Here they are." Picking up the transcript, he found the page he'd marked with a paper clip, and read to them.

> JAYWALKER: Jeremy, you say you killed Victor
>   Quinones.
>
> JEREMY: Yes, I did.
>
> JAYWALKER: Can you tell us why you killed him?
>
> JEREMY: I can only tell you what was in my mind
>   at the time.
>
> JAYWALKER: And what was that?
>
> JEREMY: In my mind, I was trying to save my life.

"In my mind," Jaywalker repeated, *"I was trying to save my life.* Unless you can say you not only disbelieve those words, but disbelieve them *beyond all reasonable doubt*— something you cannot possibly do if you put yourselves in Jeremy's shoes—this case ends right there. Because that, jurors, is the absolute, undistilled essence of what justification is all about. *In my mind, I was trying to save my life."*

Jaywalker would have loved to stop right there, on an emotional high, but he knew he couldn't afford to. There was simply too much other stuff he had to talk about. Like whether or not Jeremy had been telling the truth or lying about Sandro, Shorty, Diego, Mousey and the rest of the gang, and the fact that they called themselves the Raiders and wore black jackets with pirate motifs. He couldn't come right out and comment on the arrival of the Raiders in court that very morning; that event wasn't in evidence. But just as some things said from the witness stand were "in the ear" even when stricken from the record, so too were some things "in the eye" even when they couldn't be mentioned. Like intent to kill, which was one of the elements, or essential ingredients, to murder. And how if Jeremy had honestly been trying to save his life, however unreasonably he may have perceived things in the moment, then intent to kill was nowhere to be found in the case. And burden of proof, which was the prosecution's, not the defense's, even on the presence or absence of justification. *Especially* on the presence or absence of justification. And despite anything that Judge Wexler might tell them to the contrary, how utterly absurd it would be for them to sit in the relaxed atmosphere of an eleventh-floor courtroom twenty months after the fact and try to draw a bright line where justification ended. And extreme emotional disturbance, which in this case presented nothing but a trap for the jurors, a convenient out by which they could find Jeremy guilty of manslaughter instead of doing the hard work of deciding whether to convict him of murder or acquit him altogether.

"Don't you *dare* do that," he told them. "Neither Katherine Darcy nor I spent four full days rejecting dozens of other prospective jurors before picking you just to have you come to the only real issue in this case and have you duck it. If you think she's proved that Jeremy wasn't justified in what he did, and proved it beyond all reasonable doubt, then tell us, tell us to our faces by convicting him of murder. But if you're left with even the slightest reasonable doubt on that issue of justification, then tell us *that*.

"How do you that? Well, it's been said that the prosecutor has the last word at trial, because she gets to sum up last. It's not like during the testimony, where there was an opportunity for redirect examination and recross. No, when it comes to summations, there's no such thing as rebuttal. Once I sit down, as I'm about to do, I'm done. Even if Ms. Darcy makes an argument to you that I have the perfect answer to, the rules simply don't allow me to make it.

"But you know something? In spite of that huge advantage, the prosecution doesn't really have the last word at all. Not even the judge does. You know who does? You do. And you get to speak that last word, each of you, shortly after Mr. Craig here, as your foreman, rises from his seat to tell us that you've found Jeremy Estrada not guilty on each and every last count of the indictment. At that point the court clerk will address each of you individually, by name. She'll ask you if that is your verdict. And you'll get to look us squarely in the eye and wipe the tears from your face, and surely Jeremy's face, and probably my face, too. And at that point you get the last word. Because that's the moment you get to say as loudly and as proudly as you possibly can the words that will echo in your memory for the rest of your life.

"Yes, that is my verdict."

And then it's over.

No "Thank you." No "I appreciate your attention." No "You've been a great jury." As he always did, Jaywalker left the pleasantries to others. Instead he simply turned from the jury box, returned to the defense table and took his seat next to Jeremy. By that time he'd been on his feet for an hour and a half, give or take a few minutes. He'd put everything he had—every ounce of sweat and every drop of blood—into that hour and a half. It wouldn't have been an understatement to say that he'd been working on it for a year.

Though never as hard as he had at three o'clock that morning, when, finally more or less satisfied with what he wanted to say—*more or less* being as good as it ever got when you were Jaywalker—he'd downed yet another pot of black coffee and forced himself to memorize the first and last names of all twelve jurors. In order.

And yet as good as he felt about what he'd said and how he'd said it, and as buoyed as he was by what he took to be the jurors' uniformly positive reactions, Jaywalker sat down not just in relief and exhaustion, but in dread. Dread that all he'd said and done might not be enough to save the young man seated beside him.

23

WATCHING THE CLOCK

Katherine Darcy stood up to speak after a fifteen-minute recess. Until then, Jaywalker had barely been aware of her presence in the courtroom, so focused had he been on his own summation. True, she'd congratulated him as soon as the jurors had filed out of the courtroom, and he'd thanked her. But it wasn't until they'd reconvened and she'd stood up to deliver her own summation that he really noticed her.

And being Jaywalker, naturally the first thing he noticed was how good she looked. If Jaywalker's rumpled hair, gray complexion and the dark circles around his eyes were testimony to how little he'd slept and eaten over the past two weeks, Darcy looked as though the trial had barely fazed her, and that summing up was something she did every day of the week.

She was wearing all black, and Jaywalker had to wonder for a moment if she was trying to send the jurors a subliminal message that, like César Quinones and his wife, she was in symbolic mourning for Victor. No, he decided, a moment later. She just happened to look good in black and must have known it, to her credit. Even if it did mean wearing a long, narrow skirt in the middle of May. Then again, the courtroom was air-conditioned to a fault, so why not?

When he was exhausted, Jaywalker tended go off on absurd mental tangents like that. And at the moment he was way beyond exhausted. So he bit the inside of his cheek, dug a bent paper clip under his thumbnail and forced himself to concentrate not on Darcy's outfit but her words.

And she was good.

Not Jaywalker good, perhaps, but that could be said for pretty much the rest of the world. Still, she was comfortable on her feet and had a nice way with the jury. And she knew the case every bit as well as Jaywalker did. But while his delivery had brimmed with emotion, hers was grounded and factual. Missing from all the talk about Jeremy and Miranda and their puppy love, she told the jurors, was any possible explanation of how Victor Quinones had ended up with a bullet between his eyes, other than that offered by three eyewitnesses who were total strangers to one another, a medical examiner who knew none of the players, and a detective who might know nothing about millimeters but surely was capable of stretching a tape measure forty-five feet.

And as soon as she'd put it that way, the same jurors who'd nodded so enthusiastically during Jaywalker's summation began doing the exact same thing during Darcy's. She didn't dispute the fact that Jeremy had been treated badly by Sandro and his friends. She acknowledged that the jurors would be less than human if they failed to feel sympathy for him. And she termed the group's conduct during the barbershop incident nothing less than despicable. But then she reminded the jurors of their oaths and obligations. "What you may *not* do," she told them, "is let your sympathy cloud your reason and your emotions eclipse your judgment."

One by one, she reviewed the testimony of each witness who'd testified at the trial, leaning heavily on the observations of the three eyewitnesses, the autopsy findings, and the forty-five feet Jeremy had chased Victor before firing the final shot but had conveniently forgotten since. "He can't admit it," Darcy suggested, "because that would be the end of the case right there. But given the evidence, he can't possibly deny it, either. So he does the only thing he can possibly do. He says he doesn't remember it that way." And as she paused to raise both eyebrows in an exaggerated expression of frank disbelief, Jaywalker felt himself slide ever so slightly lower in his chair.

Darcy did agree with Jaywalker on one point. She, too, told the jurors not to use extreme emotional disturbance to compromise on a manslaughter verdict. But where he'd asked them to acquit Jeremy altogether, she urged them to convict him of murder. "What it comes down to," she said, "is that final, fatal shot. The one fired between the eyes at point-blank range. Until then, you might be able to stretch things almost to the breaking point and argue that the defendant was justified. Bringing the gun that morning, beating up Victor, maybe—and I say *maybe*—even firing the first shot. But then he closes that forty-five-foot distance, picks Victor's head up from the pavement, places the business end of the gun within five inches or less of the bridge of Victor's nose, ignores Victor's plea for his life and pulls the trigger. That, ladies and gentlemen, is where justification ends and extreme emotional disturbance goes out the window.

"That's where it becomes, if we were to use Mr. Jaywalker's term, an execution. Personally, I reject that term and all the drama it suggests. I prefer to use the term *overkill*. Because that's exactly what we have here, the use of deadly force when any conceivable need for deadly force no longer exists. But the truth is, you can forget Mr. Jaywalker's term and you can forget mine. *Execution, overkill,* it makes no difference at all. Because the New York State Penal Law just happens to have a term of its own for it. It's the very same term you'll find in the indictment, and it's the very same term Justice Wexler will use when he instructs you on the law in a few minutes. So here it is, here's what they all choose to call it—

"Murder."

Having spoken for just under an hour, Katherine Darcy thanked the jurors and sat down. It was close to two o'clock by that time, and Judge Wexler sent the jurors back to the jury room, where their lunch orders were waiting. Then he turned to the lawyers and told them to be back in forty-five minutes for the court's charge.

The charge took the better part of an hour. Wexler began by instructing the jury on the general principles of law they were to follow, including the presumption of innocence, the burden of proof and reasonable doubt. Next he defined the various crimes charged in the indictment. "Murder," he told them, "is causing the death of another person accompanied by the intent to cause death."

Then he instructed them on the law of extreme emotional disturbance and justification. He made good on his promise to limit the defense's claim of justification as much as he possibly could. "Even if you should find that the defendant was initially justified in using deadly physical force," he told them, "the statute permits him to do so only to the extent he reasonably believes such force to be necessary to defend himself. If the evidence convinces you that at some point in the encounter he continued to use deadly physical force when he no longer believed such force was necessary to defend himself, you must find that his doing so was no longer justified, and you must find him guilty."

And then, just in case any of the jurors had missed the point, he repeated himself verbatim.

He also cautioned them not to decide the case on the basis of sympathy, whether for the defendant, the victim or their family members. "Nor," he added, looking directly at Jaywalker as he spoke, "should you let your emotions overcome your reason." In the same vein, the subject of punishment was not theirs to consider; it was for the court alone to decide. Not *possible* punishment, Jaywalker noticed. Just punishment. Their verdict was to be unanimous on each count of the indictment, either guilty or not guilty. And if they needed further instructions, wished any portion of the testimony read back to them or wanted to see any of the exhibits received in evidence, they were to communicate with the court by having their foreman, Mr. Craig, send out a written note. But in no way was that note, or anything Mr. Craig might say in the courtroom, to divulge how the jury stood in terms of any votes taken on any of the charges.

"You may now retire," he told them, "to begin your deliberations."

Jaywalker looked at the clock, saw it was 3:56 p.m. It was something he would do hundreds, if not thousands, of times over the course of the hours to follow. He knew from years of experience that with the testimony over, the evidence in and the lawyers silenced, the clock would now become a major player in how things unfolded. Whether it had completely dawned on the jurors or not, they were *sequestered,* prisoners themselves after a fashion. Jaywalker liked that fact, and whenever it was left up to him he insisted that they be locked up, just so they could get a tiny taste of what it had to be like for the defendant. But at the same time he knew that sequestration could work against him, that as the hours passed and the jurors became more and more anxious to return to their families and their lives, justice could sometimes fall victim to expedience. And expedience often showed up looking an awful lot like compromise.

He looked again. 3:58 p.m.

The first note arrived at 4:49 p.m.

The receipt of a note from the jury invariably produces a tense moment in the courtroom. In order to transmit their note to the judge, the jurors must use a buzzer to summon one of the court officers, a buzzer loud enough to be heard in the courtroom. And although the jurors are instructed to buzz once if they have a note and twice if they've reached a verdict, they've been known to mix up those directions, leading to untold numbers of anxiety attacks or worse. So while this time there'd been only a single buzz, it was more than enough to get Jaywalker's butterflies moving again.

The spectator section began filling up. Family members took their places. Jeremy was brought in from the pens and seated at the defense table. Jaywalker and Darcy took their seats. Judge Wexler entered from a side door. The court reporter nodded to indicate that she was ready. The clerk walked up to the bench and handed the note to the judge. He read it twice, once silently to himself, the second time aloud.

We, the jury, request to hear again your charge concerning intent to commit murder.

William Craig
Foreman

Short of an acquittal, it was as good as Jaywalker could have hoped for. In his summation he'd stressed Jeremy's explanation for having killed Victor Quinones, that in Jeremy's mind it had been to save his life. While that testimony, if believed, was relevant on the question of justification, it also went to the even more fundamental issue of intent. If Jeremy had never intended to cause Victor's death, that was the end of the murder charge right there.

As elated as Jaywalker felt about this development, Wexler and Darcy reacted with visible disbelief. After all, didn't the evidence establish that Jeremy had lifted Victor's head from the pavement at a point when Victor had been unarmed and helpless, before delivering the final shot between his eyes at point-blank range? If ever there'd been a classic example of intent to cause death, surely that was one. How could any jury be hung up on something so straightforward?

But hung up they were.

"Bring them in," said Wexler. Not *the jury,* not *the jurors. Them.*

A court officer could be heard banging on the door to the jury room and shouting, "Cease deliberations!" A few moments later the jurors filed into the courtroom and resumed their places in the jury box. Jaywalker looked hard for some clue from them. Several made eye contact with him, a good sign. Beyond that, it was hard to read them.

The butterflies did their thing.

"Mr. Foreman," said the clerk. "Please rise."

Mr. Craig dutifully stood.

"Will the defendant please rise."

Jaywalker and Jeremy stood up as one.

"Mr. Foreman, has the jury reached a verdict?"

And even though Jaywalker's brain knew that they hadn't, his heart pounded wildly in his chest. He could only wonder at how Jeremy and his family, who were strangers to the ritual, would deal with it. Having not expected the question in the first place, they had no way of anticipating the answer.

"No," said Mr. Craig. "We have not."

"Thank you. You may be seated."

He sat. So did Jaywalker and Jeremy.

Judge Wexler read the note aloud again, barely attempting to disguise his astonishment at the jury's question. It was at times like this, Jaywalker knew, that Wexler was at his most dangerous. Grimaces didn't show up in the transcript. Appellate judges had no way of knowing if words had been spoken declaratively or sarcastically. More than once Jaywalker had gone on the record to describe in detail how a prosecutor had rolled his eyes or how a judge had smacked his own forehead in disbelief. His efforts had gained him few friends and a couple of overnights on Rikers Island. He let it go this time. With Harold Wexler, you had to pick your battles.

The jurors appeared to listen attentively as the judge reread the portion of his charge in which he'd discussed intent. "Under the law," he told them, "a person intends to cause the death of another person when his conscious aim or objective is to cause the death of that person." He told them to consider the defendant's actions and what the "natural and probable consequences" of those actions might be expected to be. Then he looked up from his notes and added, "You know, the law doesn't impose a requirement upon the People to prove that the defendant said, 'I'm going to kill you' to his intended victim, or words of that sort. So you should look at his actions, not his words or lack of them.

"One other thing," he added, his voice softening. "Jury deliberation isn't intended to be a stress test. It's intended to be a time when you thoughtfully review the evidence and apply the law. It's been a long day already, and you know your needs better than I do. You know when you're tired or when you're hungry. If you want to go to dinner now, fine. If you want to go to the hotel now, also fine. If you want to go to dinner and then come back to deliberate further, even that can be arranged. So when the time comes, let me know, and I'll be guided by your wishes." Then he told them to go back to the jury room and continue their deliberations.

To a disinterested layman, the remarks might have demonstrated nothing but a gentler, more compassionate side of Harold Wexler. Jaywalker was no layman, and he was anything but disinterested. Besides, he knew the judge better than that. Fearful that the jurors were on the verge of resolving the case with a quick acquittal, Wexler was telling them to slow down, back up and settle into the fairly lengthy, predictable process that deliberations so often became. Just as his earlier suggestion to focus on the defendant's actions had been his way of telling them to pay little or no attention to Jeremy's words, particularly those he'd uttered from the witness stand.

Once again, vintage Wexler.

The second note arrived at 6:14 p.m.

We, the jury, would like to go to dinner. After that, we would like to come back and resume our deliberations. And several of us would like permission to have wine with dinner.

William Craig
Foreman

So much for a quick acquittal.

With the jurors being taken to a local establishment for dinner and a single glass of wine each, Jaywalker was forced to be rude and decline Carmen and Julie's offer to join them at a nearby Jamaican restaurant. "They got good jerk chicken," Carmen assured him. He hadn't eaten a thing in a day and a half, but the thought of chicken, let alone *jerk* chicken, whatever that was, was a nonstarter. So instead he joined Jeremy in the pens and bummed a cheese sandwich from a corrections officer. It turned out to be nothing more than two slices of stale white bread separated by a thin layer of Velveeta, but it hit the spot. Jaywalker had done army food in his youth, and prison food wasn't all that different. Put him on an airplane in the old days, back when they'd actually served meals, and he'd been in heaven.

"So what do you think?" Jeremy asked him.

"Not bad," Jaywalker had to admit.

It was only later, when he was down on Centre Street stretching his legs and trying to get some fresh air, that it struck him that Jeremy might not have been asking him about the sandwich. But even if he hadn't misunderstood Jeremy's meaning, Jaywalker would have had no good answer to the question. At times like this, early on in the deliberations, he never knew what to think.

The jurors returned from dinner just before eight o'clock and resumed their deliberations. Judge Wexler had left word that he'd be in his chambers upstairs. Katherine Darcy checked in by phone from her office, which was located in the same building. Jaywalker, who had no chambers and no office, stuck around. He talked with the clerk, the court officers, the corrections officers and the court reporter. He tried to calm Carmen and Julie down, but the truth was, they seemed calmer by far than he was. Twice he went into the pens to make sure Jeremy was okay. Both times he found Jeremy lying on a bench, his eyes closed. Jaywalker chalked it up to sleep deprivation, rather than complacency. Still, he couldn't imagine falling asleep in Jeremy's situation. Jaywalker himself was running on fumes, not having slept more than a couple of hours over the last two days. But the idea of sitting down, closing his eyes and napping was nothing less than unthinkable.

The buzzer sounded at 8:19 p.m.

Once.

We, the jury, would like to rehear the testimony of Dr. Seymour Kaplan regarding his reasons for concluding how close the gun was to Victor's head when the defendant shot him between the eyes.

> *William Craig*
> *Foreman*

P.S. Both direct and cross-examination.

This was bad, thought Jaywalker, bad for a number of reasons. First of all, Kaplan was the last witness Jaywalker wanted the jurors to hear again. His opinion that the tip of the gun's barrel had been at most five inches from its target was as devastating to Jeremy's claim of self-defense as Detective Fortune's forty-five-foot measurement had been. But unlike Fortune, Kaplan had come off as a thoroughly believable witness. So the jurors weren't asking to hear his testimony again because they doubted him. Next there was the manner in which the note referred to the two young men. Victor Quinones had become "Victor," in what Jaywalker took to be a humanizing touch. In contrast, Jeremy Estrada had had his name stripped away completely and had been reduced to the status of a depersonalized "defendant." Then there was the inclusion of the phrase "shot him between the eyes." To Jaywalker, those words seemed not only unnecessarily gratuitous but pointedly accusatory. The jurors could have said "the final shot," "the fatal shot," or even "the head shot." But they hadn't. They'd gone out of their way to make it sound like the overkill Katherine Darcy had argued it had been. Finally there was the specification that they wanted both direct examination and cross on the matter. That was a typical enough request, and under different circumstances Jaywalker would have been heartened by it. But here it had clearly been an afterthought. Not only had it been tacked onto the note as a postscript, it had been added in a handwriting visibly different from that of Mr. Craig's. And whoever had written it apparently hadn't felt on solid enough ground to have signed his or her name beneath it.

All things considered, it was a very bad note.

It was after nine o'clock by the time the jurors got what they'd asked for, and from the looks on their faces they would be more careful next time. It had taken the court reporter fifteen minutes to locate and mark the portions of the testimony relevant to the request, another fifteen minutes to reassemble everyone in the courtroom, and a third fifteen minutes for the reporter to read the questions and answers aloud to the jury. She did so, as reporters are instructed to do, without inflection, in order to avoid favoring one side or the other, either deliberately or unconsciously. The result was, as it almost always is in read-backs, a rapid-fire monotone so flat and so uninteresting as to be positively numbing.

That said, it didn't come off as devastatingly as Jaywalker had feared. To be sure, there was Dr. Kaplan's opinion that the gun had been anywhere from a quarter of an inch to four or five inches away from its target. And in support of that opinion was his finding of "radial tearing" around the edge of the wound, indicating that the scalp had been literally lifted off the skull. But on cross, Jaywalker had succeeded in getting Kaplan to admit that he'd found no evidence of a "muzzle stamp," singed eyebrows, "stippling" or "fouling." And if the absence of those things didn't truly undermine the doctor's conclusion, it made for good listening.

At least for Jaywalker.

The jury's final note of the evening arrived at 10:23 p.m., precisely seven minutes before Judge Wexler was going to send them to a hotel for the night whether they liked it or not.

We, the jury, are tired and would like to stop deliberating. We also would like to hear, very first thing tomorrow morning, the testimony of the three eyewitnesses, Miss Lopez, Mr. Porter and Teresa Morales, regarding how after the first shot or shots, the defendant chased the victim before shooting him the last time, and exactly how the defendant fired the last shot.

Nothing else, please. And we need only the direct examination this time.

> *William Craig*
> *Jury Foreman*

This was worse, far worse.

And not just the direct-examination-only specification. While it was painful to hear, the truth was that Jaywalker had asked few if any questions about the final chase and shot, having preferred at the time to get the three eyewitnesses off the stand before they could inflict more damage. And Jeremy's testimony had never really addressed the issue. When it came right down to it, the most he'd been able to say was that he didn't remember.

No, this was worse because it meant that in the morning the jurors would resume their deliberations immediately after hearing the three most damaging portions of the eyewitness accounts, the portions that blew away Jeremy's claim of self-defense and changed the case from justification to execution.

So this was how it was going to end. The jurors would come back in the morning, listen to the three accounts and find Jeremy guilty. They might throw him a break and convict him only of manslaughter, on the theory that he'd been under the influence of extreme emotional disturbance. Or they might not. But what was the difference? Either way, he wouldn't be seeing daylight for the next twenty or twenty-five years.

The jurors were sent to their hotel. Jeremy was led back into the pens. The judge went home. The clerk and court officers began locking up. It was the court reporter who stopped Jaywalker and Katherine Darcy.

"Listen," she said. "I rotate with another reporter, and I'm not due back here until two o'clock tomorrow afternoon. If you want the transcript marked for the read-back, we've got to do it now."

Darcy seemed agreeable enough. And why not? Here she was, on the verge of a conviction in her first murder trial. And she could always go down to her office on the seventh floor, find a sofa to curl up on and catch six or seven hours of sleep. Jaywalker, on the other hand, was totally out of adrenaline, in serious danger of crashing and a long subway ride from home. But it seemed he had no choice.

It took them forty minutes to isolate and mark all the relevant portions of the testimony. Jaywalker pretty much sat back and let Darcy and the reporter do the work. They'd been her witnesses, after all, and she knew from her notes where she'd asked them what. Still, it seemed to take forever. When they were finally finished, the reporter thanked them and ducked out the side door, the only one that wasn't double-bolted shut. "Turn off the lights on your way out," she told them. "The door will lock itself."

Jaywalker took one last look at the clock. 11:43 p.m. He discovered he could barely stand up. It wasn't just lack of sleep, and it certainly wasn't lack of food: that Velveeta-on-white must have had a good two hundred calories in it, not to mention a week's requirement of sodium, guar gum, xanthan gum and food coloring. No, it was the losing, or at least the certainty that he was going to.

"You okay?" Darcy asked him.

"Yes," he said. "No. I don't know. But hey, congratulations."

"Don't be silly," she said. "Anything can still happen. They're a weird bunch, this jury."

Like she was an old hand at this.

He followed her out of the courtroom, flicking off the lights and pulling the side door closed until he heard the lock click. He knew from night-court experiences that the north bank of elevators would be shut down. Besides which, only the south bank ones opened onto the seventh floor, where the district attorney's offices were. But when he pressed the button, no little orange light came on. He figured maybe the bulb had burned out, but when he tried the button on the other side of the bank, the same thing happened.

They waited five or six minutes, elevatorless.

"You up for walking?" he asked her.

"Okay," she said. "But no funny stuff. I've heard about you and stairwells."

He smiled as much as he could, which wasn't much. But when he tried the doorknob to the first set of stairs, he found it locked. As he did with the second set. "Welcome to post-9/11 security," he said. "I guess they lock these things up at night now."

"So we're stranded?"

"Nah," he said. "Got your cell phone?"

"It's in my office."

"Great."

"How about yours?"

"Don't own one." It was the truth, a lawyer without a cell phone. But Jaywalker was a dinosaur among lawyers, a throwback to the Jurassic era, and he was determined to go to his grave without ever having had one of the damned things.

Then he got an idea. "Follow me," he said, and started walking back to the north end of the corridor.

Darcy hesitated. Some part of her must have sensed that following Jaywalker was right up there with falling in line behind a column of lemmings. But follow she did, though at a distance.

Down at the end of the hall was a door. It, too, was locked, as Jaywalker had fully expected. He reached into his jacket pocket. He might not have a cell phone, but he did have a wallet. There was no money in it—*that* he carried folded in his back pocket and secured against jostlers by a thick rubber band—but he did have plastic. He found his get-out-of-jail card, more officially known as a New York City Department of Corrections Attorney Identification. It took him ten seconds to slip the lock with it. Back in his DEA days, it would have been less than five.

"What's in here?" Darcy asked.

"Judges' chambers. And," he added, turning on the lights and rounding a corner, "*voila!* Their private elevator." He pressed the button, and within half a minute an empty elevator opened in front of their eyes and beckoned them aboard. It was much smaller than the building's regular ones, and *much* nicer. Instead of graffiti-resistant brushed metal walls, this one was paneled in what looked to be real wood. In place of industrial flooring, it sported red carpeting. A bit faded and worn, to be sure, but red carpeting none-theless. And where the building's other elevators were illuminated by harsh fluorescent bulbs glaring down through low-hanging plastic grids, this one was bathed in soft tones from invisible fixtures recessed into a ceiling a good ten feet above their heads.

"So this is how the other half lives," said Darcy, stepping in gingerly, not unlike the way Cinderella must have mounted the steps to the coach that was to take her to the ball.

"This, a black robe and a gavel," said Jaywalker. "Not to mention a special ticket-proof license plate." He followed her on and pressed One. The door closed, and they began descending silently.

"Well," said Darcy, "I want to thank you for getting us out of here. And I'll see you in the morning."

Jaywalker looked at his watch. "It *is* morning," he announced, noticing that it was actually a minute past midnight.

But evidently Jaywalker's watch was a minute fast. Or perhaps it was a matter of the elevator's automatic timing mechanism being a minute slow. Whichever was the case, the result was indisputable. Only seconds into their descent, the lights above them flickered once and went off, leaving them in absolute blackness as they gently slowed to a complete stop.

24

NICE SHOES, YOUR HONOR

"**Y**ou did that," were the first words out of Katherine Darcy's mouth.

"I'd love to take the credit for it," said Jaywalker. "But I'm not half that clever." He explained that the thing must have been on some sort of timer, and that it seemed to have been their bad luck to discover that the hard way.

"Don't the night-court judges use this elevator?" Darcy asked. Or at least her voice asked. It was an eerie feeling, talking with somebody in such complete blackness. Sure, Jaywalker had had his share of conversations in the dark and then some. But not *this* kind of dark. Not absolute, utter, unrelenting darkness. It was spooky, is what it was.

"*Don't* they?" Darcy's voice was asking.

"Don't they what?"

"Use this elevator? The judges who work night court?"

"Yeah," said Jaywalker. "But they have special keys to override the system. Like the fire department."

"Still—"

"What's tonight?"

"Oh, I don't know," said Darcy. "Get-Stranded-in-the-Elevator Night?"

"No, what night of the week?"

"Monday," she said. "Or at least it was until you proclaimed it morning."

"Is that why you wore black—"

"What?"

"—to show the jury you were in mourning for Victor Quinones?"

"Are you *out of your mind?*" said the voice.

Okay, so maybe he'd been mistaken about that. "Sorry," he said.

The voice said nothing.

"Anyway," he told it, "if it's Monday, or *was* Monday, that means there's no night court tonight. Or last night."

"Great." The voice was back. "So what do we do?"

"We start," he said, "by playing with the buttons."

He found them quickly enough simply by running his hands across the front panels of the elevator. But no matter how he pushed or pulled them, or in what order or combination, none of them did anything. With some additional groping, he located the slit for the override key and spent twenty minutes trying to turn it with one of his keys or pick it with a paper clip. Eventually the end of the paper clip broke off, sticking in the slit and making further attempts impossible. He spent twenty more minutes unsuccessfully trying to find a release mechanism for the door, and another ten assuring himself that there was no emergency phone anywhere in the elevator.

"I give up," he said.

"It's getting hot in here," Darcy said.

She was right. The elevator's air-conditioning had obviously gone off when the lights and power had. And it was the middle of May, after all, and the past few Mays, present month included, had been pretty much holding their own in the global-warming sweepstakes. Jaywalker thought about commenting on Darcy's decision to wear a long skirt but decided against it. He'd taken off his jacket, loosened his tie and turned up his shirtsleeves even before he'd played Find the Button. Then again, he tended to do those things as soon as he was out of the courtroom.

But yes, it was getting hot.

"How long can we last in here?" Darcy asked.

"Oh, at least another five minutes."

"I'm serious." And she sounded it.

"Longer than you'd think," said Jaywalker.

"What's *that* supposed to that mean?"

"That I have absolutely no idea," he admitted.

She tried calling out for a while, alternating between "Help!" and "Hello there!" She tried banging on the walls, stomping on the floor, and shaking the elevator back and forth. It turned out to be well insulated, padded and impervious to shaking.

Jaywalker took off his tie and unbuttoned the top two buttons of his shirt. Placing his back against the wall of the elevator, he allowed himself to slide down until he came to a sitting position. "Relax," he said. "You're using up too much oxygen." A moment later he felt her join him. Not quite felt her, but sensed her closeness.

"Seriously," she said. "How long before we run out of oxygen?"

"I once read you don't die of oxygen starvation," he assured her. "Carbon dioxide poisoning kills you first."

"That's comforting," she said. "Hey."

"Hey, what?"

"That was a great summation."

"Yours, too."

"No," she said. "I really mean it. By the time you sat down, half of me was rooting for your kid."

"Right. And then you got up and blew us out of the water."

"I was only doing my job," she said.

"Well, you did it very well. For a rookie."

He felt an elbow jab him in the ribs. Or maybe it had been a fist; in the dark it was hard to tell. But he readied his hand to catch it next time, just in case.

"How did you get those clowns to show up in Oakland Raiders outfits?" she wanted to know.

"I swear I had nothing to do with that," he said. "I ran into a former client, and he wanted to know all about the case. So I told him. He must've figured it out on his own that it might help if they were to make a cameo appearance."

"Jaywalker the innocent."

"Always."

"And *this* is for making a fool of Detective Fortune, who just happens to be married to my neph—"

He caught her on the word *this,* or pretty close to it. And it must have been a fist, because he caught her by the wrist. It was surprisingly thin, thin enough for him to wrap his hand completely around it and hold on. And it must have been the wrist farther from him, because when he pulled on it, the rest of her came with it, across his body and onto his lap. They kissed, or at least he did.

"That was my eye," she told him.

He tried again.

"Better."

But if making out in the dark on the floor of an elevator was Jaywalker's idea of a good time, it apparently wasn't Darcy's. "We have to get some air in here," she insisted, "before we die of carbon monoxide poisoning."

"Carbon *di*oxide poisoning."

"That's what I said."

"No you didn't," he said. "You said—"

"Whatever. Get us some air, Jaywalker."

As much as he hated to get up, he did. This time he

reached upward, for the ceiling. He figured there had to be a removable panel somewhere up there. Didn't all elevators have one, in order to get at the cables? But the ceiling was too high. He crouched low and jumped. Nothing.

"What are you doing?" Darcy wanted to know.

"Trying to get you some air."

"By doing jumping jacks?"

He explained his thinking to her. It was she who came up with the idea of climbing up on his shoulders, as he would remind her several times over the days to come.

The first impediment, as they quickly discovered when she placed one foot atop his extended knee, was her heels. The result was painful, but easily enough remedied. Not so her long narrow skirt, which made it difficult for her to bend her own knees and would have made sitting on his shoulders all but impossible.

"Don't look," she warned him.

Don't look?

He heard a faint zipping sound. Make that an *unzipping* sound. Though in the dark, it turns out, they're hard to tell apart. A moment later her foot was back on his knee, this time heel-less.

The physics of climbing onto another person's shoulders are not that complicated. The climber, after placing one foot securely atop the climbee's horizontally extended upper leg, swings the opposite leg over the climbee's back and shoulders. Holding that first foot with one hand, and now grasping the second foot with his free hand, the climbee straightens himself up and into a standing position, all the while maintaining not only his own balance but that of the person comfortably perched atop his shoulders, as well.

And that's all there is to it, except for the rather obvious caveat that in order to achieve success, the first two steps must have been properly executed.

If you've ever ridden a horse, you know how absolutely essential it is that in the initial process of mounting the animal, you place the correct foot in the stirrup. It doesn't take all that much in the way of imagination to predict the outcome when the wrong foot is used instead. Now in all fairness to Katherine Darcy, it is true that horses are generally mounted—at least when humans are doing the mounting—in the daytime, or when sufficient ambient light is present to determine which way the animal happens to be facing.

Katherine Darcy did not have that advantage.

Which explains why, when she finally came to rest perched securely upon Jaywalker's shoulders, the two of them were facing in very different directions. One hundred and eighty degrees different, to be precise.

Even in the dark, they both recognized the problem immediately, though *problem* is hardly the word Jaywalker would have used to describe the situation. But as easy as it had been to get there, no ready solution presented itself for correcting things. Think back to the horse-and-rider analogy, if you will, and imagine the rider, saddled up but suddenly facing the tail end of the beast, attempting to turn around. Okay, now try to imagine it with Jaywalker's head in the way.

"What now?" asked Darcy.

Jaywalker tried to answer, but his words came out unintelligible even to him. And it was no wonder; he was talking directly into what could discretely be described at Darcy's lower lower abdomen, and every time he opened his mouth his lips kept getting stuck on bare flesh. He tried tilting his head back as far as he could. The result was substantial pain in the back of his neck and significantly less fun for his lips. But it did enable him to speak out loud.

"Just a minute," he said. "Hold on tight." And he let go of her with one hand, in order to free it.

"What are you *doing?*" she shrieked, her weight shifting suddenly as he bent at the waist, trying to, well, make an adjustment of sorts.

"Nothing," he said.

"What *nothing?*"

"Relax," he said. "It's a guy thing."

He straightened up, resumed his two-handed grip and told her to reach up and feel around above her. "There should be a panel right in the middle of the ceiling," he told her. "Either it'll push up easily, or there'll be screws to loosen it."

"I need you to move," she said.

"Which way."

"To the left."

He moved one step to the left.

"No," she said. "The other left."

Another complication that came with facing-in-opposite-directions syndrome, as they soon discovered, was the matter of "forward" and "back." But once they'd gotten their commands and responses in synch, the rest turned out to be surprisingly easy. Within a minute or two Darcy had located and loosened the four thumbscrews that kept the ceiling panel in place, and pushed the panel itself upward and off to one side of the roof. Not only did that act succeed in releasing excess carbon dioxide and ushering in cooler—and presumably more oxygen-rich—air, it allowed for just a hint of bluish light to filter in, as well.

It took some doing, but Jaywalker managed to lower Darcy to the floor of the elevator almost without mishap, the relevant portions of them being sufficiently cushioned by the carpeting as to produce only full-throated laughter and a measure of lingering tenderness. Or perhaps the tenderness might better be ascribed to the events that would transpire over the next several hours. The carpeting, it would turn out, was in fact padded.

But not all *that* padded.

And had it not been for intervention—not so much of the divine sort as the judicial—it's highly likely that Katherine Darcy and Jaywalker would have spent the remainder of the morning happily engaged in those very same events. From Jaywalker's perspective, it would have been all he could have asked for, understanding as he did how vastly over-rated sleep and sustenance tended to be. And if Darcy's words and deeds were any indication at all, then the same could safely be said of her.

But intervention did indeed intervene.

As suddenly as they'd gone out at midnight, the lights came back on, the air-conditioning kicked in, and a humming noise started up. Almost immediately, the elevator began descending. As blinded by the brightness as he had been by the earlier darkness, Jaywalker began groping around for his clothes, grabbing his pants, his shirt and what he thought was a pair of black socks.

"That's mine," Darcy snapped.

"Is not."

"Is, too," she said. "Unless you wear a 34B."

He handed it over.

By the time the elevator settled to a stop at the first floor, the two of them were more or less dressed. And although they stood side by side, facing the door as nonchalantly as they possibly could, as though simply waiting for it to open so they could be on their separate ways, they wouldn't have fooled anyone with eyes to see. Hell, they wouldn't have fooled Stevie Wonder.

But it wasn't Stevie Wonder who was standing there

when the door opened. Knowing that much was the easy part. For Jaywalker, the hard part was trying to place the familiar-looking man staring back at him, key in hand. At least he *thought* it was a man, though the women's sunglasses and the platform heels gave him pause.

And then it dawned on him.

"Judge Sternbridge," said Jaywalker, out of sheer amazement. Because it was in fact Miles Sternbridge, the head of the disciplinary committee. Miles Sternbridge, who'd meted out Jaywalker's three-year suspension and had just last week dropped by Harold Wexler's courtroom to make sure Jaywalker had been *behaving himself.* Miles Sternbridge, in platform heels.

And yet, if Jaywalker wasn't mistaken, here was Sternbridge screaming at him.

"This is a private elevator! For judges only! What are you doing on it? And you're with another of your hookers, I see!"

Jaywalker could feel Darcy about to say something, or perhaps explode, alongside him. He put a hand on her arm, first to quiet her, then to steer her past Sternbridge and toward the door that led out to the lobby. Only then did he turn back to address the judge.

"Nice shoes, your honor."

25

YES IT IS

The read-back went even worse than Jaywalker had antici-pated. He'd arrived in court uncharacteristically late, though still early by normal standards. Several court officers went out of their way to comment that he looked rested and seemed in unusually good spirits, at least for him.

Following the *elevatorus interruptus* episode and the standoff with Judge Sternbridge, Katherine Darcy and Jay-walker had bade each other good-night and headed to their respective homes. Famished, Jaywalker had stopped off at an all-night pizza joint and inhaled three slices. It was times like that when even he had to admit that living in the big city had its advantages. Once back at his apartment, he'd undressed, pausing only momentarily to wonder where his socks had gone, fallen onto his sofa and slept like a baby for the first time in weeks, if only for a few hours.

As for Katherine Darcy, she, too, looked just fine and seemed in good spirits, but there was nothing new there. And each time she made eye contact with Jaywalker she quickly looked away, obviously afraid she'd burst out laughing.

But none of that made the read-back any easier to listen

to. Even in the rapid-fire monotone of the court reporter, the testimony of Magdalena Lopez, Wallace Porter and Teresa Morales was nothing short of devastating. Each of them had recounted how Jeremy, gun in hand, had chased Victor down and delivered the final shot at point-blank range. Lopez had described how the two of them had moved to "a different spot" just before that had happened. Porter recalled how Jeremy had chased Victor and then "shot him like three more times." And when Victor had fallen to the ground, Jeremy had "picked him up by the collar and he shot one or two more times at him." But it was Teresa's version that stung the most.

I told Victor, "Run, run!" And when he ran, the guy shot him, and Victor like went down on the ground. Then he got up, and the guy shot again, and it hit the street. Then Victor ran again, inside the park, around a bench. But he tripped. And then the guy just walked over, grabbed him and killed him.

And since the read-back ended right there, the silence that followed it was absolutely deafening. Finally Judge Wexler turned to the jurors. "You may retire to continue your deliberations," he told them, and they filed out of the courtroom. Then he told the lawyers to approach the bench.

"Still want to offer him the manslaughter plea?" he asked Darcy.

She seemed to think for a moment. She had to know how close she was to a guilty verdict. She could hang tough now if she wanted to, holding out for a conviction on the murder count. But after a moment she said, "Sure, why not?"

"Talk to your client," Wexler told Jaywalker. "Man One, fifteen years. Right now, before it's too late."

Jaywalker glanced up at the clock, saw it was 10:22 a.m.

He walked back to the defense table, sat down and began explaining things to Jeremy. Not only were they still offering him the manslaughter count in the face of a near-certain conviction, he said, but Wexler himself had softened and come down to fifteen years, by far the best offer yet.

"How much would I have to do?" Jeremy asked.

"Twelve," Jaywalker estimated.

Jeremy smiled his sheepish smile. "If it's okay with you," he said, "I'd rather take my chances with the jury."

Jaywalker tried his best to convince Jeremy that from all indications, the jurors had turned against him. Even if they'd begun their deliberations looking for some way to acquit him—and the intent-to-kill note had suggested just that—by now they'd moved on and had come to view the final shot the same way the prosecution did, as pure overkill.

Jeremy shrugged, smiled again and said, "Still…"

Jaywalker got Wexler's permission for a court visit. The court officers obligingly cleared the front row of spectators, moved Jeremy's chair to the solid wooden railing, placed another chair on the audience side of it, and allowed first Carmen and then Julie to speak with Jeremy for a few minutes. The idea was for them to talk him into doing what Jaywalker had been unable to do.

They couldn't.

Jaywalker tried once more, before catching the judge's eye and shaking his head back and forth. Wexler stood up and left the courtroom without comment. Jaywalker looked at the clock—10:51 a.m. He guessed he'd be home by one, two at the latest.

He was wrong.

The buzzer sounded at 11:33 a.m. One buzzer, not two. Though in the two seconds it took to determine that there wouldn't be a second one, Jaywalker felt his heart go into serious fibrillation. Or maybe a lost butterfly had strayed up and into his chest to flap its wings in panic. He turned to Jeremy and said, "Relax," and they shared a laugh at the absurdity of the notion.

We, the jury, would like to know if there is any way we can send the defendant a message that what he did was absolutely wrong, and criminal according to the law. At the same time, some of us strongly suspect that the defendant's actions were out of character and feel it highly unlikely that he will repeat them, or similar criminal acts, in the future. How can we send that message without violating our oaths as jurors?

William Craig
Jury Foreman

"You can't," Harold Wexler told them once they were back in the jury box. "You're not here to send the defendant or anyone else a message. Your job, and your only job, is to make a determination as to whether the defendant's guilt on each count of the indictment has been proven to your satisfaction or not. Period. As for punishment, that is a matter that is solely within the province of the court. Or to put that into plain English, that's my job.

"Now let me say this," he continued, removing his glasses and looking up from his notes. "Despite rumors circulating to the contrary, I am a human being. I listened to the same testimony that you did. I have read your most recent note and understand your concerns. You may rest assured, each of you, that if and when it comes time for me to impose sentence upon Mr. Estrada, I will take into consideration all of the facts and circumstances of this very tragic case.

"I trust that answers your question," he told them. "Now you may retire and resume your deliberations."

Not that Jaywalker hadn't argued long and hard against what Wexler had proposed to say. Wrapped in all those comforting words was an implicit promise to treat Jeremy with not only understanding but leniency. But sentencing *wasn't* "solely the province of the court" at all. By imposing strict minimum terms, the legislature had made it very much *its* province, as well. Wexler could go on as long as he liked about being a human being, understanding the jurors' concerns and considering all aspects of "this very tragic case," but murder sentences still began at fifteen to life, and first-degree manslaughter at five years, which Jeremy could surely forget about, having just turned down fifteen *on a plea.* Therefore, Jaywalker contended, the judge was playing fast and loose with the jurors, lulling them into thinking Jeremy would get at most a slap on the wrist if they were to convict him, when in fact a lengthy prison term awaited him.

"You have your exception," Wexler had told him. Which in layman's terms translated into "Shut up and sit down." And the fact was, as duplicitous as the judge was being, he was standing on pretty solid ground, and he'd no doubt known it. The genteel way in which he'd answered the jurors' question had hewed closely enough to the law—which did indeed leave sentencing up to the court and not the jury—that it would no doubt satisfy the concerns of any appellate judge reviewing the statement long after the conviction.

So forty minutes later, when the buzzer sounded not once, but twice, nobody in the courtroom was surprised. Not Jaywalker, certainly, who'd known precisely what would happen next. Not Katherine Darcy, who looked sympathetic to his concerns but obviously felt powerless to do anything about them. Not the court officers, who even as they mumbled that Jaywalker had been shafted—which wasn't quite how they phrased it—called for reinforcements, a guilty verdict being a time when even the most docile of defendants tended to act out unpredictably. Not Harold Wexler, who made a point of loudly asking the clerk what a convenient sentencing date might be. Not Carmen or Julie, who sat in the audience hugging each other, sobbing softly. Not even Jeremy, who for once lowered his head and seemed intent on studying the floor, the sheepish smile finally gone from his face.

"Mr. Foreman, please rise."

As he had on each previous occasion, William Craig stood. At the defense table, so did Jaywalker and Jeremy. By now they knew the ritual well enough that they no longer waited to be asked.

"Mr. Foreman, has the jury reached a verdict?"

"Yes, we have."

In his right hand he held a single sheet of paper, called a verdict sheet. It listed the different counts of the indictment in order, by number and crime charged. Jaywalker knew from years of experience that whatever Mr. Craig were to do with it next would be a *tell,* an indication whether the jury had convicted Jeremy of all twelve counts or just some of them. If it was all, Mr. Craig would have no need to refer to the sheet; he could simply say the word "Guilty" each of the twelve times he was asked. So, too, if all of his responses were to be "Not guilty."

"With respect to the first count of the indictment," said the clerk, "charging the defendant with the crime of murder. How do you find the defendant, guilty or not guilty?"

William Craig lifted the verdict sheet and looked at it. So it was to be a split decision, Jaywalker immediately knew, a mix of convictions and acquittals. Guilty of murder but not manslaughter, for example. Or, God willing, the other way around. It had come down to that, Jaywalker the atheist praying for the compromise verdict he'd begged the jurors not to settle on.

"Not guilty," said Mr. Craig.

Jaywalker exhaled ever so slightly and thought he felt Jeremy do the same alongside him. So it was going to be a manslaughter conviction. A victory of sorts, one most lawyers would be thrilled with, given how close they'd come to a murder conviction.

"With respect to the second count of the indictment," said the clerk, "charging the defendant with the crime of manslaughter in the first degree. How do you find the defendant, guilty or not guilty?"

"Not guilty."

A muffled cry came from the spectator section directly behind Jaywalker. Carmen or Julie. The judge banged his gavel, harder and more angrily than Jaywalker would have thought necessary.

Nine more times the clerk asked William Craig how the jury had found the defendant, of second- and third-degree manslaughter, reckless endangerment, menacing, two degrees of assault and three degrees of unlawful possession of a deadly weapon. Nine more times Mr. Craig, still checking his verdict sheet, spoke the words, "Not guilty."

Only on the twelfth and final count of the indictment was his answer different. "Guilty," he said, "with a recommendation of—"

Wexler banged his gavel repeatedly, loud enough to drown out the rest. Only when the courtroom had fallen silent, save for some muffled sobbing from the rear, did Mr. Craig take the opportunity to say "leniency."

Jaywalker and Jeremy slumped down into their seats

like a pair of marionettes whose strings had suddenly been cut.

"Do you wish the jury polled?" Jaywalker heard the judge asking him. He was about to say no, it wasn't necessary. The twelfth count of the indictment had charged Jeremy with a violation of the New York City Administrative Code that made it unlawful to fire a gun within city limits. It was an unclassified misdemeanor that carried a maximum sentence of six months in jail or a five hundred dollar fine. Jeremy had already done a year in jail, the equivalent of time served. If anything, the system owed him six months change. So no, he had absolutely no problem at all with the verdict.

But when he looked to the jury box to say that, Jaywalker saw a dozen heads nodding his way expectantly. And then he remembered. In his summation he'd made a point of promising them that it wouldn't be he or the prosecutor or the judge who would have the last word of the trial. It would be them. And now they were going to hold him to his promise.

"Yes," he said. "Yes, we'd like the jury polled."

He watched and listened as, one by one, twelve of his and Jeremy Estrada's fellow citizens stood up, looked them in the eye and, when asked, answered in a loud and clear voice, "Yes, that is my verdict."

26

PERFECT SCHMERFECT

Katherine Darcy was the first one to congratulate Jay-walker.

"Why are you congratulating *me?*" he asked her. "You got your conviction. I lost." It was true, if only in the most technical of senses. But, as always, Jaywalker was being hard on himself. He knew lawyers who would say they'd won if they got a manslaughter conviction on a murder case. Hell, he knew lawyers who'd put a hung jury in their victory column, or call it a win if they managed to keep a jury out overnight. To Jaywalker, an acquittal had always been an acquittal and a conviction a conviction. So to his way of thinking, he'd indeed lost and Darcy had won, not only beating him but snapping his winning streak at, well, whatever it had been.

But far more important than any of that stuff was the fact that Jeremy was free again, not only from jail and the threat of a lengthy prison term but, as things would turn out, from the Raiders, as well. In time Jaywalker would learn that they'd disbanded some months before the trial had even begun and had reportedly regrouped for their aborted court-room reunion only, as he'd guessed, at the urging of one Johnny Cantalupo. When Cantalupo's role in the incident would be discovered, he and Jaywalker would become the subject of an inquiry demanded by Judge Harold Wexler, an inquiry that Judge Miles Sternbridge would mysteriously recuse himself from without giving a reason for doing so. Investigators would go so far as to unseal the file of Cantalupo's drug conviction, the one he was currently on probation for. They would be hoping to find a smoking gun, as they say, some connection between him and Jaywalker. But when they'd pull the file, they would be disappointed to see that the notice of appearance didn't have Jaywalker's name on it after all, but that of some other lawyer they'd never even heard of. Some guy named Alan Fudderman. And the inquiry would stop there, at a dead end.

For his efforts on behalf of Jeremy, Jaywalker's earnings came to four thousand, one hundred and twenty-five dollars, plus three lunches, none consumed. Had he taken the trouble to keep track of his hours, which of course he hadn't, the hourly rate for his services would have come out to a fraction over three dollars and fourteen cents. And that would be without deducting some five hundred dollars for a round-trip to Puerto Rico.

As he always did, especially following a conviction, Jaywalker made a point of speaking with the jurors before they scattered. They told him they'd never given any thought to convicting Jeremy of murder, having decided halfway through Jaywalker's opening statement that the case was at worst manslaughter. One of the jurors—they wouldn't tell him which one—had briefly held out for conviction and had insisted on rehearing the eyewitnesses' testimonies. But as soon as the rest of them had agreed to find Jeremy guilty of *something,* that juror had caved and gone along.

"But how'd you settle on that administrative code violation?" Jaywalker asked them.

It hadn't been all that hard, they explained. Since the indictment began with murder and from there went to man-slaughter and a bunch of lesser things, they figured the counts were arranged in order of severity of punishment. And once the judge had tried to sweet-talk them into trusting him to be lenient, they'd decided, in the words of William Craig, that "we couldn't trust him farther than we could throw him." So count twelve it had been.

"Juries," thought Jaywalker aloud that night as he lay in bed, exhausted but still exhilarated. "No matter how hard you try, you can never really predict what they're going to do. But how I wish I had a dollar for every time they've surprised me by figuring things out and ending up returning the perfect verdict."

"Perfect *schmerfect*," said Katherine Darcy. "And turn the light out, will you, so we can get a little sleep for once?"

He dutifully turned off the light. Fortunately, the switch was within easy reach. Then again, in Jaywalker's apartment, just about everything was within easy reach.

"So tell me," he said. "What does it stand for?"

"If you're talking about that thing you've got between your legs, it seems to me it stands for everything. Haven't I told you how impressed I—"

"No, no, not that. I mean the *t* in Katherine T. Darcy. As in K.T."

"Oh, *that*. It stands for *terrific*," she said without missing a beat.

He laughed out loud in the dark, the full-throated laugh of a man without a care in the world. Come to think of it, he'd been doing an awful lot of that over the past day or so.

And Jeremy?

Following the verdict, it had taken the New York City Department of Corrections four hours to release him from custody, which was just about average. Someone in records first had to determine that he had no open cases, outstanding warrants or detainers, and—notwithstanding the fact that he was a native-born American citizen—that he wasn't wanted by Immigration. Then, this time in spite of the fact that for an entire year he'd been the only Jeremy Estrada in the entire system, a captain had to be summoned to make sure he was the right one. And finally Jeremy had to take and pass a quiz that required him to know not only his home address and date of birth, but the color of his eyes.

Jaywalker hadn't waited for him to come out, having had better things to do at the time. But two days later, Jeremy called to express his and his family's appreciation, and to say that Jaywalker had saved his life.

After that, there would be no word at all from him for a full year and a half. Which wasn't all that unusual in Jaywalker's business, where clients seemed to appear out of nowhere and then to disappear just as abruptly. But then, days before Christmas, a card would arrive in the mail, a mushy store-bought thing adorned with bluebirds and angels fluttering over a pair of newborn fawns nestled in the snow. Beneath the printed greeting, in careful manuscript, would be the words, "God bless you and thank you for everything, from both of us." And although there would be no printed names or inked signatures, whether by design or simple inadvertence, the postmark on the envelope would divulge the origin. It was from Baltimore, which, as everyone knows, is in Marilyn.

* * * * *

ACKNOWLEDGMENTS

I take very little credit for the story you've just read. It's lifted from an actual case I myself tried at 100 Centre Street some years back. While much of it—including the incident that gave rise to the case, and the trial itself—is faithfully reported, I've made a number of changes, not only to disguise the participants, but hopefully to make for a more readable and therefore better book. Unabridged trials, it turns out, can be pretty tedious affairs.

As always, I'm extremely fortunate to have had the assistance of a wonderful literary agent in Bob Diforio and a fabulous editor in Leslie Wainger, and I can't thank either of them enough. My wife, Sandy, continues to be my toughest critic but, once she finally gets around to reading what I've written, my biggest fan. Not far behind are my sister, Tillie, and her husband, Dave, my children Wendy, Ron and Tracy, and these days my granddaughters Darcy, Katie, Rachel and Amy.

Finally, let me use this space to preemptively beg the forgiveness of Tom Farber—a good friend, former adversary and these days a very good judge, I'm quite sure—for allowing me to turn him into a woman, and then some. Sorry about that, Tom.

JOSEPH TELLER

A speeding sports car forces an oncoming van off the road and kills all nine of its occupants...eight of them children.

Criminal defense attorney Harrison J. Walker, or Jaywalker, is serving a three-year suspension and having trouble keeping his nose clean when a woman seduces him into representing the killer, who happens to be her husband.

Struggling with the moral issues surrounding this case, Jaywalker tries to limit the damage to his client by exposing the legal system's hypocrisy regarding drunk driving. But when he rounds a blind corner in the case, he finds a truth that could derail his defense.

DEPRAVED INDIFFERENCE

MIRA®

Available now wherever books are sold.

www.MIRABooks.com

AN INTENSE NEW THRILLER FROM
JOSEPH TELLER

One phone call changed Jaywalker's
life forever....

Criminal defense attorney
Harrison J. Walker, better known
as Jaywalker, receives a call from
a desperate mother. Her son,
Darren, has been arrested for
raping five white women in a
long-forgotten corner of the Bronx.

A young black man, Darren is positively
identified by four of the victims as the fifth
prepares to do the same. Everyone sees this as
an open-and-shut case—everyone except Jaywalker.

As he looks deep into the characters involved in the crime
and the character of our society, what he finds will haunt him
for the rest of his career.

BRONX
JUSTICE

Available wherever books are sold.

RICK MOFINA

A young mother, thrown clear of a devastating car crash, is convinced she sees a figure pull her infant son from the flames.

In a Rio de Janeiro café, a bomb kills ten people, including two World Press Alliance journalists. Jack Gannon must find out whether his colleagues were victims or targets who got too close to a huge story.

With millions of lives at stake, experts work frantically against time. And as an anguished mother searches for her child and Jack Gannon pursues the truth, an unstoppable force hurls them all into the panic zone.

THE
PANIC
ZONE

Available wherever books are sold.

MIRA®

REQUEST YOUR FREE BOOKS!

2 FREE NOVELS
FROM THE SUSPENSE COLLECTION
PLUS 2 FREE GIFTS!

YES! Please send me 2 FREE novels from the Suspense Collection and my 2 FREE gifts (gifts are worth about $10). After receiving them, if I don't wish to receive any more books, I can return the shipping statement marked "cancel." If I don't cancel, I will receive 3 brand-new novels every month and be billed just $5.74 per book in the U.S. or $6.24 per book in Canada. That's a saving of at least 28% off the cover price. It's quite a bargain! Shipping and handling is just 50¢ per book.* I understand that accepting the 2 free books and gifts places me under no obligation to buy anything. I can always return a shipment and cancel at any time. Even if I never buy another book, the two free books and gifts are mine to keep forever.

192/392 MDN E7PD

Name _____
(PLEASE PRINT)

Address _____ Apt. # _____

City _____ State/Prov. _____ Zip/Postal Code _____

Signature (if under 18, a parent or guardian must sign) _____

Mail to **The Reader Service:**
IN U.S.A.: P.O. Box 1867, Buffalo, NY 14240-1867
IN CANADA: P.O. Box 609, Fort Erie, Ontario L2A 5X3

Not valid for current subscribers to the Suspense Collection
or the Romance/Suspense Collection.

Want to try two free books from another line?
Call 1-800-873-8635 or visit www.morefreebooks.com.

* Terms and prices subject to change without notice. Prices do not include applicable taxes. N.Y. residents add applicable sales tax. Canadian residents will be charged applicable provincial taxes and GST. Offer not valid in Quebec. This offer is limited to one order per household. All orders subject to approval. Credit or debit balances in a customer's account(s) may be offset by any other outstanding balance owed by or to the customer. Please allow 4 to 6 weeks for delivery. Offer available while quantities last.

Your Privacy: Harlequin Books is committed to protecting your privacy. Our Privacy Policy is available online at www.eHarlequin.com or upon request from the Reader Service. From time to time we make our lists of customers available to reputable third parties who may have a product or service of interest to you. If you would prefer we not share your name and address, please check here. ☐

Help us get it right—We strive for accurate, respectful and relevant communications. To clarify or modify your communication preferences, visit us at www.ReaderService.com/consumerschoice.

JOSEPH TELLER

32691 DEPRAVED INDIFFERENCE	___ $7.99 U.S.	___ $9.99 CAN.
32635 BRONX JUSTICE	___ $7.99 U.S.	___ $7.99 CAN.
32605 THE TENTH CASE	___ $7.99 U.S.	___ $7.99 CAN.

(limited quantities available)

TOTAL AMOUNT	$ _____
POSTAGE & HANDLING	$ _____
($1.00 for 1 book, 50¢ for each additional)	
APPLICABLE TAXES*	$ _____
TOTAL PAYABLE	$ _____

(check or money order—please do not send cash)

To order, complete this form and send it, along with a check or money order for the total above, payable to MIRA Books, to: **In the U.S.:** 3010 Walden Avenue, P.O. Box 9077, Buffalo, NY 14269-9077; **In Canada:** P.O. Box 636, Fort Erie, Ontario, L2A 5X3.

Name: _____
Address: _____ City: _____
State/Prov.: _____ Zip/Postal Code: _____
Account Number (if applicable): _____

075 CSAS

*New York residents remit applicable sales taxes.
*Canadian residents remit applicable GST and provincial taxes.

MIRA®

www.MIRABooks.com

MJT0810BL